Henry Zeybel

WINGS OF FIRE

Pan Books
London, Sydney and Auckland

First published in the United States 1988
by Pocket Books, a division of Simon & Schuster Inc.
This edition published in Great Britain 1989
by Pan Books Ltd, Cavaye Place, London SW10 9PG

9 8 7 6 5 4 3 2 1

ISBN 0 330 30475 5

Printed and bound in Great Britain by
Richard Clay Ltd, Bungay, Suffolk

This novel is a work of fiction. Names, characters, places and incidents are either
the product of the author's imagination or are used fictitiously. Any resemblance
to actual events or locales or persons, living or dead, is entirely coincidental.

To Jan

ACKNOWLEDGMENT

My everlasting thanks to Wilson Harris,
the brilliant Guyanese novelist,
for teaching me as much about values
as he taught me about fiction.

CHAPTER 1

FOOCHOW, CHINA, WAS Lieutenant Morris Archer's first target as a Strategic Air Command navigator-bombardier. It made no difference that the city was a commercial and industrial center or that it was the capital of Fukien province in southeast China. All that mattered was that Foochow had a population of 623,000 Red Chinese, and if the United States went to war with the Soviet Union, Archer's job was to navigate his B47 Stratojet to China and destroy those 623,000 Red Chinese with a nineteen-megaton thermonuclear bomb. That response was called Massive Retaliation. Its essence: death.

Before being certified combat-ready and being authorized to execute the mission, Archer was required to brief his portion of the Emergency War Order to Colonel Axel Turner, the bomb wing commander. A slight-of-build man, but so fit and fleet as to make a mockery of a recent fortieth birthday, Turner was base squash and badminton champion.

In the guarded secrecy of a windowless blockhouse, inside a room papered with jet navigation charts of China and the Soviet Union, Archer faced Turner and his staff, a dozen veterans of World War II and Korea. Rows of ribbons on their blue uniforms attested to their courage and prowess, represented the Distinguished Flying Crosses, Air Medals, and Purple Hearts earned in steel-saturated skies over Europe and Asia.

The starred blue ribbon of the Medal of Honor on Colonel Turner's chest stood out above the others. For it, as a lieutenant copilot, he'd single-handedly willed a shattered B17 bomber back from Germany after its pilot and navigator were killed. Aboard the freezing, dying aircraft every other crewmember was critically wounded. Turner saved those few who could be saved with a perfect gear-up crash landing on a warm and grassy English airstrip.

To Archer, his briefing culminated three years of training; yet, at the same time, it was a first step. It was as if upon finishing a marathon run, he discovered that he had merely qualified to begin the race. The men seated before him had covered far more difficult distances, had learned their skills in battles rather than in classrooms. They had led strategic bombing raids while Archer had been attending grade school, and were men of a breed he had idolized at a time when his boyhood companions had naively worshiped athletes.

Turner and his staff represented the empirical generation of the United States Air Force, a branch that had gained sovereignty from the army a decade earlier, in 1947. Their present roles transcended their pasts and, perhaps, even their imaginations. Now these men were leaders in the Strategic Air Command—SAC—the most powerful strike force in man's history, a command of such scale that it had the power to end man's history. And Archer wanted his share of that power. He envisioned himself as part of the next generation, the future sitting there where they sat now, passing judgment on those who followed.

In humble contrast to the aging warriors in beribboned blue uniforms, Archer stood before them in lusterless combat crew workclothes: black boots, gray-green flying suit, dark blue scarf. If his dress was common issue, there was

2

nothing ordinary about the rest of him. With his blond crew-cut hair, intense green eyes, square jaw, and square shoulders, Archer looked as if he'd stepped down from an air force recruiting poster. A reincarnated Hitler youth, Colonel Turner thought. There always would be a need for men of his caliber.

The staff members received him with icy formality, listened to his words with frowning concentration, dissected every detail. They knew his task as well as he knew it and silently challenged him to match their perfection.

From memory Archer described a flight that was complexly simple. From the island of Guam where the Bomb Wing was temporarily based, Archer would direct his three-man crew northward along a 1400-nautical-mile overwater route, using celestial/pressure pattern navigation. Flying at 430 knots, the crew would step-climb along the way until reaching 38,000 feet in altitude. Coasting in at the tip of Taiwan, the crew would accelerate to 470 knots, cross the Formosa Strait, and pick up the China coast at the Min River. Twenty-two miles inland, straddling the Min, was Foochow. On radar, land-water contrast made the city easy to identify, impossible to miss, day or night.

Archer felt as if he were narrating an event that already had taken place. He had actually navigated the dash from Taiwan, made the unopposed radar bomb run on Foochow dozens of times using the electronic magic of a simulator that depicted portions of China and the Soviet Union.

Staring the wing commander in the eye, Archer called out the target's ground-zero coordinates: "North twenty-six degrees, eight minutes, fifty-six seconds; east, one hundred nineteen degrees, seventeen minutes, five seconds." The recitation from memory had been questioned by Archer's pilot because it was a briefing technique that no other navigator-bombardier used. The Strategic Air Command demanded accuracy, and it demanded that accuracy be confirmed with checklists. By formulating a checklist for every possible course of action the command reduced reason to reaction.

When he finished briefing, Archer knew he'd performed perfectly. As if to confirm that thought the wing commander half smiled and said, "Anyone have a question?"

An elderly major, a short man who was wearing glasses and chewing an unlit cigar, asked, "What were those target coordinates again?"

Without pause Archer recited them exactly as before. Cupping an ear, the major followed carefully, exaggeratedly tapped the numbers in his target folder. Nodding approval, he muttered, "That's not what you said the first time."

Archer's eyes widened. "Sir, that is *exactly* what I said the first time." Before anyone moved, Archer about-faced and, in foot-high numerals, chalked the coordinates on a blackboard with enough force to have cut them into stone. Shrapnel of chalk exploded from his pounding fist. He turned, glared at the bespectacled major, and asked, "Those are the numbers, sir. Can you *see* them?"

Colonel Turner grinned. Now he recalled the last time he'd met Archer: The kid had come before him with a speeding ticket, had been caught doing 115 miles an hour on the Dallas–Fort Worth turnpike. Turner normally demanded that squadron commanders deal with traffic violations. But 115 merited special attention. He'd suspended the kid's on-base driving privileges for a month even though the state of Texas had already fined him something close to a hundred dollars. Upon hearing the additional punishment, Archer's eyes had widened with disbelief, had radiated the same mute hatred they now showed. Intelligent, angry, and—if 115 was an indicator—a touch reckless, fearless. The kid had promise, Turner thought, if only the air force could make an officer of him. . . . "At ease, Lieutenant," he said.

He spoke to the major: "Martin, I think the lieutenant suspects your hearing." Major Martin closed his target folder, shrugged. Then Turner said, "Ah—Archer. Excellent briefing. Truly." The praise didn't penetrate Archer. "But from now on," Turner told him, "use your checklists."

Looking at Archer's eyes, still glowing with hate, Turner wondered how often the pup had to get hit with lightning before he learned to come in out of the storm.

4

↘CHAPTER 2

OUTSIDE THE BRIEFING room, Captain Chuck Charles
started on Archer: "I told you not to show off." As pilot,
Charles was commander of the three-man crew. He'd
earned his wings late in World War II, too late to see
combat. Discharged at war's end, he was recalled for the
Korean conflict and flew fifty missions in B26 Invader
attack-bombers. After that, he decided on a military career,
a chain of events common to captains in their mid- to late
thirties. "Why do you always have to be different?" Charles
asked.

In reply Archer pulled off his scarf, wadded it, stuffed it in
a pocket.

"What if you have to wear that again today?" Charles
said. His tall-standing, black, brush-cut hair was dotted
with gray. A swarthy complexion and hook nose gave him a
Semitic look, made him night to Archer's Aryan day. "You
should have used a checklist, the same as everyone else,"
Chuck Charles said.

"Look, I didn't screw up. Major Martin screwed up."

"He did that to make a point," Charles explained.

"We passed! We're combat-ready!" Charles drained the joy from achievement, Archer thought. No matter how perfect the results, Charles always nitpicked details that didn't matter, exactly as his mother had done. A plea roared from childhood: "What more do you want?"

"I want us to be the best," Charles flatly stated.

"I want you to be perfect," Archer's mother echoed.

Archer looked at Dixie Smith, their copilot, who with arms folded was leaning against a wall, watching. "If you two could see yourselves," Dixie often said to Archer. Now he was saying it again through sadly smiling eyes: *Don't let him get to you*.

Red curly hair, baby blue eyes, broad shoulders, and slim hips, Dixie could have played the lead in *Oklahoma!* Seemingly he didn't have a care in the world. He was a young captain who could fly loops around Charles. Although he had a thousand hours of single-engine time, he was forced to ride copilot until he met the command requirement for multi-engine experience.

"I'm going to the club, want to go?" Archer offered.

Dixie shook his head, made his curls dance. "I'm heading to the BX," he said with a soft drawl. A blond cashier at the Base Exchange was Dixie's obsession. Every blonde was his obsession. To Dixie, reality and fantasy were nearly identical. He lived his everyday dreams.

"Don't you think it's a little early for the club?" Charles said. It was three in the afternoon.

"We're finished for today. We have tomorrow off," Archer said.

"I thought we'd get together tomorrow and discuss crew coordination," Charles said.

Raging green sparks blinded Archer. He had planned to reward himself with a morning in bed.

Dixie raised a finger: "I was going to the beach."

"We'll meet in the squadron at nine," Charles said. "We'll be finished before noon."

Dixie nodded.

"Why not make it seven?" Archer said and slammed his way out of the building.

Chuck Charles looked at Dixie Smith as if seeking an ally.

Dixie shook his head. *That's between you two,* he thought. He was simply putting in hours until he moved up to pilot and got his own crew.

On Guam's Andersen Air Force Base, the officers' club was the oasis to slake off-duty loneliness. Its bar was a teak square, thirty feet a side, which surrounded a service island pyramided with bottles and glasses. Four Filipinos tended the bar during the day, eight at night. The club rule was: If it takes more than sixty seconds to be served, the drink is free. Otherwise, every drink cost a quarter, beer or whiskey, regardless of brand or mix.

Dressed in a yellow and black flower-print Hawaiian shirt and chino pants, Dick Robertson was holding down his spot at the bar, a corner known as "Robby's Turn." His muscular bulk filled the space like a side of beef. As a joke Robby once lifted his corner a foot or two off the floor, then dropped it and set up a shock wave that sloshed every drink around the square. He still wondered how he had done that. The next day, when sober, he couldn't budge the bar an inch. More recently, he'd torn a couple of decorative life preservers off the wall and sailed them across the room. Both had impacted on the pyramid, had shattered rows of whiskey bottles and stacks of glasses. Robby had shouted, "Set them up in the other alley," and then he'd passed out.

For the enjoyment of the half-dozen drinkers around him, he was reliving the moment, laughing about the cost and his visit with Colonel Turner. "I reported as ordered and was standing tall, and the Ax said, 'I hear you've been leading a pretty wild life.' The way he said it, easy and calm, I thought maybe he was just going through the motions. I kind of relaxed, eased onto the edge of his desk, and said, 'Could be better.' Hey, did I misread him!" Robby rolled his eyes. "I'll tell you: I didn't know I could stand at attention that long. And without blinking. He got out the Uniform Code of Military Justice and started reading to me." Robby puffed up his cheeks, then exhaled loudly. "I never knew he could do all those things to somebody. Hard labor? Bread and water?"

The listeners laughed. Robby didn't mind that the joke was on him. On the ground he readily played the buffoon; in the air he was one of the best copilots. Without intending to,

7

he dared to be different. Like many navigators but few pilots, Robby sported an oversize red-and-blue-dial Rolex GMT-Master wristwatch. Clasped around Robby's thick, hairy wrist, the watch and stainless steel band were reduced in scale, appeared normal in size. Generally Dixie laughed at the huge timepieces favored by navigators and said, "Big watch, little dick."

Spotting Archer, Robby called, "There's the 'no-checklist kid.' Heard you passed; let me buy you a drink. Where's Mother Chuck? That tight-ass could use a drink too." He tapped the seat of a stool next to him, waved Archer to it. "Keep it up and you'll give Chuckie a heart attack."

"Is that a promise?" Archer said quietly and won a few nods. How fast did news travel? Archer wondered. The briefing had ended only minutes earlier. A SAC wing was like a family: Everybody knew everybody else's business.

Without being told, a smiling bartender served Archer a scotch and water, easy on the ice. After saluting Robby with raised glass, Archer swallowed half the drink while gesturing to the bartender for another round.

The jolt of the whiskey was so welcome that, for an instant, Archer wanted to weep in gratitude. The tension of the briefing followed by the unspent anger generated toward Martin and Charles had clogged his chest with icy rage. Now the golden heat of whiskey melted the block inside him, coursed through him like the warm stroke of a soothing hand, brought a shiver of relief, a self-congratulatory tingle of achievement, despite others. With tears in his eyes, he finished his first drink, brushed his nose with a forefinger, then grinned at Robby.

Robby watched with a look that said, "I understand." How could anyone put up with Charles?

Archer felt protected next to Robby, the same feeling he had near Dixie. The world avoided conflict with such easygoing heavyweights. Archer was surprised every time Robby jerked somebody's chain and mutual laughter was created; identical words from him would have mushroomed into anger.

Robby's carefree spirit and popularity were attributes Archer envied. Of course, as a copilot Robby could afford to be carefree. He was responsible for a fraction of the knowledge demanded of Archer, had no responsibilities directly related to The Bomb. And in SAC, that was the difference that counted. Knowledge not only brought responsibility, it also granted power.

Middleweight in stature, Archer ranked himself as an intellectual giant, a man far superior to Robby, Dixie, and the rest of them. But without realizing it, he depended upon men like Robby to teach him the facts about life outside the cockpit. . . .

After the club closed, Robby and Archer bombarded the patio with coconuts. Each time they blindly lobbed one of the husked missiles high over the courtyard wall, they shouted, "Bombs away," then grinningly anticipated the sound of breaking glass. Through a statistical loophole, they missed the patio's glass-top tables time after time. Finally, Robby said, "And you call yourself a bombardier!"

It was then that Robby sprawled on the club lawn and explained his philosophy of SAC, one he'd developed during three years as a B47 copilot:

"When you're a lieutenant, you're allowed to do anything you want, short of raping the wing commander's wife. She might not complain, but he'd probably get jealous." Robby hadn't figured out exactly why the system was so liberal. He'd accepted the fact that rowdiness was tolerated, particularly in the privacy of the club. *Keep it in the family,* he'd thought. On the other hand, he'd seen one lieutenant cashiered for loan-sharking enlisted men, and another dismissed from duty for writing bad checks. Both had been ground-pounders, nonflyers. "Raising hell is acceptable," he told Archer, "until you make captain." At one time Robby had thought he'd found a vague relationship between the six years of childish freedom given lieutenants and the six years of childish freedom given to Oriental babies. Then he'd laughed away his rampant reason. It was a matter of economics, he'd decided. "Just think about how much time and money Uncle Sam has invested in you," he said to Archer.

Longer than you know, Archer thought. Before entering navigator training, he'd spent a year in pilot training, had washed out during the formation flying phase of T33 jets. The first failure of his life. It was a fact he kept secret when possible. Not winning pilot wings had been a slash of fate that permanently scarred his ego. Two other lieutenants had washed out at the same time. To reaffirm their self-image, they'd bought new cars. Archer had married.

After that he spent a year learning to navigate, six months learning to bomb, a month surviving in the wilderness, and another month studying B47 systems before arriving at the Bomb Wing in Abilene, Texas. Counting leave and travel time, his training added up to three years, almost to the day. Following that, for three months he sat and waited for fate to crew him with Chuck Charles and Dixie Smith. Then the wing deployed to Guam where Charles's crew spent three more months qualifying as combat-ready.

"Big bucks," Robby said. "Nobody's going to flush that investment down the tube just because you happen to get drunk and break some thing or two." Robby sat up and nudged Archer. "And you're a navigator in the only command where navs count. Bombing and navigation are ninety percent of SAC's mission. Maybe more." Robby shook his head. "As much as I hate to admit it, in B47s the nav is the crew. A good nav can carry a weak pilot, but the best pilot in the world can't make up for a guy who can't bomb."

Clamping a heavy hand on Archer's shoulder, Robby softly said, "Look, from what I've heard, you got it, you can bomb. Charles will never let you go."

↘CHAPTER 3

BETH ANN ARCHER found contentment in sleeping until noon, found delight in awakening at the center of her own limited universe. At the same time, her late arousal was tinged by judgments of laziness. Actually, she didn't sleep straight through to midday. At six she was up to breast-feed Beverly. But that was an enjoyable obligation, like feeding herself, a continuation of flesh to flesh. The child had Beth's oval face, identical dark brown eyes, uptilted nose, and narrow mouth with pouty lips.

Beverly's feedings highlighted Beth's days, were times for her to stop and be thankful that her baby was whole and healthy. The six A.M. feeding was Beth's favorite because Beverly was drowsy then, still gently adrift on the dark sea of night. At that hour, the baby usually slipped back to sleep while feeding. The heat from the tiny mouth and the warmth from the body contact between mother and daughter produced a similar soporific effect on Beth, and after tucking Beverly into her crib, she flopped down on her own bed.

Falling into bed, Beth could hear Morris's irritation: "Someday you're going to break the frame doing that." It was her bed as much as his, she thought. More, in fact. She'd bought it while living with her parents, long before she met him.

With Morris gone, Beth had her first home alone, experienced the luxury of a house exclusively for her comfort and enjoyment, even if it was a duplex. Until then she had thought of the rooms of their two-bedroom home as shadowy low-ceiling cells. She had hunched her shoulders when entering their bedroom. Now, with Morris gone, the crypt expanded. Walls widened; the ceiling soared. Windows glowed in halos of light. Music that she enjoyed filled the air: Stan Kenton and Dave Brubeck. Hard brass and soft ivory, tension and tonic.

The comfort of the house became an extension of the comfort of her Chinese red robe, a stained, loose-hanging, quilted shell that Morris called "undisciplined." With him away, she spent entire days in the cozy cover.

Beth's life hadn't been her own during the first weeks after Morris left for Guam. Without a routine, she had depended on Morris's rules to get through a day. That had meant rising at six, feeding Beverly, then staying up. The first time she'd dropped back into bed, guilt swept over her like a fever, soaked her with sweat that dried chillingly. At any moment she had expected Morris to walk into the room and stare down at her with eyes that accused, violent eyes that made her feel responsible for all the sloth in the world. Alone in bed, she had shivered uncontrollably. The fever of guilt had been like the onset of flu, had made her fear for Beverly. Who would care for her baby if she became ill? Could she breast-feed while carrying an infection? Would fever dry up her milk? How could she be so ignorant of an act that was supposedly natural, the reflex action of a good mother?

Morris's admonitions had echoed in her head: "If you're sick, go to the hospital. That's what it's there for. It doesn't cost anything." After rushing to the base hospital emergency ward, Beth had felt ridiculous when a doctor pronounced her "sound as a bell."

12

The doctor reminded Beth of her older brother, Daniel, her only sibling, who had been a constant companion, a protective giant playmate until he left home at eighteen. Beth had been ten then and, for the first time, found herself friendless, tasted loneliness. Like her brother, the doctor was tall, thin, wore brown horn-rimmed glasses, had curly black hair that resembled hers, hair that bordered on kinkiness. His name tag said "Leonard" and Beth wondered if it was his first or last name. Upon learning that she was separated from her husband for the first time, he laughed with the same lazy manner of her brother and bluntly told her, "You'll get used to it. I see a lot of wives who are lonely, who have nothing to do but imagine the worst when their husbands are away."

As if following a checklist, Leonard offered to prescribe tranquilizers: "A lot of wives use them. Seventy-five percent of the women I see aren't really sick. They're only nervous, or bored. The symptoms are endemic to SAC."

Unconsciously Beth shook her head. How would tranquilizers affect Beverly?

Seeing her negative response, Leonard said, "Don't be afraid. They're only a way of easing over rough spots." He touched her hand. She flinched. "I can give them to you but you don't have to use them unless you feel the need."

He was no older than she was, Beth decided, no more than twenty-seven. Noticing captain's bars on the uniform collar beneath his white coat, she innocently asked, "How long have you been in the air force?"

Leonard bristled, frowned, leaned forward, and looked blackly into her eyes. His reaction caught her off guard, confused her because its intensity resembled her father's hostile stare when his authority was questioned. But he looked like Daniel. . . .

"Six months," Leonard said. "I was drafted. I don't intend to make it a career. Half the people I see aren't really sick. A partnership's waiting for me, in Washington." As if dismissing her, he turned away, scribbled in her folder.

How had she offended him? She hadn't been questioning his expertise, or his touch, Beth thought, yet she felt compelled to atone for any misunderstanding. "I'll try them," she said.

Without looking at her, Leonard said, "I don't have to give them to you. I was trying to do you a favor."

Beth nodded unseen agreement. He wasn't Daniel. Daniel had never been bad-tempered with her.

After staring at the ceiling for half a minute, Leonard wrote the prescription. "Take them if you think you need them."

Equinal. The white tablets that she traded the paper for reminded her of aspirins. She'd forgotten to ask how they would affect Beverly. It didn't matter. She'd never use them, she thought. Leaving the hospital with something tangible in hand made her feel as if the trip hadn't been completely wasted.

Beth had given birth to Beverly and then Morris had gone to Guam. "In SAC there are no extenuating circumstances. The mission comes first," he had told her. "When a wing goes TDY, everyone goes. SAC people organize their lives around their duties." Like a combination of punches, the back-to-back events left Beth stunned, added mental confusion to her physical fatigue.

Morris had favored a plan for her to stay in Laredo with her parents while he was overseas. That was the last thing Beth wanted. She had lived with them until her father suggested that she was an old maid, that he was burdened with her for as long as he lived. Shortly after, at twenty-five, she sped away with Morris, disappeared practically overnight. She had not seen her parents since then, had not visited them in two and a half years.

If she returned now, her father's first accusation would be that the marriage had failed. He would not understand the concept of TDY, temporary duty, overseas, would classify her as an abandoned woman, with child. A double burden to him.

Now Beth was happy she had decided to go it alone. Her days were her own, except for duties to Beverly. Because nobody was present to second-guess how she performed those duties, each day she found it easier to follow her own mind. She developed routines that suited her, that allowed her to slide effortlessly through a day or through a week as if gliding down a seamless tube of time.

She was pleased to discover that in self-imposed routine

14

she found freedom. Beth's actions flowed from the dictates of her body and soul, grew from emotion rather than intellect, were based on "want" rather than "must."

With Morris life was a series of preordained drills. In the morning when he arose, he expected Beth to arise with him. Together they made the bed and together they cooked breakfast. Clean sheets went on the bed every Monday because Monday was washday.

Exceptions to the early rising and breakfast rules came on weekends when he was crippled by a hangover. Then he remained in bed as long as it took to exhaust the alcohol from his system.

Now that she was alone Beth changed sheets when it suited her, left on one set for a solid month, made the covers into a burrow. And eating, too, took on a dimension of animal purity. She ate what her body craved. Peanut butter on rye toast for breakfast was as logical as a can of asparagus covered with melted cheese for a midnight snack. The random system seemed to work. She wasn't gaining or losing weight. And Beverly was gaining weight. To be certain of that, she weighed the baby twice a day. And as an extra precaution, Beth took vitamins to keep her milk nourishing.

After three months, Beth Ann Archer had found a private universe but feared it would collapse when Morris returned. She didn't look forward to being squeezed, being forced backward, surrendering her new style for old routines.

Two days before Morris was due to return, she tried her first Equinal and glimpsed an entrance into a space no one else could enter.

CHAPTER 4

THE RINGING PHONE jerked Emily Charles to conscious-
ness. She was home! What time was it? Fumbling the
receiver, she tried for a lilting "good morning." "Good"
came out a bellow; "morning" cracked in two on the rising
inflection. *Cigarettes*, she told herself. Cause or cure? Her
eyes searched the nightstand for a pack, saw the clock. Ten
after ten! David and Becky had gone to school without
waking her. David was an angel.

"Are you listening?" asked the electronic voice of Jean
Turner, the wing commander's wife.

"I missed the last part. I was pouring batter, making a
cake . . ."

"Did you order the centerpieces for the luncheon?"

"Yes, ma'am," Emily lied.

"Well, they're not here."

"What?" *Was today Friday*, Emily asked herself, *already?*

"From whom did you order them?" Jean Turner said.

Emily's mind went blank. White nothing. She couldn't

muster enough will to recall a name, any name. The line whispered at her until she answered, "I don't remember. I have it written down. I'll find it. I'll call."

"If we can't have the flowers by eleven, cancel them," Jean Turner ordered.

"Yes, Mrs. Turner," Emily said to a dead line. She recalled that she'd made a hairdresser appointment for ten. How had she remembered to do one but not the other? Now she was too late for both. No centerpieces, she thought. Scandalous.

A familiar pulse throb behind her eyebrow made her right eyelid droop. She sat on the edge of the bed for a minute, closed both eyes, and pressed the heels of her palms to her brows. Her toes grazed the rug. How tiny she was! Stretching, she swung her legs, let the nappy pile make her soles tingle. Chuck used to call her "my petite pretty," she remembered. And "my little chipmunk." How she hated that name. Lovingly, he'd teased her with it. They were almost children then. Her apple cheeks still held a glow of youth. Or was it the flush of a morning after?

In search of cigarettes, she wandered through the dining area and into the vaulted living room of the on-base Capehart house. Base housing was a mini-suburb of the military installation, a tract of single-level, red-brick and frame houses. Living there was a bonus. By forfeiting a monthly housing allowance that was approximately enough to make the mortgage payment on a middle-class house in the civilian community, a military family received a furnished home with free utilities, services, and maintenance.

Emily wasn't surprised to find the living room in inspection order: no empty glasses, no glass rings . . . ashtrays clean, cushions in place, rug vacuumed . . . every venetian blind tilted at exactly the same angle. If ever a child was perfect . . . David was more than she deserved, but exactly what she needed.

She found a carton of cigarettes in a bottom kitchen cabinet, behind mixing bowls. David never threw away her things, but he made them difficult to find. Lighting up, she searched the refrigerator for the jug of fresh orange juice she knew would be there. More of David's work. She poured half a glass of juice, topped it with vodka from a pint bottle she'd hidden behind the canned goods. Two could play the

17

hiding game. For a moment she decided not to attend the luncheon. Then, sipping the clear layer of vodka floating atop the drink, she decided she owed it to Chuck. One strike already today.

Entering the bathroom, Emily laughed out loud. The room sparkled. The house was the first practically new structure they'd ever been assigned and David kept it looking as if nobody lived there.

Finding a pair of manicuring scissors, between sips of vodka and orange juice, she trimmed her mouse-brown hair, starting with the bangs.

In the officers' club ballroom, Jean Turner greeted arrivals as warmly as if she were welcoming them into her own home. When her time had come, she had assumed leadership of the wives as confidently as her husband had taken command of their husbands. As a team, she and Axel had climbed above the mist of mundane duties, could clearly view the pinnacle of high command, an attainable goal. Among dreams of future conquests, she saw Axel standing like Hillary on Everest, wearing the four gleaming stars of CINCSAC—Commander-in-Chief, Strategic Air Command—the most powerful man in the world, after the president of the United States. Axel was born for the role: a gentle, controlling touch encased in a mailed fist, ready to strike.

Through the years both husband and wife had enthusiastically performed whatever role was assigned. From Axel, Jean Turner had learned that a person cannot develop into a strong leader without being a dependable follower. Following that principle, she had earned her place by serving as a nonsalaried worker for Red Cross Home Service and Gray Ladies, United Service Organization, Brownies, Girl Scouts, thrift shops, and wives' clubs. She had been part of more drives and sales than she could name, had walked and driven more voluntary miles than many people travel in a lifetime, had donated hours that totaled years of service.

"Jean has more uniforms than I do," Axel delighted in telling friends, "wears more hats than the commander-in-chief. And she's still the best wife and mother in the world."

Almost as an afterthought, Jean Turner had flawlessly run

a home that included three children, had done so whether Axel was away for a day, a week, or a year.

Service had been Jean Turner's destiny since she'd stood at West Point and proudly watched Axel repeat the oath of office, had mouthed the words with him when he had been commissioned into the United States Army:

> . . . do solemnly swear that I will support and defend the Constitution of the United States against all enemies, foreign and domestic; that I will bear true faith and allegiance to same; that I take this obligation freely, without mental reservation or purpose of evasion; and that I will well and faithfully discharge the duties of the office upon which I am about to enter, so help me God.

So help me God! To Jean Turner, those four words breathed life into the oath. Those four words cleanly divided Americans from the communist atheists, placed man under the guidance and protection of a supreme being rather than leaving him nakedly exposed to the ruthless power of a totalitarian state.

She loved the oath: Its sentiments were her life. Currently, however, she questioned its completeness because the Soviets also had nuclear bombs. She wondered if the pledge should be expanded to include: ". . . that I will support and defend the Free World against communism." The change would be appropriate to men of SAC. Axel had told her that SAC controlled ninety-five percent of the Free World's striking power, a volume of destruction beyond her comprehension. However, when Axel had said, "Manned bombers rule the world," she understood that he was a prince of the realm. The forty-five B47s under his command formed one wing of an air armada that within a day could strike anywhere on earth.

Every inch as fit and trim as her husband, Jean Turner would have been as comfortable in a blue uniform decked with regalia as she was in her luncheon attire of full-skirted gray wool dress highlighted by a single strand of pearls, white gloves, gray felt cloche hat, and high-heel gray leather pumps.

Her quiet outfit was perfect within the military subculture where fashion lagged behind the outside world. Military wives dreamed of the latest styles but, in reality, pictures in fashion magazines were like images transported from another planet. Owning such clothes seemed as distantly impossible as holding a moon rock. Military salaries were pegged too low to permit fad chasing. And wives didn't work—period. Therefore, last season's style was acceptable for this season, and for next season and, ultimately, for as long as the wearer chose. Timeless fashion emerged. Only neatness and completeness counted.

In step with that disregard for current styles, hair design, makeup, and jewelry also tended to be muted.

The outer shell concealed the inner being, Jean Turner believed. Her shell was virtually transparent, revealed its inner layers without compromise. A touch of rouge on square cheekbones, a thin coat of tranquil red lipstick around a controlled, dimpled mouth: the only accents on her handsome face. Let the gray hairs and the wrinkles show, she told herself. They were badges of maturity rather than signs of age.

The future of the air force was of more concern to her. How to find women to take her place eventually, to perpetuate customs and traditions? Most lower-ranking wives professed interest in the air force but lacked dedication. Emily Charles was a perfect example. Such inept women had chosen the wrong profession. Incapable of running home or family, they leaned on their husbands and, in effect, made part-time soldiers of men who were expected to put duty and country first. "Just because you're officially classified a 'dependent' doesn't mean you have to be dependent" was a catch phrase coined by Jean Turner. She knew that behind every officer stood a woman equal in stature and rank.

By the time Emily Charles arrived at the officers' club, the parking lot was full. She drove her station wagon around to the side of the building, out of sight of the main road, parked in an unpaved area, and took her chances that the air police would overlook the violation.

Not until her hand touched the handle of the club's front door did she remember gloves. The cold metal on skin made her feel naked, suddenly exposed, as if she had no secrets. *Strike two,* she thought.

She was grateful when Jean Turner didn't even glance at her bare hands, merely confronted her with gentle words spoken sadly: "No flowers."

"I couldn't find the name," Emily lied needlessly and blushed with shame for failing this martinet of a woman who saw completely through her. "I'm sorry," she said softly. The apology included falsehood and failure.

"The others from your crew aren't here." No threat lurked in the words.

"Elizabeth Smith works," Emily said.

A picture of a big blonde flashed into Jean Turner's mind, a blonde with an upswept, showgirl hairdo. To top that, she had a job that came before all else. Was this tomorrow's air force?

"And—Beth . . . Beth . . ." Again, white nothing blanked Emily Charles's mind.

Jean Turner supplied the name: "Archer." Every married officer was required to provide wing headquarters with a photograph of his wife. The pictures were annotated and mounted according to crew alignment, then passed to Jean Turner for study. Therefore, she knew everyone, greeted newcomers by name at first sight, went so far as to inquire about specific children. Now she asked, "Is Beth *still* breast-feeding Beverly?"

Beth had used breast-feeding as an excuse for missing the previous two luncheons, Emily remembered. She had neglected Beth since before the last luncheon, had no idea what she was doing. "I'm sorry but I don't know," Emily confessed. "I haven't called her for over a month." Strike three!

A nicely chilled Rhine wine, Emily thought and drained a glass before she tasted her Waldorf salad. The sherry bar had closed while she'd been talking to Jean Turner. In the same minute her empty glass touched the table a waiter refilled it. She'd positioned herself on an outer aisle, a spot convenient for service.

Once at a luncheon she'd stranded herself at a center table, had suffered through the program on one glass of

21

wine. Without doubt, the single most miserable luncheon in her life. She had ended up with a crick in her neck from craning in hope of gaining a waiter's attention. If she'd had a flare gun, she would have fired it in distress.

Emily tried to ignore the barrenness that spanned row after row of white-clothed tables. The missing centerpieces were more conspicuous than the real things.

She brightened when the waiter served broiled fillet of sole with a boiled potato and green beans. Next month the dish would be chicken with rice, for certain. Perhaps she would be sick next month. No, Chuck would be home, would insist she go. There was plenty of wine and with it Emily ate everything on her plate. When had she last eaten a cooked meal? The other night David had made something in the oven. . . . Dessert was chocolate pudding camouflaged under the name of mousse. She waved it away and pointed to her wineglass.

A plump woman at an angle across the table said, "You set such a good example, Emily," and handed her dessert back to a waiter. It was the first time since being seated that Emily had been addressed. She smiled in response. The women at her end of the table had courteously introduced themselves before grace was said. Two she had met before but they gave no indication of recognizing her. After that, they had turned to each other for conversation. Emily hadn't attempted to join in, really hadn't listened.

She wasn't feeling sorry for herself, wasn't complaining, but she'd been in the wing for half a year and she still felt like a newcomer. She'd been through the newcomer ritual before, but never to this degree. How much longer would she remain invisible? Most of the wives knew each other from former assignments; their relationships went back years and years. Cliques and pecking orders had been established in B29s and B50s and B36s, long before reaching B47s. This was Chuck's first tour in SAC. She felt as if he'd been transferred to another air force, a different nation.

Coffee was served and then Jean Turner introduced newcomers before presenting volunteers with certificates and pins. Emily asked herself, *Where did women find a thousand hours to give away?*

Next Jean Turner said, "One announcement! When the wing comes home . . ."

The women in the audience applauded loudly. Some cheered. One whistled shrilly.

Jean Turner said, "Me too," nodded to the laughter, then started over. "When the wing comes home, our men will begin a new program called Red Alpha." The code name produced puzzled stares, questioning frowns. "That means three bomber crews will be living in barracks near the flight line, twenty-four hours a day, every day of the year, ready for instant launch." The audience stirred, hummed, protested subvocally. "It's going to be a minor hardship because, even though your husband is on base, you won't be able to see him." A wave of groans rolled through the audience.

Jean Turner raised a commanding hand: "Wait. It's only one crew at a time from each squadron. The tour will last two days. The duty will rotate among combat-ready crews." She paused and gave a stiff-upper-lip smile.

A striking young blonde named Ellen Robertson raised her hand, half stood, and called out, "Mrs. Turner, ma'am, our squadron has fewer crews than the others. That means our husbands will be getting the red thing more often." Women near her looked away as if disavowing her presence. A voice loudly corrected: "Red *Alpha!*" Ellen Robertson shot back with "Red whatever" and sat down.

Only youth could be so self-focused, Jean Turner thought, so impatiently concerned. Holding her smile, she said, "I'm positive that will be worked out fairly. What I'm asking is for each of you to plan ahead. Recognize that although your husband will be able to *talk* to you on the phone, he won't be available to *do* a single thing for you. Not take a sick child to the hospital. Not fix a flat tire. Not pick up a quart of milk. Absolutely nothing."

Jean Turner was pleased to see heads nod here and there, signs of agreement and cooperation. It took but a few to accept a new concept. Then those few helped the rest to cope until a dream became a way of life.

As a sort of summary Jean Turner added, "Red Alpha will be the most important duty in the Strategic Air Command short of actual war." Her smile vanished. She flushed with goosebumps. Recognition of the enormity of her spontaneous summation struck the breath from her. Red Alpha was no dream. It was a nightmare. The aircraft would be loaded with nuclear weapons. Red Alpha was an aggressive and hostile force posture. Provocative. Nothing less.

The massed listeners dissolved into small, bubbling discussion groups.

Emily wondered if the crews had been told about Red Alpha. Too often she had carried home information from a wives' meeting only to find that Chuck knew nothing of the subject. Then a day or two later he received the information officially, through normal channels. Those kinks in the chain of command chafed him.

Jean Turner needed several seconds to force Red Alpha to a corner of her mind, to calm the ripples of seismic fear. It wasn't her job to question policy, but Red Alpha was the first item she intended to discuss with Axel. *Why?* her mind persisted in asking. *Wasn't the United States the most powerful nation on earth? Wasn't the United States secure?*

With half a mind she called for order and introduced the guest speaker, a new doctor from the base hospital, Captain James Leonard.

"Call me Dr. Jim," he said in greeting, "but don't call me after five in the evening." Intended to be humorous, the line emerged with a ring of truth that stifled laughter in the tense and distracted audience. Jim Leonard desperately scanned faces and returned smiles to the few who smiled at him. Then he went to work to make the others accept him.

Instinctively, Emily classified Leonard as immature, a brash intellectual. But he was cute. Young, and brash, and cute. At the start of his talk a waiter placed a full bottle of wine before Emily. How did he know? Mentally she blessed the waiter, called him angel.

CHAPTER 5

THE B47 WAS a stupid and blind beast of burden guided by the brain of a navigator-bombardier who sat isolated in the blackness of its pressurized head. There, in the manner of an old-time accountant bent over aged ledgers, the solitary man painstakingly extracted numbers from the yellow pages of Air Almanac and HO249 sun and star tables, meticulously compared the figures to celestial sightings made by a copilot, manually plotted the differences on a chart, and predicted the bomber's pinpoint position in space for a future time, mere minutes ahead. His computations came alive the instant the aircraft flashed through the predestined point. This celestial Bartleby's toil was mathematical logic, often precisely performed in his head with haste, and as dependent upon intuition as it was upon scientific judgment.

Such navigation without computers was art. Ghosts of

Prince Henry, Magellan, and Drake flew with navigators then.

In the Bomb Wing, there were more crews than airplanes. SAC authorized a manning ratio of 1.5 crews per bomber, a figure seldom attained even though manpower was the least expensive resource in the inventory. Nevertheless, there were more crews than airplanes and about a dozen were scheduled to return from Guam as passengers.

When Chuck Charles broke the news that his crew hadn't been assigned a B47 for redeployment, Morris Archer felt humiliated. The achievement of spanning a third of the globe nonstop was to be denied him. Instead he would drone along in a propeller-driven C97 transport, well below the jet stream's hurricane force, and waste ten hours merely to reach Hawaii; then, after a night's layover, another ten hours to reach home.

"Why *not* us?" Archer demanded to know. "Somebody think I can't navigate?" His draftsman's precision in navigation had been legend before he'd finished basic navigation training. There, Archer's meticulousness had caused one instructor to accuse him of cheating on a flight mission: "Somehow—I don't know exactly how, but somehow—you made out this log and chart on the ground. Nobody can do work this neat in the air." Archer would forever savor the moment when he had dumped his briefcase's contents on the instructor's lap, had buried the man with logs from the past, relics of invisible paths through the sky, and had said, "You mean I backed in all of these?" The hand of the accountant-draftsman reached out from each piece of paper as if casting a vote on his behalf. "Anyone clever enough to back in all of these has to be the world's greatest navigator." The incident was strange victory: Archer was happy to be accused falsely rather than to go unrecognized.

Now, knowing Charles's dislike for obscenity, Archer said, "How come we have to ride in the back of a fucking C97 *again?*" Archer already had envisioned arriving home, climbing down the ladder of a jet bomber he had navigated, taking off his gleaming white helmet, and hugging Beth, who would be waiting. His fantasy was in tatters.

Didn't Archer understand that in the military there were

situations in which explanations weren't forthcoming? Charles wondered. Then, contrary to his judgment, he tried to explain: "We were the last crew to become combat-ready."

"All the more reason we should get a plane, we can use the training," Archer said. In SAC training was the guiding light of day-to-day operations.

"There's nothing I can do. That's the way it is," Charles finally said. He was assigned to supervise the redeployment team in Hawaii, a job nobody wanted. The team left Guam first and arrived in Texas last. Charles had more reasons than Archer to get home, but he hadn't complained. Somebody had to do the job.

Dixie's eyes twinkled like Christmas lights: "This way we get to spend a night in Hawaii." He grinned, wiggled his fingers in front of his face, and sang, "Hula, hula. Hula, hula."

"All the girls there have black hair," Archer said and was startled when Chuck Charles laughed out loud. He hadn't meant to be funny. After Charles left the room, he said, "I know why we didn't get a plane."

Dixie rested his chin on his hands: "This is going to be good."

"Hey, bite it, Dix," Archer said and hesitated. Then he didn't care what Dixie thought, he had to get it out of his system: "The reason is refueling. Chuck isn't that smooth—yet." He knew he was stretching the point. To date Charles hadn't failed to offload the required amount of fuel, but he usually had needed the maximum allotted time.

"If he can't get it, I will," Dixie said modestly. He sounded like Mickey Mantle calling, "Save me a bat, I'll hit one out of here and win it."

Although vision was excellent through the B47 blister-type canopy, refueling from the copilot's rear seat in the tandem cockpit was difficult. The copilot couldn't see the point of contact. The tanker refuelling boom plugged into the bomber's nose squarely in front of the pilot, directly over the navigator-bombardier's head.

During training Dixie had displayed amazing skill in refueling from the rear seat. Making contact on his first attempt, he had remained hooked up until, after ten minutes, the instructor pilot said, "That's enough, showboat." A few minutes into the hookup, disregarding the two handles on the control yoke, Dixie had encircled the yoke's hub with one meaty paw. Thereafter, he flew the bomber in single-handed fighter-pilot fashion, simply held formation in the slot of the tanker.

At debriefing Archer had complimented him on his prowess. After all, inability to fly formation had once brought Archer's downfall. Who can appreciate performance more than a man who failed in the same act and thereby eliminated himself from further competition?

In reply, Dixie had nodded shyly, then had smiled broadly and said, "Once I get it in, I sure hate to take it out."

During redeployment, if a bomber crew failed to offload its fuel at French Frigate Shoals, it was forced to divert into Hickam Air Base, Hawaii. In accordance with SAC headquarters' microscopic grading system, the mission was scored an inflight abort. Had the plane been headed for the Soviet Union, the delay would have diminished the initial strike force by one. Although relaunch as a second-wave sortie was probable, it was not as desirable as packing maximum power into the first punch.

In describing the exactitude of the British army, Rudyard Kipling wrote: "And you are totally accountable for everything you do." SAC perpetuated that tradition. Every action counted, was compared to a standard.

Free of redeployment worries, Morris Archer learned that nothing was required of him during his final week on Guam. His idleness caused him to yearn for Beth. The single extra night he would spend in Hawaii became a sublime punishment inflicted by Charles.

Three months of furtive masturbation beneath a thin sheet at night in the crew's open-air, screen-wall quonset hut had crusted Archer's psyche with layers of loathsome gratification. How had he endured the mortification of fidelity to Beth?

His orgiastic images excluded Beth, focused instead on island girls described by Dick Robertson and on Robertson's wife, Ellen, who was a knockout.

For months Ellen was the single permanent star in Arch-

28

er's revolving constellation of imagination. The few times Archer had been near Ellen he'd found it difficult to focus on her, to speak directly to her. Her flowing blond hair looked as if it belonged on a movie star. Her glacier-blue eyes had a sensual slant, the almond shape of the Orient. But the rest of her was pure Nordic: freckled white complexion, long gracefully rounded limbs, and a wide-shouldered body with breasts so prominent that glancing at their contours made Archer feel unfaithful. But how could anyone ignore them? Whether the viewer was male or female, to see Ellen Robertson was to have thoughts knocked ajar.

Archer once overheard Jean Turner describe Ellen to other senior wives: "If that girl were any more grown up, she'd be dangerous." The words made him recognize that beyond her startling breasts and dazzling eyes, Ellen's body was childish, boyish, slim, and hipless. The realization opened endless fjords for his mental explorations. Was she narrow everywhere? How did she accommodate the bulk of Robby? Did he hurt her? Did he please her? And she him? Who else had ventured within her?

Archer was certain that Robby would answer his questions, if he found nerve to ask them. But it was more exciting not to know. Knowledge limited imagination.

Dick Robertson loved to tell of how he had met Ellen: "I was a junior at Syracuse, just turned twenty-one. I saw her at a dance. What a mood she gave off." He did his routine of puffing his cheeks, then exhaling loudly. "One minute she was pure ice. Then the next, hot, hot, *hot* fiery stares. Lightning practically shot out of her eyes. I couldn't guess where it came from: love or hate, sex or rage. Nobody was asking her to dance. Nobody dared. So . . ." He sneered confidently. "I went over. We danced two dances, slow dances. She plastered herself to me. In a second I had a rod-on that was like a flagpole between us. We danced one more slow number and she was ready. We went to her house, her parents weren't home. We did it in the front hall, right on the floor. Then we went up to her room and did it again. Everything was beautiful for both of us, until . . ." Robby paused and grinned as if caught with his hand in a cookie jar. "Until she told me she was fourteen."

Robby's candid attitude about his wife's sexuality quietly shocked Archer, who couldn't imagine discussing Beth in similar detail.

Chuck Charles thought that all of Robby's values were hopelessly out of kilter. He encouraged Archer to ignore the man and his ideas. The vibrations between Charles and Robby were beyond Archer's wavelength. He had never heard them exchange a greeting, had watched Charles excuse himself from groups that Robby joined. As often as Archer had irritated Charles, he had yet to experience the physical threat that Charles's eyes radiated toward Robby. At times the air seemed to crackle with static from his stare.

Uncharacteristically, Robby too lost several degrees of cool when Charles was near. His Jovian composure deteriorated to nervous, fleeting, eye-cutting leers. His stature shrank.

After a time Archer thought that he glimpsed what irritated Charles. There were evenings when Robby could piss off the pope, not necessarily with topic, but with philosophy underlying topic. Since his first night on Guam, Robby's favorite pastimes had been whoring in Agana and bragging about it at the bar, in detail, usually to Archer.

"She says she's sixteen, but . . ." Robby raised a shoulder, flipped a hand to express doubt. "What equipment!" The puffed cheeks and exhaled air. "Titties like honeydew melons. Why don't you go with me later?"

The question had come up before and Archer had thought about it. While in pilot training at Hondo and Laredo he'd lived the weekends in Mexican whorehouses.

"All that tight golden flesh," Robby said.

A challenge that for months had rested submerged on the bottom of Archer's mind unexpectedly rose to the surface and burst from his mouth: "How would you like it if Ellen cheated on you?" Like a rebounding radar beam, the image of Beth cheating on him with some faceless lover echoed back.

"There's no such thing as cheating," Robby stated. He wasn't getting lured into some stupid philosophical dead-end discussion that led nowhere and proved nothing, he thought. "A man does what he has to do."

"And what about a woman?" *What about Beth?* reechoed.

"Women are different. They don't have the same needs," Robby said. He finished his drink, set the glass down hard. Standing, turning to Archer, Robby said, "I'm heading downtown right now. You want to go?"

Archer met his stare. "No," he said emphatically, without excuse, and experienced the majesty of moral superiority. As long as he remained faithful, he could believe Beth was faithful.

↳CHAPTER 6

Exactly a minute and forty seconds behind schedule, Colonel Axel Turner landed the first redeployment B47 at Dyess Air Force Base. Upon touchdown, a white drogue blossomed from the bomber's tail to help slow the craft. Moments later, with the bomber in the middle of its rollout, the copilot poked a flagpole with a half-size replica of the wing flag up through the sextant port. The banner was Turner's trademark, was flown and shown by every airplane he boarded.

When the flag popped into view above the canopy, unfurled and snapped in the airflow, a sergeant in the control tower announced over radio, "The Ax is back," then covered his deviation from standard procedures by quickly adding, "Welcome home, sir. We missed you."

Beneath his oxygen mask Turner smiled. No need to crush misdirected esprit, he thought and said, "Thank you, tower. It feels good to be wanted."

In the tower, the guilty sergeant pretended to wipe sweat from his brow, then grinned at his coworkers.

While steering the B47 Stratojet along a taxiway toward the VIP parking slot in front of base operations, Turner spotted Jean standing next to the base commander, Colonel Doyle "King" Royal. The whole welcoming committee had turned out to greet him, he noticed. As if recognizing that he saw her, Jean raised a hand in greeting. Then Axel Turner gave his undivided attention to a wand-wielding ground crewman who parked him.

After setting the brakes and cutting engines, unstrapping from seat and parachute, and peeling off oxygen mask, helmet, and life preserver, Axel Turner rested a minute before massaging and then combing hair that was wet with sweat. Across the chest and along the arms, his gray-green flying suit was stained by a thin white crust of salt, the residue of inflight refueling labors.

At his age, eleven hours in the seat was too long, he thought. His back ached, felt tender around the kidneys. Not enough fluids, he told himself; but, no input, no output. Despite how sleek she looked from the outside, the B47's internal design was contrary to nature: There was no room for a man to move about. A crewman didn't even get out of his seat to urinate. Instead, he wiggled his pride through layers of straps, rested its head in a plastic cone attached to a rubber tube, then hosed away while hoping that the tube didn't kink or clog or that the overboarding vent didn't freeze shut. No inflight malfunction was more intimidating than a backfiring relief tube. And although a tiny toilet was stowed aft of the copilot's seat, to Turner's knowledge, no man had ever emptied more than his bladder inside a B47. A design to defy nature, he concluded.

Then he recalled that at age fifty-three, Henry VIII had sat encased in steel for four days while directing the capture of Boulogne. A separate god watched over ancient warriors, he thought.

The others aboard the bomber—the navigator in the nose, the instructor pilot in the copilot's seat, and the crew's regular copilot on a step in the two-foot-wide aisle—waited patiently for Turner. Air-force custom dictated that the senior officer was last to board, first to disembark.

By then, the second aircraft in that day's six-plane bomber stream was on final approach and Axel Turner paused to watch. The plane rounded out five feet too high, glided two or three seconds too long. Then its wheels slapped the runway in a puff of white smoke. The plane porpoised ten feet into the air before its pilot slammed it down in a cloud of burning rubber.

Turner's landing had been as soft as an angel's kiss.

"At least he put it down in one piece," Turner said, not unkindly.

First man down the ladder, amid popping flashbulbs and clicking shutters, Axel swept Jean into his arms, solidly hugged her against him, gently kissed her lips. Pleased to see tears of joy in her eyes, he said, "I love you," for her ears only.

She nodded in agreement, held back words that she feared would bring weeping. Healingly she ran fingertips along creases pressed into his cheeks and forehead by oxygen mask and helmet, tracing the fading ghostly outline of the inhuman, faceless intercontinental warrior who functioned beneath modern technological armor. "I love you too," she finally managed to say and smiled shyly, yet invitingly, reflected happiness that made her glow as girlishly as the day Axel had first met her.

"I have to talk to King," Axel told her. "I should be home in an hour."

"Is it about Red Alpha?" she asked.

He nodded. "The name's been changed to Quickstrike." He touched her hair. "An hour, at most."

"Make sure we have a few hours alone before the gang gets back from school."

"Hours?" he whispered and grinned. Still smiling, he turned, shook King Royal's hand and flashbulbs popped anew.

As base commander, Royal functioned like a housekeeper who maintained facilities necessary for the wing to operate. As wing commander, Axel led the combat forces. Royal answered to Axel.

Axel's main question for King was how soon the Quickstrike facility would be ready. While taxiing, he'd glimpsed its construction site, an ugly brown hole alongside the parking apron.

"Two months," King Royal said.

"Dammit," Axel Turner complained to the world at large, "the Russians already have put up two sputniks!" Axel Turner didn't enjoy the feeling of running in second place.

On October 4, 1957, the Soviet Union had surprised the world by launching a three-stage T2 rocket that placed a 184-pound satellite into orbit, the first man-created celestial body. The satellite's "beep-beep" signal had been received by radio stations around the globe, monitored like the heartbeat of a newborn colossus. Mother Russia had birthed a second twentieth-century revolution.

One month later on November 3, the Soviet Union had orbited Sputnik 2 with a passenger, a dog named Laika. The satellite had weighed 1,121 pounds—nearly warhead size.

Gravity's rainbow had taken on a thermonuclear hue.

And the United States had not put so much as a ping-pong ball into orbit.

"I need that building, King. Someday soon, one third of the bombers in this wing are going to be on Quickstrike, every minute of every day."

"You're preaching to the choir, Ax."

Both men knew that it took less than thirty minutes for an ICBM to lift off from the Soviet Union, glide across the polar ice cap, and slam into an American base or city. To have time to race beyond the radius of weapon effects, bomber crews had to be airborne in less than fifteen minutes after warning. Missiles were replacing the bombers in the game of intercontinental Russian roulette.

"You never cease to amaze me," Axel Turner told Jean. "Every time is as wonderful as the first time."

"Can you really remember that long ago?" she said.

He frowned and pretended to think to himself for several seconds, then smiled, nodded, kissed her lips.

"As wonderful as the first time after the war?" she asked.

They were snuggled beneath a down-filled comforter large enough to overlap three people. One side of the comforter pictured a perfect enlargement of an Iron Cross appliquéd from tiny patches of shimmering black and white silks. Axel had bought the enormous cover for a carton of cigarettes, in

Germany, immediately following the surrender of the Third Reich. He had gone there as part of a team to survey the effects of strategic bombing. Upon his return to America, the first time Jean and he had made love, they had wrapped themselves in the comforter. The union had been a reverent, happy yet sad, mystical experience.

Now, he recalled that time when he had returned from Germany and he said, "Things were a little different then. That had been after years. This was merely months."

"Liar!" she called and laughed. "You said *every* time is as wonderful as the first."

"That's true," he said, "but some times are *more* wonderful," and he kissed her breasts.

"If you think you'll get out of this by doing me again, you're right," she said and bent her head to kiss him.

Afterward, he said, "As wonderful as the first time!"

"Which first time?" She caught him peeking at his watch: "Have a date?" He stared beyond her without answering. She said, "Things are getting bad, aren't they?"

He shrugged, glanced into her eyes. For the briefest moment she thought he was going to cry. She had seen him cry once, at his mother's funeral. He had appeared so vulnerable then, exactly like now. As much as she had understood his need for release back then, she hadn't been able to watch him, hadn't been able to comfort him.

Suddenly the spasm passed and she thought he resembled his father. For the first time, the idea of his someday becoming aged entered Jean's mind, alerted her to his mortality. How was it possible? So soon? There was so much more ahead for them. He was her virile, vibrant lover, her valiant warrior. Her eternal man. Now, suddenly, mortality burst upon him like an aerial bomb.

Axel sighed. "We were always so far ahead, and now, overnight . . ."

"What about Quickstrike?" she asked, not knowing exactly what she meant.

"It's a reaction." She knew he hated reactions. He was born to lead.

"I know we're still ahead," he said in a tone meant to convince himself more than anyone else. "God forgive me,

36

but sometimes I think we should strike first while we have the power to wipe out the communist threat forever." He rubbed his eyes with the backs of his hands, as a sleepy child might do.

Jean cradled her husband in her arms, rocked him gently, suppressed an urge to croon to him.

CHAPTER 7

MORRIS ARCHER, DIXIE Smith, and a planeful of other officers and enlisted men stepped off a C97 at Dyess Air Force Base and were greeted by pitch-black night. Not a single soul awaited them. It was two in the morning and, obviously, some command-post controller had failed to notify wives of the plane's arrival.

"Want me to call Liz?" Dixie said to Archer. "Or you want to call your wife? No use bothering both of them."

"I don't care," Archer said. Too bad the officers' club was closed. At this stage, he'd just as soon get drunk as go home.

"I'll call Liz," Dixie said.

When Elizabeth Smith arrived an hour later, she was dressed as if it were the middle of the day. The thought that she had taken time to put on makeup while he had sat and waited made Archer see sparks. It took all of his willpower to nod a greeting.

"Miss me?" she asked Dixie.

"Every day," he answered.

And Archer wanted to shout, "But not every night. Let me tell you about Dixie's blond receptionist in Hawaii, and his cashier friend on Guam."

Seated alongside his bags piled in the back seat of the Smith's Cadillac sedan, Archer felt like another piece of baggage during the drive into town: Dixie and Elizabeth ignored him. Or did he ignore them?

Beth, wearing her Chinese-red robe, cautiously opened the door. Her first sleepy words were: "What're you doing home?"

Archer said, "Well, I'll go away and come back later, when it suits you."

"No, no," she said softly and wrapped her arms around him, hugged him with cheek resting on his chest. "I'm still half asleep."

In her body she carried the heat from the bed and it penetrated Archer. He recognized every curve of her body touching his. Yielding softness made him break out in anticipatory sweat. He found her mouth and kissed it, lapped long drinks from a well that was his, a private oasis in his self-demarcated sexual wilderness.

"Gentle," Beth said, "little kisses."

Heedless of her words, he lowered her to the floor. She was naked beneath the robe and his tongue burrowed into her deepest heat. Within frantic minutes, she quivered, sighed, and whispered a blessing. Then he was atop her and months of anguish drained from his body to hers. So little after so long, he thought and craved more than was humanly possible.

While he drifted inside her, Beth had the delusion that Morris was a nighttime stranger, a phantom lover without soul, one who would disappear by daybreak. Dreamy encounter without consequence. Uninhibitedly she requested, "Kiss me, down there, again."

On their wedding night she had told him, "Even if you didn't love me, I'd pretend you did." After all, he had rescued her from her dragon father. Then she had confessed that she'd never experienced an orgasm. Oh, she'd experienced good feelings, little ripples that she thought might be an orgasm. . . . Of course, before Morris, she had had only one lover, a furtive shadow, a substanceless figure that lurked outside her father's sight. And with Morris, she had reached no climax until, after they had been married for a year, she allowed him to kiss her down there. And that had been the key to "unlock the box," as she now unashamedly thought of the experience. For the rescue and for what he so willingly did to her, for what he was so willingly doing to her right at that moment, she owed him more than love. Loyalty, or obedience, perhaps.

They talked almost until it was time for Beth to breast-feed Beverly. Morris summarized the Guam months: emphasized his role in making the crew combat-ready, justified his insubordination before Colonel Turner, complained of Chuck Charles's supervision, described how much he missed her, and related the unfaithfulness of other husbands.

Beth nodded and smiled sadly. To her, his adventure sounded unhappy. She wondered why he remained in the air force. Was SAC more important than happiness?

Then he unwrapped gifts: pearl necklace, pearl bracelet, pearl earrings. The pearls were large and lustrous; each one shone like a tiny moon, Beth thought. The necklace and bracelet were triple strand and Beth wondered how much he had spent on them. They were far too formal. With what could she wear them? There were practical gifts that would have pleased her more. New clothes, for example. Or a larger house, different furniture, things for Beverly.

After fastening the pieces on her, Morris began to make love to her again. But he sensed a coolness in Beth and, wondering what he had done, or had not done, he asked, "What's wrong?"

"Nothing," she said.

"Don't you want to make love again?" She had been satisfied twice and he only once.

"It's not that."

"Then what is it?"

"Nothing, really." She made the mistake of glancing at the bracelet.

"You don't like the pearls!" He had spent his entire per diem on them—money that guys like Robby and Dixie whored away.

"It's just that they probably cost so much. . . ." He pulled away from her, drew back so quickly that she felt air rush between them, felt a chill sweep over her.

"They cost three hundred and I bought them with per diem, free money. They'd cost twice as much in the States." Didn't she understand his sacrifice?

Three hundred dollars! The sum was greater than she'd imagined. Three months' rent, she thought. "That would have bought a new sofa and two new chairs," she said. They still used furniture she had bought before they married. She wanted to be rid of those fashionless relics, rid of those reminders of a past that she detested.

Archer glanced about the room, breathed heavily. He had wanted to please her. . . . Everything looked disarrayed. Clothes, sheets, blankets draped over everything. "You want new furniture, you don't even take care of what you have," he said loudly. His voice woke Beverly, who began to cry, who hadn't cried in days.

Beth shrank. They'd had the argument before, more than once: She was a poor housekeeper, a very poor housekeeper, nothing like his mother. Why had she looked at the bracelet? Why had she uttered a word? Her single sniper round would be answered by a barrage of words, salvo after salvo loaded with accusations and subtle threats. How could she escape the domination of men? Was she never to have a say in her own life?

Before going to Beverly, she slipped into the bathroom and swallowed an Equinal, then, for good measure, a second. In half an hour she would be safely bunkered against any onslaught, wouldn't care if Morris dropped an atomic bomb on her.

❧ CHAPTER 8

AFTER SLEEPING THROUGH the day, Archer awoke and found no meat, no potatoes for supper. How could one woman be so totally disorganized? His mother had gone shopping every day of her life, had lived to serve his father. Beth sighed when Morris slammed shut the refrigerator. "I'll go to the store right now," she offered.

"Hey, you had plenty of time while I was gone." She wasn't getting away with trapping him into baby-sitting. His tone lightened: "I'll go out to the commissary. I don't mind." He would stop at the club for a drink or two, he told himself. If he felt like it, he might eat there too.

He smiled, kissed Beth's cheek, said, "See ya."

Abilene was a nothing place, Archer thought while he drove toward the base. A nothing place with nothing people. Nevertheless, the Abilene town fathers had given the Department of Defense an empty sack and the DOD had filled it and handed it back.

Dyess Air Force Base was set on scrubland in a direction that Abilene never would have expanded toward. The tract had been a lure to hook government jobs and dollars for Abilene's population. The lure of land had succeeded twice.

Prior to World War II, the town fathers leased 1500 acres to the federal government for construction of Camp Barkeley. After the war began, the government built an army airfield adjacent to the camp.

Peace brought disaster. Both military installations closed. Within a year, *Life* magazine described Abilene as a modern ghost town.

The Korean War prompted town fathers to cast out land as a lure once again. In 1952 the air force nibbled at the offering, proposed reopening the airfield if the city would donate 3500 additional acres. Within weeks, Abilene citizens raised nearly a million dollars to purchase the extra acreage. Early the following year, Congress appropriated thirty-two million dollars for construction of a permanent SAC base.

The first military unit arrived at Dyess in the fall of 1955. The first B47 Stratojet touched down in January 1956. Morris Archer arrived mid-1957.

Archer was taking a shortcut through the base housing area when, at an intersection, he saw Emily Charles standing on the sidewalk, peering into automobiles that slowed for a yield sign. Archer stopped his car, pushed open the right door: "Need a ride?"

She blankly looked in at him for several seconds before she said, "Oh, it's you." Then she darted into the car as swiftly as a mouse, scampered across the front seat, and settled, practically nested, pressed against him. Startled, he drew back from her, yet, reflexively, he reached out and shook her hand. "I was hoping somebody I knew would come along," she said. "I totaled our car yesterday."

"Were you hurt?"

"I don't think so."

Archer laughed at her answer, and after several seconds, she raised her eyebrows and smiled. He wondered if she had been drinking. He saw a network of tiny red veins in her cheeks, unpowdered cheeks. Without a mask of makeup, the rest of her face was invisible to him.

She said, "Chuck's still in Hawaii, thank God." After a pause: "What's your wife's name again?"

When he told her, she raised her eyebrows and nodded. "And you're Morris."

"Right." He grinned. She had to be drunk. How else could she have trouble recalling his name; they'd met at least half a dozen times before. "That wins you a free drink."

"I can use it," Emily said. "Vodka and tonic, please."

Archer laughed at her quick acceptance.

At the club, Emily and he took a booth and again she sat so that their legs touched. Before the first round arrived, Archer had an erection. He ordered a second round at the same time the waitress set down the first.

"Buy me some Kools," Emily said.

Archer ordered two packs.

"Do you buy everything in twos?"

Archer smiled crookedly, the spendthrift playboy caught in the act. "And I *do* everything twice," he said. Then he swallowed half his scotch and water in one gulp.

Emily blinked her eyes: "You drink too fast."

"Only the first one." He finished the drink and nothing happened: The jolt with its golden glow failed to find him. Diluted alcohol was no match for the excitement of her leg pressed against his. Why hadn't he ordered a straight shot or, better yet, a double to start the day?

"Does Beth drink?"

"Sometimes. Not much." He didn't want to talk about Beth, didn't care to be reminded that he was married. To change the subject, he talked about flying, told Emily stories that illustrated his skill as a bombardier.

She startled him by saying, "Chuck wrote about how good you are."

To Archer the words were an embrace, a revelation of secret recognition of equality—perhaps superiority. He wrapped an arm around Emily's small shoulders, hugged her body against his, felt her breasts press against his chest, and said, "If Chuck would relax a little, we could be one helluva crew." He surprised himself by telling a story that complimented Charles's flying ability, interpreted routine as spectacular.

44

By then, they'd had a couple more drinks. Archer felt confident. Emily had seemed to enjoy his stories, had laughed at all the right places. And her leg still rubbed his, ankle to hip.

She said, "You remind me of Chuck, talk about nothing but airplanes."

The comparison stung him. He wasn't Charles. With the courage of several drinks inside him, he studied Emily for the first time, boldly stared into her face.

She was a tiny creature. Short, chopped brown hair that looked as if she cut it herself. Uneven hair, uneven black eyes, cockeyes. Narrow face, twitchy little nose, sharp little teeth. A brown mouse. She sipped from her glass and Archer pictured her gnawing an ear of corn, holding it with her tiny hands, her tiny arms close to her tiny body. He pictured her, in the same pose, nibbling at his erection, giving little squeaks of delight. He recalled the saying, "Big woman, big pussy; little woman, all pussy."

He said, "If you don't want to talk about flying, what do you want to talk about?" and he took her hand.

She stared at him with a mask as blank as the one she had worn when he had offered her a ride. When she failed to answer his question, Archer pressed her hand against his erection and whispered, "Let's talk about this."

"Don't," she told him but made no effort to pull away.

"Just hold it," he said, "please," and felt fingers curl, grasp firmly. Her burning grip squeezed the alcohol in his body up to his brain, set his face afire, left him light-headed, breathless. With heart throbbing, he said, "Let's get out of here." He stood and swayed.

The blank mask said nothing, rose like a bodiless specter. He led her outside as easily as leading a child.

In the parking lot, certain nobody was in sight, he dared to kiss her. Inside the car, he kissed her again, drove to behind the club, parked, hid. For a moment he wished for Dixie's huge Cadillac instead of his tiny Chevy. Tiny car, tiny woman, he thought and took Emily into his arms.

Again he grew hot, dizzy. This wasn't right. But it was Beth's fault that he was doing this, her indifference that drove him to it. Frantic kisses. The heat of closely murmured "don't's" filled his ear, urged him on. Frantic undressing. He raised her above him, momentarily held her aloft like a partly clad statue, or a trophy, then sat her atop him, straddling him. Her murmurs became sobs.

In her eyeless face, teardrops found a path beneath closed lids, rolled down powderless cheeks. He kissed tears and tasted bitter union. "What's wrong?" he said.

Tearstained mask of sorrow, face of regret reflected back at him. Illicit conquest, hollow triumph.

"What's wrong?" he pleaded and felt himself wilting, dying inside of her.

In an attempt to salvage something from the encounter, or perhaps to reassert his manhood by justifying his predatory lapse of self-control, or perhaps simply to rescue himself from God-knows-what fate if she ever told Chuck and word got back to Beth, Morris Archer telephoned Emily Charles the following day.

"Who?" she squeaked after he identified himself.

"Morris Archer!" Was she drunk?

"Oh, yes. Thank you for the ride to the club."

Was she being sarcastic? "About last night," he said, then cleared his throat. "I'm really sorry."

In a tiny voice she told him, "I guess I should apologize too. I blacked out at the club." Archer thought she was joking until she asked, "Did you bring me home?"

"Yes," he whispered. Why had he called? What if she now put two and two together? "Well, if we're *both* sorry. . . ."

They laughed together, self-consciously.

"I guess that makes everything all right," she said.

"Yes," he said. But did it?

46

⤚CHAPTER 9

The December 6, 1957, issue of the *Abilene Big Country Journal* carried the following story on its front page:

> WASHINGTON—The Soviet Union's production of long-range jet bombers is increasing, high authorities in Washington revealed today. A previous report that the Soviets had halted production of manned bombers and were concentrating on long-range ballistic missiles was incorrect, official sources said.
>
> The Soviet emphasis on long-range manned bombers significantly changes the intelligence outlook. Nikita S. Khrushchev, Soviet Communist party chief, recently declared that manned bombers were virtually obsolete after he contended that the Soviet Union has perfected an intercontinental ballistic missile with a range of 5000 miles. Mr. Khrushchev stated that the manned bombers of the United States Strategic Air Command would be powerless in war against Soviet ballistic missiles.

The exact size of the Strategic Air Command fleet is classified, but it has been estimated at 2000, including both heavy and medium bombers.

No figure estimates as to the present number of Soviet bombers were available. However, an increase in bomber production indicates that the Soviets might have approached or even surpassed the United States in bomber strength.

A year ago, intelligence sources reported that the Russians had about 1000 heavy and medium jet bombers, and were expected to reach 2000 by mid-1959.

In the past, Soviet production estimates have been used to justify the rate of United States bomber production.

Accepted information about Soviet capabilities has not always turned out to be reliable, a high source conceded. However, Russia's ability to increase bomber production concurrent with its onset of long-range missile production represents a formidable military capacity, the source stated.

The December 7, 1957, issue of the *Big Country Journal* was headlined: VANGUARD BURNS ON LAUNCHING PAD; FAILURE ASSAILED AS BLOW TO INTERNATIONAL PRESTIGE. One of the accompanying stories read:

COCOA BEACH, FLA.—A Vanguard rocket bearing the first United States satellite exploded in flames and burned on Cape Canaveral beach yesterday. The rocket flew for four seconds and reached a height of four feet.

Remarkably, the satellite-bearing third stage of the rocket, which was embedded inside the nose of the second stage, was thrown clear and survived the crash. The third stage will not be usable. However, the satellite itself, which weighs barely four pounds and is about the size of a softball, was undamaged.

Authorities at the launching site said that "what we know is the end of a chain of events and we are trying to find out what happened—what caused it." They said that the failure was "undoubtedly a failure of some individual part" rather than one of overall design.

Project Vanguard leaders emphasized that the program had in no way been affected by the October 4 and November 3 Soviet successes. Project Vanguard's success has been entrusted to the Naval Research Laboratory.

↘CHAPTER 10

In the beginning, only three Bomb Wing crews were on around-the-clock Quickstrike duty, constantly ready to race to their nuclear-armed bombers and be airborne within fifteen minutes. Quickstrike marked the birth of an alert system that was to endure decades beyond the career spans of the men who initiated it.

To keep the system flexible, crewmen were exercised daily upon orders from SAC headquarters at Offutt Air Force Base in Omaha, Nebraska. The orders passed through a network of command posts that stretched to every base, worldwide, where SAC aircraft were positioned. Day or night, without warning, crews were sent racing to aircraft on practice scrambles that demanded a variety of responses.

An "Alpha" scramble, for example, required crews merely to climb aboard the airplanes and verbally report to the base command post that they were in position, ready for further instructions. On a "Bravo" scramble crews went a

49

step further, started engines in preparation for taxiing. And on a "Coco," the crews taxied the bombers to takeoff position at the hammerhead of the runway and simulated launch by taxiing down the runway at fifteen-second intervals. Every exercise was closely monitored, each crew timed, response times logged and compared to a standard.

There was no exercise in which bombers took off. That came later.

Naturally, there were messages—codes beyond Alpha, Bravo, and Coco—for launching the bombers on Emergency War Order missions. One such code ordered the bombers to fly as far as the Positive Control Point, geographical coordinates north of Canada, where the crews turned around if, en route, they did not receive additional instructions. According to SAC planners, this maneuver was a protective reaction that temporarily removed the Quickstrike force from imminent danger. The planners knew, however, that the Soviet leaders would view the maneuver as a direct threat, the equivalent of a stiff forefinger to the breastbone. Once Quickstrike aircraft were airborne, other bombers were generated into their slots.

Ultimately, there was the Go Code, the message that authorized crews to expend nuclear weapons. The Go Code was comprised of only two letters. When those two letters matched the two letters sealed inside a black plastic packet that was chained around each Quickstrike aircraft commander's neck, a packet that remained sealed until after a crew received a Go Code message, then war was certain. Once received and validated, the Go Code could not be rescinded.

Like a command barked by Big Brother, the crews were scrambled by the imperative "ah-ooooo-gah" of klaxons located across base. Each Quickstrike crew had its own automobile with rotating beacon mounted on the roof. When the klaxons blared their pulse-raising signal, Quickstrike vehicles had right of way over everything on the road.

After two or three scrambles, crewmen's reflexes became like those of sprinters awaiting a starting gun. Consciously and subconsciously, they listened for the blare of the klaxons, anticipated the signal to respond, to move, to begin the race. In a short time, reflexes were honed even sharper,

50

were conditioned to react to the first note of electronic command.

Regardless of what a man was doing, the klaxon call instantly moved him in the direction of his vehicle, sent him toward his airplane, headed him for his target.

Men caught in bed leaped to their feet, stepped into prepositioned clothes that waited in line, finished dressing while on the run.

Men caught in the shower lathered from head to toe, didn't pause to rinse or even turn off the water. Trailing suds, they leaped into flying suits and boots and dashed for the flight line.

Men in the middle of a moving morning constitutional broke it off and ran.

Quickstrike waited for nothing.

Not until reaching the airplane and talking to the command post over radios did a crew learn the type of scramble, learn whether it was tasked for an innocent exercise or for an Emergency War Order launch. Each scramble was a possible beginning of mankind's end.

Copilots bore the responsibility for message traffic. After reaching the planes, pilots and navigators tensely waited while copilots copied, validated, and decoded messages, then shouted findings that moved everyone to action.

One afternoon during the first month of Quickstrike, Morris Archer stood on the entrance ladder of a B47 bomber and watched Dixie Smith furiously copy a transmission. It was the crew's second day on duty, its second scramble. Suddenly Dixie frowned, tossed his checklist aside as if he would never again need it, and called to Chuck Charles, "Start engines. Taxi." He snapped his head toward Archer and shouted, "Fire! Close it up and let's get out of here."

Fire? Archer didn't relate the word to a scramble. Had he missed part of some briefing? What did Dixie mean? Commence fire? Attack! "Close it up and let's get out of here" could only mean that they were launching, going to war.

Archer's emotions soared as if a whirlwind had swept him

51

aloft, had sent him sailing away on the most exciting flight of his life, very likely the final flight of his life. Dixie's face held a concentration that Archer had not seen before. *Good-bye, Beth,* Archer thought and dropped to the ground, dropped into the eye of screaming turbines, helped the crew chief to pull chocks and grounding wires, unplug cables, move the ground power unit. Loose the bomber from the shackles of earth!

The kerosene taste of jet exhaust suddenly filled Archer's mouth, gagged him, produced thick, hot mucus; his chest heaved as if he had just raced a mile. The aircraft next to them was already moving, turning, blasting him with its vibrating backwash of fire. Seen through the heat, the taxiing bomber broke into a thousand pieces, reformed, and shattered again.

Archer sprinted, leaped onto the ladder of his intact bomber, frantically pulled up the rungs behind him as he climbed, jerked closed the outer door, pounded its lock into place. He felt the bomber lurch forward. They were on their way!

The jolt from the bomber's lurching start tripped a psychosomatic switch: For a millisecond, Archer's heart stopped, downshifted as if slipping into overdrive. His heated mind coolly saw the twelve hours ahead, hours that would change the world forever. Those twelve hours were his destiny. To fulfill them, he had to pace himself, had to be deliberate, perfect. Everything depended upon him.

Methodically, he slid closed and sealed the inner door, felt the slight ear pop of the beginning of pressurization. He turned to glide forward to his position in the nose, mentally pictured his target. . . .

Dixie grabbed Archer's shoulder and shouted, "There was a fuel spill on the ramp. The fire trucks are washing it away. The command post wanted us moved in case there was a fire."

Archer barely understood Dixie's words, had anticipated confirmation of his thoughts: Attack! War! Then he realized that "fire" meant "fire," nothing more. Another exercise.

❧CHAPTER 11

THE FIRST DAY that Chuck Charles's crew was on Quick-strike, Beth Archer went to the base hospital to see Dr. Jim Leonard. She'd learned his full name when she'd made the appointment a week earlier, on the day after Morris told her of the upcoming duty.

Beth had anticipated the meeting more and more as the week passed, began to feel as if she were going on a date. She didn't understand her feelings: Jim Leonard had been rude the time they'd met. She wanted to see his face, she decided, a face that was printed across her mind like a portrait in the family album, the face of Daniel, her companion brother and childhood protector.

What she wanted as much as seeing Leonard's face was a refill of her Equinal prescription. She still had pills, but there was no way to tell how long they would last. Her usage was dictated by Morris's attitude, and his mood swings were unpredictable.

Since his pique over the pearls, however, he had been more considerate than usual, had shown an almost reptilian patience toward her. Twice, he had recognized when he was being hypercritical, had paused in midsentence, had said, "I'm sorry. Forget it."

Still, she imagined his anger stalking her like a jungle creature, poised to slash her to pieces if she wandered one step off a thorny, twisting, barely visible trail. Would she ever get untangled, be able to run freely through life? Apprehensions over the unknown drove her to drugs as surely as face-to-face confrontations.

Morris had been jubilant about being scheduled for Quickstrike. When she failed to match his enthusiasm, he said, "Don't you care about my career?" She froze, could not take the next step. "Don't you care about my life?" her inner voice silently begged.

When she didn't reply, he walked her out on their half porch, sat her on one of their two lawn chairs, asked her to wait. He went back into the house and, a minute later, reappeared with a tumbler of scotch, sat beside her, covered her restless hands with one of his. She shivered.

He said, "Are you cold?" She shook her head, wanted him to explode and get over with it. It was too late for her to fake enthusiasm. "Do you want me to get you a sweater?" Again, she shook her head.

He sipped his drink without taking his eyes from hers, licked his lips, told her, "Quickstrike is the most important duty in the air force, in any service, probably in the entire world. Nothing in history matches it." His eyes unfocused and he looked through her, far beyond her. "One crew—our crew—has so much power—so much responsibility. . . ."

He stretched his neck, stared into the distance as if he were looking beyond the curvature of the Earth, as if he could see all the way to his Soviet target.

Finally, another sip. And he said, "Would you care for a drink? I forgot to ask."

She said, "Yes," but she wanted a tranquilizer.

"Really?" he said and smiled. "You really want a drink?"

Was he disappointed in her? "No," she said. How could she guess what he wanted of her? "I don't care," she told him.

His smile grew sad. "But you should care," he said

54

somberly. He finished his drink in one swallow. "Quickstrike," he whispered. Were there tears in his eyes? "Alpha and Omega."

Morris stared at the sky while they sat mutely, sat until he declared, "Time for a little more ground refueling."

Beth turned the Chevy down Hospital Road and felt as if she were leaving the base and the air force behind. The three-story, red-brick hospital stood apart from other buildings, loomed up from the prairie like a solitary monolith. Isolated haven from pain.

The hospital should be separate, Beth thought. Doctors were doctors, not soldiers, or sailors, or airmen. No wonder Jim Leonard had been upset when she'd asked how long he'd been in the air force. He probably had thought that she was questioning his ability as a doctor.

She made her way to the outpatient clinic. On schedule, she was ushered into his office, a small, sterile room with walls conspicuously bare of diplomas. Leonard stood, bowed his head for an instant, gestured to a wooden chair beside the desk.

He was taller than she remembered, not as thin. But he still looked remarkably like Daniel, features as well as hair. And his dark brown eyes matched hers.

As if reading her mind, he said, "Same eyes."

She cocked her head. "What?" she said coyly.

"We have the same color eyes."

She studied him before she said, "The same hair too." Then, to shield herself, she told him, "My baby daughter has them—the same color eyes, and hair." "Are you certain you're not my brother?" she wanted to say but the joke would require a detailed explanation.

Jim Leonard lowered his eyelids. It was as if a curtain dropped, only to immediately spring open on a different scene. Abruptly he asked, "What seems to be the problem today?"

Beth felt that a friend had vanished and a stranger had taken his place. Her folder lay spread on the desk before him. Did this stranger expect her to expose her life as fully? Her mouth opened but she could not speak the lines she had rehearsed.

He leaned toward her and said, "Are you taking the

55

tranquilizers I prescribed?" He looked exactly like Daniel. The question was spoken in a tone that sounded as if he actually cared about her answer. Was it her imagination?

"No. Yes. Sometimes. I didn't take one today."

"Do the tranquilizers make you drowsy?" It wasn't her imagination; there was sympathy in his voice.

"Yes. No. Not really. They relax me, help me to . . ." Tears filled her eyes. To what? To live with Morris? She couldn't say that.

Jim Leonard closed her folder, flipped it shut with a single finger. "Do you need a refill?"

"No. Yes. Please. Yes."

He slid a pad in front of him, scribbled on the top page, tore it free, and handed it to her. His eyes were chocolate sweet, his voice mellow: "I hope you won't consider this improper. I wonder if you'll have lunch with me."

Had she heard him correctly? Lunch?

"I owe you something," he said. "You're the only patient who ever made me lose my temper."

She tended to affect men that way, Beth thought.

"I mean," he said, "the only patient I ever lost patience with."

She smiled at his boyish attempts to explain himself, his concentration.

"That's not right either," he said. His hands fluttered. "That sounds confused. Look—" he gestured like an umpire calling a runner safe—"it wasn't your fault. I was upset over something the hospital commander said to me. And then you happened to get in the way." He groaned. Lifeless hands fell to the desktop. "I mean, you happened to show up."

Beth had guessed that they were nearly the same age. Suddenly she felt older, motherly.

He took off his glasses, pinched the bridge of his nose. Daniel used the same gesture to calm himself. "To get back to the subject," Leonard said, "may I buy you lunch?"

Beth resisted an urge to shout, "Yes," and said, "It's only ten o'clock. What about . . . others . . . ?" What was her mind doing?

"You're my last patient this morning." He shrugged, lolled his head to the side, making a comical face. "Don't ask me. I don't make the schedule."

56

That made her laugh.

"Just a sandwich, somewhere simple?" he suggested.

He drove downtown and they ordered cheeseburgers and french fries and malts at a drive-in restaurant, exactly as if they were on a high school date.

"I almost phoned you once, to apologize," he said.

"Why didn't you?"

He pushed out his lips and scratched his head, the expression of a monkey in a zoo. Beth smiled before she recognized that he wasn't pantomiming. His answer was spoken sincerely: "Because you're married. I thought you'd get the wrong idea."

"What do you think now?" How had she asked such a bold question?

"I don't. I'm surprised we're here." His response was a letdown. What had she expected?

While they ate, Beth learned that Jim Leonard was thirty, a few years older than she'd judged. "I lost a couple years after high school," he said. The day after graduation, he had married his high school sweetheart. "We had to get married," he said casually. "But we would have married anyway. We expected that I'd be drafted, and I expected to end up as one of the troops trying to invade Japan. The future looked grim. Then the A Bomb fell and the war ended overnight and I never was drafted, ended up working as an orderly in a hospital instead."

The teenage marriage had failed. "Anne still wanted to be in high school, going to football games and basketball games and dances, and I didn't. My father convinced me, if I was going to work in hospitals, I might as well work as a doctor." Jim Leonard's father was a doctor, and his father's father was a doctor.

Poor little rich boy, Beth thought.

Anne and their twelve-year-old son, James Eliot, the fourth, lived in Baltimore. "Jimmy's going to the same schools I went to. Good schools." To Jim Leonard, good schools meant private schools. "My father keeps an eye on him, expects him to become a doctor too.

"Anne's remarried now, to an older man, a friend of my father." He smiled. "Now, she acts very, very mature, more mature than I feel. In a way, I still love her. She's a good mother. We just married too young. We were children."

Beth liked him for those statements. Lasting love. Appreciation of motherhood. Blameless failure.

Because he had been in school, he had been deferred from the draft during the Korean War. "I missed all the wars; then, after the world was at peace, I got drafted into the air force, and into SAC, of all places." He shook his head in wonder.

With the appetite of a teenager, he finished the french fries that she had not eaten, then drained the last inch of her malt.

CHAPTER 12

THE UNITED STATES Vanguard rocket's explosive stillbirth sent painful tremors across America. SAC bombers were suddenly more valuable than ever.

"First, they called it Red Alpha. Then, Quickstrike. Now, it's Alert," Axel Turner said from the padded depths of his leather swivel chair that tilted backward until he rested his heels on the edge of his oversized cherrywood desk.

"Maybe if they stopped playing with the name, we could get on with it," said King Royal from one of three chintz-covered armchairs arranged in a half-moon on the opposite side of the desk. He was there as a sounding board, which, to his way of thinking, meant he supported Turner's line of reasoning, unless that reasoning went too far astray. Advocate and anchor, he thought, and puffed on a Cuban cigar slightly larger than a twenty-millimeter cannon shell. The cigar's aroma beat that of fine wine, he thought.

Royal glanced around the office. Turner's austerity embarrassed him. The artwork on the pale blue walls (a blue that looked faded rather than pastel) would have been perfect for the room of a twelve-year-old airplane enthusiast: cheap color prints of bombers and tankers mounted in black, wooden, standard-issue frames. Except for a blue cardboard nameplate with silver embossed letters that read COL. A. TURNER, there was nothing to personalize the room. A commander deserved more, Royal thought. In comparison, his own office was plush: two couches, end tables with brass lamps, marble-top coffee table, onyx ashtrays, Persian throw rugs, several Dufy prints. "A sheik's oda" was how Turner had laughingly described the room the only time he'd seen it.

Along with the name change from Quickstrike to Alert, SAC headquarters tasked each B47 wing with adding fourth and fifth crews and bombers to the Alert posture. This meant that instead of spending two days a month on Alert, crews were committed for at least four.

"We're headed for one third Alert, King. Fifteen airplanes from every B47 wing in SAC."

Royal anticipated his boss: "But not one missile."

"Right!" Turner hammered a fist on the padded arm of his chair. How had the Soviets moved so far ahead with missiles? Personally, Turner didn't believe the Soviets had the delivery capability, especially not in number. He suspected Khrushchev was bluffing. However, only the previous week, during a conference of wing commanders held at Offutt, he'd listened to CINCSAC—the Commander-in-Chief, Strategic Air Command—explain the situation. . . .

"High-altitude reconnaissance by U2 has found ICBM launch sites, or what we construe to be launch sites, located midway between Moscow and Leningrad, and southwest of Perm," CINCSAC said. Behind him, on a wall-size projection of the western Soviet Union, electronic arrows stabbed the two locations. The steel-gray eyes of CINCSAC swept the audience, pierced to the soul of each wing commander. "There are one hundred launch pads in the two areas." The steel in his voice matched the steel in his eyes. "Photographs show evidence of a missile at each pad, but . . ."

CINCSAC's case-hardened demeanor softened; his steel eyes took on a brushed cast. ". . . we cannot confirm how many of the missiles are operational, if any. We are certain that several of the missiles are empty shells, decoys. Gentle-

60

men, it's possible that all the missiles are decoys." CINCSAC paused, let the idea sink in.

Then he snapped ramrod straight, stood to his full height, towered above his subordinate commanders. From his starry height, he flung down a challenge: "Is any man here willing to make that assumption, to take that risk?"

Rigid silence acquiesced to whatever followed.

"If the Soviet Union has, say, seventy ICBMs," CINCSAC said as if talking to himself, "it can target two weapons against each of our wings. If one out of two missiles is reliable, then, without Alert, thirteen hundred B47 and two hundred fifty B52 bombers die on the ramp thirty minutes after Khrushchev pushes the button."

The conclusion was obvious. After the missiles struck, the United States would have no threat to counter the follow-on Soviet bombers that would be targeted against cities. With its population facing annihilation, the United States would be forced to surrender.

CINCSAC had explained the Alert concept: Within a year, one third of the United States strategic bomber fleet would be brought to armed standby. Unbeknownst to him, by mid-1961, by direction of the president, Alert would expand to include half the bomber force, arm over 700 aircraft for instant launch.

His not to reason why, Turner thought. If he didn't care to play Alert, CINCSAC quickly would find somebody to fill his role.

Turner recognized that rank was a mantle on loan to the current wearer. Symbolically, other officers had worn Turner's eagles long before Turner was born, and other officers, as yet unborn, would wear the same eagles when Turner was long dead—he hoped. At times he feared the future didn't extend much beyond today. What kind of world was he building for his children?

In the manner that rank was a mantle on loan, command also was borrowed property. "If ever I get canned," he once told his wife, "I'm not going back to the office, ever." He made certain that everything there belonged to the government. He would bid his farewells by letter, a noble gesture that would save his subordinates from having to hide the guilt or the pleasure in their final stares.

When a wing commander failed, it generally was for

reasons beyond his immediate control. No one individual was to blame. Several navigators, for example, had a bad day and missed the target during an Operational Readiness Inspection and, as a result, no matter how faint the trail, supervisory error was traced back through the staff until reaching the wing commander.

Supervisory error was an occupational hazard that put a bomb wing commander into the same category as a football coach. If the team failed to produce as expected, the coach's head rolled. It was easier to blame one man who symbolized authority than to scrap the entire team.

Days earlier, at the meeting for wing commanders, Turner had watched CINCSAC stride into the conference room unannounced and order everyone to remain seated. With four stars of his rank gleaming on each shoulder, he'd said, "Will the commander of the B47 wing at Charger Air Force Base stand."

The tall figure of Colonel Harry Jamison had risen quickly, had focused on CINCSAC with pointerlike attentiveness.

"You're not boss anymore." CINCSAC's voice hadn't hesitated: "Get out of here."

Before the trembling glances of his colleagues, Jamison had exited with downcast eyes. Broken and finished. No redemption possible. No explanation necessary. Overnight failure after twenty-plus years of devoted service. And the remaining men had breathed silent sighs of relief, sighs of resurrection, for the destruction of one had touched all.

CINCSAC then had introduced Jamison's replacement and the new commander had slipped into the vacated seat before it cooled.

If a wing commander held the ultimate responsibility, he also held the ultimate authority on his base. The authority provided the leverage to produce. Turner wondered if he would have the nerve to fire King Royal as dramatically as CINCSAC had fired Jamison. Why did he think that? They went back a long time together. Turner lowered his feet from the desk, hunched forward. "King, when will the Alert bunker be ready?"

"A matter of days." By pleading with contractors, Royal and the base civil engineer had gained three weeks in finishing the structure. Of course, they'd paid overtime, plenty of overtime, but, for once, funding hadn't been a problem. SAC headquarters wanted it yesterday, and that was that.

Royal was about to say, "Please, don't push anymore on the subject," when Turner told him, "You and your men have done an outstanding job. See that your civil engineer gets a Commendation Medal out of this."

"Why, I thank you, Ax," Royal said and sat up straighter. A man was never too old or too experienced to appreciate being complimented on a job well done. "And my civil engineer thanks you."

"Everything on this base is to focus on Alert," Turner said. "Be sure your people understand that. The bombers are the only reason we're here."

↘CHAPTER 13

Cʜᴜᴄᴋ Cʜᴀʀʟᴇs ᴋɴᴇw his value to the air force. A self-made officer, he had won wings and, along with them, commission through the rigorous Aviation Cadet Program. After World War II, he'd left the air force when his country no longer needed him and, five years later, returned to duty without complaint when his country again called.

Since that time he'd spent nearly two years isolated from Emily and the children: one year in Korea, the other on Shemya, a radar station at the end of the Aleutian Islands chain, a speck of land midway between nowhere and forever. Shemya had been difficult because, by then, Emily had developed problems, was blacking out and losing track of hours, sometimes days. But he'd performed as duty required until an air-force doctor had dictated recall two months early.

The recall was the only stain on his record until Emily forced another. While he was supervising the redeployment team in Hawaii, she wrecked the station wagon, sideswiped four parked cars in the middle of the night before plowing into a telephone pole. It was her second arrest for driving while intoxicated. Colonel Turner brought Charles home a week ahead of schedule. When he saw Emily, Charles hugged her, gently asked, "Are you certain *you* are all right?"

She said, "I think so," and tried to apologize.

He stopped her, told her, "Don't worry, we'll work it out together." He wished he could be with her, watch over her always. "The important thing is that you're not hurt." He would guard her from harm and danger. "Everything else can be repaired, or replaced." She was sick, drank because she was lonely; all else sprang from that.

Charles had volunteered for SAC, had expected the assignment to solve his problems. A fresh start in a new command, and all that. Emily had agreed.

With ten years of active duty behind him, he was trapped, could not afford to leave the service, could not throw away that much time at his age; in ten more years he would qualify for a lifelong pension. But his five-year break in service worked against him, made him an old captain, reduced his long-range value to the air force. Those five dead years haunted him. Another ghost from his past was his lack of a college degree. Without that slip of paper, he was considered a middle-aged drudge when compared to the highly educated boy wonders the air force now eagerly sought. A short time ago, he marveled, as a newly commissioned pilot, he too had been a boy wonder! Had his drop through the trapdoor of five dead years left him hanging in a limbo of failure? Or had the fall landed him in a psychic grave?

His status as a reserve officer was at the bottom of his problems. That status most likely would limit him to the rank of major and force him to retire at twenty years. Still, he was not assured of either likelihood. In three or four years, when eligible for promotion to major, if passed over in favor of more highly qualified captains, he would lose his commission and be released from the officer corps. After that, the only way to gain pension was to serve the remainder of the twenty years as an enlisted man, to become servant to those who once served him.

65

Many officers in the same reserve category bitterly called themselves "Christmas help."

Charles's salvation lay in a spot promotion, a system unique to SAC, a system whereby bomber crewmen were rewarded for sustained outstanding proficiency by being promoted "on the spot." Initiated in December 1949, and destined to continue until June 1966, spot promotions were held by approximately one of every fifteen SAC crewmen.

If promoted to spot major, Charles's chances for normal promotion would increase. But, more importantly, if he held the spot for six months (spot crewmen who failed to maintain high standards forfeited their promotions), then, even if passed over for normal promotion, he would someday retire with a major's pension.

Superimposed on Charles's salvation like a shadow of misty light, a black halo, was the temperament of Morris Archer. Archer's skills might get Charles promoted. Crews were ranked primarily by bomb scores, and Archer had the talent to be the wing's best bombardier. But was deliverance worth the trials of Archer's moody, capricious, volatile episodes? Was there a hidden price to salvation bestowed by a malefactor?

Archer escaped Charles's understanding. As a distinguished ROTC graduate, he had been handed one thing Charles coveted, a regular commission. Without proving himself beyond a civilian classroom, he had been awarded status that guaranteed at least the rank of lieutenant colonel and a twenty-eight-year career. At times, the logic of the air-force selection system escaped Charles's understanding.

In frustration, Charles tore into Archer's records, found the history of a man-child. Archer had been an honor student in college. His grades on the nine Air Force Officer Qualification Tests were impossibly high, a solid string of eights. Stung by those facts, Charles felt diminished, inferior by comparison. He partially recovered after first reading Archer's training report from navigator school. On rereading, he saw the report as ambiguous, was driven to track down, by telephone, Archer's reporting officer, a lieutenant named Carl Jessup.

"Archer?" Jessup said. "God, yes, I remember Archer. His temper was the talk of the base. He couldn't accept the slightest reprimand, couldn't see himself as doing anything wrong, or incorrectly. He would just tell a person, 'Fuck you.' He didn't care who it was. Except for me. I was his rater. He'd take criticism from me, take whatever he had coming." Jessup laughed. "He was intolerant of anyone who—in *his* opinion—was not overly proficient at his job. If an instructor was the least bit uncertain, Archer turned the man off, I mean conspicuously avoided participating in any kind of activity. One instructor named him the 'Thousand-Mile Stare.' He upset lots of people." Jessup laughed loudly. "Of course, a few of our fat cats probably deserved it."

After a pause, Jessup said, "As funny as this may sound, I liked Archer. When he was motivated, I mean when he really got interested in something, he was impossible to beat." As an afterthought, he asked, "You see that Marilyn Monroe movie, *The Seven-Year Itch?*" Charles hadn't. "Well," Jessup said, "old Marilyn comes walking out of this theater and she says to Tom Ewell, 'I felt so sorry for the monster. He just wanted to be loved.' That reminded me a lot of Archer. I don't think he ever had a real close friend."

Book-learning smart, Charles thought, and for the first time, he sat in wonder at the depth of another man's education. A child of the Great Depression, Charles had inherited his share of national poverty upon finishing high school, had been thrust headlong into the responsibilities of adulthood: first, blue-collar lathe operator; then, soon after, soldier, flyer, guardian of the nation's heritage; and, concurrently, husband and father. His life had been hopelessly distorted by the overpressures of the times.

Archer's life had been caressingly molded by the hopes and dreams of aftermath, by newfound wealth and technology. Years of education had been piled upon years of education: college upon high school, pilot and navigator and bombardier training upon college. As a result, Archer's entry into manhood had been delayed, his childhood prolonged under a guardianship of institutions.

To Charles's amazement, Archer's training report from the Advanced Navigation Reconnaissance and Bombardment school denied Jessup's words. It read: "Lieutenant Archer has proven himself extremely resourceful and as an officer possesses very good judgment. In the classroom he always is well prepared to discuss the course material. In flight his work is flawless. He makes friends easily and gets along well with his fellow officers and instructors. Lieutenant Archer's attitude is best during a particulary difficult problem. He likes challenging situations and is able to deal with them effectively."

How had Archer done that? What sort of chameleon was he? Could he shift his psychological coloration that easily? What threat altered his psyche?

Filed ahead of both reports was the training report that eliminated Archer from pilot training. It was void of a "word description of the student." The white block was a mysterious hole in Archer's record, made Charles feel as if a segment of Archer's life had been punched out and discarded.

Had Charles known the events that disqualified Archer, he might have decided that he was dealing with a person who had no right to be a crewmember.

Archer was eliminated from pilot training after eleven months of instruction because he was unable to fly formation in the T33, the final phase of training. In formation flying, every pilot did what the leader did, without question; responses had to be instantaneous. A formation of four was expected to move through the air as tightly bunched as the fingertips of a cupped hand.

Throughout air forces of the world, the degree of blind faith in the leader was conclusively demonstrated every few years when an elite aerobatics team (comprised of from four to nine airplanes) *flew into the ground in formation,* destroyed itself while following its leader.

Archer was not comfortable flying closely alongside another airplane, waiting to duplicate another man's actions. From the beginning, his instructor, Lieutenant Wink Evans, insisted he never was close enough to the lead airplane. Evans' constant "Tuck it in, tuck it in" reverberated in Archer's mind day and night.

One afternoon, angered by Evans' nagging, Archer tucked it in with a wild yaw that caused the two aircraft to touch. Wing tip tank brushed tail as Archer's plane overshot the other. "On the ground, right now," the lead instructor, a captain named Sullivan, ordered. There was no physical damage to the airplanes; but the mental stress was incalculable.

After they parked, Sullivan and his student ran across the ramp to Archer, who had just climbed from the cockpit. "What the hell were you trying to do?" Sullivan shouted and backed Archer against the fuselage.

"You could have killed us," his student shouted.

Archer turned his head away, noncommittally stared down the ramp.

"Listen to me," Sullivan said and jabbed a knuckle against Archer's sternum.

The knuckle was a hot iron, a brand of guilt. Its stigma flashed green flames across Archer's vision. He blindly slapped the branding iron aside, hunched his shoulders, shouted, "You fucker, touch me again and I'll kill you."

Wink Evans leaped between the men, nodded when Sullivan said, "Get him off the flight line."

Every instructor knew every student's problem, Archer thought. And every instructor backed up every other instructor. He was puzzled when Wink Evans didn't hand him a pink slip, a failing grade, at critique. Instead, Evans told him, "You've had as much instruction as I can give." He watched Archer for nearly a minute.

That's it? Archer thought and his deepening frown spoke for him. Evans pointed a finger, thought twice, dropped his hand to his side. "I could guess you made that wild maneuver deliberately, but it would be only a guess. As I said, you've had all the instruction I can give you. Tomorrow, you take a check ride."

So that was it? Archer saw he had no chance to pass on the following day. The instructors were going to wash him out. He'd never before failed at anything.

With contained agony, Archer went to the officers' club bar and drank. He drank until he blacked out his life.

He awoke on the floor, in the hallway outside of his dormitory room, barely had time to shower and change clothes before reporting to the flight line.

His evaluator was a captain he had never met, a crisp man who scarcely spoke. While the hangover plucked jittery nerves, Archer conducted the aircraft preflight under the evaluator's silent gaze. "Why go through this?" Archer wanted to shout.

69

In the air, the evaluator remained silent but Archer knew he was failing. His touch was as leaden as his spirit. He flew so loosely that the lead aircraft seemed miles away. "Can you tuck it in a little more?" the evaluator said.

With the resigned finality of a man diving from a sky-scraper, Archer unfocused and flicked the control stick hard right, banked his jet toward the lead trainer.

As the two airplanes rapidly closed toward the same spot in the sky, the evaluator screamed in self-defense, "I have it," and snatched the stick from Archer's control. He was an instant late. Wing tip fuel tanks of the two aircraft slammed together. The orange tank on Archer's airplane sprang up at an obscene angle, then tore loose. The airplane whipped in the opposite direction, undershot the leader, snapped into a left wing low, descending attitude before the evaluator regained control.

I'm not going to be a pilot, Archer told himself and knew that tomorrow he would hate himself more than ever.

CHAPTER 14

To untrained eyes, a city appeared as pinwheels of flashing dots that blurred into globs of light, an illuminated Rorschach blot; energy reflected from man-made structures blended; buildings fused one into another, melted into ghosts formed by the rhythmic antenna scan on a twelve-inch cathode ray tube, radar scope, cyclopean eye of the isolated B47 navigator-bombardier.

SAC leaders called the B47 navigator-bombardier a "three-headed monster" because his skills encompassed those performed by three men on older warplanes—navigator, bombardier, radarman.

A three-headed monster with but a single eye.

Yet to that trained single eye, radar ghosts were recognizable, identifiable. Within the radar scope's flashing pinwheels, constant shapes resided. To that eye, each city was a distinct image.

Oklahoma City, for example, was a "seven," or, as Morris

Archer saw it, a "hangman's scaffold" complete with dangling noose.

Like the eye of a connoisseur of Persian rugs, a radar bombardier's eye stared deep into its subject. In a city's radar image, it discerned patterns within patterns, focused on ever-narrowing interior designs that led along a boulevard, isolated a neighborhood, moved down side streets, located a specific building and, finally, pinpointed a designated corner of that building as aiming point, ground zero.

Although crews were delivering forces that would lay to rest radar ghosts for miles around, still, accuracy was paramount. A perfectly placed bomb ensured *maximum* destruction of life and property, the essence of massive retaliation.

Paradoxically, a bomb that landed within 3500 feet—more than half a mile away—from the aiming point was considered "reliable," was judged an acceptable release.

Striving for pinpoint accuracy, a radar bombardier pored over maps and vertical photographs and radar pictures of a target city, studied details with the intensity of a man house-hunting in preparation for moving there.

Target study was an obsessive delight.

Later, when Archer proved himself and was assigned Moscow as an Alert target (in those days the most difficult targets were assigned to the most proficient crews), his ego roared off like a rocket.

Archer was fascinated by the top-secret target study maps of Moscow that showed every building, down to individual homes, each structure numbered and labeled. And there were radar photographs, taken by delicate high-flying U2 reconnaissance aircraft with wings thinner than angels', aircraft unknown to the rest of the world, secrets within secrets.

In the heavily guarded, windowless Alert bunker, Archer unblinkingly studied the Moscow target folder, ran his hands across the maps, tried to grasp the mysteries of the foreign capital.

He learned that his bombardier role was predicated upon year after year of rehearsals. Actions supplemented thoughts only in the isolation of a radar simulator that depicted Soviet territory. (To make rehearsals as real as life, the air force replicated the western USSR on large plastic and metal plates; when submerged in a shallow tank of water and scanned with an electronic beam, the plates produced radar returns like those seen from the air. That equipment was connected to a booth that duplicated the navigator's station inside the B47.) Hidden, earthbound, Archer played out bomb runs on wartime targets, artificially evaporated Moscow and the Kremlin times uncountable.

Every day, in all weather, Strategic Air Command crews made high-altitude attacks on cities across the United States, silent attacks on unaware citizens six miles below.

No weapon was released.

Instead, a bomber crew simulated weapon release with a break in an electronic tone. A ground-based radar site tracked the bomber's course, simultaneously inked it on a plotting board with a recording pen. At the tone break the pen lifted, left an empty space on the board.

By plotting geometric vectors calculated from course, groundspeed, time of fall, airspeed, heading, trail, and wind, site personnel penciled an imaginary impact point for the imaginary weapon. They then measured the distance from that pencil point dot to the target which was represented by a tiny inked X, an X refined to a second of latitude and longitude. Distance between dot and X was miss distance, called "circular error" and measured to the nearest ten feet. On the rare occasion when dot superimposed X, circular error was zero and the bomb was called a "shack."

The term "shack" carried over to radar bomb-scoring sites from remote bombing ranges where dummy shapes were dropped. There, targets were gigantic circles painted on the ground and at the bull's-eye sat a frame structure no larger than an outhouse. A perfect drop hit the house, "got the shack."

ALPHA ROMEO CHARLIE HOTEL ECHO ROMEO

The world revolved about Archer when he heard Dixie Smith call those words to bomb plot: "Crew, ROMEO Three Niner. Type run, ROMEO Four. Target, DELTA. Altitude, three seven point zero angels. True air speed, four five zero. Navigator's name, Archer, I spell, *alpha romeo charlie hotel echo romeo.*"

And Archer was "on," center stage, playing a ten-million-dollar pinball machine. All eyes watched him. His scores were the prime factor in determining Charles's crew's reliability and, subsequently, its ranking within the wing. Archer's guiding touch . . .

During bomb runs the hand of the bombardier flew the B47 by means of a tracking handle, a phallic joy stick that controlled both crosshair placement and autopilot. On a run, which lasted approximately seven minutes, a bombardier repeated a series of actions that became more rapid, more compressed in time as the run progressed. The copilot began counting down five minutes before release: "Three hundred seconds to go." To the best performers every second was valuable, contributed to resolving the wind problem and to refining the aiming point.

The very best performers tended to be neurotic perfectionists who acted reflexively yet questioned the accuracy of every move they made.

In Archer's case, during a run his body became a mechanical device that unresistingly responded to the criminal part of his mind, the part that made decisions and reacted upon first sight. When the hangman's scaffold at Oklahoma City came within fifty miles, for example, that part of his mind pushed his hand to the tracking handle and drove radar crosshairs onto the terminal building at Will Rogers Airport or onto the state capitol in the heart of downtown. It was the natural thing to do.

Meanwhile, a second segment of his mind hovered over the first. Like a fagin, it systematically evaluated every move and with the iron discipline of a fanatical schoolmaster, or perfectionist mother, was alert to the slightest imperfection: "Stop being lazy. Put the crosshairs on the *exact* center of the capitol," it might shout. This savage teacher's corrections left the criminal with nervous doubt, ego-defacing guilt. The culprit questioned his ability to continue. Couldn't he do anything right? What would he do wrong next?

Like a benevolent Supreme Court judge, a third section of Archer's brain impartially observed and reviewed what had taken place. It confirmed the teacher's reprimand while excusing the culprit mind that committed the offense. After all, the culprit hadn't meant to be lazy.

74

Action, judgment, and review were accomplished in the same moments that a normal person required to perform the basic task. Light speed of brain hampered only by subsonic emotions of body. Three-headed monster ... three personalities ... three minds within a single body.

During the final minutes of a bomb run the radar eye narrowed to a wedge-shape view. Its antenna scanned right and left across the target area. Located in the nose of the B47 below the bombardier's feet, the beating antenna sent vibrations up the bombardier's legs, pulsed a separate countdown to release.

"Sixty seconds to go," Dixie Smith called from the copilot seat.

Regardless of how the run had developed to there, in that instant the fear of a gross error alerted the schoolmaster and the judge. They systematically reviewed the previous minutes, restudied the case while the criminal continued to operate the body. He checked the oxygen flow control lever at 100 percent, gave his machine a deep breath of pure energy. The airplane was at 37,000 feet.

"Airspeed, four five zero," Chuck Charles said.

The schoolmaster converted the speed to meaningful terms: "Seven hundred and sixty feet per second." Archer's eyes mechanically compared their ingrained image of the city to the image that appeared on the radar scope. His culprit mind reconfirmed the accuracy of crosshair placement. The schoolmaster nodded approval.

"Fifty seconds."

"I'm direct," Archer said. "I'll take second station."

"PDI centered. You have the airplane," Charles told him.

Archer's right hand flipped a switch that transferred control of the bomber to him. His eyes never left the radar scope. His right hand slid back and grasped the smoothly rounded joy stick. His left hand flitted across control knobs that adjusted antenna tilt angle and receiver gain, refined the radar picture.

"Forty seconds."

On radar the building that Archer desired drifted out of a ghostly mass. He felt momentary physical relief. His minds were crammed with sizes and shapes and patterns of buildings surrounding the one he chose. Everything was as it should be, his minds agreed. "Going right," he said and milked the joy stick gently to the right, moved thin white electronic crosshairs from the center to the northeast corner of the building, a distance of a millimeter on the radar scope. The aircraft turned almost one degree. Radar shapes and patterns were harmonious. The criminal definitely had the correct target. The schoolmaster nodded; the judge smiled.

"Thirty seconds," Dixie said.

"Straight and level," Charles reported. "On airspeed."

Archer switched camera controls so that the radar screen was photographed every other rather than every fourth scan of the antenna. His right foot was motionless over the interphone floor switch, but inside his left boot toes invisibly tapped at 200 beats a minute.

Everything was ready.

Suspicious minds nodded wary accord. His body hunched over the radar scope, froze in anticipation. To see Archer at that moment was to view a statue, a dead man.

"Twenty seconds." Dixie read from a checklist: "K-2 Auto."

The dead came to life: Archer's right hand unguarded and armed the automatic weapon release switch. Then the hand flashed back to the joy stick, stroked it, squeezed it, but held it in the null position. His mind reconfirmed shapes and patterns. The crosshairs were exactly where they should be.

"Ten seconds. Tone on."

Archer activated the electronic signal and scanned the bomb control panels. Everything was set. His eyes returned to the radar. Crosshairs exactly where he wanted them? He did not depress the interphone switch but said, "That's it. That has to be it." The schoolmaster frowned at the hint of doubt.

"Five seconds."

Too late to change anything, the schoolmaster thought. *It had better be right.*

"Bomb doors coming open," Charles said. The doors spread in the time it took to speak the words. The open doors broke the clean aerodynamic sweep of the B47, made the warplane tremble in flight.

Three seconds remained until release. In that time, Archer's eyes recorded the data before him: the radar picture with crosshair position, the true heading, the true airspeed, the readings on the wind dials, and the Greenwich Mean Time to the second. His eyes stopped on the time-to-go meter, which showed one second. The moment passed. A red light blinked on; the electronic tone cut off. "Bombs away," Archer called and, reaching high over his right shoulder, pulled the shield-guarded, red-painted emergency bomb release handle in case the computer failed at the critical instant. The emergency bomb release handle over-rode all systems, jettisoned whatever hung in the bomb bay.

"Tone off," Dixie confirmed and Charles racked the airplane into a breakaway maneuver that gained maximum separation of bomber and bomb, increased the crew's chance for survival.

Charles turned so tightly that gravitational and centrifugal forces held Archer immobile, kept him from writing the data his eyes had recorded. In the score was his future.

⬥ *CHAPTER* 15

F ROM THE *Abilene Big Country Journal,* 1958:

U.S. LAUNCHES FIRST SATELLITE INTO ORBIT

CAPE CANAVERAL, FLA., January 31—An army Jupiter-C rocket today reaffirmed the United States' international prestige by placing a satellite into orbit around the Earth.

At 10:45 P.M. the Jupiter-C made a perfect liftoff. The roar of its engine filled the Cape Canaveral area. The sight and sound brought cheers from spectators along nearby beaches. The rocket never wavered on its skyward course.

Jupiter's "payload" of instruments weighs about eleven pounds and is contained within a 7.5-pound protective steel case. The rocket's final stage after burnout weighs 12.67 pounds, giving a total satellite weight of 30.8 pounds.

"The satellite and the final third-stage rocket were designed to remain together and circle the Earth as one unit," a spokesman explained.

For spectators, there was an apprehensive fifteen and three-quarter seconds' delay between the firing command and engine ignition.

The firing command brought an agonizing silence to those who were watching. Nothing seemed to happen while liquid oxygen vented as a cloud from the juncture of the seventy-foot rocket's first two stages.

Inside the Jupiter-C, the fuel tank was pressurized three seconds after the firing command.

Then, seven seconds later, the boom that supplied dry ice to the rocket's battery system dropped away.

Engine-priming fuel ignited almost invisibly.

At fourteen and one half seconds after time zero, the main stage engine roared to life with a tremendous golden orange burst of flames that sprayed in all directions.

Liftoff occurred without further hesitation.

NAVY VANGUARD PUTS SECOND SATELLITE INTO ORBIT

CAPE CANAVERAL, FLA., March 17—A 6.4-inch satellite sphere was placed into orbit today by a navy Vanguard rocket. The three-stage rocket lifted from its launching pad at 7:15:41 A.M. and flawlessly soared beyond sight.

The satellite was the United States' second and the world's fourth. The apogee (highest point) and perigee (lowest point) of its elliptical path were 2513 and 407 miles above the Earth.

Although the altitude figures far exceed those of the three previous satellites, their significance was dimmed by the small weight of Vanguard's satellite, only 3¼ pounds.

In comparison, the United States Explorer II weighed 30.8 pounds. The Soviet Union Sputnik I was 184 pounds and Sputnik II was 1120.

Despite their small sizes, the American satellites have superior instrumentation and are expected to make greater contributions to science. Furthermore, they have a predicted lifetime of two to four, or even ten, years.

Sputnik I fell from orbit and disintegrated upon reentering the atmosphere in January. Sputnik II is expected to survive no more than another month.

THIRD U.S. SATELLITE IN ORBIT; SHORT LIFE
PREDICTED

CAPE CANAVERAL, FLA., March 26—The United States' third artificial satellite was fired into orbit today by an army Jupiter-C rocket.

Designated Explorer III, the new satellite was expected to have a maximum life span of only two weeks because the last three rocket stages did not fire at the planned angle to the Earth.

The satellite weighs thirty-one pounds. . . .

1.5-TON SOVIET SATELLITE FIRED INTO ORBIT

MOSCOW, May 15—Soviet Premier Nikita S. Khrushchev announced that the Soviet Union today launched a new space vehicle that weighs nearly 1.5 tons. He said that the achievement proved again that his nation has "outstripped the United States in science and technology."

Mr. Khrushchev made his statements at a Soviet-Arab friendship meeting in the Kremlin. He compared the United States' satellites to oranges alongside the Soviet Union's monstrous Sputnik III. He said: "I do not want to belittle the United States' efforts, but I cannot conceal my joy at my country's success and progress."

Later, Mr. Khrushchev told his Kremlin audience that the Soviet Union did not intend to use its progress "to the detriment of mankind either directly or by blackmailing others."

Figures released by Tass, the Soviet government news agency, said the cone-shaped missile is nearly six feet in diameter and twelve feet long. It weighs 2925.53 pounds, Tass reported.

U.S. CONCEDES LAG IN MISSILE STRENGTH

WASHINGTON, May 16—The Soviet feat of launching a 1.5-ton satellite would not be duplicated by the United States for at least two years, an official source estimated today.

Rocket specialists here agreed that the most recent Soviet

launch into orbit was made possible by using a modified intercontinental ballistic missile.

Not until 1960 at the earliest will United States Air Force intercontinental missiles of equal size become available. Initially the United States missiles will be capable of launching satellites weighing one ton. Ultimately the payload will be increased to several tons.

❧CHAPTER 16

"R ED BASTARDS," AXEL Turner whispered to himself when he finished reading the intelligence report on the orbiting ton-and-a-half vehicle. That clinched it as far as he was concerned: if the Reds could throw up that much, they had to have ICBMs.

Amazing, he thought. A nation that a generation ago was illiterate now stood ready to conquer space. What had Khrushchev said? "Whether you capitalists like it or not, history is on our side. We will bury you." Red devil bastards.

Words that had lived inside Turner since his Presbyterian boyhood sang in his memory: *He hath loosed the fateful lightning of His terrible swift sword. . . .* He refused to believe that such almighty power was intended for the glorification of the ungodly.

He flicked the intelligence report onto his desk. Black manifesto . . . ultimatum . . . challenge? *I have read a fiery gospel writ in burnished rows of steel: "As ye deal with my contemners, so with you my grace shall deal; let the Hero, born of woman, crush the serpent with his heel, since God is marching on."* Christianity had to triumph, he told himself.

SAC was salvation.

No army would ever conquer the Soviet Union, invade and inhabit. The only alternative was to destroy the colossus from the air, use the massive god-given power of SAC.

He tilted his chair, leaned his head back against the welcoming cushion. He tiredly knew his constructions were frameless daydreams. There was nothing he could do directly.

The question of the limits of his power had arisen during the annual recertification of Major Amos "Pappy" Trembly's crew. From an aberrant cell of his imagination Major Clark Devon, a member of Turner's staff, had come up with a deranged supposition.

He'd said to the crew: "Suppose you're on Alert, out at your airplane, and Colonel Turner comes running up and hollers, 'Take off. Hurry. Go bomb Russia.' What do you do?"

"Does he give us a written message?" copilot John Duggen had asked.

"No."

Duggen had another question: "Does he authenticate his order?"

"No. There isn't time."

"We don't do anything," the navigator, Lieutenant Hal Zorn, had said. Duggen had nodded agreement.

"But he tells you that ICBMs are inbound. He orders you to get off the ground, to go to Russia, to hit your target," Major Devon had elaborated.

Zorn had again said, "We don't do anything."

"You mean you're just going to stand there and die?" Devon had said heatedly.

"Now wait a minute, Hal," white-haired Pappy Trembly had said, "I'd take off if—"

Zorn had shaken his head.

"—if I knew missiles were headed my way, but—"

"No," Zorn had whispered.

"—but I'm not sure I'd go beyond the positive control point, unless . . ." He'd squinted in concentration, then all in a rush had said, "Lord, yes. If the United States was

83

under attack and Colonel Turner told me to go, I'd go—all the way."

Zorn had sighed.

Trembly had put a hand on Zorn's shoulder, had gently explained, "The order came from Colonel Turner. He's the wing commander."

"That's not good enough," Major Devon had said.

Trembly had turned loyal eyes toward Turner. "Sir, you're my commander. I follow your orders."

"Wrong," Devon had insisted.

"Why?" Trembly's word had been an angry buzz of pain.

At that point Turner had interceded. "Amos, I appreciate your vote of confidence, but the procedures are explicit."

Trembly had stood stiffly erect, retreated into a shell of dignity, posed like an old soldier who was devoted to his superior, an old soldier who didn't agree with the impersonality of modern command and control.

Caught up with his supposition, imagining more than he had expressed, Devon had shouted, "Can't you see? What if Turner's insane?" Then Devon had taken a loud breath, had said, "I mean, what if Colonel Turner is temporarily unstable? I mean, he too has to follow procedures." He'd held up one finger. "Major Trembly, you don't react until you—" he'd waved the finger— "get a *valid message* in the *proper format* and—" he'd jabbed two fingers toward Trembly, had shouted— "it *authenticates.*" He'd raised clutching hands to heaven. "How many times do we have to explain that?"

As much as Turner disliked Devon's example, he had to admit the premise was correct. Turner did not possess the codes necessary to authorize a strike. Certainly, using an authenticated message, he could launch the Alert bombers under his command, start them toward their targets, but they remained tethered by an electronic leash. They turned back at the positive control point if the Go Code did not reach them from some higher authority.

Even CINCSAC lacked the ability to strike an enemy under normal circumstances. And by the time decision-making authority funneled down to him in some nightmarish emergency scenario, most of the country would be gone.

Only the president had power to authorize the expenditure of nuclear weapons.

Turner lowered his feet from the desk, walked to a row of

84

windows that overlooked the flight line, admired the neatly parked silver ranks of swept-wing warplanes. And the words came back to him: . . . *writ in burnished rows of steel* . . .

As he'd done more and more often during the past months, he questioned the course mankind had chosen. He didn't like the end he'd seen.

In the office from which he commanded a strike force of forty-five bombers capable of delivering nearly a thousand megatons of destruction, Colonel Axel Turner knelt, pressed his palms together in front of a chestful of ribbons that described his warrior prowess, then bowed his head. He called to God, prayed aloud that Strategic Air Command bomber crews would never have to prove their unqualified uniqueness.

Axel Turner was no exception. For Strategic Air Command leaders, the May launch of Sputnik III was a brutal aftershock to two months of psychic overkill that began in March when a B47 crew bombed South Carolina.

↘CHAPTER 17

Among crewmen the bombing of South Carolina became known as "The Kukla, Fran and Ollie Show" because the navigator's name sounded much like Kukla. The B47 crew had descended to 10,000 feet to practice "manual inflight insertion" which the irreverent called "aerial intercourse."

The exercise required the navigator to insert a nuclear mass into the bomb. To reach the weapon he crawled through a dark passageway that linked crew compartment to bomb bay. Normally a tight fit, the channel became even tighter because the navigator wore parachute and flight helmet in transit.

Inside the shadowy, yellow-green bomb bay, the navigator stood on a foot-wide fold-down ledge and went to work. The olive-drab bomb that filled the bay was an early-generation thermonuclear device, a primitive behemoth lacking in sophistication.

To begin, the navigator unscrewed the weapon's nose

plate to reveal a yellow sphere of explosives. The sphere's outer design resembled the pattern on a soccer ball, except that each section of the pattern was much larger. The navigator disconnected wires attached to detonators implanted in the sections nearest him. He then lifted out these sections, which were wedge-shape, high-explosive "lens mold" charges designed to focus trigger force inward. In that manner he cleared an avenue to the hollow core of the bomb.

Next, he reached back into the passageway and unclasped the lid from a three-foot-tall canister known as a "bird cage." Suspended inside the cage was a dull gray nuclear component—a mass of heavy metal, the "m" in "$E = mc^2$." Not quite as large as a bowling ball, the mass had the weight of ten balls.

The navigator lifted the "ball" component by screwing a crowbar-size rod into it. The ball-rod contraption was as unwieldy as a hundred-pound barbell with all the weight on one end. Transferring the ball into the hollow heart of the weapon was a critical procedure: If the navigator struck the mass against the detonator of a still-in-place charge, there was chance of an explosion. And as every crewman admitted, "One inflight explosion could ruin your whole day." After the ball was seated, the navigator unscrewed the rod and set it aside.

Then he repacked the wedge-shape charges as tightly as pieces of a jigsaw puzzle and reattached electrical leads to their detonators. Lastly, he screwed on the bomb's nose plate.

The weapon was alive but not breathing, complete but unarmed.

To accomplish the final step in preparing the weapon for a full-scale thermonuclear yield, the navigator returned to the crew compartment. There he operated black boxes that closed fuzing circuits inside the bomb.

"Kukla" finished the insertion after experiencing difficulties familiar to all B47 navigators: balancing on the foot-wide ledge; gently manhandling the clumsy ball and rod; breathing the thin oxygen at 10,000 feet; building nervous tension while playing with the detonators. It wasn't the first time he'd performed the inflight feat, and on the ground he'd practiced it at least once a quarter since he'd been in SAC. Nevertheless, he was fatigued by the effort.

While laboring to return through the narrow passageway, he paused to catch his breath and, for no reason except that which fate decreed, reached overhead and thoughtlessly grasped for support. He got hold of the cable that connected the navigator's shield-guarded red-painted emergency bomb release handle to the U-shape hook that clutched the sling holding the bomb. He suspended his weight from the cable. The first twenty pounds of pull unlocked both the U-hook and bomb bay doors.

The bomb fell onto the doors, its weight spread them, and it continued its fall to earth.

The unarmed weapon landed in the yard of a farmhouse in Mars Bluff, South Carolina. It tore a crater seventy-five feet wide and thirty-five feet deep. The top was blown in and a side was blown off the rambling one-story house. Six civilians were injured. Five other houses and a Baptist church were damaged.

A traveling salesman who was riding along the highway about a quarter mile from the house said that the concussion was so great that it turned his car around on the road.

The air force issued a statement:

A B47 from Hunter Air Force Base, Savannah, Georgia, on a routine training flight, accidentally jettisoned an unarmed nuclear weapon due to a mechanical malfunction of the plane's bomb lock system. A high-explosive component of conventional TNT in the nuclear triggering device did explode. This explosive is carried in all nuclear weapons. There was no atomic explosion and there is no danger of an atomic explosion. The potential danger in an incident of this type is possible contamination of a small area if the high-explosive charge completely destroys the weapon.

Only the day before, a month-long search by the navy for a missing nuclear weapon had been declared a failure. In February the weapon had been jettisoned into the sea off Savannah Beach, Georgia, after a B47 collided with a jet

88

fighter at 35,000 feet. The bomber landed in damaged condition. The fighter pilot bailed out safely.

Command-level response to the bombing of South Carolina was instant anxiety: Every crewman became suspect. If a man could drop a bomb accidentally, why couldn't a man drop a bomb deliberately?

↘CHAPTER 18

SAC COMMANDERS AGREED: Crewmen's human frailties constituted the major weakness in the control of weapons. Corrective actions were necessary.

Until then, in windowless blockhouses, crewmen attended quarterly classes in which instructors taught the innermost details of nuclear weapons, ploddingly reviewed fuzing and firing circuits from the time a weapon was armed, through release and free fall, detonation and explosion. On its first morning of each Alert tour, a crew operated black boxes in a nuclear weapon simulator and proved it could arm a weapon, select a burst altitude, and cope with malfunctions that demanded knowledge of the bomb's inner workings.

What could be done by a misguided man with such detailed working knowledge? Could a latent pacifist neutralize his crew's weapon and thereby negate a strike? Could a madman overcome safety devices and detonate a weapon on the ground?

Overnight, commanders decided that crewmen no longer had a "need to know."

As quickly as production permitted, self-contained bombs that required no inflight assembly replaced the old weapons, which were dismantled. Supposedly the new bombs were tamperproof.

To control this next generation of weapons, navigators received a single magical black box called the T-249 that had a two-position wafer switch and a press-to-test light. A navigator flipped the wafer switch from "Safe" to "Arm" and the light came on, indicating the bomb had armed. Or the light failed to come on, indicating perhaps that the bomb had failed to arm. Whichever, the crew dropped the bomb. "Don't worry about it," weapon instructors advised. "Improved design has made malfunctions virtually impossible. Chances are the problem is somewhere other than inside the weapon."

By that time, weapons had ceased to have insides as far as crewmen were concerned. Instructors refused to answer questions that went beyond turning the T-249 wafer switch or pressing-to-test its light.

"I like this new system," Dixie Smith said one afternoon while on Alert. "Drop it and pop it. No need to clutter your mind with details."

"It never was your worry," Archer said. "I want to know what happens when I drop a weapon." Crewmen were being reduced to delivery boys, he thought.

Dixie smiled. "You're never going to drop that thing. Khrushchev isn't as stupid as he looks." He laughed. "Neither is Ike."

Knowledge was power, Archer believed, and by being denied knowledge he was made less powerful—whether he dropped the bomb or not.

After the bombing of South Carolina, on training flights whenever a weapon was aboard, B47 crews were ordered to keep the locking pin installed in the U-hook. The locking pin acted like a safety on a gun, made it impossible to drop the weapon, even with the emergency bomb release handle.

Thinking out loud about the new directive, Robby Robertson told Major Clark Devon, "I'd hate to crash-land with that big mother behind me."

Devon, who combed his thick black hair straight back, had a brusque forwardness in dealing with crewmembers: "If you're willing to fly with the bomb, you have to be willing to die with the bomb."

Robby said, "I'll eject first."

"If you do," Devon said with a grin of malevolent superiority, "you'd better be certain the plane crashes a million miles from nowhere." Robby exemplified Devon's every dread: He was an uncouth slob, a brainless appetite, a thoughtless gorilla paid to fly. "Otherwise, it's your court-martial, fly boy."

Devon considered himself too intelligent to be on a crew. He was a Naval Academy graduate. At the time of his interservice transfer, the lure of rapid promotions within a newly created service had been overpoweringly inviting. Now he wondered why he'd swapped the knots-per-hour leisure of ships for the knots-per-minute hurry of planes, why he'd forsaken navy gentlemen for air-force barbarians. During the short time he'd navigated B29s, he had been horrified at the intellectual shallowness of crewmen. Few could carry on a meaningful conversation. Most had never read a serious book, or seen a play. To his wife, he'd described his crewmates as "trained apes who are happiest when they're eating, sleeping, or defecating." He was too intelligent for that life. On a crew, Clark Devon could benefit a handful of men; on Turner's staff, he could think for the entire wing.

Following the bombing of South Carolina, in his zealousness to anticipate future problems, Clark Devon originated the staff versus crew encounters of "What if . . . ?"

The confrontations began after SAC headquarters introduced "Red Dot" and "Blue Dot" and "Green Dot" messages to Alert. The colored message formats provided commanders with more options and gave them tighter control over crew responses during Emergency War Order situations, as well as during exercises.

Devon recognized a weakness.

At a daily seven A.M. Alert crew meeting, Devon asked Pappy Trembly, "What if, during a scramble, your copilot makes a mistake while copying message traffic?"

With loyalty to copilot John Duggen uppermost in mind, Pappy said, "I don't think that's possible."

"Then," Devon said, "what if your copilot—and I don't mean Duggen—what if some *substitute* copilot passes false information to you?"

Pappy blinked rapidly. The questions were strange, new. How was he being tested? Feeling a loyalty to flying comrades, he said, "I don't know anyone who would do something like that. Do you?"

"Perhaps," Devon said and gave his grim toothy grin. "What if a copilot somehow steals the Go Code and passes it to you instead of the real message. Could you detect his deception?"

Pappy stared at Devon, couldn't answer. In his mind, anyone who so much as conceived such questions was guilty of some sort of crime.

An answer hadn't been necessary. Colonel Turner had been at the morning meeting and, within the hour, had telephoned SAC headquarters. As a result of the first "What if . . . ?", copilots no longer were the sole point of contact.

Thereafter, procedures for handling message traffic were taught to every combat-ready crewman. Furthermore, each man was required to prove proficiency by taking a test every day that he was on Alert. The test consisted of a taped transmission, which changed daily. Each man copied and authenticated the transmission, then answered questions about how he would respond to it.

The only passing grade was a perfect paper as Pappy Trembly was first to learn when he miscopied a single letter. For corrective action, Devon scheduled Trembly to attend a four-hour communications class with men who were upgrading to combat-ready status.

"Four hours of beginner's class? I never heard of such a thing," Pappy said. "Look at my worksheet, I got the message right."

"But your response was incorrect," Devon told him. "Getting the message is one thing. Knowing what to do with it is another."

"But I know what to do with it."

"You didn't prove it: You wrote down an incorrect response."

Pappy struck his pose of self-righteousness. "I made a mistake."

"Exactly," Devon said with a grin as gleaming as a scythe. "And no mistakes are permitted."

Stiffly, Pappy said, "Major Devon, I protest. I'm not going to sit through four hours of classes because I copied one wrong letter."

"Then we'll discuss it with Colonel Turner as soon as we find somebody to replace you. Until this is settled you're excused from Alert duty."

Excused from Alert duty? Was he no longer combat-ready, Pappy asked himself, just like that? Devon had struck at his soul. Crew duty was his life. Did he dare challenge Devon in front of Colonel Turner? Pappy Trembly's respect for command overpowered him. He quietly said, "I don't think Colonel Turner should be bothered with a problem this small." The only thing the class would cost him was an afternoon nap. "I'll attend the class," he said.

Later, in the Alert lounge, Bobby Bushman, a captain copilot, said, "They should give Pappy a tiny lollipop to pin on the ribbon of his Combat Crew Readiness Medal for being such a sucker."

"Who's the enemy?" Bobby Bushman asked when the Duress Code came into use. The Duress Code evolved from the newly instituted Two-Man Policy, which prohibited one man from being alone with a nuclear weapon. Even in pairs crewmen were not permitted access to their Alert bomber until they exchanged codes with an armed guard by verbally adding or subtracting single-digit numbers to total the "number of the day."

From that system came the Duress Code, a two-digit number for use by a crewman who was being forced to board an airplane. Guards were instructed to kill anyone standing directly behind a man who spoke the duress number.

After Clark Devon explained the system at morning Alert Briefing, Dixie whispered to Archer, "Don't do anything crazy the next time we walk out to the airplane and Chuck happens to be behind you."

First the staff didn't trust the crewmen, and now crewmen

were expected to distrust each other, Archer thought. How long until they were chained in lock step?

Quickly, Devon explained that day's "What if . . . ?" "You've lost your radios. You're outbound across the United States. All along your route you see columns of mushroom-shaped clouds. You reach your positive control point but have no Go Code. What do you do?" He studied the audience with narrowed eyes, like a schoolteacher trying to decide who wasn't listening. When he had everyone's attention, he said, "Captain Charles?"

"Depending on my fuel reserve, I'd hold over the PCP and try to contact somebody for the Go Code."

"All right, you go into a holding pattern," Devon said, "but all your radios are still inoperative. While you're orbiting, three B47s headed in the direction of Russia come along and pass you. A pilot in one of the planes waves his arm, like he's saying, 'Follow me.'"

Charles thought before he emphatically said, "In a case like that, I'd follow him."

Devon closed his eyes and shook his head.

Charles said, "Why not? You said we saw bombs exploding, the U.S. was under attack. And then three airplanes went beyond the PCP. They had to have the Go Code."

While Charles argued, Devon continued to shake his head. Now he opened his eyes: "I didn't say a word about bombs exploding. I said that you saw mushroom-shaped clouds. The clouds could have been cumulonimbus build-ups that your mind converted to mushroom shapes."

"What about the three B47s? Are you going to say they didn't have the Go Code?"

"It's possible."

"Anything's possible," Charles muttered.

"Exactly. What if those three airplanes lost their radios too, and their crews reached the same incorrect conclusions you reached about the clouds? Then you know what happens? You follow them and the four of you start World War Three."

Crewmen believed that their primary duty was to attack the enemy, Devon thought. The propensity of a warrior was to prosecute war. But in a thermonuclear world, that bent needed restraint. Unchecked enthusiasm was deadly, two-

95

edged. The Strategic Air Command was principled to prevent war, to preserve peace. The command motto was "Peace is our profession." The four words were printed in foot-high letters on a sign at the base's main gate. Couldn't crewmen read? Couldn't they understand that fundamental message?

Charles said, "Major Devon, I think you should know that many of the crews feel your questions are farfetched and—"

"Nothing is farfetched," Devon said levelly. "You have to expect anything. The trouble is that you people don't think. If you don't have a Go Code, you don't go. It doesn't matter what the rest of the world is doing. How can it be clearer?"

By creating confusion he showed the crews clarity, Devon thought. His mind was filled with madness bred of madness ever since he overheard a B47 aircraft commander brag, "When the time comes, the crews will win the war despite the plans. We'll do what has to be done." The boast proved to Devon that, despite his teaching examples, there was no guarantee that crews wouldn't do exactly what their emotions dictated when the world was afire and they were on their own.

↘CHAPTER 19

IT WAS AN olive-drab, early spring West Texas morning. The sun died behind a late burst of polar jet stream that whipped down from the plains carrying half of Oklahoma inside it. The temperature dropped twenty degrees in an hour. Man and beast hunched back to the wind, sought only shelter.

Emily Charles, however, was driving through South Abilene on her way to a destination she was about to forget. She heard a radio newscaster report:

"Two B47 Stratojet bombers crashed today. Reportedly, all crewmen on the two warplanes were killed. The air force is withholding details of the accidents until next of kin are notified."

The two planes were the fifth and sixth B47s to crash within a month. Three of the first four had exploded shortly after takeoff, had killed everyone aboard.

Emily felt a tightness in her chest. Chuck was flying. A cold stone pressed against her heart. She stopped the car in the middle of the street, rested her forehead on the steering wheel. She knew Chuck was involved, had no doubt about it. Next of kin, she thought, and with face hidden by circling arms, she donned the widow's mask of grief. Probably, somebody was already looking for her.

Memories of failures made her sob. She hadn't cooked breakfast for Chuck that morning, hadn't so much as crawled out of bed to kiss him good-bye. And she loved only him. Had always loved only him. What were his last words? Had he hugged her and whispered "I love you"? How could life end so suddenly? Why hadn't she felt what was coming?

When Chuck had been in training for Korea, Emily had seen an aircraft accident. Rather, she'd *heard* the accident. She'd been playing in the wives' club monthly bridge tournament when a heavy vibration that tingled the soles of her feet, had rattled the officers' club windows and made glasses jump. "Dear God, that wasn't a crash," somebody prayed. Ruthie Gordon had leaped up and led everyone out to the patio. At a distant end of the runway, Emily had seen a strand of greasy smoke trailing downwind. *A soul evaporating into broad daylight,* she'd thought. Along with other wives, she'd cried.

After a time, Ruthie Gordon had confessed, "I know it's Gordo. I didn't say good-bye this morning." Two women had hugged Ruthie before a third had put an arm around her and rocked her. Yet another had offered a handkerchief. But not a single woman had attempted to dissuade her from her conviction. It had been as if in offering up her husband for sacrifice she had spared all others.

Ruthie Gordon's good-byes had earned her the title of "Uncouth Ruth the Belle of Duluth" from the men in Chuck's class after one of them saw her kiss Gordo and say, "I hope you crash and burn, bastard." Smiling, Gordo had gently tapped her jaw with a fist, had answered, "Up yours, old twat." In her defense Gordo had explained, "Her good-byes are like actors saying, 'Break a leg.'"

Ruthie had been right that day: It had been Gordo who'd crashed. Nevertheless, several hours had passed before she'd been officially notified that he was dead. In the weeks that followed, Ruthie had gone to bed with most of the men in the class, or at least with the ones who had wanted her. Those men had affectionately rechristened her: "Uncouth Ruth" became "Gordo," the living extension of their dead flying comrade. After the class graduated, Ruthie had disappeared.

Emily sat up when a young man rapped on the windshield of her car. He opened the door: "You all right, ma'am?"

"My husband had an accident," she said.

"Oh?" He looked inside the car. "Where is he?"

"I don't know," she said.

The man raised his eyebrows: "Well—see—I'm sorry for your troubles and all, but you're blocking traffic." Through the rearview mirror Emily saw waiting cars. "Want me to move this for you?"

Emily slid over to the passenger seat. The man drove the car into the parking lot of a drugstore. He jerked a thumb toward a Texaco station across the street: "I have to get back to work." He stepped out of the car. "If you need a phone or anything, come on over."

"Wait," Emily said. She rummaged in her handbag, found a five-dollar bill. "Here." She handed the money toward the man.

"I didn't do anything to deserve that."

"It's the smallest I have."

"Then you keep it."

Emily smiled sadly, waved. She recognized the drugstore in front of her. She was in River Oaks. The Archers lived nearby. She reached beneath the front seat, pulled out a half-full pint bottle of vodka, and carefully puckering her lips, she took a long sip. The dashboard clock told her it was a quarter after ten. She took another sip. At a time like this Beth Archer needed comfort, Emily decided. She wondered how much life insurance Morris owned.

Beth was wearing her Chinese-red robe when she opened the door. "Did I wake you?" Emily asked. "Can I come in? You got any orange juice?"

While Beth watched, Emily helped herself to glass, ice, and juice, took a bottle of vodka from her handbag and mixed a drink. Even Morris didn't drink this early in the day, Beth thought. The woman looked pale and pasty-faced. What did she use for face powder, all-purpose flour?

Emily tasted her drink, sweetened it with a dribble of vodka, then said, "I have bad news. Two more B47s crashed today."

99

Beth sat down at the kitchen table. "That's why you're here." She wondered why the air force had chosen Emily, of all people. Shouldn't they have sent an officer, like in the movies? Or would he come later?

Emily nodded, the tiny nervous head bob of a chipmunk. "One of the crews was Chuck's. The report said they were all killed."

A flush radiated over Beth. "Morris?" She had an impulse to telephone Jim Leonard before a frigid calm froze her spine. How had it happened? Most of the accidents had been associated with takeoff, she knew. Morris had told her that the sixty-second takeoff run was the most dangerous part of a mission. He'd talked about it only yesterday: "All that inertia. Once you pass decision speed, there's no way to stop. You can't put on the brakes. When you reach the end of the runway, you either have flying speed or you don't. There's no place left to go except up. You horse the airplane off the ground and hope it flies. There's so much stress right then. . . ." Had he meant metal stress on the airframe or mental stress on the airmen?

She'd asked him, "Are you afraid when you fly?" and she'd had to wait for his answer.

"Sometimes, a little. I don't trust Chuck. In an emergency, I'd rather have Dixie doing the flying." He'd grinned like a trapped wolf: "At least the pilots have a chance." She'd known what he meant: The pilots ejected upward, could bail out at ground level; the navigator ejected downward, needed a minimum of five hundred feet of altitude to have a first chance of surviving.

Beth asked Emily, "Did they crash on takeoff?"

"I don't know."

"What?" What was this woman saying? "What do you mean?"

"I don't know how they crashed. Nobody's called me yet."

Wait, wait, wait, Beth thought.

"Have they called you?" Emily said. She drank half her drink, then giggled. "I drink like your husband."

"How do you know what happened?" Beth said.

"I heard the radio and right away I knew."

"What did you hear?"

"The radio said two B47s crashed, and everybody was

killed, and next of kin hadn't been told yet. But I *knew* right then. It had to be Chuck. I forgot to kiss him good-bye." She told Beth about Ruthie Gordon.

The woman was an idiot, Beth thought and wanted to punch Emily's face, to shut her mouth. Beth was fed up with drunkards.

Emily was describing how Ruthie Gordon had made a pass at Chuck when Beth sprang and shoved with both hands, slammed Emily against the refrigerator. Emily's glass struck the bridge of her nose, sloshed drink and ice cubes over her. Emily's head hit the refrigerator door and she dropped to the floor like a bundle of laundry. Beth ran from kitchen to bathroom, locked herself in, groped down through Archer's odors—T-shirts, shorts, socks—and, in a bottom corner of the dirty clothes hamper, found her bottle of tranquilizers.

Placing a pill far back on her tongue, Beth tasted its familiar bitter relief, was about to swallow when she thought, I'm no better than Emily. She spit the pill into the toilet, poured the remaining pills after it. She wouldn't be like the rest of them. She wasn't lonely. She wasn't nervous. She wasn't bored. She was angry.

She slipped out of the bathroom and into Beverly's room. Again, she locked the door. Beverly was quietly playing with her delicate toes. Beth's nervous static arced across the room and Beverly's face knotted. Beth swept up the child, automatically cooed, "Baby, baby, baby Bev. My baby Bev." Beverly cooed in reply, "Ma, ma, ma."

Beth sat down on a straight-back wooden kitchen chair. How often she'd yearned for a cushiony armchair in that room. Morris called her desire an unnecessary indulgence. Beth offered her breast to her baby.

Later, when she came out of the bedroom, Emily was gone. Beth telephoned the command post and a controller comforted her with facts. The B47s that had crashed were from Pease and Pinecastle. To Beth the names sounded as distant as Jupiter and Mars.

With the uncanny precision of a sleepwalker who glides harmlessly through darkest night, Emily blindly made her way through Abilene and across base to her house. Did she steer her automobile or did the automobile steer her?

101

Emily was curled into sleep on the living-room couch when Charles came home. "Mom's feeling bad," David told him. "She got hit on the nose. I put an ice pack on it." He hugged his father's waist. "Supper's in the oven. Your favorite, meat loaf."

"Another merit badge dinner," Charles said and returned the hug. "Did Mom say how she got hurt?"

"No. I don't think she remembers."

Son was father: black brush-cut hair, swarthy complexion, hook nose. There was a vitality in the son's carriage, an alertness in his stance that the father had once possessed but now had forfeited to the real and artificial gravities of flying, to the weight of survival equipment, to the burdens of adulthood.

"Beck's in her room, doing homework," David said.

"How long's Mom been asleep?"

"Since I got home. You have a good mission?"

"We had the best—I can't imagine a better flight. Everything went exactly right."

"I'm glad." David smiled sickly. "We heard at school, two more crashed today."

"I know."

"I didn't tell Beck. You don't have to fly for a while now, do you?".

"Right, no flying for a while. We go on Alert in a couple days."

"I'm glad. Hey, you have time to shower. Supper'll take another hour." David smiled proudly: "I'm trying skillet bread too, right out of the Scout Manual."

Archer had had the best day of his short career. He'd flown a celestial leg to Salt Lake City and had ended up as the only bomber on the site. He'd racetracked, made six runs in less than two hours, and every score was under a thousand feet. The last two were 150 and 120. His performance was equal to a baseball player hitting four doubles or triples before finishing the day with two homers. Six big ones!

At debriefing, bomb-nav specialists laughed when Archer told them, "If nobody minds, I think I'll marry that airplane."

Archer didn't get angry when Charles said, "I was surprised by the last two scores. You were cutting the racetrack too short. You gave me a few minutes of worry."

"So what's new," Dixie said and, with a grin normally reserved for blondes, told Archer, "Keep doing this and we'll end up at Bomb Comp."

Archer waved him off. That subject was for private daydreams.

Archer felt so confident that he didn't stop at the officers' club on the way home. He was tempted. He wanted to hear the comments about his scores. He was king for today.

Beth met him at the door. Her eyes were slightly unfocused. If he hadn't known better, he'd have sworn she'd been drinking.

"God, what a day I had," he said.

"Me too," she answered.

He laughed, thought she was joking. She was still in her red robe. He wanted to tell her every detail of his mission, but beneath the robe his hands found nakedness, wetness.

"Take off that flying suit," she said. "All those zippers, they're like barbed wire." Her voice sounded overmodulated, fuzzy, blurry, as if it came from a cheap radio.

His flying suit and shorts were around his ankles when Beth knelt and took his semirigid penis into her mouth. "Oh, yes," he sighed in gratitude.

He didn't get completely hard before he went off. She swallowed all he ejaculated, the first time that she had done such a thing for him. Why now? His legs barely supported him. And while he shivered, she crept backward, stretched out on the couch. With eyes closed, she spread her robe and her legs, opened herself with calculating fingers, exposed her coral inner body to him. "Eat me," she whispered.

Was this Beth? Archer didn't recognize the base desire. Had a fantasy come to life? He held back, wanting to see her eyes. "Look at me," he said.

"No," she moaned. "Just eat me, please."

He stooped before her and she clasped his golden head in two hands, pulled him into her.

Ghosts stood no vigil that night in the mind of Morris Archer. Flames from the wreckages of six B47s were extinguished after Beth had told him about Emily's visit. At first he had been angry, had picked up the phone to call Chuck. Then he laughed and said, "So now I'm dead," and the act of speaking the words was an unburdening.

In retrospect, the counterfeit self-control he had generated to climb into the B47 coffin-crematorium now took on a genuine quality. He saw that he had a justified right to fear death.

He remembered Beth asking, "Are you afraid when you fly?" and he had answered, "Sometimes, a little." In truth, had he allowed himself to dwell on his fears, he would have been terrified. And why not? Only a fool would not be afraid after six B47s exploded in flight and fell from the sky for no known reason. A sane man might envision a similar thing happening to his airplane. And a sane man's conclusions would be based on facts, not cowardliness.

Two B47s had crashed on March 14, one on March 31, one on April 14, and two on April 15. The loss rate equaled sixty-six a year. If it continued, theoretically every B47 parked at Dyess would be lost before 1958 ended.

Almost overnight, the problem was solved. Engineers X-rayed and magna-fluxed the B47 fleet and found fractures in many wing roots. Under takeoff stress such wings tore loose. Every bomber was given new life with a "boiler plate" modification: Metal braces were installed to beef up the fractured areas.

In later years, Archer would look back on his fears and recognize that a valiant life was not predicated upon a devil-may-care sense of immortality. A courageous man accepted that life was fragile. He approached danger with respect and deliberateness. He knew that defeat or destruction was as probable as victory or survival. His daring was premeditated. And when a man emerged a winner, he was humbly joyful. There was no stigma attached to happiness.

Beyond that time, Archer came to understand that true heroism was not a onetime Medal of Honor event. True heroism was a day-in, day-out struggle against reality, and everything that reality entailed—the bitter and the sweet events connected with being husband, lover, father, provider, leader, and follower.

❧CHAPTER 20

Beth Archer sat at her kitchen table and drew a pencil line down the middle of a sheet of coarse tablet paper. The paper's gritty texture reminded her of being a little girl with pigtails in a sleepy-warm one-room grade school in Laredo. Was it yesterday or a lifetime ago?

Morris was on Alert again. Alert or flying. His life. Her life.

She drew a plus sign atop the left-hand half of the page and a minus sign atop the right. Was she still in school? Beneath the minus she listed "Alert" and "flying."

She dreaded Morris's return from Alert. He was desperately high-strung, filled with a frightening, nervous urge. She had better be ready, in the mood or not.

One time when he arrived home she had been out shopping for the two-inch-thick sirloin steak she knew he wanted for supper. When she'd entered the house, he was sitting in the unlighted living room, holding a bottle of scotch. He'd corked the bottle, stood, and with head lowered and shoulders hunched he'd stalked her. She'd felt herself shrink as he approached, had expected him to swipe out, knock her down, and devour her. At the last moment, she'd held out the wrapped meat: "I was shopping. I knew you'd want steak."

He'd snorted, brushed tensed muscles along her flank, glided around her, his breath heavier than his tread, whispered, "Swell," and eased out to the porch, sat there until she went to him and coaxed him inside.

He'd reminded her of the high school bullies she'd known, mostly slick-hair Mexican boys who moved frictionlessly, drifted a breath away when passing, touched only with their eyes. Clicking tongues: "Chickie, chickie." Her black hair, her dark eyes drew them to her. She'd once heard a sigh, "India hermosa," in her wake. She had hated them, had felt defenseless against their suggestive smirks.

After she'd coaxed Morris back into the house and after they'd made love, she'd found a fist hole in the bedroom closet door. "I don't know why," he'd said. "I exploded. Nothing seemed right."

He wouldn't tell her the cost of replacing the door. She guessed it equaled the price of a new chair. Like his scotch, Morris classified the door as " a man's expense."

It was a wonder that any crewman saw the world clearly, was totally sane, Beth thought. She could never live by their rules: always perfect, not permitted a single mistake on the ground or in the air. And yet, in a perverse reversal of logic, the same perfect men willingly flew airplanes that were obviously imperfect, that blew up at any minute, that killed them all.

SAC's values distorted everything Morris touched. Her. The house. Beverly. He expected them to be in inspection order at all times. Poor Beverly, Beth thought. How would Morris treat her when she grew older, made innocent childish mistakes, was less than perfect?

On the paper before her, below the plus sign, Beth wrote "Beverly," the single constant factor in her life.

Did the plus sign equal love?

Then, still in the plus column, Beth wrote "Morris" followed by a question mark.

Below the minus sign she wrote "house" and "new furniture," and under "new furniture" she wrote "new couch (green)" and "new bedroom suite." She heard Morris telling her they didn't have that much money and she realized that she could make lists all day but they wouldn't solve her problem. As much as she denied the fact, she was lonely. Or was she unloved?

She stared at the question mark after Morris's name. It had appeared automatically, subconsciously, represented a confrontation she could not yet openly face. She traced over the question mark, wove the limp single strand of doubt into a sturdy rope of challenge.

Then, impulsively, beneath the heavy sickle she had drawn, she wrote "Jim." She wanted to sit down and quietly discuss the past two months with him.

She felt hopelessly overwhelmed: Her life's core was fear and death. She was involved in national and international events and, regardless of how small her role, she wasn't trained to cope. Why had Morris chosen SAC?

She believed everything would be clearer if she could have a long talk with Jim. Since the time they'd lunched together, she had seen him once. . . .

He'd walked up to her outside the base exchange and said, "We have to stop meeting this way." They agreed it was her turn to buy and went to the snack bar. Beth was carrying Beverly, and Jim offered to hold the child.

"I thought you weren't allowed to carry babies," Beth said. Morris frequently told her that regulations prohibited men in uniform from carrying babies, groceries, or umbrellas.

"I think that's right," Jim said and took Beverly. "If I get caught, what're they going to do, draft me and ship me to a remote base in Texas?"

They ordered chocolate malts, extra thick, and Jim insisted on paying: "It's my upbringing. If you paid, I'd feel like a gigolo. I could never look you in the eye again." He looked into her eyes, and said, "That would be my loss."

They found a table and Beth took Beverly. They tasted the malts, agreed that they could be thicker, that it was impossible to make a malt too thick.

"So what do you do when you're not an air-force doctor," Beth said, "nights and weekends?"

"If I'm not on call, weekends I usually go to Dallas." In

answer to her frown, he said, "I have a friend there." In for a penny, in for a pound, he thought and added, "A stewardess for Delta."

"I thought doctors dated nurses."

"Like in books?" He lowered his voice to a narrative bass: "Nurse Sheila and Dr. Jim's eyes met across the operating table, above the shimmering sunset scarlet of Mr. Dick's inflamed appendix. Or was it Mr. Appendix's inflamed dick?" He stifled a laugh, made a visor with his hand.

Beth said, "I hope you know the difference, for Mr. Dick's sake," and made him laugh out loud, show his teeth.

"It isn't that funny," Beth said. For perhaps the first time in her life she felt like an adult talking to another adult.

"It is if you've been in an operating room." He explained: "An appendectomy is often a beginner's first operation. It's supposed to be easy. You've been trained, been through anatomy—but still, the first time you have a living, breathing person in front of you—a person who you're responsible for—and you're actually *inside* this trusting person's body—well, every imaginable doubt creeps into your mind. It's easy to forget everything you've been taught.

"I saw a new man grab the little finger of another doctor, an older surgeon who was assisting, coaching more or less. I guess the new man thought he had the patient's appendix because he called for a scalpel. You see, the appendix is about the size of the little finger. Anyhow, the new man called for a scalpel and the old surgeon very calmly told him, 'Please don't slice that off, it happens to belong to my right hand.'"

They drank malts for a while, exchanged satisfied glances.

He asked if she was using the tranquilizers. When she said, "Once in a while," he told her, "I shouldn't've given you those. You're a more confident woman than I thought."

"There are times when I need them," she said. Spontaneously she told him about Morris's return from Guam, about his anger over her reaction to the pearls. She left out the sex and the story seemed incomplete.

"There's unrecognizable tension after couples have been separated for months," Jim said. "He loves you and he probably felt rejected."

"No, no," Beth said, "you don't see. We'd already made love. The pearls—the way he hung them on me. Then he wanted to make love again—it was like he was *paying me*. It wasn't love." She covered her mouth with a hand. None of it had been love, not for either of them, she realized now. Strangers familiarly uniting in coldly sanctified acts. "You can pretend and you can push things aside," she said to herself, "but that doesn't solve anything." At that moment she didn't feel very confident.

Jim teased a napkin from the overstuffed table dispenser, took off his glasses, and carefully polished the lenses. "Sex doesn't always have to be love," he said, "especially after people have been apart for a long time." As soon as he finished he recognized that he hadn't said what he'd meant.

"You don't see," Beth told him.

"Yes I do. I take back what I said. When two people are really in love, sex always includes love—somehow, somewhere love is there."

"Then maybe we aren't really in love," Beth said.

Jim Leonard massaged the bridge of his nose before putting on his glasses. He wasn't qualified to comment, he thought.

Beth stirred her half-finished malt: "You want this?"

"No. Thanks."

His refusal disappointed her. Had she scared away the teenager she'd seen before? She asked, "Who's Nurse Sheila?"

"A name. Somebody made up."

Beth asked about the stewardess from Dallas, learned that Jim had met her on a flight, that she had visited Abilene one time and hadn't liked it. "There's nothing to do here," he said. "We ended up spending the weekend in—my house."

Beth stared into his eyes and smiled. "Was love there?"

"Come on . . ." Then he too smiled. "Yes, there was love, in a way."

"Are you going to marry her?"

"I can answer only half that question. I don't think so. No." He grinned a weak, melancholy grin. "I don't know her half. She probably doesn't either. She won't admit it but she still loves a pilot she used to date. Now he's married to somebody else." The grin faded. "She still sees him."

Her questions had hurt him, Beth thought. But at the same time she wondered about the stewardess and how she managed making love to two men. Jim's tangled love affairs could make a novel, she thought. She wanted to know more about his life. "Why do you live downtown? I thought bachelors had to live in the BOQ. Or are doctors special?"

"Anyone can move into town. It's just that a bachelor doesn't get housing allowance as long as there's room in the Q. I get the allowance because I pay child support. Even if I didn't, I'd still live downtown to get away from the base."

Beth asked where he lived. She was speechless when she heard he had a duplex in the complex where she lived. She didn't tell him they slept two blocks apart.

She'd dreamed of Jim Leonard that same night.

She was in her bedroom, but it was furnished in wish-book style: window draped with lime-green lace; canopy bed topped with lace and ribbons; forest-green satin sheets and lime quilt.

It was daylight. She thought she was with Morris. He was kissing her breasts, little kisses, tickling with his tongue. She stroked his head, and instead of Morris's crew cut, she touched what felt like her hair. She looked down and saw Jim.

Through the venetian blinds sun-warmed stripes crossed their naked bodies, camouflaged them into one. Where did she end and he begin?

Beth was delighted and frightened. Where was Morris? On Alert? Flying? Crashed?

Thin bands of shade made them into a zebra. They rose and fell, trotted gently on the dark green satin veldt. Hands as soft as spring grass caressed her. Long, lean fingers traced delicate patterns, left fingerprints of pleasure outside, then inside.

The pleasure was unbalanced by uncertainty. She shook her head and said, "But don't stop," after he asked, "Can you come this way?" Or had her imagination asked the question?

If only she knew what had become of Morris. Then, perhaps, she could relax.

↘CHAPTER 21

Major Clark Devon frequently recited his personal axiom of doom: "The end of the world will come at night when the United States is asleep."

At two A.M. on a hot July night, Strategic Air Command crewmen were called from their beds to begin a buildup that placed every bomber on Alert.

Chuck Charles and Dixie Smith were waiting at the squadron building when Morris Archer arrived. "You're logged in," Dixie said. "Chuck saw you drive up. We got Line Twenty-two, generates at X plus twelve, two this afternoon."

"What do we do until then, go to breakfast or go home?"

Charles said, "Maybe later." He looked at his watch. "Right now we have an intelligence briefing at the base theater."

Stern air policemen dressed in sharply creased blue uniforms that included blue berets, white scarves, and ivory-handled revolvers guarded the theater doors, verified the identity of every man who entered.

Among the crewmen there was friendly shoving at the doors and in the lobby. At least a dozen men asked, "Where's the popcorn?" But inside the auditorium, the men quickly found seats, conversed quietly.

"Lebanon" was the word most heard. For two months the West had watched while Gamal Abdel Nasser, president of the United Arab Republic, had fomented unrest across the Middle East. The question had been: How long until the West faces up to him? Under the Eisenhower Doctrine, the United States was committed to rescue Middle East nations threatened by a "country dominated by internal communism." To Western observers Nasserism equaled communism. The man was evil.

A few weeks earlier, in a secret briefing, Archer had heard an intelligence officer report:

"Nasser is a syphilitic. Almost all Arab males of his age have syphilis. They acquire it either congenitally or, as young men, contract it from prostitutes. National poverty prevents proper treatment. Usually there is no treatment. Therefore, five to thirty years later, the syphilis reemerges in an advanced stage. Nasser, who is forty, now shows signs of tertiary syphilis. As a result, his political activity runs in cycles: When he's well he works constantly, feels he must get ahead or make up for lost time; when he suffers attacks he is incapacitated by lack of concentration and impaired judgment."

At exactly three A.M., a voice called, "Gentlemen, the commander." The audience jumped to its feet an instant before Colonel Axel Turner strode down the left aisle of the theater, said, "Be seated, gentlemen," and took his place in the center of the first row. "Carry on," he said.

On stage, Major Clark Devon stepped to the dais and loudly asked, "Is the auditorium secure?" Each officer in the audience looked at the men on both sides of him. If he saw an unfamiliar face, he was expected to stand and thereby challenge the stranger. After several seconds during which everyone remained seated, an air policeman in a rear corner answered, "Sir, the auditorium is secure."

The houselights dimmed and Devon said, "Colonel Turner, gentlemen, the classification of this briefing is top

112

secret." A slide that read TOP SECRET flashed on the screen. "In light of recent developments in the Middle East, President Eisenhower ordered United States military forces to Defense Condition One at zero-seven hundred hours Zulu today." A new slide read:

DEFCON 1
X-HOUR 0700 ZULU
(0200 CDT)

"By X plus twenty hours all B47s in this Bomb Wing will be on Alert." A new slide listed the normal Alert sorties plus line numbers up through forty-five with generation times progressing in roughly half-hour increments. "Captain Fenner for intelligence."

Pale, thin Leon Fenner moved swiftly to the dais, nodded, and a map of the Middle East filled the screen. He said, "Colonel Turner," and read from a handful of teletype messages.

"At the request of Lebanon President Camille Chamoun, at thirteen-hundred Zulu today, nine thousand United States Marines will land south of Beirut International Airport." Several listeners applauded. "A task force of seventy U.S. naval vessels, including three aircraft carriers, will be standing by offshore.

"The presence of United States forces in Lebanon is intended to stabilize two months of internal unrest generated by Druse rebels who are supported by the United Arab Republic, composed of Egypt and Syria.

"Earlier this month, Secretary General Dag Hammarskjold denied need for a United Nations police force to seal the border between Lebanon and Syria. President Chamoun claimed the border was a mass infiltration route for UAR rebels. Following Hammarskjold's denial, both Turkey and Iraq offered support to Lebanon."

Fenner flipped to another page. "At the request of Jordan's King Hussein, the United Kingdom today will deploy two thousand paratroops into Amman, the capital of Jordan, as a measure to strengthen the Jordanian government.

"Six months ago, Jordan aligned with Iraq and formed the Arab Union. King Hussein is cousin to King Faisal the Second of Iraq."

Another page and Fenner's voice lost its brittle edge, became funereal. "In Iraq, pro-Nasser rebels yesterday stormed the Baghdad palace and reportedly killed the royal family. It is believed that King Faisal the second, his cousin and ex-regent Amir Abdulillah, Premier Nuri al-Said, and their families were murdered. Naked corpses with their heads, hands, and feet cut off were dragged through the streets and hung from lampposts." Mutters of discontent rose from the audience. "Foreigners have been attacked in the street.

"Brigadier General Abdul Karin Kassem proclaimed a new republic for Iraq and named himself leader of a military cabinet."

Another page: "Between twenty-five and forty Soviet divisions, supposedly on summer maneuvers, are massing along the Turkey and Iran borders."

Another page: "United Arab Republic President Gamal Nasser reportedly has flown to Moscow to meet with Soviet Premier Nikita Khrushchev."

And a final page: "In Moscow, one hundred thousand people marched on the United States Embassy building and smashed front windows with barrages of stones, bricks, and ink bombs."

With an expression strained by the weight of all he reported, Fenner looked at Axel Turner. "Sir, that concludes the briefing."

Turner wondered why intelligence officers seemingly carried the responsibility for the events they described. Did the selection process choose hypersensitive men for the job? Or did the process isolate consummate actors?

Turner thanked Fenner, adding a nod like a royal pardon, then stood and faced the crewmen. As he spoke he moved across the front of the theater as lightly as a featherweight boxer, yet his compact frame exuded the power of a heavyweight. "I hope we someday look back on Lebanon as we now look back on Suez," he said. "Practice scrambles are canceled until we are downgraded from DEFCON One. There's no telling how long we'll be in this posture." His steady eyes extended confidence, sincerity. "Whatever happens in the next few days, or weeks, I have the utmost faith that each of you will perform the mission exactly as planned. Carry on, gentlemen."

114

The audience stood at attention while he exited up the aisle.

Charles said, "Our plane is supposed to be ready at two. Before that, we have preflight and target study. Let's go home now. Stick by the phone. If you don't hear from me, we'll meet back at the squadron at nine-thirty."

Morris Archer raced home and woke Beth. He used general terms to talk around secrets, and much like a schoolboy with newly acquired knowledge, he recited all he knew of a world on the brink. In a convoluted way, he made himself the focal point of that world. Was it possible he believed the United States was mobilizing for his glory?

Beth wanted to say, "Who cares what foreigners do to each other? Why must we get involved? Are we as mad as they?" But she feared hostile reaction to her honesty.

While it was still dark, they halved and squeezed oranges, fried Canadian bacon, poached eggs, toasted English muffins, brewed tea, to produce a last supper for daybreak.

Then Morris deliberately packed a B4 bag, made Beth wash and iron extra clothes while his mind flew beyond family and home. He *knew* he would reach and destroy his target. He envisioned refueling and rearming at a poststrike recovery base in Iran, then flying a second mission, a restrike sortie, to erase a target that miraculously escaped the first-wave attack. Destroyer of miracles, he thought. Following victory, what odyssey awaited?

Meanwhile, Beverly woke and Beth cared for her too.

There wasn't time to make love, barely time for a farewell kiss after Beth chauffeured him back to the squadron. Chaste warrior consigned to battle, capable of extreme and terrible acts but with conscience and heart limpid.

Not until a decade later did Morris Archer understand that different men had entirely different views when toeing the edge of the same precipice. At such a moment, a man's vision revealed his nature, his relationships with those things he loved.

In that future time, Morris looked back and saw Dixie Smith returning home, slipping into bed as easily as if he had risen only for a drink of water. Later Dixie asked Liz to be late for work, knowing that jobs didn't matter. They

115

made love. Then over Danish rolls and coffee, he told her that the Arabs were slaughtering each other again. "Again?" she said. "You mean *still*." He nodded and told her that Russia was on one side and the United States on the other, still. She said, "Not still, *always*." They had a second cup of coffee while he explained that he would be gone until the turmoil ended. "That could be forever," she said. "It'll never stop." Then they made love a second time before they went to their separate meaningless jobs.

Looking back, Morris saw Chuck Charles walking in to Emily who was sitting in bed with one cigarette between her lips and another smoking in the ashtray. Emily's face was a shadowy mask of doom cut by a blood-red mouth. She said, "When they call in the middle of the night, it has to be bad."

Comfortingly, Charles told her, "No worse than usual." The usual was bad enough, he thought. "This time it's the end of the world," she said. "Should I tell the children?" Chuck made her a drink to relax her. They talked and she grew calm, persuaded him to mix one more. The mask of doom faded, lingered in outline of fatigue.

The children woke at sunrise. The family sat down to a breakfast of cereal and toast. Emily was carefree and doting, except for a pause when she hugged Becky fiercely and trembled. David pushed back his chair, called, "Mom, you all right?" From his Boy Scout first-aid training, a list of stroke symptoms filled his mind. After the children went out to play, Emily made love to Chuck with a desperate schoolgirl passion, embarrassed him because he did not consider the situation to be final. Nevertheless, her ardor reaffirmed his belief in her devotion and dependence. To him, her life was as valuable as his. Her display gave him hope that someday she would again value his life equally.

The Lebanon Crisis was a replay of the Suez Crisis, with one major difference.

In 1956, Bulganin spoke for the Red Bear, hinted of "countries that are so powerful they need not attack by naval or air power" but could use swifter means, "such as rocket technique." United States intelligence declared the implied Soviet nuclear rocket threat to be a bluff.

In 1958, Khrushchev was the Bear's voice and bluntly warned: "The USSR cannot remain indifferent to what is happening in the . . . immediate vicinity of its frontier. We know that the USA has . . . hydrogen bombs . . . an air force and a navy. But you well know that the USSR also has atomic and hydrogen bombs . . . and ballistic rockets of all types, including intercontinental ones." United States intelligence did not doubt him.

The crisis ran its course without United States Marines becoming involved in fighting between rival Lebanese forces, historically opposite sects who would for years ahead clash again and again. However, America's neutrality established a precedent that permitted a following generation of marines to invade, observe, and be murdered by the same religious fanatics.

In early August, SAC demobilized to a normal DEFCON 5 posture and the Soviet army backed off from the borders of Turkey and Iran, after the United Nations General Assembly adopted a resolution sponsored by all the Arab countries that called for mutual respect for each other's sovereignty. In September the Lebanese insurrection ended: Fouad Chehab was elected to succeed Chamoun.

The dead became more fertilizers of history; the events, ashes of memory.

During the long, tense days of the Lebanon Crisis, Archer stood like a priest on the frontier edge of a new religion, a dozen-year-old religion prepared to sacrifice mankind. A religion with no heaven, only hell. Impatiently he listened to the thoughts of others without understanding what was said.

The Alert facility lounge was a public confessional where men interpreted their dilemmas aloud, sought confirmation of personal beliefs. Never had Archer heard crewmen speak so candidly, but never, in his experience, had they so tightly circled the abyss.

Archer felt trapped in history, but not a history he wanted to remember ten or twenty or thirty years hence, not a history that would grant him the honor as an old man on his deathbed of proudly saying, "I was there when it happened. I made it happen." He was in a child's dream and an adult's reality.

All about him, men seemed suddenly of a different caliber. Or was he seeing their true quality for the first time?

Pappy Trembly, for example, shuffled from person to person in the lounge and said, "Better to waste your time doing this than to shoot it all in twelve hours." Were his words absolution to counter Archer's belief? Didn't the old fool understand that Russia would never go away? That nothing was accomplished by sitting? Archer had not trained merely to wait.

Bobby Bushman asked, "Are we really going to kill millions of Russian peasants just because thousands of camel jockeys hate each other?" And he spoke heresy: "Bulganin had the right idea during Suez. He said Russia and America should line up on the same side and kick ass."

Charles argued: "We're trying to settle religious differences with political force. It won't work."

Then, one afternoon, chubby Mick Riordan announced to a small audience, "I question whether I'll actually drop the bomb if the time comes." Riordan carried a rosary in a thigh pocket of his flying suit, often sat with right hand thrust into the pocket, fingers barely moving, lips occasionally twitching. Silent prayers for whom? "I guess I won't know what I'll do until I'm on the bomb run, at the target." He was smiling when he spoke the words.

"He shouldn't be on a crew," Archer said to himself. "He's unstable." Within a subculture where obedience and perfection ranked foremost, Archer's evaluation was absolutely correct. Yet had he unwittingly condemned everyone but himself?

Despite the knowledge that his religion was the true religion, Archer felt distant among peers. It was as if he and they coexisted on a landscape stretched between two worlds. His dark realm was antithetical to their light. How had he become alien in a land where he sought eventually to reign?

↘CHAPTER 22

Emily waved good-bye to Chuck and held back tears. She
knew she would not see him again in this life. It wasn't fair:
they'd survived Korea, made it through the B47 crashes,
and now they would die . . . for Lebanon?

A long time ago she had read an article about a Doomsday Clock, about how it was set at eight minutes to
midnight. In her mind the Doomsday Clock stood taller
than any man, rested on a black tombstone isolated on a
field of night that stretched beyond sight. The clock's
numbers were tar black, except for the twelve, which glowed
redly, pulsed like a trembling heart, gave the clock's livid
face a ruddy heat. The clock's hands were skeleton arms
that ended in bony pointing fingers. The rigid short arm
aimed skyward, dead on twelve. Emily could see the long
arm creeping forward, nearing alignment with the short. Its
forefinger was a minute from midnight, heartbeats from
finality.

When the finger closed that tiny gap, they would die.

Fatalistically, death appealed to Emily. Without Chuck she did not care to live. He was the only person on earth who understood her, who loved her unstintingly.

She tried to imagine her death. Nothing from her harbored life provided reference for the brutal blast of a thermonuclear bomb. She thought of being touched by the sun, of suffering the fatal pains of a thousand sunburns. The imagined pain—pain beyond endurance—raised gooseflesh down her arms, made her shiver. She decided she would rather be disintegrated by invisible rays. Her body would glow. Her bones would show through her skin like X-ray pictures. She would evaporate into thin air. How badly would disintegration hurt? How long would it take? Did pain matter if everything disappeared when it ended? She feared a final agony.

God must be a hundred-proof son of a bitch to give men such a weapon, she thought. She looked about, fearful that somebody might have read her mind. She wouldn't want Becky or David to hear such thoughts. Softly she said, "Dear God, I'm sorry." But she wasn't to blame, she realized. The thought wasn't hers. She'd heard it from Steve. Her encounter with him came back like a nightmare . . .

Chuck and Emily were new to Dyess, had been there less than a month, when Chuck was named Officer of the Day. The duty required him to spend the night at base headquarters.

Alone and bored, Emily went to the officers' club and bought a fifth of vodka. It was toward seven o'clock, and as she'd expected, the after-work crowd had cleared out of the bar. She decided to have one drink.

She was waiting to order when Robby Robertson sat down beside her, introduced himself, and offered to buy. She had never seen him before, would to this day swear that he'd called himself Steve Stevenson.

His broad smile made her smile. His face looked as innocently happy as a snowman's: round, unlined, scrubbed pure white, with dark coal eyes and a cherry nose. His hair looked damped, as if he'd just taken a shower. He used an after-shave lotion she didn't recognize, a heavy odor that she enjoyed. Dressed in white shirt, gold-and-blue rep tie, blue blazer, and gray flannel slacks, he resembled every air-force officer she knew. Uniform out of uniform.

One drink led to another, as long as he bought. Emily had little cash, didn't dare run up a bar tab on top of charging the fifth of vodka.

They got drunk while he performed predictably. She listened to him talk about himself (he told her he was single, but had a steady girlfriend), about flying (he said he was a bomber aircraft commander), and about sex.

"What do you like to do in bed?" he asked.

"Watch TV," she said.

"So do I," he said. "Let's go watch some TV."

Despite his bluntness, she kept him at a distance. She didn't black out completely, later was able to reconstruct most of what happened.

She protested but he followed her home. They necked standing up in the carport. His tongue tasted bourbon-sweet. He lifted her off her feet and carried her into the house. They still had clothes on (were they on the couch or on the bed?) when David ran in and began hitting Robby, shouting, "Get off my mother."

Somehow she talked David back to bed. She and Robby had a nightcap—huge drinks that took nearly half the fifth of vodka. She felt her feet tingle, and then she was frightened: They were naked in bed and his hairy body looked as heavy and shaggy as a buffalo. She expected him to fall on her, stampede over her, crush her. . . .

Instead, he dropped no weight on her, barely touched, barely penetrated her. He moved in short jabs, rapid half strokes. In less than a minute, he snorted, pulled back, and came on her pubic hairs. Then he was off the bed, dressed, and gone. Had he said good-bye?

Emily hugged her pillow and slept.

When Chuck woke her in the morning, the first thing that caught his eye was the big red-and-blue wristwatch on the nightstand. He picked it up, sadly stared at it until Emily cried tears of self-hatred. He let her calm herself before asking, "Do you remember who this belongs to?"

"I met a pilot at the club. A big man with straight black hair. He bought me drinks. His name's Steve. I think he's in our squadron."

Chuck sat on the edge of the bed, took one of her hands in

121

his. This was the first time in nearly four months that Emily had strayed, he thought. The demands of moving, packing and unpacking, had occupied her days. And he had been available to share her nights. How could she be lonesome again, so soon? In one night? He despised her spiritless willpower, her unfaithfulness. At the same time, he wished he could retire today and spend every tomorrow with her. He stroked her hand. His gentleness made her cry again. Why wasn't his tender touch enough?

For the first time she honestly lied about another man. It seemed the necessary thing to do after the many encounters in which she hadn't been able to recall her actions. "I remember driving home and thinking that somebody was following me. But I don't remember anyone being here." Did those words hurt Chuck any less? She cried harder than before: She had betrayed herself as well as him.

Nobody named Steve fit the description Emily had given. Chuck Charles carried the watch to work and questioned the squadron adjutant. "Only navigators wear a watch that big," the adjutant said, "navigators and Rob Robertson."

His description fit.

The schedule showed Robby's crew was mission planning the following day. No need to hurry, Charles decided, a guilty man remained guilty forever.

The next day when Robby took a break, Charles slipped into the crowded mission planning room and placed the wristwatch atop a form Robby was completing. Let the accused convict himself, Charles thought and took a seat in a far corner of the room, watched from behind a magazine.

Robby returned, immediately saw the watch. He scooped it up, read the serial number, smiled. "Where did this come from?" he asked. Nobody answered. He slid the band over his hand and snapped it snugly around his wrist. He had convicted himself as surely as if he'd stretched a noose over his head and cinched it.

Robby looked about the room. After several seconds his eyes met Charles's stare.

Charles lowered the magazine and the set of his mouth made Robby's mind race, turbocharged. For an instant Robby mentally denied that he had left the watch *there*. He never took off the watch in public, he told himself, removed it only when he undressed for bed. And then he knew that habit had betrayed him.

In a normal voice that crossed the noisy room as directly as a beam of light, Charles told Robby, "Come outside."

Robby trailed after Charles, saw no alternative: He'd been caught red-handed. He expected a fight, but there was no way he could throw the first punch. Already he felt defeated. Even if he won the physical battle, he would lose whatever administrative war that followed.

The moment they exited the building, Charles turned abruptly. Robby raised his fists.

He added proof of his guilt with every gesture, Charles thought, and with hands at his sides, he stared scornfully at the younger man until he lowered his fists. There was no need to explain to this hoodlum that Emily was sick, vulnerable. No need to say that regardless of what happened, past or future, Emily was the woman that Charles loved, his wife and mother of his children. A hoodlum had no respect for the values of others, would never understand reason. A hoodlum knew only force.

Charles said, "If you ever again so much as talk to any member of my family, I'll beat you until you wish you were dead."

The unemotional certainty in Charles's warning made Robby recognize that there was nothing to dispute. Although he outweighed Charles, Robby had no desire for a fight. Charles possessed the burning strength of the defender of a cause. Robby had the numbing, debilitating disadvantage of chilling guilt.

"You're a hoodlum," Charles said. "Keep out of my way." He stepped toward Robby and Robby moved out of his path, watched him enter the building, took a deep breath of relief.

He'd gotten off far lighter than he'd expected, Robby thought. But he had to watch his behavior around Charles. He wondered what he would have done had the roles been reversed. But that was impossible, he knew: He couldn't picture Ellen going to bed with Charles. Then he wondered if Charles had been afraid of him. No, he told himself, the man was righteous. Righteous men knew no fear.

123

❧CHAPTER 23

Morris had hinted to Beth that the world would end, then left her—unprotected mother with child—for days, hopelessly waiting.

She listened to the radio and wished for a television set. Like a threatened animal, she listened intently to every unusual sound, every engine noise. Wouldn't she be able to hear the bombers if the entire fleet launched? At night odd noises would wake her and she would lie absolutely still, holding her breath, straining her ears. She felt blind; her ears were her contact with the outside world.

By the third day of the Lebanon Crisis, Beth regretted throwing away her tranquilizers. She circled a treadmill of unanswered questions. Where was Morris? Why didn't he call and tell her what was happening? Had the bombers deployed elsewhere? How long would the uncertainty continue?

She telephoned the command post. A controller read an

official statement, apologized for not being permitted to tell her more: "By order of the president, the Strategic Air Command has assumed its highest state of readiness until the present crisis in the Middle East is resolved."

Against her judgment, Beth telephoned Emily Charles.

"I talk to Chuck every day," Emily told her. "He's here, at Dyess." Beth heard her drink. It was eleven o'clock in the morning. "Do you know we're all little chipmunks?" Emily asked.

Beth interpreted the question as a reference to the song, "We're All Little Chipmunks." "I never heard it," she answered.

In a toneless voice, Emily said, "We're all little chipmunks and we're going to die. We'll all be angelmunks. God will protect the children. He won't allow them in the war. They won't die."

Emily was beyond drunkenness, Beth thought. "You should call Chuck and tell him—"

"I can't tell Chuck anything. I might lie to him."

"But you should tell him about the angelmunks," Beth said and wondered if she should call Morris instead and tell him of Emily's problem. Would he care? Would she dare? She was afraid to phone the Alert facility. She'd done it during his first time on Alert and had been intimidated by Morris's angry breathing. He'd spoken in the hissing dragon voice of her father: "Look, you have no idea how busy I am, like right now. So, starting now, I'll call you when I have time. All right?" Chuck was more considerate than Morris. "Call Chuck and tell him," Beth advised.

Emily said, "I have the power to sense things through the bottom of my feet. I feel a storm coming. We'll all be little angelmunks."

"Please, call Chuck," Beth urged and said good-bye. In the face of insanity, Beth felt helpless. What could she do for Emily? What could she do for herself? Men who made thermonuclear war had no conscience. Her insight made her fearful for unprotected women and children everywhere —American, Russian, Lebanese.

Having nowhere else to turn, after a lapse of three years, Beth called home. Her father answered and she said, "Hello, Daddy," as if she had talked to him the day before.

"Beth Ann?" He sounded cautious. To him the telephone was a bearer of bad tidings, a poisonous snake, something he did not care to handle. "Here, I'll let you talk to your mother."

"Beth Ann," her mother said, excited, flustered. "I been thinking of you. We got your pictures of the baby."

"Beverly," Beth said.

"She looks like you when you were little." Then, realizing the phone call was out of the ordinary, knowing that a long-distance call never had a purely social motive, she asked, "Are you and your husband getting along?"

"Morris," Beth said. The question woke Beth to the fact that there was no way she could explain her predicament. In her mother's world, wives did what their husbands commanded. Subservience made a marriage successful. "Everything's fine," Beth said.

"Linda Williams and Bob parted," her mother said. Linda had been Beth's best friend in high school, had married shortly after graduation. "He moved somewhere up north. To Dallas, I think. Linda got the three children, lives back with her mother." Linda's father had run away while her mother was pregnant with a third child, Beth remembered. "People say Linda drove him off, always wanting more than she needed, same as her mother."

The double lesson was so transparent that Beth smiled sadly. Why had she called? What knowledge had she expected her mother to provide? Her mother knew no more of life than she did. Beth said, "Mama, I love you." She had seen her mother as distantly different. Now they appeared closely akin, stood side by side, were perhaps exactly the same woman on the same spot. Without filtering emotion through intellect, Beth said, "Would you like to come visit?"

"Yes," her mother answered and, in the same breath, added, "But I can't leave Homer. Who'd care for him?" Her mother asked, "Couldn't you come here?"

"I can't. Who'd care for Morris?" Beth said, intending the response as a sarcastic joke that mocked both of them.

Her mother missed the irony, said, "I know. I know." Then she asked, "Write more. Please."

Beth promised and there was nothing else to say.

* * *

On the fourth day of the Lebanon Crisis, Morris at last phoned, sounded as remote as if he were on an island in the middle of the Pacific Ocean.

"Are you mad at me?" Beth asked. Was he angry because they hadn't had sex before he left?

"No. I have a lot on my mind," he said. "We're so busy . . ." It wasn't true. After the first-afternoon flurry of target study and preflight, the days were as empty as the outer reaches of space. There was not even the mad dash of a daily practice scramble to break the monotony.

The major diversion was inspecting the airplane three times a day: morning, afternoon, evening. Each time the crew approached its B47, Dixie acted surprised: "Look, it's still here!" Once a day they stared through a plastic plate on the weapon to ensure that the arm-safe switch was in the safe position.

The rest of the time they waited. They sat. And talked. And ate. And slept. In the confines of the underground bunker they lived buried alive.

"Do you want me to come out and see you?" Beth asked and was relieved when Morris said, "I don't think so." It was too hot to sit in the car, he thought. Of course, if Beth didn't have Beverly and they owned an air-conditioned car like Dixie . . .

Every night around sundown, Liz drove by in the Caddy and picked up Dixie who was waiting at the gate. They parked on a street away from the Alert bunker, out beyond the sentries and barbed wire but still within sight of the airplanes. Dixie always came back smiling.

Morris reconsidered, suggested to Beth, "Why don't you get a sitter for the baby and come out alone."

"I hate to leave Beverly with a stranger," Beth said. "She's upset for days after. Besides, most sitters charge too much."

The expense convinced Morris. "And it's so hot," he added. Trapped in the frigid comfort of the Alert bunker's central air-conditioning, he forgot that Beth depended on a laboring, secondhand evaporative cooler stuck in the bedroom window to hold the duplex's temperature down near eighty degrees.

Together they convinced each other not to do what they didn't want to do.

If it were Ellen Robertson, Morris thought, he wouldn't care if they sat in a steambath. . . .

The same as Liz Smith, Ellen drove to the Alert facility every night. Whereas Liz silently drifted in with the shadows that accompanied sunset, Ellen roared in like a flaming rocket. Traveling too fast, she braked noisily, then revved the engine and beeped the horn whether Robby saw her or not.

After she left, Robby trudged into the lounge, flopped into a chair, and sighed. "Once I got out of college, I'd've bet the moon I'd never again do it in a car." And he chuckled contentedly.

Just the night before, Ellen had beeped at Morris, who was outside the fence, pacing. He walked over, leaned against the car and was about to offer to find Robby when Ellen said, "What do you guys do in there all day?"

No answer came to Morris's mind. His eyes had locked on Ellen's legs. She wasn't wearing stockings and her skirt was hiked up, bunched around her thighs. The legs were perfectly smooth, lightly tanned. She smelled soapy fresh, bathtub clean. Morris felt a rising erection.

"You don't sleep together, do you?" Ellen asked and laughed.

Morris said, "Yeah. Right now it's crowded, four to a room . . ." before he understood what she had meant. He felt foolish, and insulted.

Ellen brushed silky blond hair from in front of her face. "Wonder what would happen if a woman got locked in there all night?" she said and stared through the windshield. Her loose-fitting, unbuttoned shirt showed that she wore no bra. Morris's fingers curled with a desire to cup her free breasts. He wondered if she wore panties and it dawned upon him that she had driven there half naked, prepared to play. The thought made him rock hard.

His mind split into three. One segment fed upon close-ups of her golden beauty, incorporated them into a daydream of explicit sexual actions performed right there. The second part of his mind rebelled against her smug beauty, smarted from the slap that suggested he was homosexual; it wanted to humiliate her, dominate her. The last fraction imagined her prowling darkened halls of the Alert bunker,

128

slinking from room to room. He said, "Any woman spent the night in there, she'd make a million dollars."

"Even if she was old and ugly?" What a curious question to be spoken by such young and beautiful lips.

"No. Any old and ugly woman would make only five hundred thousand," he said.

Ellen laughed, then turned her blue eyes on him. He felt spotlighted, bathed in a shower of glorious light. She had placed him center stage, given him confidence.

Ellen said, "Remember the joke about the woman who had to sell it because her husband lost his job? The first night she came home with forty dollars and twenty-five cents. Her husband said, 'And twenty-five cents! Who gave you a quarter?' She said, 'All of them.'"

They laughed together.

Morris's mind dissolved into the shallow flow of the conversation: "You heard the one about the whore . . ." Was he bold to use that word, especially without Robby present? ". . . the whore who had Saint Vitus' dance?"

Ellen nodded and together they repeated the punch line: "Okay, boys, turn her loose."

Morris said, "How about the whore with the glass eye?"

"I know that one," she said coldly. "It's crude." The spotlight went out, the play ended. "Here comes Robby," she told him.

"A guy's five minutes late and right away somebody bird-dogs his wife," Robby said and faked a punch at Morris.

"We were talking about what you guys do all day," Ellen said.

"Nothing," said Robby.

Ellen nodded: "That's what Mo said." When Robby moved to the passenger side of the car, had his back turned, Ellen looked openmouthed at the spotted bulge in the front of Morris's flying suit, then winked.

Morris went underground. Locked inside a toilet stall in the community bathroom, he fantasized half-dressed Ellen onto the center of the Alert lounge floor. Crewmen filled the room. Morris was ringmaster of the circus that followed.

CHAPTER 24

EXCEPT FOR CATNAPS on the couch, Emily had been awake since Chuck had gone on Alert. The four days were less than a minute on the Doomsday Clock. To Emily there was no sense of time passing, no dimension to those few seconds that remained.

The inverted eye of a portable television silently scanned the world, had been on watch continuously since Chuck departed. Emily had turned off the sound, deafened herself to the outside. She'd added a degree of psychic blindness to life by turning the television on end. She'd tilted the set so it would be easier to view when she was lying down. Then she'd left it in that position. Now when she sat up or reclined in the opposite direction, the world was made up of swimmers and floaters, and some who stood on their heads, unrecognizable faces and bodies, silent patterns of coal dust and ashes.

She lived within an isosceles triangle formed by couch, toilet, and refrigerator. David and Becky had surrendered that space to her, made it her inner sanctum. When they passed along its boundaries, they soundlessly watched her as if they were something from the fringe of television, watched her as if she were a ghost perhaps, the specter of Emily. Were any of them still alive?

Indeed, at times Emily felt she no longer existed physically. She craved nothing: not food, drink, or smoke. In shutting out the noise of the world, had she forfeited her right to speak, to respond, forfeited her right to need a mouth?

Every so often David entered her sanctuary, served her a sandwich she did not taste, gave her a kiss she did not feel. He tidied up around her, treated her like an invalid. One day he brushed her hair. Another day he changed her blouse. Was she an ailing ghost, most fragile of all beings? Or had David become parent and Emily child?

What a fragment of a woman, she thought. Roleless, damned creature . . . neither mother nor wife . . . How many strange men had she been with? She did not know her own history. How could Chuck love her? She didn't deserve his love. What she deserved was to lose him. God knew, Chuck didn't deserve the burden of her . . . albatross . . . millstone. . . . With a wife like Jean Turner he could be a general, she thought.

Drunk with fatigue, Emily felt tired to her soul, dissipated, as completely burnt out as a dark star. She was oppressed by a constant vision of the remorseless figure of death standing on the horizon, blocking every path to the future, black-shrouded skeleton of pain pitilessly stroking the seconds until midnight of Doomsday.

She thought of Becky and David and the bomb became staggeringly cruel, unfair beyond reason. Even God didn't have the power to spare the children, she thought. Why couldn't they somehow survive, live on to make a new, innocent world?

Becky and David . . .

Years before, she had seen one photograph of the bomb's devastation—one photograph from Hiroshima—and it was all she had needed. She had felt an instant, hopeless compassion for children everywhere and the feeling had remained inside her, arose and overwhelmed her whenever the bomb was mentioned.

Now she envisioned a nuclear weapon fireball that enveloped the base and their home, envisioned her children with their hair afire, being seared by flames. . . . She heard Becky and David scream and cry. With their clothes burned off, bodies quilted with blisters and melted eyes running from their sockets, they groped toward her in rigors of pain, and she shrank from them. Their hideously ugly faces were copper-red and charcoal masks of dripping flesh. Lipless mouths gulped air for scorched lungs. Their rubbery fingers and toes were fused, webbed. Her skin crawled at the thought of their alien touch.

These bleeding and charred bodies were not the children she loved. These newborn monsters carried the fiery brand of the underworld. God would not accept them into heaven. They too were damned.

While Emily waited in animated repose, time continued its everlasting dance, glided forward and backward in her mind, waltzed to the cosmic tune of eternal pain.

One minute she was a rosy schoolgirl on a merry-go-round, her schoolgirl mind vexed by the riddles of first dates and first kisses, class rings and going steady. In that mind she was still virgin, tortured by the knowledge that she would give away her virginity before she met Chuck. Oh, how she longed to save it for him. But in a springtime orchard with apple blossoms floating overhead, drifting in white silhouette before a full-faced moon, she tasted sweet wine and straw, smelled new earth, was born and died in an instant of sharp, tiny pain. Good girl/bad girl. Her dilemma left her fitful, unhappy, dissatisfied. Her self-control—lack of control—was her never-ending nemesis, her self-destruction.

In the next minute Emily was passenger in her coffin, blanketed with flowers. Chuck stood over her and wept. Children together, they never would be silvery grandparents together with grandchildren tinier than she. David wept too. But dauntless Becky stood tearless, accusing; her expression asked, "Why? Why did you do this? Why did you leave me?" "When you're older, you'll understand. Don't judge me now," Emily tried to explain but her mouth filled with bitter red tulips.

She tasted the earth they laid upon her, tasted damp

moon shadows, closed her eyes to blind memories, undecipherable passages that she had endured as penance for being a woman. And in her final resting place she knew she would not be at rest. It was not the world that was poor and empty; it was something inside her soul . . . worthless . . . miserable . . . wretched. . . . Was her inferiority born from self-perpetuated guilt that gave appearance to her existence, called attention to herself?

Leaving Chuck was the final abnegation of self, final denial of a love object she long had expected to lose. Now she never could lose him. By forfeiting herself she would hold him forever. For her, tomorrow would not come.

Emily navigated the left edge of life's final triangle, reached the bathroom and found a bottle of Equinal in the medicine cabinet. She poured the pills onto her palm. About forty. She searched the cabinet, found another bottle, an older prescription with a dozen or so pills. Fifty should do, she thought.

She walked the back edge of the triangle to the refrigerator, found a jug of orange juice. David, as always, she thought. He would forgive her. She clutched the jug to her chest, felt it chill her heart.

"Vod-ka, vod-ka. Vod-ka, vod-ka . . ." Her mind sang the word to the melody of "The Volga Boatmen" as she trudged in tempo along the triangle's third side, shortest side, invisible final side.

She sat on the floor, where she could reach everything on the low coffee table before her. Less than half a fifth of vodka remained . . . enough. She'd hardly drunk anything. . . .

Ice. She'd forgotten ice. She wasn't getting up again. The orange juice was cold enough. She ritualistically mixed a drink: vodka, orange juice; taste; dribble more vodka. She slipped an Equinal between her lips, washed it down with a sip of her drink. She'd never had trouble taking medicine, even as a little girl. She'd pretended pills were candy.

After the third pill she began to cry. In her life there had been many times when she had cried alone. Her empty passion for acceptance weighed upon her as coldly as a glacial ridge, pressed as relentlessly as the passing days that crumbled her existence, crushed life from her. Tears coasted the slopes of her icy cheeks. She touched them and they turned to brands of guilt on her fingertips. Her tears produced only pain, she thought. Pain from tears, not tears from pain. She cried in self-pity and in self-defense. She remembered crying somewhere in a car, recently.

She saw the past as if watching a grainy, poorly lighted motion picture, an arty black-and-white movie filled with shadows and symbols. She was in a small car with Morris Archer. He was kissing her, undressing her while she begged him to stop. Then she closed her eyes, shut out the unfaithful world.

Morris had phoned her the following day and he'd apologized. At the time, his call had puzzled her. Now she knew. . . .

She took two more tranquilizers, then telephoned Beth Archer, who answered on the second ring and said, "Morris?"

"Yes. I called to say I'm sorry about Morris," Emily said.

"Emily?"

"Yes. I'm sorry for what I did."

Was Emily apologizing for wrongly reporting the plane crash, Beth wondered, after all this time? She looked at the bedside clock, saw it was nearly midnight. The mistake wasn't worth talking about. "Morris and I discussed it," she said. "We decided to forget it. You were drunk."

"You discussed it? Forgot it?"

"Yes."

Yes? And why not? Hadn't Chuck always forgiven her lapses? The difference, Emily thought, was that she cringed inside a blank haven of self-induced amnesia while Morris stood openly exposed. Beth was more saintly than Chuck. "You're such an outstanding person," Emily said, "you'll probably become an angelmunk princess."

Beth said, "Good night, Emily."

"Wait. No matter what you hear about me—do you know a pilot named Steve?" said Emily.

"No. I have to go—"

"No matter what you hear, please, remember I'm a loving person."

"Emily, it's midnight," Beth said and hung up. The woman was a basket case, she thought.

* * *

Midnight. Doomsday. The world finally had overtaken her, Emily thought. She poured half the bottle of tranquilizers onto her palm, transferred them to her mouth with a vacuum movement of her lips. She tried to swallow them dry but couldn't; the attempt brought new tears to her eyes. Now she would have a sore throat. She washed down the pills with her vodka and orange juice.

She dried her eyes on her wrist, then sat up straighter, fluffed her hair as if preparing for a meeting. She had one more apology to deliver. Emily dialed Jean Turner's number.

CHAPTER 25

EMILY'S TELEPHONE CALL was the perfect ambiguous conclusion to a totally ambiguous day, a day that Beth Archer reflected upon for months.

As it developed, Beth would have been happier if Morris hadn't phoned. Before hanging up, he said he expected a day off at the end of the first week of the crisis. She dreaded that single day, knew he would cram a week of sex and drink into less than twenty-four hours. Beth had to talk to someone and decided it would be Jim Leonard, the one sane person she knew.

That evening Beth escaped the house before the phone sounded a second time. She had been closing the door when the phone had stopped her, ringing out like an escape alarm.

With the phone still ringing in her imagination, she pushed Beverly's stroller to Jim's door, and when he opened it, she smiled and said, "I was going for a walk. I thought you might like to walk and talk too."

"I don't know if I can do both at the same time," he said.

He was barefoot, wearing a madras shirt and khaki shorts. Out of uniform he appeared taller, darker. He was without glasses and seemed younger, matched the face of Daniel in her childhood memory. He squinted. "You live around here?"

She pointed. "Two blocks down. Upstairs of the empty lot."

He grinned. "Come in for a minute. Let me find some tennies, turn off the stove." He dashed away, left the door open.

Beth parked the stroller and hefted Beverly. The living room reminded her of a men's club: glossy, overstuffed leather and dark, polished wood. The house had an aroma of garlic and Italian spices.

"I'm building lasagna," he called from another room. "You had supper?"

"No. Yes. No. I wasn't hungry."

Jim reappeared, carrying scuffed tennis shoes. "Let's hold the walk, have some supper first." He was breezier out of uniform, bouncier, more relaxed, Beth thought. Was he happy to see her?

She sniffed the air, said, "How can I refuse?"

"Want a glass of wine?"

"If you do."

"I don't drink. Doesn't do anything for me," he said.

Jim effortlessly made her an equal partner in the kitchen: He asked advice on cooking, followed her suggestions. And he listened to her other words, showed interest in the problems of her life. Beth wondered if the evening was a sample of an affair between married people. After all, he'd been married once, had learned how to behave. *What a curious notion,* she thought. It suggested that a first marriage was merely a training course for what followed in life. And what of an affair? Was it nothing more than temporarily playing house with a partner who was considerate? If the partner wasn't considerate, what was the sense in being there?

By the time they finished eating, Beth felt that Jim understood her better than Morris ever would. She had been primed to talk and she had held back nothing, had told him of Daniel's love, of her mother's passivity, of her father's tyranny, of Morris's rescue, and of Morris's obses-

137

sions, demands for perfection, his ultimate tyranny. "Before you were married, didn't you recognize your father's traits in Morris's behavior?" Jim asked and she immediately answered, "Yes." But she hadn't expected him to direct them at her, she realized. Had she fooled herself? Had she fled from one oppressor to another in the name of love?

As counterpoint to her story, Jim named her father "Draco" after she called him "a dragon." And Morris was renamed "Sagittarius," the Archer. Jim nearly christened Beth "Andromeda," the Chained Lady, before he decided the symbolism cut too close to the truth. "And who am I?" Beth then asked, as if reading his mind.

"Cassiopeia," he said, "the queen more beautiful than the water nymphs." And he told her that, in legend, the nymphs were jealous and their father, Neptune, took vengence for Cassiopeia's beauty by flooding her realm and sending a sea monster to ravage the land. An oracle declared the country could be saved by sacrificing Cassiopeia's daughter, Andromeda. Therefore, Andromeda was chained to a rock near the sea where the monster could devour her.

"I feel more like Andromeda," Beth said.

"But Perseus came along and killed the monster and saved Andromeda," Jim explained. His conscience stopped him from finishing the story: "And Perseus married Andromeda."

It was nearly ten o'clock when they finished washing dishes. By then Beverly was asleep. Jim turned on the television: "Let's see if the world's still in one piece."

Beth didn't want the evening to end, didn't want to lose the comfort of Jim Leonard. It would be easy to watch the news and then drift off . . . to where? What about Morris? Was this another dream?

On a grassy landscape of Beth's mind stood a tall monument of flawless white stone that had stood ever since Beth could remember, that represented principle, represented a woman's fidelity to her husband. If she was unfaithful, the monument would crumble and vanish, could never again be rebuilt. Beth knew that losing the vision would cost her integrity, would be like losing part of her identity.

They sat side by side on the couch and Jim casually took her hand in his, wove his fingers between hers. Something in her stirred. Morris seemed distant. She turned her head and

Jim's brown eyes were inches away. She closed her eyes. Did he kiss her or did she kiss him? She thought: *I can count all the men I've kissed; a kiss is still something special.*

Jim moved closer and they shared tiny kisses, the kind that she enjoyed most, the kind that Morris seldom gave. This wasn't a dream. . . .

Beyond her mind's flawless monument the dark green satin veldt of her fantasy fanned out into an endless land where she could romp freely, without fear . . . with Jim. Could she dare such an adventure? Never look back? In her loyal heart she knew she could not, could not be like Jim's girlfriend in Dallas, could not love two men at the same time. Choosing Jim meant forsaking Morris. She wasn't prepared to do that.

Jim sensed Beth's surrender, or a beginning of surrender, or perhaps his sensitivity toward her vulnerability made him sense her indecision and share her torment between principle and desire, and he thought, *I can't give you what you need.* He'd gone too far, he decided, and his kisses became playful rather than passionate.

Beth felt the change and opened her eyes, wondered, *Doesn't he want me?* Paradox of virtue and desire. She recalled all the compliments he had paid to her. She knew he liked her. "I think I feel the beginning of love," she said and the boldness of her words struck her mute. Was she forcing him to commit himself? Was she that anxious?

He smiled sadly and brushed her cheeks with his fingertips, stroked her face with long, lean fingers.

She saw that his hand and his eyes were not related, saw a veil of armor inside his stare. Had she misread everything? Her tongue regained life: "Don't you like me?" She hated herself for the question.

Wearing the same sad smile, Jim said, "Wouldn't it be better if we stayed just friends?"

Just friends? Then that was the end of it, she thought. A formal friendship was nothing. For an instant she felt relieved, felt as if she had suddenly spotted a camouflaged trap in the fantasyland of her mind, had sidestepped pulverizing danger. Then she was on the verge of tears: Just friends meant good-bye, no tomorrows. He'd never call her. And she'd never dare call him. They'd meet only by chance and then she'd be too embarrassed to do more than exchange greetings. She felt rejection, betrayal. And the onset of anger. Why had he led her on?

"Beth, I can't give you what you need. Not now. Whatever you're looking for in me, you can find in Morris. You just have to work at it." If that were true, he thought, then why was she there with him?

Was he accusing her? Beth wondered. Was he placing the blame for her unhappiness on her? Was he saying it was her fault that Morris was a tyrant? Was he hinting that she hadn't tried? Damn him. He didn't understand her at all. Angry energy surged through her. She felt as she had when she'd faced the idiotic babble of Emily Charles. "You're no different from Morris," she shouted. "You men are all alike, all on the same side." She was sick of trying to satisfy men, sick of trying to guess what they wanted, sick of men telling her what she wanted, what she needed. "Damn you and Morris both," she shouted.

Jim's sad smile spread into a grin: "I'm no different from Morris?" He laughed and reached for her.

Beth shoved him away and scrambled to her feet. Why was he laughing at her? What was funny? Was he crazy too?

"Wait," he said. "Listen. Am I the first man who's paid attention to you since you decided Morris doesn't love you? Am I?" He didn't wait for an answer. "And now, do you want me to rescue you from Morris? Do you?" He supplied the answer: "You do. Right." He shook his head. There was no armor, no defense within his brown eyes. "And then what? What do you want then?"

"For us to get married," she almost said. The thought made her face burn. She was married. And that marriage had not been a solution. If Jim had stripped-off her clothes, she could not have felt more exposed than she did in that moment. And then vulnerable nakedness became insight. He was the first to show her affection since she had begun to feel unloved. And now she did expect him to rescue her, only this time she would be saved from a former rescuer. She smiled and tears came to her eyes at the realization of the comedy of her own design. She again was transferring responsibility for herself from one man to another.

She did not know exactly what she wanted, but she did recognize that in some way she desired to be free, desired to control her own destiny. Her anger transformed itself into joyful power and she suddenly wanted to run, to skip, to leap, to fly. She hadn't felt such exuberance since leaving the playgrounds of childhood. Was her life again going to belong to her?

"Let's wake Beverly—don't worry, she'll be all right, she won't cry—and let's go for a walk, or a ride, or get a malt. Do something," she ordered. "And then you can take us home."

Beth felt as if she had once more found her brother Daniel.

CHAPTER 26

JEAN TURNER WAS nearly ready for bed. She made certain that Frank had shined his father's shoes and that Delano had precisely placed insignias on his father's clean uniform for the following morning. She believed that by having daily duties a child developed a sense of responsibility, and by performing duties that benefited others a child learned to be a team member: two sound leadership principles. As mother-leader, Jean ensured that tasks were understood, supervised, and accomplished.

Once at a lawn party when daughter Eleanor had been serving sandwiches to guests, a general's wife had told Jean that children shouldn't have to do chores that reduced them to the status of servants. Jean had boldly but quietly said, "But I set the example. I cook and clean house and do laundry for them."

Jean stretched out on the floor, curled her toes under the edge of the bed in preparation for her fifty sit-ups, the last thing she did each night. Fifty sit-ups in fifty seconds was her goal. Her record was fifty-three seconds.

Axel had been asleep for an hour, had turned in after the ten o'clock news and a phone call to the command post. "If we fly off to war, they'll go without me," he'd said after the call, had spoken as if it were the first time he'd had the notion. Jean had hugged him and said, "Somebody has to stay home and comfort the women and children." Then, as if together recognizing that home was the most dangerous place of all, they'd held each other, had assured each other that the crisis would end soon. "Nobody wants that kind of war," Axel had told her.

Jean was waiting to begin her sit-ups, watching the bedside clock's second hand climb toward twelve, when the phone rang with the impact of a starter's gun, made her jump to her feet. A furious adrenaline rush gave her a nervous, clammy touch of terror. She said, "Hello," expected the call to be for Axel. War or peace?

A small mouse voice said, "Mrs. Turner? This is Emily Charles."

Axel turned over and, with eyes closed, held out an open hand. Jean patted his shoulder, whispered, "Not for you."

"I called to apologize for the time I was supposed to order flowers," Emily said.

The price of being a commander's wife, Jean thought.

"It wasn't the florist's fault. It was all my fault. I forgot to order them."

"You're forgiven," said Jean Turner.

"And I forgot gloves that day. I'm sorry."

"I'm certain you won't forget in the future."

"Mrs. Turner, you're so perfect, you're sure to become the angelmunk queen."

Jean Turner had been prepared to end the conversation. "Angelmunk queen" stopped her. In a nonjudgmental tone, she asked, "Emily, have you been drinking?"

"A little. Did you see the clock? It's red midnight and I can't say good-bye to Chuck because I'm afraid I'll lie to him. I'm sorry I lied to you." She paused. "God bless you for forgiving me." If only she could be like Jean Turner . . . Emily's feeling of inferiority brought tears to her eyes. It was too late to change, too late to turn back; red midnight

143

was final. She placed the telephone receiver on the couch. Would Chuck forgive her? Would he understand?

"Emily," Jean said. Had she hung up? "Emily," she called. There was no dial tone. During her time in the air force, Jean Turner had received equally strange calls, from wives and husbands, had been asked to referee family spats, to locate wayward spouses, to lecture adults and children. Axel received his share too. But he refused to switch to an unlisted number, said crank calls were one more cost of being boss.

Jean stretched out on the floor and, when the second hand reached twelve, began her sit-ups. Her well of nervous energy made the exercise effortless. After thirty sit-ups in twenty-five seconds, she was barely breathing harder than normal, knew she would do fifty in under fifty seconds, considered trying for one hundred in one hundred seconds. Thirty-seven, thirty-eight . . .

"Angelmunk" flashed in her mind and she jumped to her feet, grabbed up the telephone directory. From a previous assignment, she recalled a wife who had spoken of a "homedevil," had believed that a demon was using household appliances and fixtures to torture her: The demon shocked her with the refrigerator, burned her with the stove, scalded her with hot water from the kitchen and bathroom faucets, shot fire at her from light sockets. That woman had been hospitalized. Angelmunk was too close to homedevil. Something was very wrong with Emily; if Jean was the only person who knew, then she was responsible for Emily's welfare. For a woman who was alone, the hours after midnight held too many unknowns, too much fear.

Emily poured what remained of the Equinals onto her palm, pushed them into her mouth, rinsed them down with her drink. One at a time she found pills that she'd dropped, picked them off her lap and off the rug and swallowed them without drinking. The simple task took more and more effort and concentration until, finally, she was moving like a deep-sea diver, felt she was working her arms through an ocean of lead. For a long time she was thirsty, but lifting her glass seemed impossible, even if she used two hands. She closed her eyes and saw yellow flames, saw a soot-black father-creature leering, flicking his oily forked tongue at her. Behind him, deep purple shadows overflowed with beasts. . . .

Emily's telephone stayed busy for twenty minutes and Jean Turner called the operator who reported that there was no conversation on the line.

Jean nudged Axel: "Something's wrong at the Charles's."

"Call the police," he said.

"Not that kind of wrong," she said. "I can check on it, be back in a minute."

Maybe it was an air-police task, Jean thought, but Emily had reached out to her. She walked three short blocks to Nebraska Street and saw that the Charles's house was the only one lighted. She brought to mind the Charles children . . . Becky, the youngest . . . David, who was in Scouts with Frank.

No time for amenities, she thought and tried the front door, found it locked. She went to the kitchen door, turned the knob, and the door opened. She entered while telling herself that the air police would have broken down the front door, wakened the neighborhood.

Jean noticed the vodka bottle and the empty pill bottles before she saw Emily curled into a fetal ball behind the coffee table. In this country, in their profession, how could a life grow that sad? Jean wondered. Yet the scene was similar to images that had been hovering in the background mist of her mind.

Jean studied the empty bottles, tried to guess how many pills Emily had swallowed, wondered if tranquilizers were enough to kill her, surmised they were, then wished she had spent more time helping in the pharmacy while a hospital volunteer.

Jean unraveled Emily's body, saw that she was breathing with shallow intakes that were too far apart. She felt Emily's slow pulse, then shook her fiercely but got no response.

How dare Emily kill herself! To Jean, the suicide attempt became a personal affront: One of her soldiers had deserted ranks; discipline had gone amiss. Fleetingly, she considered phoning the emergency room and ordering an ambulance. Then she decided that she had started it and she would

145

finish it; she knew as much as the ambulance drivers. Her mind recited a leadership principle: Know your men and look out for their welfare. Emily was her charge.

She lifted Emily with a fireman's carry, snatched her off the floor as deftly as an eagle grabbed up a fieldmouse, carried her to the bathroom, and placed her in the tub.

Tough problems required tough solutions, Jean thought. She found a douche bag and hose in the bathroom closet and then went to the kitchen for milk and liquid dishsoap. She mixed milk and soap in the bag, hung the bag from the shower curtain rod. She undressed Emily, then stripped down to her underwear and climbed into the bathtub.

Emily did not want to swallow the hose and Jean considered the semiconscious resistance to be a good sign. If there was punishment in the treatment and pain in the cure, Emily deserved them for trying to abandon two children and a husband. With Emily's upper body clamped between her legs, Jean force-fed the rubber tube to her.

Emily could barely hold her nose above the surface of the swirling gray and white liquid, swirling liquid marble. Her head was afloat in an enormous black pot. She reached out and lifted her right breast above the marble level. Her fingers felt the breast; her breast felt the fingers wrapped around it. Yet the hand was attached to nothing; the breast was severed from her body. She dropped the breast, grasped her neck, felt that it too was connected to nothing. Then she recognized other pieces of her floating in the pot and she wanted to scream but she couldn't scream because her mouth was full, all of her parts were full, swollen, about to burst. Her eyes bulged and she choked on terror. She needed to scream. If she did not scream, she was going to explode. . . .

Emily's groans awakened David. Never could he have imagined the scene he encountered in the bathroom. The room looked like a torture chamber, smelled like a sewer. "Mrs. Turner? What're you doing?" If the woman strangling his mother had been anyone else, he would have attacked her. "You're killing my mother," he shouted. "Stop."

What did they look like? Jean didn't care. She forced a

146

grim smile, said, "Your mother drank the wrong thing and this is necessary to cure her."

Rubbing her eyes, Becky walked into the bathroom. At the sight of her naked blue mother, she screamed and continued to scream. Was her mother dead?

Jean commanded, "David, everything is under control. Get Becky out of here."

David wrapped his arms around his screaming sister, carried her out the door.

"Make some coffee, David." Keep him busy, Jean thought. "We'll be finished in a few minutes."

"Should I call my father?" David shouted.

"No, not now. Close the door. Everything's under control." But at what price to the children?

Emily was on hands and knees in her body's waste, spitting blood and thinking that her throat had been clawed open by fiends or had been pierced by the embalmer's scalpel. She knew her situation was real; she could smell, touch. But she was afraid to open her eyes. Through pain that she felt to the soles of her feet, she asked, "Am I dead?" and a woman's voice harshly told her, "Not quite yet."

❧CHAPTER 27

I THINK I'VE been to hell," Emily Charles told Dr. Ruben Gomez during one of the daily therapy sessions that Jean Turner had arranged. Gomez had objected that a daily program was impossible, that as the base's lone psychiatrist his days were filled. Jean had told him, "Expand yourself. Skip lunch or something. Emily's husband works twenty-four-hour days, back to back."

Jean had been an overpowering presence in Gomez's office, more spirit than woman or man. Was hers the spirit of military aggression, a sublimated lust for battle, or the spirit of humanly concern manifested in instant action, or both? Gomez might have better appreciated her nature if he hadn't been put under siege. How did a captain ask the wing commander's wife to back off? As a draftee, he was air-force property for two years; her husband had power to make the years pleasant or unpleasant.

With perfectly timed intuitive insight, Jean Turner had given Gomez the opportunity to capitulate gracefully:

"Doctor, I know you understand long hours and hard work from medical-school days. The work you do here and now is for others, for their futures." She'd smiled knowingly, confidentially. "You certainly can't be in the air force for the money." Then she'd provided the white flag for his surrender: "I'd consider any extra effort to be a personal favor."

This woman attacked on all sides, Gomez had thought. In rapid succession she had launched a frontal assault of challenge and sarcasm, a feint of compliments and altruism, and an encirclement of bribery. The final maneuver had captured Gomez because he believed that "making points" was the foundation of military life. He'd ceded the hour a day to Jean/Emily while knowing that he could steal the time from other patients. Had Jean recognized the basis of his submission?

With professional insight, Gomez believed he understood Jean's involvement. By rescuing Emily she had returned a soul to the world. In a deeper sense, Jean had symbolically delivered a late-life baby.

It was far better that he counsel Emily than have Jean attempt it, Gomez decided. Before departing his office, Jean had studied the dishwater-gray walls, the window with its bleached-bone-white venetian blind, the blackish-green fake-marble linoleum floor, and the flaking bargain-sale gray metal furniture; she'd asked, "Is this where you meet patients?"

"I'm afraid it is," he'd said.

"It's cold and impersonal," Jean had said.

"It's government issue," Gomez had replied.

The next day, the office was refurbished: wheat-color walls, earth-tone drapes that hung from ceiling to floor, clay-orange wall-to-wall carpet, stone-gray overstuffed chairs in glove leather, charcoal-brown leather couch.

To Emily, the made-over office was curiously dark, curiously veiled, yet imbued with an odd luminosity of hope. Her appointment was at noon, and entering the office was like passing from day to night, drifting into an artificial umbra.

Emily's first words to Gomez were: "I never dream, but maybe that's because my whole life has been a nightmare."

Ruben Gomez had curly red hair, delicate features, was as fair skinned as a fresh peach. He wore a wedding band twice normal width. His posture was so relaxed that his slight frame molded itself to the contours of his chair, disappeared into the leather. Yet his eyes remained vivid, radar alert, and sometimes he cupped a hand behind one ear, cocked the ear to attention. His face held the vibration of a smile that never vanished, a hint of confidence that Emily first interpreted as smugness. Gomez was years younger than she had expected. In the beginning, she felt she was talking to a child, someone slightly older than David.

Emily learned to appreciate Gomez's subtle smile as a form of neutrality—containing, perhaps, a touch of benevolent dispensation. The hint of his smile told her: "I am interested. As a person, you have value to me."

But hadn't Chuck always related to her in the same manner?

In response to her first words, Gomez said, "We needn't concern ourselves too much with the past. Yesterday isn't that important. Tomorrow isn't that important either. Today is what counts."

He was wrong, Emily thought. Tomorrow held her greatest fears.

In the middle of her initial visit she sat for twelve and a half minutes (Gomez timed her)—one quarter of the session—without speaking, until he asked, "What have you been thinking about?"

"About my children—Becky and David—about them graduating from high school, going to college, getting married, having children of their own." She thought: Tomorrow could be the setting for dreams as well as nightmares.

Gomez viewed Emily as a classic case: an alcoholic with a reasonably benign history as "bottoms" go, but a final bottom that was a singular, traumatic, nearly fatal event. He had read about such cases but had experienced only one, a highly respected public figure who hanged himself and was cut down barely in time. During recovery, the man had told Gomez, who then was an intern in Atlanta, "I died. I'm not the same person I was. I paid for every mistake I ever made."

Emily told Gomez: "I feel my whole body was torn apart

150

and put back together." *Put back together in the right order, with the bad parts left out,* she thought. "I feel I paid for every wrong I ever did."

"My father sold furniture, owned his own store. He went to market once, when I was nine, and while he was away I told a teacher that he drowned in a boating accident. I said the boat turned over and they couldn't find his body. The teacher wrote a sympathy card to my mother.

"When father learned what I'd done, he spanked me so hard that he hurt me and my mother had to keep me in bed for a week. She threatened to divorce him over it. Every day my father cried and begged me to forgive him. His tears made me feel guilty."

"The first boy I went steady with turned out to be no good. His name was Bernie Cox. If he caught me talking to another boy, he'd call me names and punch me, really hard, on the arms and back. Even when I wasn't flirting, he'd claim I was and he'd punch me just the same. He called me 'hot pants' and 'bitch.'

"One night, in a restaurant, we got into a fight—an argument. He was angrier than I ever saw him. I was afraid he was going to beat me up. After we ate, I handed him his class ring and ran outside. While he was paying the bill, I pretended to faint, right in the middle of the sidewalk. When I came to, I pretended I couldn't walk.

"Bernie knew I was doing it to get away from him and he started shouting, 'She's not sick.' There was a crowd around me and everyone got upset with him and told him to be quiet, which made him madder at me. Finally he got so mad that he punched me—" with a finger, Emily traced a gentle arc along the curve of her jawbone—"right here. He hit me so hard, I saw stars, really. All I could hear was ringing. I was afraid I'd be deaf.

"A policeman was there and he lifted Bernie right off the ground, carried him away and handcuffed him to an iron fence, and made him sit in the dirt.

"Then the policeman took me home and left Bernie sitting there, chained to the fence, looking through the bars like a dog.

"When my parents heard that Bernie hit me, I wasn't

allowed to even talk to him anymore. My mother kept me in bed for two days."

"In high school I knew a girl who . . ." *Who did it with all the football stars,* Emily thought. ". . . who said, 'Women give sex to get love; men give love to get sex.'" But that girl hadn't been truly in love with any one person, Emily remembered. "She drank a lot and said, 'It doesn't count if you're drunk.' I guess I always believed her."

"Does that philosophy include your attempt to take your life?" Gomez asked.

"I don't know if I was drunk then."

"I did it with an air policeman once—a sergeant—so he wouldn't give me a ticket. Chuck was overseas . . . I'd been drinking . . ." Emily avoided eye contact with Gomez while she confessed. Then she looked straight at him: "There isn't anything more to say about it."

There were days when Emily felt her life had been staggeringly miniaturized, as if everything had been compacted into the frame of a television set, reduced to the recurring conflict of a soap opera.

On those days she laughed at everything. Her mind said: Nothing matters.

On one such day, Gomez was talking but Emily couldn't hear him. Cushioned by delightful feelings, she was too frivolous to shuttle across his band of night, to ponder his words, herself, anything. To her, it was the first day of summer vacation . . .

Then Gomez gestured mystically, waved his hand in an S pattern, and for a moment a wall of the room turned transparent, became a cornea, and Emily saw Chuck flying through the air, hawk with flesh of iron, skin of steel.

Had Gomez's mystical gesture revealed a secret eye of love within her? When the session ended Emily hugged Gomez in appreciation for his unwitting gift.

"It's enough to be a wife and a mother," Emily said. "That's what Jean Turner is."

"Do you think she's good at those tasks?" said Gomez.

"I wish she'd been my mother."

"In a roundabout way, you could consider her your mother," Gomez said. "She gave you life."

Emily smiled. "But I'm not a child now."

They sat silently for long seconds before Gomez asked, "Would you like to be a child again?"

"Yes." *Wouldn't everyone?* she thought. "But that's impossible."

Gomez thought: Unlike most patients, ambivalent feelings didn't puzzle Emily; she accepted facts at face value, accepted contradictions without question. He hoped that time would change that. Her tests indicated that she was too intelligent not to question conflicting emotions.

Emily said, "Jean Turner can't do a thing about tomorrow."

Gomez laughed. "That's true. But she can accomplish plenty today."

A month into therapy, Emily told Gomez, "I took a drink of vodka last night." She paused. "Then I spit it out."

"Why did you take the drink?"

"I wanted to feel its heat . . . I don't know."

"Why did you spit it out?"

"I knew you'd ask that. Did I want to prove I'm in control?"

Gomez answered with a quizzical tilt of the head.

She said, "Sometimes you're no help. You're too smug. Sometimes—I don't know—I don't like you."

"Only a saint could love everyone all the time."

"You never met Chuck. He's so nice, I could scream. He's perfect when things are at their absolute worst."

"What things?"

"Things—you know—*me*. My god, he's so understanding, he drives me crazy. Sometimes I wish he'd hit me, or beat me . . . especially when I deserve it. He's so good, I hate him." She began to cry tears from an inner pain. "I hate him for no reason. He's all I have in the world. Why do I hate him?"

Regardless of the depth of her introspection, the half-alive world of alcoholism remained a puzzle to Emily, a maze of stupefying proportions.

Her future labor seemed insurmountable: to remain sober

153

in a world that was drunk. Yet tenuous freedom bred fear of recapture. Would she again be caught? Would she someday drink again? Gomez claimed one drink would destroy her. Was he correct, would one drink lead to another? How much control did she have? Not enough, she knew, not enough. Her experimental sip of vodka had been an insane act. She had been lucky to survive it. She came to fear the very idea of drinking, feared it would kill her.

She did not want to die again.

As dry days accumulated, Emily developed a deepening sense of accomplishment, a self-congratulatory inner glow that satisfied beyond alcohol. She concentrated on daily achievement, on the simple fact that if she swallowed a single sip of alcohol, tomorrow would be Day One all over again and her beautiful string of perfect days would be snapped, ruined beyond repair; for her, time again would stop. She couldn't face that. She already had wasted enough of her life.

Although she would not be certain for years to come, and perhaps not entirely certain even then, perhaps never entirely certain, Emily made herself believe that she would not drink again. Yet, in the beginning, it was hope more than belief that sustained her; only as time progressed was hope converted to faith.

During one phase of reeducation Emily shouted at Chuck, "Why did you accept me for all those years? Why didn't you try to change me?"

With calm logic, Chuck answered, "Em, honey, you can't change other people. If you love them, the best you can do is care for them and wait for them to change themselves."

He hugged her to him, whispered, "I used to pray that you'd change. David did too." He kissed the top of her head. "These last weeks have been as happy as any I can remember."

Emily felt a drop touch her hair. She raised her head and saw that Chuck was smiling, crying tears of joy. Tears that brought her joy.

CHAPTER 28

ON JULY 19, 1958, days after the start of the Lebanon Crisis, the United States Air Force unsuccessfully launched a three-engine Atlas B intercontinental ballistic missile from Cape Canaveral. Once again, failure was spectacular. The *Abilene Big Country Journal* reported:

> With a tremendous burst of flame and smoke at the base of the rocket, the Atlas rose from the launching pad in what appeared to be a perfect liftoff.
>
> Moments into the flight the huge rocket began to wobble from side to side. The wobble increased in intensity and then the monster rocket disappeared in a puff of smoke that resembled the cloud of an atomic explosion.
>
> From the cloud's mushroom crown a black wedge of metal raced upward, trailing a jet of flame.
>
> Then the streaking broken tip of the Atlas disappeared in a fireball that arched over and plunged earthward, like a meteor.

Two weeks later, on August 2, the air force successfully launched a 100-ton Atlas B, America's first intercontinental ballistic missile. The Atlas thundered skyward with 350,000 pounds of thrust, enough to throw its payload 6300 miles, the distance from middle America to Moscow, and beyond.

Would this modern Atlas bring down the sky upon mankind?

Before the Lebanon Crisis officially ended with the withdrawal of the last United States forces from Beirut on October 25, the Strategic Air Command was preparing for its Tenth Annual Bombing and Navigation Competition, a World Series of strategic prowess that matched crews from United States Air Force B47, B52, and B36 aircraft as well as from Royal Air Force Valiant bombers.

One hundred sixty-four crews from forty-one bomb wings competed, staged out of Castle and March Air Force bases in California. Each crew flew a single mission that consisted of radar-scored bomb runs on San Jose, Boise, and Butte, followed by a night celestial navigation leg that terminated at a set of geographic coordinates near Phoenix. Each USAF and RAF strategic Bomb Wing was represented by its four best crews and four best airplanes. Those crews were selected a month before Bomb Comp which took place in mid-October.

As commander, Colonel Axel Turner had final say regarding which four crews represented his Bomb Wing; nevertheless, he called together experts from his staff to help make the decision. The men met in the conference room of the intelligence building, a windowless cinder-block structure across the street from wing headquarters which housed Turner's office. On the way to the meeting Turner concluded that the more privileged to secrets he became, the more time he spent hidden indoors, distanced from the warrior's milieu.

Secrets begot secrets, Turner thought. As a bomber pilot in World War II he'd known only short-lived secrets of unitary simplicity. Back then, the point of attack was the single daily variable, for the Germans knew the Fortresses flew from England by daylight whenever weather permitted. Today, the geometry of Cold War secrets had a molecular complexity: One secret attached itself to another and another until facts became a superstructure of forbidden knowledge. The minor details of a single nuclear weapon perfectly illustrated the complexity of Cold War secrets. Shape, length, diameter, weight, yield, cost . . . With one or two such details, an expert could calculate the others and, from those, could determine related data, such as range of delivery vehicle, accuracy of the vehicle, target priorities, size of stockpiles. . . .

Turner failed to recall the astonishment with which, not that long ago, he had received the secret news that the British had developed a 22,000-pound high-explosive Block Buster or Earthquake bomb. It was for the Lancaster. A Fortress couldn't lift it.

The half-dozen experts Turner had requested came to attention when he entered the conference room. King Royal also was there. Royal had no authority regarding operational decisions but Turner wanted him present as a sounding board. Both men knew that success at Bomb Comp would boost everyone's morale. Not only crewmen would share the glory, but base support personnel and civilians of Abilene as well.

"Be seated," Turner said, and avoiding the head of the table, he took a chair midway down the table, next to Captain Leon Fenner. Before each man were typed sheets of statistics with SECRET stamped in bright red ink at the top and bottom of each page. The sheets listed the bombing and navigation scores for every crew in the —th Bomb Wing during the past two quarters.

"Anybody doesn't know why we're here?" Turner said and glanced at each man. "I've studied the list. I want to know what you think." He slid back his chair, as if to remove himself from the group.

Tied at the top of the list were the crews of Lieutenant Colonel Frank Santucci and Captain Chuck Charles. Charles's crew ranked that high because it led everyone by a wide margin for the most recent quarter.

"I always thought the top four went automatically," said Captain Fenner. "They're the best."

"That's not true," said Major Clark Devon.

Fenner wasted no time. "In that case, Major Devon, who do you object to?"

"To whom do I object," Devon said. "The issue isn't to

whom I object; the issue regards the image of the crews we send to represent the wing."

Major Fred Martin nodded agreement.

"We want crews who not only have earned the honor of competing, but also deserve the honor," Devon said. "In other words, we want officers and gentlemen, not mere technicians."

Major Martin said, "I agree. Scores aren't everything."

One mind in two bodies, Fenner thought and picked up the list, studied it for a few seconds, looked at Devon, asked, "Do you object to Colonel Santucci's crew?"

For a nonrated company grade officer, Fenner had balls, Turner thought.

Devon said, "Not in the least. Colonel Santucci's crew has proved itself time and again." Both Santucci and his navigator, John "Wells" Fargo, held spot promotions to lieutenant colonel.

Fenner again looked at the statistics, said, "Do you object to Captain Charles's crew?"

Devon looked at Turner, said, "There I have definite reservations."

"I do too," said Martin. After attending Archer's Emergency War Order briefing, Martin had classified him as a "wise-ass lieutenant." Since then, every time Martin had heard Archer speak, his opinion had been reinforced.

Technicians were what Bomb Comp was all about, Fenner thought. It was the same as war: Bombs on targets were all that mattered. The end results didn't require gentlemen. Besides, Charles's crew was new blood. His navigator was a lieutenant, closer to Fenner's heart than the older majors and lieutenant colonels who had been to Bomb Comp in the past but had not won. "May I ask, what are your reservations regarding Captain Charles's crew?"

Devon studied each man in the room, with the exception of Turner and Royal, cleared his throat, and said, "I expect what I'm about to say will remain in this room. I feel Charles's crew is potentially unreliable, in every sense of the word." He addressed Fenner: "Charles has family problems. How do we know he won't have to return home in the middle of competition? Then what? You know, he didn't finish his duties in Hawaii, had to be replaced on Alert during the first week of Lebanon . . ." Devon shook his head. "And his nav is erratic. Too unpredictable."

"I don't have good feelings about Charles's nav," said Martin. "He's capable of doing something unpredictable, something that could completely wipe out the wing's chance to win."

Fenner said, "I beg your pardon, sir, but you're judging that man on feelings rather than on facts." His words made King Royal smile. "Is that fair?"

Martin adjusted his glasses and removed an unlit cigar from the corner of his mouth. "Despite what you think, Captain, Charles's nav hasn't proved himself over a long enough period. If he's as good as his current average, he'll stay on top and we can send him next year." He squinted at Fenner. "You've never been to target study with him, never seen how he has his own way of doing everything. Charles can barely control him, doesn't try to change him. To win at Bomb Comp a crew must be completely standardized. Every man has to go by the book."

Turner eyed his other three experts. "You gentlemen have thoughts on the subject?"

The three officers were from maintenance and their spokesman, a lieutenant colonel, said, "We're here mostly to recommend the best airplane. We don't know the personalities of the crewmen. But, in my opinion, the wing should send the best operators, regardless." His two associates nodded agreement.

Devon shook his head in disbelief.

Martin spoke for him: "As I said, there's always next year. He's only a lieutenant."

"So were all of us, once," Fenner softly said.

King Royal's voice drifted down from the far end of the table: "I don't know the personalities either, but to me it doesn't matter; Charles's nav was the best in the wing last quarter, by far. Why, with those numbers he might have been the best in SAC." Royal paused, looked inward, convinced himself. "That pup's hot, gentlemen. He could bring it all home."

"Sir, with due respect," Devon said, "we work with these people day after day. . . ."

Turner slid his chair forward: "Anyone have any complaints about the third, fourth, and fifth crews?"

Nobody replied.

While Turner looked at the list, Devon silently mouthed the words "I'll see you later" at Fenner, who frowned.

"All right then," Turner said, "no more objections." Bomb Comp was only one mission, Turner thought. Luck was as important as skill. A flash in the pan was as apt to win as some calculating old timer. Wells Fargo could do his usual reliable job and finish in the middle of the pack. He'd done so before.

This was the last Bomb Comp he'd experience as a wing commander, Turner thought. Why not go for broke? What did *he* have to lose? His immediate future was decided, couldn't be changed by Bomb Comp results. If he selected Charles's crew, the decision would irritate Devon, but occasionally Devon had to be forced to lose one in order to be kept in line.

Turner said, "Let's give Charles a shot while his nav's hot. Next year he may be burned out and we'll have wasted him." The heat and pressure of Bomb Comp would temper Morris Archer or cook him in his own juices, Turner thought. He liked the idea of trial by fire, corrected his thought to "trial by warmth." San Jose, Boise, and Butte were a lot less punishing than Berlin. This way, Charles, or rather his missis, would be tested too. From what Jean told him, he expected Emily to meet the challenge. Turner said, "We'll go with the top four crews on the list."

Did Fenner dare to smile?

If the choice was so obviously foregone, then why had Turner called this irksome meeting, Devon wondered and searched his mind for ulterior motives.

Turner leaned toward the maintenance experts. "Now let's talk about the best airplanes. And don't forget, the outfits that win the Fairchild Trophy and the Best Overall Crew Award will split twenty promotions among the enlisted maintenance troops."

Devon resisted asking, "Do you mean we should send the crew chiefs who are most *deserving*?"

CHAPTER 29

MORRIS ARCHER'S PLANNING to escape from Chuck Charles ended with the announcement that their crew was selected to represent the —th Bomb Wing at the Tenth Annual Bombing and Navigation Competition.

Archer had been ready to request a crew change the day after Jean Turner saved Emily Charles and Chuck was replaced on Alert. Archer didn't know the exact reason for the substitution, but it made him angry: If Charles got a day off, then he and Dixie deserved a day off too. If Lebanon wasn't more important than Emily, then why was the whole fleet sitting Alert?

Emily was giving the crew a bad reputation, Archer thought.

He was more convinced he wanted a change when Charles returned to Alert three days later, on the day the crew was supposed to have off but didn't because of rescheduling that Archer blamed on Emily. Charles called

Dixie and Archer to his room, privately told them, "Emily took an overdose of tranquilizers."

Archer said, "I'd never let Beth use those things. Anyhow, she doesn't need them."

Charles looked at Dixie and said, "It was an accident."

Archer sneered inwardly. Down a suicidal wedge of his mind's eye, a beam of sight as narrow as a bombing radar scan, he saw truth: The overdose was no accident; Emily had tried to kill herself, and, probably, she was drunk when she did it.

"She all right now?" Dixie asked, and after Charles nodded, he smiled approvingly, returned the nod as if he truly cared.

"I'd prefer you didn't discuss it with other people," Charles said.

Archer was repelled by the tears in Charles's eyes. Was Archer's lack of compassion a denial of Chuck and Emily, or a denial of himself?

Minutes later, Archer phoned Beth and said, "Emily Charles tried to kill herself. That's why Chuck was replaced. She takes an overdose of tranquilizers and he gets three days off. I'd better never catch you taking those things." Charles was to blame as much as Emily. "He treats her like some kind of queen . . ." He wouldn't put up with Beth acting that way. ". . . when she's nothing but a drunken whore."

"Oh?" Beth said. The idea of Emily being a whore overcame Beth's annoyance with Morris's veiled threat concerning tranquilizers. If he knew . . . Beth again remembered Emily's visit, recalled her saying, "I drink like your husband," a curious declaration that had floated in Beth's mind since she'd heard it. Beth expected Morris to explain why he called Emily a whore. When he didn't, she said, "She must have done it on the night she called here, around midnight."

Why had Emily called Beth? Archer wondered and felt himself being backed into a defensive position. Had Emily remembered the night he took her to the club? Had she played true confessions at the last minute? No, Beth would have called and confronted him with something that dramatic. Guilt fueled anger and instinctively he attacked.

"Goddamn her. Where does she get off calling that time of night? What did she want?" And he wished that Emily had killed herself. His fascist mind saw death as a final solution.

Beth didn't understand why Morris was angry. "Emily only said she was sorry for what she did," Beth said.

"And what did she do?"

"You know, she came over and said you'd crashed."

Archer told Beth, "I don't want you talking to her. She doesn't know what she's saying."

Emily had said she was sorry, Beth thought. What was wrong with that?

That night, while talking to Jim Leonard on the telephone, Beth asked, "Did you ever cheat on your wife?"

The question surprised both of them.

Jim said, "Do you mean with just anybody, or do you have someone particular in mind?"

"I don't know what made me ask that."

"I believe in the old forsaking all others," Jim said.

Compulsively, Beth asked another telephone question, an impersonal survey question: "Did your wife ever cheat on you?" How easily technology reduced manners.

"You mean beyond the household servants?" There was an awkward pause, then Jim said, "Are you having a change of heart? I can be there before you hang up."

They laughed like two veteran conspirators, two plotters who recognized that danger was behind them. But what was behind the question? Leonard thought. Did she suspect Morris of being unfaithful? Wasn't it natural for Beth to be suspicious, after having drifted so close to her own infidelity?

So that Bomb Comp more closely resembled war conditions, SAC Headquarters forbade practice runs on the three target cities and waited until two weeks prior to competition to announce coordinates of the designated ground zero (DGZ) points. As a result, Janus-faced warriors from SAC and Bomber Command had identical limited study time in which to transpose friendly cities into hostile targets. As was expected in thermonuclear battle, a crew's first view of a target would also be its last.

In the —th Bomb Wing, Major Fred Martin was in charge of Bomb Comp target material. When Martin arrived at his cubbyhole office on the day that target information was to be released, Morris Archer was waiting. It was fifteen minutes to seven, a quarter hour before the work day officially began. "I'd like my target folder," Archer said.

"Which one?" Martin asked.

"Bomb Comp. What else?"

Martin stared back: "Those folders aren't ready yet."

"What do you mean . . ." Archer imitated Martin's voice but with a girlish tempo: ". . . 'Those folders aren't ready yet'?"

After Turner had ruled in favor of Charles's crew, Martin had decided to give Archer another chance. *And now this?* Martin wanted Archer out of his office, wanted to brew a pot of coffee, then sit down and quietly drink his first cup of the morning. Nevertheless, he attempted to be civil: "We haven't selected the offset aiming points. The folders will be ready after lunch." He turned his back to Archer, opened a drawer of one of the many four-door file cabinets that took up two walls of the crowded office, and reached inside for a can of coffee. Suddenly his back felt vulnerably exposed. Abruptly he turned. He wished they weren't alone. "I have work to do," he announced, "work on the offset aiming points."

In radar bombing, designated ground zero was not always the aiming point. Frequently a bombardier aimed at the brightest radar return close to the DGZ. The bright return was called an offset aiming point (OAP) and was not the spot where the bomb was expected to land. (The OAP distance was measured in feet, east/west and north/south, from the DGZ.) While the bombardier aimed at the vivid OAP, a ballistics computer compensated for the offset distance and aimed the weapon at the DGZ.

Offset aiming had one disadvantage: Computer errors multiplied as the distance between DGZ and OAP increased. The problem related to angles. For example, a theoretical bullet from a theoretical rifle whose sights were out of line by a single degree would miss a bull's-eye that was ten feet away by two inches; the same theoretical bullet would miss the center of the moon (240,000 miles away) by four thousand miles.

164

Archer wasn't in the mood to wait. "Maybe we don't need offsets. Let me see what you have."

Martin had not yet seen the target information that had arrived the previous afternoon by registered special delivery mail from the 3908th Strategic Standardization Group; he had been unauthorized to open the package until this morning. He felt no need to explain the rules to Archer. Instead, he addressed Archer as if he were talking to a child: "Don't need offsets! Don't need offsets? But you always need offsets. When have you every made a run without using offsets?"

"At least once every quarter," Archer said. He was quibbling. Although SAC regulations required a quarterly bomb run in which the DGZ was the solitary aiming point, bombardiers still cranked offset distances into the computer as a backup, in case they had a mental lapse and couldn't find the DGZ.

"You know what I mean," Martin said and felt himself overheating. He mentally damned Archer for pumping up his blood pressure. "The folders will be ready after lunch." What he then tried to make sound like a warning came out like a plea: "I have work to do."

Archer said, "I'd like to see the targets."

"Not now."

"Why not?"

"Because they're not ready."

Archer recognized his mother's reason that equaled no reason, the illogical "because" that equaled arbitrary and selfish reasons. "You mean *you* aren't ready," he said.

Unjustly accused, Martin said, "Get out of here, Archer. Leave me alone." He pulled a cigar from his breast pocket, stripped off and crumpled its cellophane wrapper into a ball, threw the ball at a wastebasket and missed. He bit the tip off the cigar and spit it toward the basket. The tip hit the wall and fell to the floor, out of sight behind the basket.

"You missed," Archer said, "both times." Martin stood where he was and rolled the cigar between his fingers. Archer said, "Aren't you going to pick them up?"

"Goddammit, get out of my office. You'll get a folder when I say so. If not today, then tomorrow." Martin felt his pulse growing stronger and stronger. "If not tomorrow, then . . ."

Archer's eyes unfocused and he saw an aurora of flashing green flames. He leaned on Martin's desk, rested his weight on clenched fists.

". . . whenever I get around to it."

"Shut up," Archer shouted. "I want shit from you, I'll scrape it off your teeth." He pounded the desk with both fists. "Give me my folder."

Martin was stunned by the vehemence of the insult, by the violence of the demand. Martin could not comprehend how a junior officer could be totally without respect, totally void of tradition and values. Was this a sample of what was in store from now until Bomb Comp ended? At this rate, Martin would have a heart attack before it was over. Martin looked at Archer and saw a man afire, a figure blazing with rage. Archer would consume himself and those around him, Martin thought.

To calm himself, Martin sat down at his desk, lit his cigar, puffed dense smoke into the oven air of the confined space, caused Archer to make a face of distaste and to dodge advancing clouds.

Martin considered himself to be more intelligent than Archer, far more experienced, smart enough to rid himself of the nuisance. But how? Simply give Archer what he wanted . . . ?

Martin stepped to a locked file cabinet, worked the combination dial, opened the top drawer, and withdrew a tightly sealed package. He shredded the package's wrapping in opening it. Inside were five identical folders. He replaced four folders in the drawer, slammed it closed, and spun the dial. He thumbed through the fifth folder before he threw it on the desk in front of Archer and slapped a classified document receipt atop it. "Sign the receipt and you're on your own. You can compute offsets or not," Martin said. "Play the game by any rules you want. It's all yours. Just sign the receipt."

Archer's eyes narrowed. He flicked aside the receipt, picked up the folder, and thumbed its pages, saw familiar lists and photographs. Obviously the folder contained Bomb Comp target data. Did it have everything he needed? Was he clever enough to analyze the information, to assimilate it? Did it matter? How could he refuse the offer? By backing down, he would admit he desired Martin's assistance and advice.

His ego signed.

Martin touched a finger to the receipt, then pulled back his hand. Was the contract binding? "You're on your own," he said. Were the words fact or question? Had Martin in some uncontrollable manner been manipulated into a pact with a demon?

Absentmindedly Martin reached down for the ball of cellophane. When he looked up Archer was gone. The receipt remained. Was it valid?

Later, Martin told Clark Devon about the exchange and was surprised when Devon said, "Guys like Archer are too busy directing traffic when there's not a car in sight." It was a statement Martin might have used to describe Devon.

Were they all stamped from the same mold?

To Morris Archer, Bomb Comp became more engrossing than war. During the two weeks prior to the event, he studied maps, photographs, and radar predictions of San Jose, Boise, and Butte more assiduously than he perused Moscow and the Kremlin, read every detail with eyes and fingertips, overlaid contours of targets onto contours of brain.

The target cities burned into his sight until wherever he looked faces of the cities looked back. He could not avoid their stares, identified their patterns in shadows on a rug, in careless folds of a towel, in crumpled wastepaper, in swirls of his wife's curly hair. Echoes of ground zero visions that he absorbed would remain in his memory for a lifetime: the main terminal building at San Jose Municipal Airport on California's Guadalupe River; the Idaho State Capitol that flared like a beacon at the end of broad Capitol Boulevard; and tiny Butte's mile-high St. James Hospital cradled in the curve of Silver Bow Creek. Why would he remember them? How would he ever forget them?

In rehearsing for Moscow he was limited to studying his secret role in the isolated security of the intelligence blockhouse, but for Bomb Comp he had a script that he carried everywhere, studied day or night. He rehearsed endlessly for a wordless drama that he would flawlessly (he hoped) perform a single time, an unhesitating performance as conclusively brilliant as the rising of a sun.

Within his dreams of glory, however, the nightmare of abject and dismal failure persisted and Archer's insecurity intensified because criminal, taskmaster, and judge unanimously agreed that failure would be totally his.

CHAPTER 30

In the weeks before Bomb Comp, Morris Archer treated Beth like an extra, a bystander incapable of understanding the dramatic magnitude of his starring role.

Was his inattention toward Beth the result of misunderstanding? When Morris boasted, "I have—we have our own airplane, one that no other crew can touch," Beth didn't know what to say. Morris reminded her of a teenager with his first automobile. Did she cause him to believe she did not care?

He was home every night. The four chosen crews were excused from Alert in order to fly, to sharpen their bombing coordination and to boresight their aircraft. Despite apparent freedom, Morris's schedule was rigidly structured. He flew on alternate days, and when not in the air, he studied targets. At night, when he drank at home, he kept his Bomb Comp target folder beside him as if it were holy scripture, referred to it frequently.

One night he asked Beth to read along while he recited data. On the third target, in an effort to break the monotony, the boring numerical dirge of his flawless recitation, Beth said, "That's wrong," after he intoned the Butte target coordinates.

Morris's response made Beth laugh: he swiveled his head left and right, back and forth so rapidly that he reminded her of a malfunctioning robot, out of control.

"What's so funny?" the robot predictably shouted. "What are the coordinates?" He automatically recited the numbers again while he reached for the book.

Or was he reaching for her? Beth saw metallic white lips. Her joke had backfired. "No, I'm sorry, you were right," she said, clicked the apology he was programmed to expect. "I read the wrong line. It was my mistake."

He jerked upright, stood and looked down, a hovering gargoyle. "Don't play with my mind. All you have to do is follow what I say." He took the book from her.

"I'm willing to help," she said. "I'm sorry I made a mistake." She held out her hands in supplication, ready to accept the book's return.

His plated eyes ignored her. She was incompetent, uninterested, he thought. He walked out to the front porch, looked to the stars. From the time he'd signed Martin's receipt he had known that he was on his own. Nobody cared as much as he cared—not Charles, not Dixie, not Wells Fargo, nobody . . . except, perhaps, Colonel Turner.

In the moment when Turner came to mind a shooting star raced low across the horizon of Archer's vision. More than a coincidence, his ego declared. With target testament gripped tightly in both hands, Archer was infused with abnormal confidence, silently dedicated his efforts to Turner, the demigod before whom he once had stood in shocked anger (and shame), unfairly doubly punished. He saw himself in the future, standing in honor, totally redeemed. Self-consigned martyr, Archer wished that Turner knew he labored alone, independent of Martin and others.

Archer's isolation was a predicament born of his nature. Lost in the cult of disaster, this ordinary man was a unique being within the myopic range of his single mind's eye.

Was Archer's isolation escape from reality or transcendence of life? Did he exist on a rarified level of involvement, a stellar plateau of commitment? Was it possible that his virgin warrior soul was the true soul of future man, the soul needed to achieve tomorrow in a thermonuclear world? Was the loss of virginity the end of mankind?

Or was Archer the egocentric forerunner of the Now Generation, the Me Generation in which each person was his own guiltless self-proclaimed deity guided by self-aggrandizement?

When each man became savior unto himself, then any ordinary life could meaningfully culminate in man's destruction of mankind; any man could produce a cataclysm to garner satisfaction of his ideology's strength over another's.

Terrorism would flourish, produce day-by-day world destruction.

Egocentricity would be the core of limitless power.

With Morris home every night Beth was not free to phone Jim Leonard, and now she needed his comfort more than ever. Morris treated her like an object, a vessel, an unfeeling receptable. She served primarily for frequent mechanical sex, greedy and selfish sex, careless sex. Oblivious to her needs, Morris made no effort to satisfy her. Wrapped inside her, he remained rapt in his own recall. Was she being punished for indifference?

She could have been satisfied so easily, would have been content if they dispensed with sex, would have been content if Morris held her tightly and told her, "I love you."

But he contributed nothing. He filled her yet left her empty.

The one time she had asked for attention, had flirted and practically begged for attention, he'd said, "Leave me alone. I have a thousand things on my mind. Can't you understand? Bomb Comp is the most important thing in my life. Don't you know what it means if I do well?"

The most important thing in his life was not her. The thought repeated itself to Beth: litany of rebuff, litany of rebuke.

Beth was relieved when Morris flew away to California. At the same time, she was left with the greatest burden of her life: She was pregnant and felt husbandless.

She had sensed her pregnancy in the moment of conception, had experienced the same dynamic upsurge of insight she had felt when they'd conceived Beverly—a palpable swelling tide of indescribable force that flowed from body to mind, that linked primitive instinct to modern intellect.

That first time, with Beverly, they had been at advanced navigation school, had driven to San Francisco for Saturday night, had splurged and stayed at the Mark Hopkins Hotel. She still remembered the room's green drapes: Their color matched Morris's eyes, eyes that took on a dazed cast when she'd asked, "Did you feel something special?" after they'd made love.

"Yes. What . . . ?"

"It was an earthquake," she'd said and laughed when he'd sat up, tried to get out of bed. She'd held on to him, pulled him down. "No. I'm joking." She'd explained, "What you felt . . . we made a baby."

He'd frowned.

"I'm not joking now," she'd said.

"How can you tell?"

"I don't know. I felt it. I just know."

After she'd missed her period and confirmed that her intuition was correct (but had she ever doubted her intuition?) she had pictured herself as an ultrafeminine, very mature, and astute woman.

And now again, two days ago, before Morris left for California, he had been inside of her and she had felt it—the conclusive current from body to mind, the amalgamation of souls—but she'd said nothing, knew Morris had felt nothing.

And now that he was gone, Beth asked herself, Was the current the same this time? From Beverly she had received a flow that coursed deeply, felt softly stuffed with dreams and happiness, with the warm electricity used to run a Ferris wheel or a merry-go-round. But this time the flow crackled coldly, stabbed her with sharp jolts of guilt, with the grim surge used to shoot voltage for electrocution. Was the cosmic difference a sign of the baby's sex? This time had they struck a son, a robot warrior child in the mold of Morris? Had they made a terrible mistake?

* * *

172

On her first evening alone, Beth walked to Jim Leonard's house. He opened the door and she told his handsome face, "I'm pregnant."

His eyes opened wide, his jaw dropped. "Hey, you got the wrong house, stranger," he said and slammed the door.

In the seconds that the door was closed Beth was blinded by tears. Then Jim was beside her with his arm around her shoulders, supporting her. "I don't want to be pregnant," she said. Would she have felt differently if the baby had been Jim's son?

CHAPTER 31

At the Tenth Annual Bombing and Navigation Competition no bombs fell but the most deadly enterprise took place beneath banners that proclaimed PEACE IS OUR PROFESSION. Did the competitors believe that peace was the most difficult and abnormal state in which to live? Did they resurrect their forfeited lives by transforming everyday imaginings concerning danger, death, and world destruction into ritualistic duty?

Charles's crew was assigned to bomb on the first day of competition. Clark Devon distributed the —th Bomb Wing schedule shortly after the crews checked into the March Air Force Base Bachelor Officer Quarters.

Rookie Archer was to be the sacrificial lamb, Dixie Smith thought. He would be first man across the targets and when he returned the old birds would pick his brain.

Charles saw what Dixie saw, and knowing Archer would too, he went to Archer's room to pacify him. He found

Archer sitting at the desk, target folder spread before him, a new bottle of Cutty Sark scotch beside it. "We're flying tomorrow," Charles said.

Archer shook his head in long, slow arcs.

Charles spoke, then wished he could retract his words: "You don't intend to drink all of that tonight?"

Archer stiffened slightly, then hefted the bottle, opened it, drank a mouthful that he chewed while he replaced the cork and handed the bottle to Charles. Archer walked to the closet, took a second bottle of Cutty Sark from the shelf, and placed it on the desk in the ghost ring of where the first had stood.

Charles read the message: No matter how many he took, more were always available. A lesson he'd long ago learned from Emily. Echoes from yesterday threatened his tomorrow. Was Archer preparing to throw away everything? The open target folder indicated otherwise, but it failed to register; Charles's sober mind was confused by years of exposure to alcohol. He said, "A lot of people are depending on you."

Fuck all of them, Archer thought. Tomorrow he would bust their balls. No matter what happened in the air, afterward he wouldn't tell them shit. He owed them nothing.

Charles placed the first bottle alongside the second. "Wait until tomorrow and I'll help you with these."

Archer's head again traced long, slow arcs.

That night Archer kept watch on the two full bottles, dozed, endured his nightmare of abject and dismal failure, arose twice to sit in the bathroom and study his target folder.

He had refined and refined and refined until his mind was so beautifully systematized that target recognition was a reflex. Terminal building, capitol, hospital sparkled at him like guiding polar stars from the electronic firmament of each frozen city. Swirling sky above, static sky below. One guided him to the other.

Meanwhile, in the adjacent bed, Dixie Smith barely moved, occasionally snored in a soft buzz that stopped when Archer loudly imitated it, harmonized and overpowered it. Archer asked himself why Dixie wasn't out with some strange blonde. Was it possible that Dixie cared about tomorrow? Cared about winning?

Winning. The word leaped out at Archer, frightening him, and he tried to shut off thoughts about results. He feared that waking dreams of success foreboded failure. In his mind a universal counterweight of defeat balanced too many hopes for victory. Wasn't that a natural force? Was it possible for any man ever to grasp as much as he secretly desired?

He began to think of failure, of things that could go wrong—things other than target identification—all the things beyond his control, beyond anyone's control. A starless, oppressive vacuum descended upon him and he broke into a panting sweat of fever, smothering self-hating sweat of fear.

To flee the black void of failure, he scanned his memory and rediscovered golden fantasies of Ellen Robertson, pornographic interludes that had sustained him through nights of Guam and Lebanon Alert, and he gave his mind and body to the pleasures of her gentle caress.

The same as on any day before an evening takeoff Charles's crew wasted hour after hour.

At the officers' club for a late breakfast, they ended up waiting for a table because every other crew seemed to have the same plan. Afterward they wandered through the base exchange before returning to their rooms to finish waiting and to suit up for the mission.

Archer tried to nap but ended up thumbing through his target folder. Dixie read *Hondo,* a paperback he'd bought at the exchange. When he finished, he flipped the book to Archer: "The way that L'Amour guy writes, he makes you feel like you're right there."

Archer read a few pages of the novel but couldn't get interested. His eyes grew heavy and he fell asleep minutes before Dixie announced it was time to dress. The effort of pulling on boots brought Archer the late afternoon tiredness always felt on such days. "I wish we were coming back instead of going out," he said and Dixie nodded a "Me, too."

Wells Fargo drove them to the flight line in a new, blue, four-door Pontiac. Local dealers provided two automobiles for each competing wing as a thank-you for the large volume of business the air force brought to the community year after year.

Charles's crew arrived at its airplane four hours prior to takeoff time. Just before Fargo stopped the car, Dixie laughed and then Charles laughed and Archer asked, "What's so funny?" Dixie and Charles pointed to the airplane.

The Stratojet's tires—main gear and outriggers—were painted with white sidewalls. Archer asked, "Is that legal?"

The crewchief approached Charles and saluted: "She's ready to go, sir."

"Nice wheels," Dixie said and grinned.

"It was my idea," the crewchief said proudly, "and Colonel Turner approved it. She's the only bird like that in SAC, sir."

Did Turner have a sense of humor, Archer wondered, or was this a joke at their expense, one he didn't understand?

With the help of maintenance specialists who normally weren't present—specialists who led and trailed the crewmen, opened and fastened panels for them, practically performed the crewmen's duties—the crew finished the preflight inspection ahead of schedule. On the way to base operations, Archer complained, "They didn't need us. I could have slept another half hour."

Filing a flight plan also took less time than normal. Everything was canned. "I could have slept another *hour*," Archer said. *Hurry up and wait,* he thought, *the SAC way.*

They were the thirty-third airplane in a seven-hour-long bomber stream. They were cleared to follow ten minutes behind the plane ahead of them. The preplanned route covered 2500 nautical miles and flying time was five hours, fifty-seven minutes. The three bomb runs took place in the first three hours.

They had finished filing and were eating hamburgers and french fries and milk shakes in the base operations snack bar when Axel Turner walked up to the table and said, "Keep your seats, please." Nevertheless, they stood and he nodded to each, called them by name, "Chuck. Dix. Morris," had a broad smile for Dixie. Everybody liked Old Dix, Archer thought enviously, and again imagined having Dixie for his aircraft commander.

"The airplane's in perfect shape," Charles said, eager to please.

"Nice sidewalls too," Dixie said and made Turner smile again. They all sat down.

"Well, Mo, do you have everything you need?" Turner asked.

Here he was two hours from takeoff and Turner asked *now* if he had everything he needed. . . . Archer honestly did not know how to answer.

Charles waited for a reply until the pause grew embarrassingly long, then said, "We're ready, sir. Right, Morris?"

Archer shook his head. What did they want him to say? He grinned a scarecrow grin and nodded, then shook his head again.

No? Yes? No? What was happening? Charles wondered. Had Archer been drinking?

Turner leaned forward and spoke directly to Archer: "Feel comfortable with the targets?"

"Yes, sir. Very much so."

"The offsets suit you?"

Did Turner want the truth? Archer had worked and reworked offset aiming point computations, had determined figures that seemed reasonable, then had not trusted his computations. Inherent errors were only magnified by offset aiming. He'd decided to make direct runs on the three designated ground zeros. His study had convinced him it was possible. Only briefly had he considered stealing offset aiming data from one of the other navigators; his refusal to use anything that originated from Martin had stopped him. Archer decided the truth wouldn't hurt him: "I don't have any offsets."

Turner and Charles sat back in their chairs. Turner heard Major Martin describing Archer: *He has his own way of doing everything.* "What do you mean?" Turner said.

"I don't trust what I came up with."

"You don't trust Major Martin's offsets?"

"I never got Major Martin's offsets. He never gave them to me. Major Martin hasn't helped me one fucking bit."

Charles glanced away abruptly, closed his eyes as if he had

been struck a stunning blow. He turned back, confronted the scene before him with a stricken look, seemed to shrink until his flying suit was a loose gray-green shroud.

Dixie's astonished eyes lit up as if he'd spotted a curvy blonde. Each time he thought he'd seen it all, Archer surprised him with a performance more outlandish than before.

Turner again heard Martin's warning: *He's capable of something that could completely wipe out the wing's chance to win.*

By then Archer was ablaze. Green flames blocked the edges of his vision. Before the fire consumed him, without preamble, in a rush, Archer told the story of his encounter with Martin, related it factually so that there was no hero or villain, ended with, "But it doesn't matter now. I can run all three targets direct. I know the aiming points better than I've ever known anything in my life." How often did one have an opportunity to plead his case before the demigod to whom he'd pledged his effort? As evidence of his ability he blindly recited San Jose target data.

Turner abhorred the pettiness of Archer's story, was disappointed with Martin more than with Archer. Then he saw that he had forced the confrontation. In choosing Archer he had violated his own creed: officers and gentlemen first, technicians last. But, at this point, he had to live with his decision.

Turner raised a hand that simultaneously stopped Archer and blessed him. "I believe you," Turner said. "I know you can do it."

The words of faith flew straight to Archer's heart, ordained his success.

Dixie smiled and gave Archer a thumbs-up. Charles closed his eyes for a few seconds, then opened them and smiled distantly, as if he were merely spectator to an event beyond his control, perhaps beyond his comprehension.

Was this a scene from the future? Were intelligent and mature men fated to sympathize with the tantrums of adult children? Or have whims of eccentrics always moved the world?

⟍CHAPTER 32

AFTER TAKEOFF FROM March Air Force Base, they climbed southward before turning to the northwest and paralleling the Pacific coastline. In so doing, they unwittingly followed the course of El Camino Real, the royal road that stretched from San Diego de Alcala to San Francisco Solano, the trail of twenty-one Spanish missions dedicated to saints.

Nearly two hundred years earlier the missions had been spaced a day's journey apart as resting places for travelers. Now Charles's crew spanned them in an hour and, along the way, enacted the destruction of San Jose.

Archer naively walked electronic crosshairs along El Camino Real, unwittingly stepped them from shrine to shrine—San Fernando Rey de Espana, San Buenaventura, Santa Barbara, Santa Ynez, San Luis Obispo de Tolosa, San Miguel Arcangel—line of angels leading to Nuestra Senora de la Soledad, initial point for the final lineup to the target.

San Jose came within the fifty-mile range of the radar crosshairs and Archer felt miraculously blessed with eyes of supernatural power. Had he been leisurely driving an automobile north on the Monterey Highway he would not have viewed greater detail as he entered San Jose. Fairgrounds . . . university . . . civic center . . . pinwheel radar reflections of man's culture pointed the way to him, guiding stars of frozen earthly firmament. The thin, black, reflectionless flow of the Guadalupe River washed Archer's vision, drifted his powerful eyes to designated ground zero: the main terminal building of San Jose Municipal Airport.

Had he been less powerfully focused he might have been aware that the exact aiming point was revealed to him from the tremendous distance of maximum crosshair range. However, on this night of miracles, he transcended doubt. Colonel Turner's command blessing—"I trust in you"— had granted him Olympian courage, had silenced the nerve-racking, harping voices of shrill taskmaster and sarcastic judge. The criminal innocently performed alone.

The thousand eyes of night winked at Chuck Charles through the bubble of the bomber's cockpit. Thirty-five thousand feet below, the sparkling southern California coast reflected the sky. Charles checked heading and airspeed as the bomber approached Soledad, waited to turn to bomb run heading and then transfer steering control to Archer. . . .

Charles flinched anew at the recollection of Archer's outburst concerning Martin, wondered about Colonel Turner's true response. The story had been a surprise to Charles, but it shouldn't have been. Archer had a knack for making everyone look bad. Turner's words of trust had sounded artificial to Charles, but had buoyed up Archer. Of course, Archer heard only what he wanted to hear, saw only what he wanted to see, said only what he chose to say. He was the monkey trio—hands clasped over ears, eyes, and mouth— rolled into one, Charles thought. How did he get that way?

Charles was never to learn that answers related to Archer were not within his province. Within the realm of adulthood the two men were alien to each other. When Charles died, he still would be baffled by Archer's behavior.

A recurring idea crossed Charles's mind: If tonight's results were neither spectacularly good nor spectacularly bad, if they were merely acceptably average, he would seek a crew change, request a different navigator. In that situation he and Archer could part on equitable terms, without prejudice.

Emily had suggested the change. "There are too many cooperative people around for you to put up with his antics. You don't need the heartburn he gives you. You don't deserve it," she had said.

He decided that Emily was correct. Charles owed himself and his family the energy he wasted on Archer.

About a month after Jean Turner saved Emily, Charles had been struck with paralyzing exhaustion while at home, soaking in a hot bath. Without warning he was totally enervated, felt as if his muscles had been pulverized. Although he'd never experienced the sensation before, he recognized the exhaustion for what it was, feared neither stroke nor illness. Sprawled in the tub, he pictured Gregory Peck, in *Twelve O'Clock High,* unable to hoist himself into the belly of a B17, a self-inflicted casualty of his own excessive demands.

Dead battery, Charles's mind mockingly told him.

After limp minutes, he had mustered strength to pull himself out of the tub, to inch his way to the bedroom, to slide his wet body beneath a sheet. Emily already was asleep, the house at rest. His final thought was one of relief: There was no reason to worry about anyone.

He slept nearly twelve hours. Emily had woken him with a steaming breakfast tray. "Up and at 'em, sleepyhead. You're missing the world." Then she rushed away to her appointment with Dr. Gomez.

Charles was still in bed when she returned, undressed and crawled in beside him, asked, "How's my Hawk today?" He grinned at the name, was pleased by it.

"I love you, Hawk," she'd said just this afternoon when he'd phoned her. She'd been baking a chocolate cake for David and Becky, had promised to have another waiting when he returned. "Maybe I'll bake an extra for Doc Gomez," she'd said. Her counseling sessions had been reduced to twice a week. "He said to tell you, *'Buena suerte.'* He's interested in your success."

Flattered by Gomez's concern, Charles had felt as if he'd been told he'd popped up in another person's dream.

* * *

. . . they were over Soledad and Archer said, "Give me fifteen right." Charles tilted the steering yoke and the North Star moved off one o'clock, shifted closer to the twelve o'clock position along the bomber's nose. He waited a couple of minutes, until he was certain they were inside crosshair range of San Jose, then asked, "How's it look?"

"Yes," Archer said.

Charles fumed. What kind of answer was "yes"? At times Charles was exasperated enough to root against Archer's success.

"Three hundred seconds to go," Dixie Smith said from the copilot seat. He wanted to ask, "How's it look?" simply to see if Archer again answered "yes." Archer was a pisser who would foul any stream, who never considered that someday he might need to drink from the same stream, Dixie thought.

In preparing for Bomb Comp, Charles had given Archer more latitude than ever and in gratitude Archer dropped a big one smack in Charles's lap, right in front of Colonel Turner. Dixie wondered how he would react if he were in Charles's seat.

"Two hundred and forty seconds to go," Dixie said and when Archer did not acknowledge the call he asked, "How's it look?"

"Yes," Archer said and made Dixie laugh.

With an eerie sameness the B47 swept across San Jose, Boise, and Butte. The airplane flew unswerving courses from point to point—Valley Falls, Follyfarm, McCall, Gibbonsville—smoothly sliced the stratum of night, the black layer between firmaments, cut a wake of foamy contrail ribbons that vanished in minutes and left the heavens unscarred by man. Like magnets the terminal building, the Idaho Capitol, and St. James Hospital drew the bomber to them, appeared as beacons on Archer's radar.

Rehearsal proved itself by refinement, refinement by perfection.

The eerie sameness was exaggerated by Bomb Comp rules that provided no results to the crews inflight. On a normal mission, minutes after release, bomb plot controllers radioed a coded score to a crew. Bomb Comp results were telephoned only to a scoring committee at March.

Without a score, a tangible sign of success (or failure), Archer felt no sense of accomplishment, no sense of completeness after crossing a target. Trapped inside his cage of destruction, he saw his tasks as void of finality. Would actual thermonuclear warfare be the same? he wondered. Would he fly thousands of sightless miles to drop an unseen weapon on an unseen target to produce unseen results? Was his destiny merely to destroy an electronic echo? Was he a flesh and bone robot, a breathing mechanical part of the bomber?

Why, on the verge of possible triumph, did he experience such a hollow feeling? Would actually delivering the bomb be a psychic dud? Would victory be hollow? Did a robot mind contain an empty universe?

Frustrated expectations depressed and tormented him. Did the vague possibility of failure force him to discredit his entire role?

The criminal automatically performed computations for the night celestial navigation leg while taskmaster and judge silently reflected upon the completed bomb runs.

Colonel Turner, Major Devon, and the crewchief were waiting for the bomber when it parked. Archer unstrapped before the brakes were set, climbed down the ladder before Charles and Dixie finished their postflight.

Archer saluted Colonel Turner and asked Devon, "You have my scores?"

"Colonel Turner has them," Devon said.

Archer looked expectantly at Turner who said, "Wait until Chuck and Dixie get here."

There was a problem, Archer instantly decided and his chest froze. The criminal in his mind rapidly reviewed the bomb runs, saw guilty actions that a few minutes earlier he would have classified as innocent. But the taskmaster and judge reserved comment, knew that Archer had performed flawlessly. Then the criminal knew that error had to be the fault of the equipment, had to be beyond his control. That wasn't fair, Archer thought and suddenly he hated his job, hated the uncertainties of his air-force life. If he could have, he would have resigned his commission in that moment.

Then Chuck and Dixie were beside him and Colonel

Turner handed a slip of paper to Chuck, who held it so they all could see while Dixie shined his flashlight on it. The slip of paper read:

Charles

420/270

0/0 Shack

0/0 Shack

4.1 NM

"Oh, dear God," Charles said in disbelief and gratitude.

"Are you serious?" Dixie said and looked at Turner who smiled and nodded. Dixie grabbed Archer around the waist, lifted him off the ground, spun him in a circle, and let loose with a rebel yell.

"The first twin shacks in comp history," Devon said.

The crewchief squeezed Archer's hand in both of his, pumped it vigorously. "Thank *you*, sir," he said several times.

It was impossible to top such scores, Archer thought and realized he'd won. There was no doubt. He felt vindicated from every criticism ever lodged against him. The results proved that he was the absolute best.

"The bar's closed," Turner said, "but when you finish debriefing there're several bottles of mission whiskey waiting in my quarters."

Archer stayed drunk during the next three days of competition. In his stupor he passed on every detail of the targets as he'd seen them, described them to Devon and Wells Fargo and anyone else who cared to listen. The one time he saw Fred Martin, he laughed in his face and gave him the finger.

He telephoned Beth the morning of his success, awoke her. "I got a four-hundred-twenty-footer and two shacks," he said and the facts sounded like a made-up dream. "I'll win best in bombing, probably best in navigation, and definitely best overall."

Beth's praise was unstinting but not generous enough to satisfy Archer. "I'm the best," he told her, "and you hardly care."

As it turned out, 27 of the 164 crews had a navigation circular error of less than four miles. Most of them were B52 crews. "They goddamn well ought to be able to navigate," Archer said bitterly, "they have two navigators doing the job of one, and an extra guy who does nothing but shoot the sextant." However, with Archer's bomb scores, the —th Bomb Wing easily won the Best Wing Bombing Award.

At the awards ceremony held in a hangar before a billboard-size scoreboard that listed every crew, Charles, Dixie, and Archer were called forward to receive plaques designating them as best in bombing and best overall in bombing and navigation combined. CINCSAC made the presentations. Before handing out the plaques, he told the audience, "This is a unique trio of professionals. One perfect bomb might be considered a touch of luck. Two perfect bombs are a tribute to crew dedication and determination, and to maintenance proficiency."

After handing the men their plaques, CINCSAC gruffly said, "Two of you are improperly dressed." Archer looked down at his uniform, checked that insignias were aligned, buttons buttoned; he found no discrepancies. He looked at Dixie, who raised his eyebrows and shrugged. Charles frowned, equally puzzled.

CINCSAC said, "You two are out of uniform—*Major* Charles and *Captain* Archer."

Archer stopped breathing. He had suspected that a spot promotion was possible, perhaps in a few months when the next quarterly list was published. He had not considered receiving it right there, *right on the spot.*

Charles told CINCSAC, "I can correct half the problem, General, put one of us in proper uniform." He unpinned the double track silver bars from his shoulders and pinned them in place of Archer's single silver bars, instantly confirming Archer's promotion.

CINCSAC said to Dixie, "Isn't it time Axel gave you your own crew?"

Dixie smiled: "Thank you, General."

The three men saluted and, in step, marched off the presentation platform.

Was it imagination or did Archer actually feel the solid weight of the extra bars, the comforting weight of new rank on each shoulder. His mind leaped ahead. Would Beth understand what he'd accomplished? What would Robby think? And Ellen? Then he was jealous. What he had was not enough. If Charles deserved to be a major, then he too deserved to be a major. After all, he was creator of the miracles.

⤵CHAPTER 33

Beth Archer quickly learned the finer points of RHIP—rank has its privilege.

Promotion to captain jumped Archer from the lower half to the top of a long list of company grade officers awaiting base housing, skipped him over lieutenants who had been on base before he arrived. In a few weeks she would have her own home, Beth thought happily, ignoring a twinge of guilt for breaking in at the head of the line.

Promotion to captain brought more money too, increased Morris's base pay from three hundred thirty-five dollars a month to four hundred fifty-two. With concurrent raises in flying pay and housing allowance, the gain totaled almost two hundred dollars a month, Beth discovered. Now, perhaps, they could afford new furniture.

Best of all, Beth felt an uplift in esteem. Was it true that a wife wore the rank held by her husband? Her first ego boost came at the base exchange after a cashier saw Beth's identification card. The cashier, a short Mexican woman to whom Beth normally wouldn't have spoken, said, "It was wonderful what Captain Archer did, Missus Archer. My husband helped fix the airplane Captain Archer flew in Bomb Comp and got promoted too. He's so happy. We're so thankful."

The woman's smiling face was dark and pretty, but chubby. Her body was sagging toward the center. She typified all the Mexican girls with whom Beth had gone to high school. *Too many meals of beans and tortillas,* Beth thought, *and too many children at an early age.*

In response to the thanks, Beth smiled with queenly grace, as if she had helped bestow the reward upon the woman's husband, said, "Our thanks to you." The cashier blushed, then hid her face in her hands.

A few afternoons later, Jean Turner honored Beth with a visit. Although Beth was flattered by the attention, she was uncomfortable facing Jean Turner one to one. Dressed in a freshly pressed navy-blue linen suit, Jean appeared imposingly stern, practically regimental. Then Jean lifted Beverly onto her lap, kissed the child's cheeks, cooed, made Beverly laugh, and suddenly Beth saw Jean's gray hairs, her delicate wrinkles. *She could be a grandmother,* Beth thought.

Jean said, "It may sound egotistical but in my mind every air-force baby is my baby, the same way that every air-force member is a member of my family."

Over cookies and tea, Jean said, "We must stick together. Beneath the difference in rank you and I are sisters, in the same way Axel and Morris are brothers. We're all brothers-and sisters-in-arms."

Jean made another declaration that Beth thought about for days: "There are times when I place the air-force family ahead of my personal family. My children understand. I've taught them that people who have talent and positions of authority owe a debt to the less fortunate." Beth tried to imagine what she had to offer to those less fortunate, recognized no debt. She could imagine how Morris would react if she gave a stranger priority over him. He resented it when she put Beverly first.

Before departing, Jean told Beth: "Emily Charles now has the responsibility for organizing wives' club luncheons. I'm very proud of her. I hope you can help her with ordering flowers and choosing menus."

189

"I think I can find time," Beth said in hopes of seeing Jean again. Was Jean Turner's cosmopolitan image what Beth always had longed for in a mother?

For her first Dyess wives' club luncheon Beth bought a new dress, with Morris's approval. Jean Turner complimented her on the dress and, in front of Emily Charles, praised her choice of centerpieces.

Emily frowned at Jean, said, "You never complimented me for my centerpieces," and the two women laughed, didn't bother to explain the humor to Beth.

Beth had been surprised by the sight of Emily. The word "beautiful" had come to her mind but hadn't been quite right. Emily mimicked Jean Turner's poise but without Jean's rigidity. Later, Beth decided that "serene" was the word she'd been looking for, and displaying an astute insight she wasn't aware of, she told Morris, "Emily acts like a civilian among soldiers. She's a guest at her own party."

Following the "wine course," as Jean laughingly described the before-lunch drinking, Beth ended up at a table with wives of junior captains and lieutenants, none of whom she'd met before. She was clearly the most fashionably dressed. The conversation worked around to spot promotions.

"I heard the funniest story about two captains who were spot majors up at Little Rock," a stout woman said. "After a bad bomb, they lost their spots and the next time they entered the club bar the piano player played 'Autumn Leaves.' He sang—" and the stout woman softly sang— "The falling leaves—drift off your shoulders—those golden leaves—have disappeared. . . ."

The listeners laughed, including Beth. She hadn't considered that Morris could lose his promotion. *That would be a nightmare,* she thought.

Another woman said, "We have a friend who *refused* a spot."

Several women murmured disbelief.

"Truly," the woman said. "His name's Perry Rozanski. He's a captain, a *really* sharp navigator. A short while before the quarterly spot list came down from SAC, he requested a crew change. He couldn't *stand* his AC, a bossy old major.

190

"When the list came out, *both* of them were on it: Perry to major and his AC to LC.

"Perry *refused* to put on major leaves.

"After a week, his squadron commander called him in and gave him a pair of major leaves. Perry handed them back and said, 'I don't want those. I want a crew change.'

"Meanwhile, the AC threw a *tremendous* promotion party, with a buffet and everything. It cost him three or four months' worth of his pay raise. You see, he'd expected *never* to make lieutenant colonel, was convinced he'd retire as a major.

"Perry kept wearing his captain bars, so, after another week, the wing commander called him in and *ordered* him to put on the leaves, told him there would be no crew change as long as he and his AC held spots.

"That convinced Perry that he was stuck with his AC, the way things stood. So . . . on the next mission, Perry dropped three bombs out in the boondocks. He told us, 'I was supposed to be running Amarillo and I hit somewhere in Oklahoma.'

"The next quarter neither one of their names was on the spot promotion list. Perry got his crew change the day the list came out."

"I don't believe that story," Ellen Robertson said from the next table. She was turned around in her chair, obviously had been eavesdropping.

"Don't argue with *her*," a brunette at Beth's table whispered. "She's a troublemaker."

The woman who told the long story faced Ellen. "The story's true. We know the man—we've known him for years—Perry Rozanski."

"Perry, fairy, I still don't believe it," said Ellen. "Nobody walks away from a promotion to major."

"You wouldn't understand," the whisperer said. "I'm sure some people would lie, cheat, and steal for a spot, if they were eligible." As a copilot, Ellen's husband didn't qualify for a spot promotion.

"Balls to you," Ellen said and turned her back on Beth's table.

"What's that supposed to mean?" the whisperer asked. "She's so rude, I don't see why anyone sits with her."

191

"Spot promotions are unfair," another woman said and set off everyone at the table.

"A man's either combat-ready or he's not. On Alert everybody does the same job."

"Weren't spots designed to reward the crews who were assigned the most dangerous targets?"

"Alert changed all that. Now a spot crew might not even be launched."

"The whole system needs to be reworked. Everyone ought to share in something like Alert pay."

"That would be fairer than giving the money to just a few. . . ."

"Money *and rank.*"

"That's really unfair," a woman who spoke for the first time said directly to Beth.

The bitterness in the woman's voice made Beth lower her eyes. Why were they being cruel to her? Her shiny esteem felt tarnished.

The woman who told the long story said, "Maybe we ought to change the subject. I don't think all of us are comfortable talking about spots."

Did the social gathering possess a lynch-mob mentality: When the victim was dead, was he forgiven? As helpless as a man dangling from a rope, Beth beamed down a smile of gratitude for the coup de grace that ended her torment.

The luncheon ended with a long talk by the base judge advocate, a quasi-lecture that refuted "the civilian belief that military justice is to justice as military music is to real music." "Military justice is extremely swift but extremely fair," he concluded repeatedly while putting several wine-sodden listeners fast asleep. The moment he sat down, Beth headed straight to her car. Ellen Robertson intercepted her in the parking lot. Since Bomb Comp, Beth and Morris had exchanged dinners and evenings of drinking with the Robertsons.

Ellen saw tears in Beth's eyes. "Don't pay any attention to what those cows say about spots," Ellen said loudly. "They're jealous. A lot of women are more vicious than men. Some of them would make better pilots than their husbands. You turn the other cheek and you only give them a new target to hit."

Beth nodded, touched the corners of her eyes, and quietly

thanked Ellen for her support. Ellen was not a person she would choose to fight, Beth thought.

What a piece of fluff, Ellen thought while she watched Beth carefully drive away. What did Morris see in her? She would have bet that Beth did it only with the lights out. Morris needed more than that, Ellen thought. His wiry, boyish body was something. And Morris's pouts were sadly funny, resembled a James Dean kind of sullenness, the kind a woman wanted to comfort.

↘CHAPTER 34

T HE MILITARY AFFAIRS Committee—a group of businessmen from within the Abilene Chamber of Commerce—
proclaimed the B47s at Dyess to be the best bombers in the
world. In recognition the committee feted the Bomb Comp
crewmen, the maintenance men, and their families at a
cookout at the A. J. Sykes ranch.

The Sykes ranch house sat northwest of Abilene, beyond
Anson, at the end of a miles-long blacktop private road that
lost itself amid overwhelming openness, a plain of solitude.
Everlasting wind curled its way across the wide-open land,
wound in among brown grassy swells, ruffled yellow sun-
baked ridges. Local wags claimed that the wind blew so long
and so hard at times that on a drive-in movie screen it once
blew Roy Rogers off his horse.

The panorama offered no rewards or punishments, only
consequences.

There was beauty, however, in this apparently sterile
land, a desert plain beauty wherein sunrise blasted startling

reds at one end of a daily spectrum that faded into sunset's comforting shadows, that wide purple band of subtle shades that shifted tint by tint with each passing stroke of twilight.

It took a long time for an outsider to understand such obvious but subtle beauty, to recognize moment-to-moment blendings in sunlight's blinding rays or in moonlight's invisible shadows. A man had to live beneath the open sky day and night, live inside the dome of barrenness before he appreciated the high plain landscape.

"Who'd want to live out here?" Archer said. "The only good thing about the place is that there's plenty of parking space, if you don't get stuck in the sand."

Most Abilene businessmen were cowboy-lean sons of the soil, as dry and solid as the thin oaks that dotted the arid Big Country land. With tenacious grasp they'd dug roots into the desiccated plain, determined that nothing would stunt their growth. They were survivors who had endured fierce economic droughts of government reductions and tornado winds of unpredictably fluctuating military appropriations.

Despite their hospitality, Archer felt he was an outsider among them, was simultaneously flattered and made uneasy by their attention. He found commonality with those who drank by matching their glasses of bourbon with his of scotch. Then, after several drinks, he challenged their principles. "I thought the law said it's supposed to be dry around here."

"It is dry," a tall, rawboned man drawled. "Look out yonder. "It's so dry there that the trees chase the dogs."

The men within their small circle laughed slowly, savored the squelch while they cut their eyes back and forth from Archer to the joker.

Archer excused himself from the group. If the drinks hadn't been free, he would have found Beth and gone home. What had that bunch of hicks ever done except mooch from the base?

How would he have responded if he'd known that the joker had been an infantry lieutenant who survived besieged Bastogne?

Beth roamed through the throng at the Sykes ranch. For the third morning in a row she'd awakened with an upset stomach. With Beverly she'd had no problems, no doubts.

Beverly had been a love-child, she thought. What was the baby now inside her?

She'd expected Morris to pay more attention to her after Bomb Comp ended. But he spent his free time drinking, called it "celebrating." Like today. The minute they arrived he went straight to the bar and joined a crowd of men. He knew she wouldn't dare to follow.

What good was a promotion, or a pay raise, or a larger house if she didn't have a husband who loved her?

At the far end of a covered patio larger than their entire duplex, Beth came upon a grill that was ten feet long and six wide and was half covered with three-inch thick T-bone steaks. Twice as many more steaks were stacked, waiting, on a nearby table. The mound of raw meat made Beth's stomach churn.

Two bearded chefs danced around the grill, pranced as spryly as if circling a partner at a square dance. Wearing chef hats forced over ten-gallon cowboy hats, they used long-handled tongs to toss and turn steaks. From bottles of Jim Beam bourbon they splashed whiskey onto the cooking meat. Columns of flames shot up from the bed of white-hot coals. One cook touched the brim of his hat and told Beth, "Down that end's the done ones, ma'am." He pointed to a pile of charred meat.

Beth's stomach rumbled. Everything was far too large, and far too done, burnt to a crisp, ruined, she thought. "I can't begin to eat one of those," she said softly. She wanted to lie down, get away from the greasy odor of seared fat.

"Don't fret, miss," said a man who'd overheard her. He had a smiling ferret face, wore a leather coat, snakeskin gambler's hat, snakeskin necktie, and snakeskin boots. "Half of these we throw away." He forked a steak from the pile of charred meat, dropped it on a platter-size plate. "Look here." He held the steak close for Beth's inspection. "See?" The steak was in three layers, held together by toothpicks. A thick middle slab was surrounded by outer layers blackened by fire. The snakeskin man peeled away the black meat and revealed a nearly two-inch thick T-bone cooked to pink and juicy perfection.

"Hell, that one's too done," the snakeskin man said and scraped the plate into a garbage can. He reached for another steak and Beth excused herself.

If she was going to be sick to her stomach, she preferred to be alone. Around a bend in a nearby arroyo, she found a shady spot on a slab of rock.

She had been stretched out on the slab for only a minute when a short woman cautiously rounded the bend, called, "Are you all right, Missus Archer?" Not until the woman walked closer did Beth recognize her as the cashier from the base exchange, the Mexican who recently had waited on her.

"I'm tired," Beth said. "I'm afraid I'm pregnant." The unexpected confession to another woman brought relief, even if the woman was a stranger. More so because the woman was a stranger.

The woman smiled. "I watched you talk to that man in the leather and then you headed here . . . you didn't look good. I thought maybe I could help." She rolled her dark eyes. "Then I thought maybe I seen wrong and you weren't sick. . . ." She giggled. "Maybe you were headed to that man." She ducked her head between her shoulders like a child who expected a slap of reprimand.

Beth rocked her head from side to side. "That's the last thing I need."

"This your first baby?"

"Second." Because the woman made her the center of attention, Beth felt as if she were talking to a servant. She could say anything without being held accountable.

"Your first baby boy or girl?"

"Girl. Beverly. She's fifteen months old."

The Mexican woman nodded, held up three fingers. "I have three sons. I lost my baby girl."

"I'm sorry . . ."

"Así es la vida."

"How old are you?" Beth asked.

"Twenty-two." The Mexican woman smiled bashfully. "I was fifteen years when my husband married me." She took off her coat sweater, folded it into a square, slipped it beneath Beth's head, then sat down beside her. "You need rest," she said and gently stroked Beth's hair.

If only Morris would touch her that gently, Beth thought.

"I didn't have to get married," the woman told Beth. "On my wedding night, I was *una virgen.*"

197

Beth closed her eyes: "So was I." The Mexican stroked Beth's hair while she slept. The servant became equal.

In a dream Beth gave birth to a son. Propped on her elbows, she was reclining on a hard, oilcloth-covered examination table. She was alone. The delivery was as effortless as a bowel movement. Did she push the baby into the world, or did it crawl from her? Or did she shrink from the newborn, withdraw her body from around it?

She watched her son ooze from her with reptilian slowness. His face was masked by a vivid red birthmark (burnmark?) across hooded eyes that glowed greenly, without pupils.

Beth shivered at sight of the face. The mouth was stretched open, lips drawn back, prepared to bite with sharp teeth, shark's teeth.

The creature's shoulders were coated with swamp-green alligator skin. Claws scratched her tenderest flesh as they slipped from her.

Then the moist creature lay motionless between her legs. Its abnormally long penis looked headless, was a dangling flap of loose pale skin. Beth could not stop herself from pushing away from what she had birthed. Was it alive or dead?

She felt a responsibility to cradle it in her arms: It was her son. But she could not bring herself to touch it. The thought of breast feeding those razor teeth made her tremble. *She was afraid of her son.*

She touched herself where the claws had raked her and found blood on her fingers. Already it had hurt her. She could never love this thing.

She wished it dead, then felt guilty for her wish.

Toward evening Morris Archer found himself standing next to Julius MacDuff, the patriarch of modern Abilene. "My mother was a Jew and my father a Scot," he'd overheard MacDuff tell Colonel Turner earlier in the day, "but darn little of their teachings rubbed off on me. It didn't take me long to decide that saving was for others and that a man needed to spend money to make money. However, it took a little longer for me to understand that it's safest to be spending another man's money." He'd cackled softly, dryly.

MacDuff had amassed his wealth first in oil marketing and later in real estate speculation.

Now he leaned close to Archer and, in the confident voice of a fellow victor, said: "Strategic warfare is big business, Captain. Abilene's citizens more than paid their dues in that business. When we scraped together the million dollars that bought the acres we donated to the air force, we bought ourselves a ride ticket that's good forever. Dyess will never close."

MacDuff lowered his voice: "I suppose you've heard we'll be getting another B47 wing in January. Axel will pin on his brigadier star and move up to air division commander."

Archer hadn't heard any of the facts, hadn't heard so much as rumors, but he nodded agreement while resenting that a civilian knew such important news before the military population.

"Yes, sir, Dyess will never close," MacDuff said. "When B47s become obsolete our base will get B52s, and when 52s phase out our base will get the best bombers that follow. You can argue about missiles all night long, Captain, but strategic bombers'll be around forever. Too many powerful people are interested in them."

To emphasize his next point, MacDuff tapped Archer lightly on the shoulder: "I believe the right man could spend most of his military life at Dyess, make a bunch of friends, build up investments in local property, maybe own part of a business or two. He might retire only as a lieutenant colonel or so, but he could retire as a rich one. Yes, sir, strategic warfare is big business, very profitable."

Julius MacDuff gave Archer a gap-tooth smile. "None of it's hurt you, has it?" Within his question was an unspoken question: Was Archer a man worth keeping in Abilene, a man to enlist, a hard worker who would help a city expand? "You're a captain two years ahead of schedule," MacDuff said.

Archer heard none of the enticements. Instead, he was offended by the implication that his promotion was anything less than a deserved military honor. His promotion had nothing to do with big business. He didn't want to believe that SAC was merely big business. The scotch inside him spoke: "I earned what I have. I didn't buy it."

MacDuff stared through steel-rim spectacles, locked tired, experienced eyes on Archer.

Archer stared back, read nothing in the aged man's face. Was he angry? Insulted? Patronizing? He looked indifferent.

Another outsider who understood little about minor roles in history, MacDuff thought. He was dealing with a child of a man and could burn him down with the slow smoldering eyes of unemotional certainty. This child-man had never faced a real challenge, such as the survival challenge of constructing a new future for an economically destroyed city. Archer was a wrecker, not a builder, MacDuff decided. May God in his infinite wisdom never find cause for this or any nation to depend upon the likes of Morris Archer, MacDuff silently prayed.

In MacDuff's lined face Archer still recognized no counterforce. Was this old man staring at him or beyond him? Involuntarily Archer broke the eye-to-eye deadlock, turned his head, searched behind himself. He found nobody, nothing. *Had MacDuff been attempting to see inside of him?* Was that possible?

MacDuff recognized Archer's confusion and understood that he was dealing with a man who took everything personally.

MacDuff knew that there was no way to quantify the impact a base had on a community. The relationship went beyond dollars and pennies. The air force sent a boy down from New York, for example, and he met an Abilene girl and a new chemistry developed. They taught each other new habits and values, changed each other in ways that could be good and bad. Or maybe the air force sent a married man and his family from California and they moved into an Abilene neighborhood and, again, their habits and values affected the Texas way of life, maybe upset the local traditional way of doing things. For better or for worse a lot of futures were altered.

Abilene was the buckle on the Bible Belt. To win the air force, its citizens had gambled with their fundamental beliefs. They'd hoped that their ways were strong enough to survive the alien influx. When MacDuff had said, "Abilene's citizens more than paid their dues," he'd meant that they'd risked more than money.

To explain all of that to Archer was a waste of effort, MacDuff sensed: Archer would classify himself as one of the aliens and would receive the lesson as a slap in the face, consider it another display of Texas chauvinism.

Later, on his way to his automobile where Beth waited, Archer passed Colonel Turner. Emboldened by scotch, he said, "Bomb Comp results sure didn't hurt you any, *General.*

Turner looked displeased, said, "You've been talking to Julius."

"No, Julius has been talking to me," Archer said.

"It's not supposed to be officially announced for several more days."

"Well, I guess he thought I deserved to know. I guess I had something to do with it."

Did Archer actually believe that Bomb Comp results influenced his promotion? The man was preposterous, Turner thought. If he too hadn't had more drinks than normal, he would have laughed and walked away. But, under the conditions, he decided to educate Archer. "My promotion was decided before I selected the crews for Bomb Comp," he said. "But if it hadn't been, Bomb Comp results wouldn't have influenced it. You don't understand the game."

"Then how come we got spots and—"

"Shut up and listen," Turner said. Archer's spot was a gift from CINCSAC, he thought, but whether or not Archer kept that gift was up to The Ax. Should he tell Archer that? Would it have any benefit? What would he gain by flaunting his power before this low-ranking officer? Turner decided he'd had too much to drink. He should have ignored Archer's reference to *"General."*

"Well! I'm listening," Archer said. "Say something."

"You are an asshole," Turner stated and walked into the night.

Archer found himself trapped inside a green explosion, bound in a fire of hatred. He wanted to chase after Turner and . . . what? Punch him? Ruin what little he had? Or was it already ruined? He was powerless. He had won promotions for everybody and still he was at the bottom of the heap.

He stumbled to his car, forced Beth from behind the steering wheel, and drove home like a mad man. By the time they reached the duplex, Beth was huddled beneath the dashboard, hysterical.

CHAPTER 35

THE NEXT MORNING while Archer was trying to sleep off a hangover, Beverly sneaked into the bedroom and with a tiny forefinger raised one of his eyelids. He stared at her through a single bloodshot eye and she said, "I love you, Dada." It was the first sentence she spoke to him. Or was it the first time her words registered in his mind?

The anger that had filled his throat upon being disturbed now dissolved in humility. Was this his first recognition of Beverly as a fellow being?

The truth was that he hadn't wanted a child. Beverly's birth was something that happened, a task that had to be accomplished, another exercise like a practice Alert scramble . . .

When the time came, far into the night, Beth had shaken him awake. She was having contractions; she thought her water had broken. He responded mechanically, slipped into his clothes and carried what she handed him to the car.

On the way to Hendrick Memorial Hospital, he took a

shortcut and found himself bouncing violently on a washboard surface, a street under repair. The jolts made Beth groan loudly. "You came this way deliberately," she accused.

"It was the shortest way," he said. "I didn't know——"

"You did," she shouted. "You did it deliberately."

He slowed to a walking pace, searched for the smoothest path, still the slightest bounce made Beth cry out. He didn't know what to say in apology, felt guilty although innocent. By the time they traveled the two blocks under repair he was coated with a nervous, metallic sweat.

At the hospital a flight of nurses snatched Beth from him, swept her from sight. He was made to fill out forms. Then he paced until shortly after daybreak when a nurse sternly told him, "You can see your wife for a minute," and led him to a darkened room with enameled flamingo-pink walls that he would remember always. They surrounded him like glistening, sweating, pulsating flesh. A moist greenhouse heat brought out his metallic sweat again and he tasted his body's odor. The room's atmosphere seemed to compress him, smother him. Was the room a grotto of death or a womb of life?

Beth was on a high hospital bed, tangled in a white sheet, thrashing from side to side. Her eyes were closed. She looked as if she'd been laboring in the sun, he thought. Her face was flushed and puffy. Beads of sweat as round as teardrops stood out on her forehead. Her clenched hands tugged at her soaked nightgown. "It hurts," she moaned each time she turned.

What was he supposed to do? Did she know he was there?

Suddenly she lay still, opened her eyes and calmly ordered, "Get me a drink of water."

The pitcher on the bedside table was empty. He filled it in an adjoining bathroom. By the time he poured a glass of water Beth was thrashing again. He waited for her to pause, then offered the drink.

"I don't want that," she said. "What's wrong with you?"

"But you asked for it," he said.

"You're so dumb," she shouted. "I don't want it. Get it away from me." Then she rocked from side to side and moaned, "It hurts so much."

He was not trained for this, he thought, had no experience

in childbirth, no idea of what to do. Should he take her hand and kiss it? Stroke her hair? How could he comfort her? Her unprecedented belligerence made him afraid that anything he did would irritate her. Therefore, he did nothing except watch her display of pain. He was grateful when, a few minutes later, a slouching, shuffling nurse told him he must leave. Then she tiredly said, "Birthing is a woman's burden," and made him feel more inadequate, more despondent.

From the waiting room he phoned the squadron, explained to the scheduling officer what was happening. Archer was supposed to be mission planning that day for a flight the following morning. "Maybe I can be there by noon," he said.

The scheduler said, "Forget it. I'll give the mission to another crew. Take care of your wife. And I hope it's a boy."

Archer was embarrassed for needing so much time. Then he sat and waited, alone. Was Beth the only woman having a baby that morning? Or had the other fathers gone to their jobs? How useless he was, he thought. What a tiny role he played. Why was his presence necessary?

Around eleven o'clock the first man Archer had seen since entering the hospital appeared, draped in a green surgical gown. Was this a domain of women, strictly for women? The man was Beth's doctor, a man Archer had not met. Beth had insisted on a civilian doctor, and after the base hospital administrator provided a certificate that paid for the option, Archer agreed. Beth alone had found a civilian who suited her.

Now the doctor said, "Mr. Archer?" and, when Archer nodded, shook his hand and told him, "You're the father of a healthy baby girl."

Archer again nodded, dumbly, didn't think to ask about Beth's condition. *The baby was born: the drill was ended.*

Archer's unenthusiastic response caused the doctor to say, "I'm sorry if you're disappointed."

Archer squinted questioningly.

"I thought maybe you were hoping for a boy," the doctor said.

"No. A girl's fine. A baby's a baby," Archer said and laughed hollowly.

Two hours later a nurse led him to a bright, pastel-green

room where Beth was propped up in bed with Beverly in her arms. For the first time he saw his daughter and was amazed by the sharp definition of her tiny, perfectly formed hands. He had expected a newborn to be less than complete, less than fully developed. He awkwardly held her for half a minute, thought that both he and the baby were uncomfortable, then returned her to Beth's arms. . . .

As it turned out, the only service he provided haunted him: Beth didn't forgive him for taking the torturous shortcut.

Was it surprising that it took Archer so long to recognize his daughter? Beverly was Beth's child, Beth's responsibility until she reached out to him: "I love you, Dada." Did the words offer him a new identity?

He answered, "I love you too, Beverly." She tried to pull herself onto the bed. He boosted her aboard and she ended up sprawled on his chest, nose to nose.

With a single finger she touched the stubble on his chin, said, "Dada."

Through his hangover, he tickled her chin, said, "Beverly." *Monkey see, monkey do,* he thought. "Say—Morris."

"Mama," Beverly said.

Archer shook his head and hundred-proof voltage lightninged through his skull. "Oh," he said.

"Oh," Beverly said.

Archer laughed through the pain: "Right. Oh. Oh shit."

"Oh . . ."

"Sh-h-h-h-h-h, that's enough." He smiled at the idea of her swearing. "Say—Morris. More-iss."

Tiny bow lips hummed: "M-m-m-m-m . . ."

She was a miniature of Beth, he thought. He saw nothing from him in her. He carefully nodded encouragement: ". . . iss. More-iss."

She repeated his name and he kissed her. "I love you," he said and when she answered, "I love you," he hugged her tightly.

Beth entered the bedroom: "Beverly, I told you to keep out of here."

"She's all right," Morris said but Beverly already was squirming from his arms. He squeezed her, held her against her will.

"Let her go," said Beth. Her expression was at once calm

and tense, as though she wore two faces, two masks imposed upon each other. Beneath a cap of curls she was resigned mother and expectant child, sad Beth and happy Beverly.

"She was all right before you came in." Beverly whined loudly, made his head throb. He lost the desire to argue and allowed her to slide from the bed. He felt limp. "Look, I'm sorry about last night," he said.

At the memory of the ride home, Beth turned her head aside. In recent months Morris had mentally battered her, but she didn't classify mood and word attacks as abuse. If such mental cruelty was abuse, then every woman Beth had ever known could be classified as abused. Last night was different. Although Morris did not touch her, she knew she had been physically abused. If he had bloodied her with his fists, she would not have felt more violated. He had meant to injure her, she thought, and she ought to flee for her own protection. Laredo seemed her only refuge, however, and going there was like escaping from one desert island to another. "You were insane," she said.

"I had too much to drink."

"It was more than that."

Archer silently agreed.

Was his self-destructive mode a robot's response to inevitable failure? While on his final flight at pilot training school he had consigned himself to death with a careless flick of the control stick. Void of emotion or violence, the sudden act of resignation resembled the short circuit twitch of a mechanical man. For the first time since that moment, failure again awaited him.

Was Archer's self-destructiveness the component that made him the perfect thermonuclear warrior? Was mankind's inevitable failure predicated upon human robots willing to sacrifice themselves in order to produce such failure?

Particles of episodes from the cookout gorged Archer's drugged mind: Smiling salesmen presented him with their cards, offered tremendous discounts until the gap-tooth face of Julius MacDuff pushed them aside, as if to remind Archer that the deals were the dregs of the big business of strategic warfare. An opportunity he had seen the day before reappeared in his mind and he sat up in bed, asked Beth, "Want to go shopping later?"

"For what, groceries?"

"Furniture. For the new house." They already knew the house they were getting, one being vacated by a retiring captain.

The expectant child took control of Beth's face, won over the resigned mother. "Do you mean it?"

"Anything you want," Archer said, "in about two hours," and he gently lowered his head to the pillow, closed his eyes.

Did Morris at last understand her discontent? The expectant child kissed him lightly on the cheek.

In the background the resigned mother scowled in disbelief. Why was Morris being generous? Was this an expedient to pacify Beth, to atone for his attempt to injure her? What did new furniture matter? Would they ever actually move into the new house?

After three years of marriage Beth did not know Morris. Or was it that she knew him and did not love what she knew? In those years she had not identified with him in a single manner. She did not see through his eyes or hear through his ears or speak through his lips. His questions were not her questions, his answers not her answers. Didn't true love entail becoming part of another, uniting *me's* into *we?* She doubted that Morris would pause if she declared that he did not recognize her as a part of him. He was an entity, he would say, who needed no identification with others. He had yet to accept her, yet to accept Beverly.

Why did the expectant child within her think that now was different from the past?

True to his word, Morris awoke and escorted Beth while she selected new living-room, dining-room, and bedroom furniture, all to be paid for on time and all to be delivered when they moved into base quarters. Were the purchases a generous end to a dream? Or were they a bribe to enlist future allegiance?

Later in the week the Archers became a two-car household after Morris bought a black 1959 Thunderbird. Were his splurges self-indulgence or another form of self-destruction?

CHAPTER 36

THE EVENING WAS a play in which Beth had acted before. For this performance the cast was on the Robertsons' stage.

Morris played Bartender who kept glasses filled, seldom allowed them to fall below the halfway mark.

Robby was Chef who, with florid concentration, tended the backyard grill, repeatedly added coals and shouted, "How soon? How soon you girls gonna be ready?"

Ellen was Ellen. Beth was Assistant. In the kitchen, the two women prepared twice-baked potatoes, biscuits, and salad, worked at a pace dictated by Ellen's indifference.

"Em Charles is a loon," Ellen said. Morris again had repeated the story about Emily's announcement of his death.

Beth didn't care to argue but, to her, Emily was a different person from the woman Morris and Ellen thought they knew. In the course of luncheon planning sessions, Beth had come to regard Emily as a friend.

"Rob says her husband's a pain."

"I don't know him very well," said Beth. "Morris doesn't like him."

"But I'll bet he likes Morris. I won't lie to you—" Ellen smacked her lips— "I wish Rob had a spot."

Beth leaned against a cabinet. "I'm so tired of hearing about spots . . ."

Struggling for airspeed shortly after takeoff, a B47 vacuumed toward them from the south, filled the house with turbine roar, rattled windows, then dopplered away to the north.

"When they were falling out of the sky, every day I expected one to land here," Ellen said. "Rob would go fly and I'd tell him not to drop in for lunch."

The Robertsons' home was a two-story frame house in Tye, a mile from the north end of the Dyess runway.

"When you've been at the base hospital," Beth said, "have you ever met a doctor named Jim Leonard?"

"Tall, lean, kinky hair, wears glasses?"

"He has hair like mine."

"Yeah, I know. Is he a Jew?"

Beth took offense. "Do I look like a Jew?"

Ellen shrugged. "He talked to the wives, came on like a wise-ass, then had to back off." She threw a handful of flour into dough that was sticky. "I thought he was sexy." She threw in another handful of flour, kneaded halfheartedly. "This look okay?"

"Spread some flour before you roll it, it'll be all right."

"Hey, I don't roll biscuits. I drop 'em. They taste the same." She added a sprinkle of flour. "So what about this doctor? You hot for him?"

Beth laughed self-consciously. Had she given herself away that easily? At navigation school she had considered the northern wives to be boldly outspoken; Ellen topped them all. "One time when I wasn't feeling very well, he gave me some medicine that helped a lot."

"Tranquilizers?"

Beth flinched. "I don't use them anymore."

"Or any less, huh? Everybody takes them."

"Do you?"

Ellen looked down her nose. "I told Rob, when I have to

210

be put to sleep to cope, then it's time to stuff SAC—and the air force."

While porterhouse steaks were grilling, Robby entertained Morris. "Last week when we went to Marietta to pick up a plane, I picked up a Georgia peach."

Marietta, Georgia, was the home of the Lockheed plant that modified the B47 Stratojet. Boeing designed and developed the bomber but, because the purchase contract called for 1600 airplanes—at three million dollars a copy—in order to meet deadlines the Lockheed and Douglas corporations were called upon for simultaneous production. Very, very big business.

(In a strange manipulation of resources, the B47 phaseout program incredibly began in 1957, the same year the final B47 rolled off the production line. Then every week for the next eight years four B47s would be reduced to scrap until by 1965 the Stratojet would be a memory.)

"A redhead," Robby said, "ripe for picking. Met her in a bar. Said she was a housewife doing a little light hooking for kicks. She offered to blow me for ten bucks. So, in the middle of the afternoon, we tiptoed up to my hotel room. First, I got her to strip. She had big bazongas, liked to bounce them, show them off. She rubbed them all over me before she gobbled my knob, swallowed me all the way to the hairline.

"In about a minute and a half I was ready to go off, so I told her, 'I changed my mind. I want to put it in.' She says, 'Why the hell not.' While she's getting out of her panties, I turn and fire a load in the other direction, then turn right back and plug in, pound her until I get off again." Robby laughed. "How 'bout that? Two for one. But that's not all."

He stared intently at the cooking meat. He never turned a steak more than twice. "Perfect," Robby said and rapidly flipped the steaks with tongs. "Never stab a steak," he told Archer, "until you sit down to eat it."

He checked the time on his wristwatch.

"Back to the redhead," Robby said. "She tells me I look like a real stud and maybe, for another ten, I'd like to offload in her mouth. I said, 'Why the hell not.'" Robby leered. "But, I told her, she had to make me come or I wouldn't

211

pay. She went down and went to town." Robby puffed his cheeks, exhaled slowly, relished the memory.

"She worked me over from head to tail." He grinned. "Finally, after about twenty minutes, she looks up and says, 'The hell with you. You got a dry ball or something.' I told her, 'I'm just trying to save some for when I get married.' "He laughed loudly. "You should have been there, Mo."

Morris nodded, smiled, wondered what kind of sex Robby got from Ellen. Just before Robby took the steaks off the grill, Morris asked, "What do you know about Charles's wife, Emily?"

For a moment Robby's eyes glowed as hotly as the coals. Then with a stone-cold blank look he said, "Are you interested in *her?*"

"No. She's—that would be—"

"She's bad news, that's what she is," Robby said and turned his attention to piling steaks on a platter.

As Beth had expected, her steak was undercooked. She ate the edges then watched Robby and Morris share what she pushed aside.

The actors moved to Robby's den for the play's finale. Morris set the stage: On a coffee table he composed a still life of two bottles of Cutty Sark, water pitcher, and ice bucket.

Still playing Bartender, Morris poured a scotch and water for Ellen. Beth passed. Morris was making the drinks stronger, his habit as evening progressed. A fraction of an inch remained in one bottle and Morris tipped the bottle to his lips, drained it. "Dead soldier," he said and handed the empty to Robby who read the label while Morris opened the full bottle. He poured two half glasses of scotch, dropped an ice cube in each.

Beth was tired of the same dull plot. The play was an excuse for getting drunk. Now they would settle into man talk, drink more, repeat stories she'd heard, flying stories that made them appear champions. All the while the baby-sitting bill would grow and grow.

Tomorrow Morris would sweat in bed until the poison vented from his pores, was exhausted by his body. Their bedroom would stink like a distillery, reek of dissipation.

She was tired of the pointless, selfish routine. *My god, Jim Leonard didn't even drink beer.*

Robby sank into his recliner and cast an innocent lure. "I tell you about the time I went to Taiwan on R and R?" Robby had visited the island while the wing was deployed to Guam.

Morris hadn't taken R and R. He'd saved his money to buy pearls for Beth. She was wearing the earrings. They glowed like tiny satellites in abandoned orbit around her feral face.

Robby pressed ahead. "One morning, around four o'clock, I found myself in this hotel restaurant with—well, I won't mention any names in order to protect the guilty." Robby grinned. "But we all know him." Morris grinned. "Let's call him 'a friend.'"

Robby explained that the only other customer in the place had been a heavyset, richly dressed Chinaman who was seated a couple of tables away. Robby and his friend had known the Chinaman was monitoring their conversation, but Robby's friend hadn't cared, was on stage recalling sexual exploits from before: "One cute little thing offered to blow me—two hundred dollars for an hour, she said—and she promised not to take it out of her mouth the whole time."

The story caught Beth's attention. Ellen looked sleepy, or bored. She'd probably heard the story before, Morris thought.

Robby continued: "My friend said he told her, 'For two hundred an hour, *I'd* do that.'"

Robby said they had been in the middle of a chuckle when the Chinaman had walked over, made a little bow, and said, "Excuse me, please. I overheard your offer. Perhaps we can work out an arrangement?"

Robby and Morris laughed. Ellen smiled. Beth asked, "Did your friend do it?"

"Would you, if a Chinese woman made the offer?" Robby laughed. "Two hundred an hour." And he laughed again.

Beth shook her head.

"What if she offered a million dollars?"

"He's setting you up," Morris said.

Beth dismissed Morris with an untamed look that he had never seen, a look that said, "I can take care of myself."

Morris said, "I was only trying to——"

Beth smothered his words with her own: "If I agree, I'm committed. From there all we do is haggle over price."

Robby stared at Beth, let intimidating eyes creep down her body until she crossed her legs and started a foot bouncing. Then he said to Ellen, "How 'bout you, babe?"

"Whatever you want," Ellen answered. Who could take Rob seriously? she thought.

Morris laughed loudly. "You'd go down on a Chinese woman?"

"Twenty minutes later you'd be hungry again," Robby said. The men laughed.

Ellen smiled. Blond hair veiled her face. Stretched lazily across the couch, she looked tumbled. Morris remembered Beth stretching on the couch, opening herself to him. He pictured Ellen doing the same and felt an erection commence.

Ellen whispered, "For a million dollars . . . what wouldn't I do?"

Robby asked her, "Go down on Beth?"

For a second Ellen froze, briefest arctic pause, then melted, smiled, stroked hair from face and winked at Beth. Beth's bouncing foot shifted into high gear.

What the hell was going on? Morris wondered. Suddenly they were into territory he'd never navigated. Forbidden land?

"How about Mo?" Robby said to his wife.

Morris Archer's heart missed a beat. He felt as if Robby was speaking from within his mind, could see fantasies of countless encounters, night shades of sex. In the next instant he was tossed in time, felt like a ninth-grader playing Post Office, a man-child who couldn't bear to hear the next number called. Would he be chosen?

"For a million dollars?" Ellen said. "Blow Mo?" Her eyes held a sleepy promise, bedroom eyes that made her twice as desirable. She focused those bedroom eyes on Morris Archer.

"Two million?" Archer bid.

"Why not nothing?" Ellen said. "Give Mo a slow blow—for nothing."

Morris's heart flew away. He read desire in her look, in her words.

214

Beth's foot stopped.

"Drunk," Robby said.

"If I did," Ellen asked, "would anybody find out about it, besides Mo and me?"

Robby snorted. "That make a difference?"

Ellen nodded.

At the same moment Beth said, "No. It's absolute. Living with yourself is what counts."

"Ahhhhh," said Robby, "so there're things you wouldn't do regardless of the payoff, even if you knew you wouldn't get caught."

"That's right," Beth said. She looked to Morris for support. "Right?" Was she asking him to appreciate her refusal of Jim Leonard?

"If you say so," he told her, his reverie broken. Could she see that his mind and heart had been inside Ellen?

Robby perched on the edge of his seat. His eyes widened. In front of his chest, the fingers of one hand spread and curled as if supporting a heavy crystal ball. "Beth," he said, "assuming you'd never be convicted—never even suspected —for a hundred million dollars, tax free—in gold, if you want—would you kill Morris?"

"No," Beth said instantly.

Robby continued as if she hadn't spoken. "Killing him wouldn't have to be a violent act. It could be something as simple as pressing a button—and he dies painlessly."

"I told you, no," Beth said. "The idea is stupid."

"It's just a game," Robby said and sat back. "How about you, sugar booger," Robby said to Ellen, "would you throw the switch on me?"

Ellen smiled. "For a hundred million?" Her smile widened. "It wouldn't have to be impersonal, or painless."

Robby roared out a deep-chested, apeman laugh. He said, "El knows: Money is god."

"Love is," Beth said softly.

"Money buys food and drink and sex," said Robby.

"And weapons," Morris added.

"Amen. And weapons," Robby repeated, "for SAC, to fuck the Russians."

"Amen," from Morris.

"Add 'em up, that's happiness," said Robby.

"Drunk," Ellen said.

Robby moved out of his chair with predator speed, crossed the room in two strides, caught Ellen's head in one paw, and pulled her face to his. He could break her neck with one hand, Beth thought. He looked into Ellen's eyes, said, "Drunk," then kissed her mouth. She hung in his grasp until he gently placed her head on the couch.

He stepped to the center of the room and raised his hands overhead. Beth expected him to pound his chest, waited to hear a tomtom echo. Instead, he dropped his hands to his thighs, slapped them with gunshot cracks. He turned to Morris: "Would you, Mo? Same conditions I offered Beth. Be honest."

Morris grinned: "Would I kill me?" Two could play Robby's game. "That's what you asked Beth."

"Don't be cute," Robby said. "You know what I mean. Come on, be honest."

"No fear of punishment," Morris said. No accounting to anyone, except himself. No mother. No Charles. No Turner. No SAC. A million—no, a hundred million dollars for one life. One wife. Ridiculous. He was prepared to trade a million lives for nothing, he thought. "Kill my wife for a hundred million," he said, "tax free?" He shook his head: "Never." Then he aimed a finger at Beth, unconscious gesture. He smiled and his mouth said, "But promote me to colonel . . ." Involuntarily he squeezed the trigger.

Beth raised her hands, made shields to deflect his psychic bullet.

"Ka-pow," said Robby. "You're dead, Beth."

Beth felt a piercing impact on her ego. Morris's senseless hate struck her like a single devastating bullet, tore open her heart, drained her last drop of love for Morris Archer. In the hollow eye of his imaginary gun barrel she saw his enormous frailty, saw the blindness of his unfeeling material quest. "You hurt me," she cried and sprang to her feet. "I always knew you never loved me." With speed greater than Robby's, she was out of the room, out of the house, and into the car before Morris reacted.

"She took my Thunderbird," Morris called from the front door.

"Easy come, easy go," said Robby. "Have another drink."

"I'm going to bed," said Ellen. "Don't wake me when you come up."

Robby nodded, gazed distantly until she left the room. Then he asked, "Captain Archer, if Beth stood to gain a hundred million tax-free dollars, would you pull the switch on yourself?"

The curtain fell.

But elsewhere it rose on another stage, another play.

❧CHAPTER 37

WHEN BETH REACHED home, she did not have money to
pay the baby-sitter. "I'll bring it to you tomorrow," she
promised. How much had Morris spent on scotch to take to
the Robertsons? she wondered.

She picked up sleeping Beverly and fled her home, ran to
her only friend, Jim Leonard. She expected Morris and
Robby to chase her, feared for her safety at the hands of two
drunken beasts.

She burst in on Jim Leonard as if he were the cause of her
problems. She whispered accusations she wanted to shout at
Morris: "He doesn't love me. He doesn't love Beverly. He
hates everybody and everything except himself."

She put Beverly in the bedroom, returned to the living
room, paced. "You should see Morris around Robby. He
puts on a swagger, puffs up his chest. . . ." She pictured
Morris aping Robby's gargantuan build, inflating his body
to emulate Robby's bulk. As if size made the man, she
thought. "They look like Laurel and Hardy," she said.

Jim caught her wrist and she dropped into the contour of the couch, beside him. Her downturned face and upturned hands looked waxen, gave her the unposed posture of a discarded mannequin. Was Jim's task to infuse her with new life?

He wrapped a hand around the back of her vulnerable neck and massaged deeply. Beth sighed, leaned into him. He kissed the top of her head. Beginning with a desire to right an unintentional slight, he had grown to feel responsible for her. Was he destined to be a Dr. Lonelyhearts for unfinished women who had failed elsewhere?

His intellect enjoyed the bittersweet role of protector. The intimacy of sharing another life's problems made his life more meaningful. But wasn't that what being a doctor was all about? Helping those who could not help themselves. Sharing pain. Finding hope for the hopeless. Fulfilling those duties had always been his family's destiny. Did he actually have a choice when it came to helping others?

"What am I going to do?" Beth said. Since the Bomb Comp celebration at the Sykes ranch, she had been pursued by the recurring nightmare of the son in her body. From behind his livid birthmask, sightless eyes glowed greenly at her. She had recognized that the child's face was a mutant reproduction of Morris's mask of superiority, mask of hate.

Were her dreams an omen? A horrible possibility had overwhelmed her: Had Morris somehow been dosed with radiation from the nuclear bombs on Alert? As a result, was she carrying a transmogrified child?

How could she bring an alien into the world? Wasn't the mutation a brand of Morris's passion for destruction? She would never love such a creature, would wish it dead one day at a time. Better to kill it outright now. "I don't want my baby," she said.

For the briefest instant Jim Leonard thought Beth was talking about Beverly. Then he understood his role in the drama.

He continued to massage her neck. She was punishing the child, condemning the child for the sins of the father, he thought. Or was she punishing the father? "How does Morris feel?" he asked.

"He doesn't know I'm pregnant."

"Would you want to do this if it was Beverly?"

219

"No. With Beverly—I was innocent then."

Did she mean that Morris's association with the bomb had tainted her with his guilt?

Jim felt her tense beneath his grasp. "I don't want another Morris Archer on earth," she said vehemently.

"Are you so positive it's a son?"

"Yes," she said. She could feel the monster clawing inside her womb.

Jim circled her with his arm. "What you ask, I don't know if I can do it."

She looked up at him, closed her eyes, and kissed him firmly on the lips. "I trust you," she said softly, "no matter what you do."

Was she offering herself in payment? Did she think he would take advantage of her in that way, at this time? Did she think he could be manipulated so easily? He was disappointed with her.

"That's not what I meant," he said harshly. "I can *do* the procedure. The procedure's no problem." A dilation and curettage, D and C, he thought. He'd done it before, twice, while an intern, for desperate unwed nurses. But Beth was married. Was the decision truly only hers?

"But the procedure's illegal," he said. She knew that or she would not be depending on him, he thought. He could avoid the problem by recommending a doctor in Washington who, for four hundred dollars, would manufacture an excuse for performing the procedure legally. But what good was that? Beth never could design an excuse that would satisfy Morris for a trip of that distance or an expense of that amount. Beth was as cornered as the two nurses he had helped.

In his memory those nurses now appeared as hardened women, sexual veterans, totally unlike Beth, who was a sensitive girl. Would he someday recall her differently? Would his guilt destroy her innocence?

He remembered a discussion with his father on the night before he graduated from high school. He'd told his father that Anne was pregnant. Had he been fishing for the same conclusion Beth was seeking? His father had said, "The solution belongs to the person who has the problem." Which made the decision his, Jim had thought at the time. Of course, Anne had wanted to get married.

How his sense of honor had changed! Or had his compassion been broadened by additional options?

"There are consequences," he said to Beth, "problems you might have a hard time coping with afterward. Not medical problems. Mental problems." *Regret could never bring back a child*, he thought.

She responded by burrowing her face into his shoulder. *Was she trying to escape his words?*

"No solution is without pain," he said. *Was he talking to her or to himself?*

"You don't want to help me, do you?" Beth said.

"That's not true. Basically I'm an instrument." *Would his father agree on that?* "But if you suffer, I don't want to be the cause."

"I hate Morris," Beth said. "I don't want to have his son."

Jim hugged her gently. "Maybe you shouldn't make up your mind when you're so emotionally involved," he suggested.

His advice was as substanceless as the air he expelled to speak it. For as long as Beth lived, the thought of Morris Archer would provoke an emotional response within her.

❧CHAPTER 38

Morris and Robby passed out in the den. Before that, Morris had wanted to chase after Beth; Robby had told him, "She expects that. Be cool. Show her you can get along without her." Robby had suspected that Beth would not go straight home and he hadn't felt like driving all over town searching for her.

Before sunrise, Ellen woke them. She ran into the den wearing a sheer baby-doll nightie and blowing a police whistle. Morris clapped his palms over his ears, shouted, "What the fuck?"

Through tossed blond hair, Ellen made a long face and looked down her nose at the bulge of Morris's morning erection. She gave him another scream from the whistle and a fast look at her naked breasts beneath the transparent nightie. Her breasts bounced. Did she like to show them off, rub them all over? Morris wondered.

She ran from the room, shouted, "Eat a big lunch."

"What's wrong with her?" Morris said.

"You should hear it when she hammers on a frying pan," said Robby.

Robby was going on Alert for a week. He changed into a flying suit, grabbed a suitcase, and was ready. On his way to the base, he detoured to take Morris home.

Morris's Thunderbird was in the dead-end driveway alongside the duplex. There was no garage, no carport. The back door of the house was unlocked. Morris walked through empty kitchen and living room, looked into empty bathroom. No Beth. In the bedroom, the bed was made. A green rage swept over him. *Hadn't she slept there? Where was she?* He slammed open the door to Beverly's room.

Seated in a straight-back kitchen chair, Beth was holding Beverly. The door's banging against the wall frightened the child and she began to cry.

The cry was a siren wail that pierced Morris's head. Whistle. Siren. Tone. Klaxon. Insane noises ruled his life, commanded that he respond instantly, regardless of what he wanted. "Shut her up," he shouted. He hated the baby. He hated its mother. "I'm going to work," he shouted and pulled the door closed with another bang. His life wasn't his own, he told himself.

He was an hour late and Chuck Charles wanted a reason. Archer said, "What difference does it make?" They weren't scheduled for Alert, or flying, or mission planning, or class. It was a dead day: check in, go home.

Dead unless you were Chuckie Eager Beaver, squadron training officer, Morris thought. Charles was seated behind his gray desk in his puke-green cubbyhole, reviewing stacks of diarrhea-brown training folders, appropriate eyewash for inspectors who visited once a year and looked everywhere.

"Major Smolik expects you up at wing to replot celestial," Charles said and triggered a chain reaction. Inside Morris's chest a fireball erupted, expanded in a rush, threatened to burst his skin. His body swelled until the fireball surged upward, filled his head, created overpressures inside his skull. Nausea took him. Dizziness followed. Then fatigue. "Why me?" he said. Why couldn't life be simple? All he desired was to ejaculate and to sleep.

Charles said, "You're not scheduled for anything. Major Smolik called down for help. I volunteered you."

"Maybe I'd like a day off," Morris said. Instead he was

being exiled, being sent to Siberia, sent to the salt mines. His central nervous system was a network of short circuits, sparking synapses misdirecting flashing green impulses. He felt too sick to argue.

In agony, he went to wing headquarters, and alone behind another dead gray desk in another puke-green cubbyhole, he spent the morning eyeballing more than calculating. He wasn't in the mood to perform his usual surgical butchery on another man's work, to slice open a mission and expose every minute error so that in the end pages of computations ran blood red from the scalpel lead of his superior grading pencil.

Instead, he generously penciled faint red check marks alongside numbers in long rows on celestial computation forms, lightly traced over plotted lines on maps rather than measured their accuracy. He catnapped when the need struck him. And he daydreamed of blond Ellen, alone at home, in her nightie.

At noon, when Major Smolik left for lunch at the club, Morris phoned Ellen. "Hi. This is Morris."

"Morris who?" she said.

He waited. "Archer," he finally told her.

Comedienne patter: "Archer? Archer! Smooth-face character with a beard. A naviguesser. Ace bum-badier."

He didn't like her humor. He considered hanging up. It was all wrong. "Did I leave my watch there?" he asked.

"No," she said.

There was a long pause.

"What're you doing?" he said.

Bored voice: "Talking to you. Almost."

He heard her breathing. He pictured her fondling her breasts. "Want to have a drink?"

"Nope."

Suddenly he was nervous. Was it from frustration or uncertainty? Husky, trembling voice: "Can I come over?"

"Why not?"

"See you in twenty minutes."

"If I'm here." She hung up.

It was wrong, all wrong. Where had he found the nerve to call?

He didn't pause to put away the mission spread in front of him. In the car he knew he rightfully should be homing on

224

Beth. His mind swirled with thoughts about Beth, about Robby, about consequences. Last night Ellen had asked about anybody finding out. *Give Mo a slow blow.* Whatever happened, he'd keep it secret. And if nothing happened, he still wanted it kept secret, saw no need for Beth or Robby to know. There was too much chance for misunderstanding.

He parked behind the Robertson house, out of sight of the road. He stepped from the car and his stomach rumbled. Hunger? Nerves? The deep-seated fatigue of a waning hangover and the edgy craving for sexual release made him weak and strong at the same time.

He tried the back door, found it locked. He circled the house, glanced in windows that blankly stared back. Was the house watching him? Was Ellen inside? He rang the doorbell before seeing that the front door was open an inch. He waited half a minute then pushed the door wide and called, "Ellen?"

There was no response. He stepped inside and carefully closed the door. He moved noiselessly from living room to dining room to kitchen, felt like a burglar who had chosen the wrong house. In a disappointing way that he did not fully understand until years later after he had played and replayed the day in his memory, he saw nothing of value in the rooms; he had been inside a typical lieutenant's rented house. Why did men accept such vast responsibility and allow their families to be so poorly rewarded?

In the den, empty bottles and half-filled glasses remained from the previous night. But no Ellen. Was she upstairs? In bed? Waiting?

Squeaking boards violated the midday lull, announced his progress as he climbed the stairs. His breathing and pulse accelerated as if he were ascending into rarefied air, entering another atmosphere, the environment of another planet, or perhaps another sun.

A strange doubling of reality took place, as if his actions were occurring within a mirror fantasy. It was his mirror-fantasy self who climbed the stairs, who sought Ellen. Had fantasy become reality; reality, fantasy? He felt no responsibility for his mirror apparition, a conscienceless other self.

Ellen was not in the first room Morris came to at the top of the stairs. Within the room, sewing machine, patterns, and material covered a makeshift table assembled from plywood and shipping crates. Dozens of cardboard boxes stood in stacks against one wall. The transient-looking room was a natural part of every military household. Did any service family ever completely unpack?

Morris found Ellen in the second bedroom.

Covered by a sky-blue satin sheet, she was propped by pillows. Her bare freckled arms rested outside the sheet, formed a white cross in front of her. Backlit by a pale late-autumn sun, her blond hair was a shimmering golden crown. Aurora!

She was wearing a black sleep mask with startled oversize white eyes painted on it.

Was her pose a joke or was she the sleeping princess of Morris's fantasies?

He stepped into the room, found the atmosphere there even rarer: His breath momentarily escaped him. He moved silently, weightlessly to her side, gently kissed her lips. Awakening kiss?

She blindly returned his gentle kiss and made him bolder. He ran his tongue along her lips. An instant later her tongue traced the outline of his mouth. His tongue found hers, hers his. The delight of their contact made him dizzy. How could such a sharp tongue be so soft?

He caressed her folded arms; they unfolded and her hands caressed his arms. He burrowed a hand beneath the satin sheet, cupped each perfect, silken breast in turn. When she worked a hand beneath his shirt and did the same, he suddenly understood the rules of the dreamy game.

Or was she mocking him? Was he realizing his fantasy with a puppet?

Whichever the case, it did not matter to Morris. "I've dreamed about you," he said. He had loved her from half a world away. "I've—" She pressed a hand across his mouth, shook her head. *Silence? Another rule of the game?* He wanted to object but by then his hand had traveled farther down her body, and in a like manner she was gripping his erection.

He undressed. Then he turned back the satin sheet, rolled back the blue sky and was dazzled by a newfound sun. As helpless as a nameless cosmonaut falling silently through space, he gravitated headlong into her radiant nether blondness. An instant later her sightless mouth found him. He would never get his fill of her, he thought.

Later, face to face, he moved to enter her and she pulled away, broke silence: "Not there, you can't come in me there." Then she shifted slightly, offered him a place he never had dared to enter. He touched the new opening with exploratory fingers and she nodded approval. He thrust slowly, discovered an entry tighter yet more yielding than fantasy. "Go slow at first," she whispered. Penetration into the unknown overloaded his imagination, magnified his vision, made the act more powerful than the performance. In his chest, a bellow swelled and collapsed.

He died inside of her for the first time, for the hundredth time.

For him the game was over. He reached for her mask. She caught his hand in midair, stopped it as surely as if she had been looking at him. He was at a loss for what to do next. Did he need to look into windows of eyes to confirm that this partner was Ellen? "I love you," he said and she again pressed a hand across his mouth.

He touched her hip and she slid away from him, groped for the sheet, and pulled it over her. "Tomorrow," she whispered.

The word was a catalyst to mix the emotions of his heart and mind. *Tomorrow. And the days after* . . . Sexual fantasies stretched across his future memory: Yesterday's dreams became a long row of tomorrows. Robby would be on Alert for a week, he thought, and there were endless weeks of Alert beyond that. "In the morning, before I go to the base?" he said.

Ellen nodded.

He kissed her a dozen times while he dressed, showered a dozen more kisses on her before he left.

In the car, he had an unexpected desire for Beth, grew an erection in seconds. Was his lust another psychic counterweight, a need to balance ownership of his property against his violation of another man's claim? Or was his lust a desire for the secret ego gratification of possessing both women on the same afternoon?

Just as unexpectedly he wondered if Ellen would visit Robby that evening. He pictured them half naked in their car and grew jealous, felt betrayed. At the same time, he understood the scope of what he had done. If *he* felt jealous, how would Robby feel? If Robby—or Beth—ever found out . . . hell would break loose.

Then he tasted Ellen on his lips and threats of hell vanished. His hands exuded an oxygen of sex, memories of her inner warmth. Mentally gripped inside her, he wanted to drive a thousand miles an hour—back to her, for no speed was enough to escape the pull of her gravity. Morning seemed as distant, as unreachable as the moon.

In a moment of clarity, he decided to swing by the base and talk to Charles, set up an excuse for being late in the morning.

After Morris's Thunderbird was out of sight, Ellen telephoned Robby at the Alert bunker: "I'm not coming out tonight. I'm too upset." She took a deep breath. "Morris Archer was here a little while ago."

"And?" Robby listened to her breathing deeply, then loudly asked, "What did he want?"

"What do you think?"

"You tell me."

"He wanted sex," she shouted.

"Was he drunk?"

"I don't think so." There was a long silence. "Maybe that's what saved me. I talked him out of it."

"You sure all you did is talk?"

"Goddamn you . . ."

"What did he try to do?"

"What do you think?"

"I don't know." She heard a barely controlled rage in his voice. "Tell me," he said.

"He tried to make me do, you know, the things you talked about last night."

"Did he hurt you?"

Finally he was concerned about her, Ellen thought. She made him wait, made him ask again: "Did he hurt you?" "A little," she said. "He pushed me around. . . ." Like you do, she thought.

"That son of a bitch, I'll break his neck."

She could depend on predictable Robby, Ellen thought.

228

CHAPTER 39

NEITHER MORRIS NOR Chuck saw the first punch. When it landed, they were standing outside Charles's office and Morris was explaining why he would be late in the morning: "There's something I have to do in town and I'll probably be an hour or—"

Robby's overhand right seemed to fall from the stratosphere, dropped on Morris like a missile warhead, impacted flush on his mouth. Robby threw a second overhand punch that missed Morris's rocking head, glanced off his chest.

Chuck heard the smack of the first punch, saw blood fly from Morris's lips. Then he saw Robby on the attack. Chuck ducked low, went in under Robby's second punch, submarined the larger man, caught him below the knees, and jerked his legs out from under him. Robby landed flat on his back, the air going out of him. Chuck pounced atop him, pinned his arms, doubted that he'd be able to hold him once he regained his breath. Chuck soothingly said, "Take it easy. It's over. You're not hurt."

By then Morris had regained his balance. He wiped his numb chin, looked at his hand, saw blood smeared across his fingers. He tasted his blood in the same moment he saw Robby on the floor, helpless. "Motherfucker," he screamed and, with a reflex of violence, kicked Robby in the neck. He'd meant to kick him in the head but had been too eager.

Chuck came off the floor, drove a shoulder into Morris's stomach, and half-carried him into his office, and dumped him into a chair, and said, "Stay here." Then he stepped back into the hall and pulled the door shut behind him.

Robby was rising off one knee, had the three-point stance of a football lineman about to charge. Chuck pointed a finger, ordered, "Hold it, Robby. I have no quarrel with you." Robby sank back to one knee; he had no quarrel with Charles.

Behind Chuck, Morris opened the door. Chuck turned, took two quick steps, placed firm hands on Morris's shoulder and waist, then walked him, practically danced him back into the office before he kicked his legs out from under him. Morris sat down hard on the floor. "Now stay in here," Chuck said and returned to the hall, again slammed the door.

By then, other men had arrived, stood watching, muttering speculations. "Robby, go to the lounge, wait there," Chuck said, "please." Robby said, "This isn't over." He walked away, rubbing his neck.

Chuck opened the door to his office. Training folders were scattered on the floor. Morris was sitting on the desk, holding a handkerchief to his mouth. "Let me see," Chuck said.

The L-shape cut looked as if Robby's punch had compressed the lower lip against the canine tooth. "It looks like a hole all the way through," Chuck said. "It'll probably need stitches. Any teeth loose?"

Morris worked his tongue inside his mouth, then shook his head.

"Major Charles," the squadron adjutant reported from the doorway, "Robby's gone to see Colonel Turner."

Chuck said. "In case anyone's looking for us, we'll be at the hospital emergency room."

On the way to the hospital Chuck asked, "What's this all about?"

"I don't know," Morris said. He could find no connection. Hardly an hour had passed since he'd left Ellen.

In the emergency room, a corpsman cleaned the lip, said, "That should be sutured, sir. I'd say three stitches."

"Then stitch it," Morris told him.

The corpsman made notes on a form, asked, "What was the cause of injury, sir?"

"An unprovoked attack by Lieutenant Robertson," Morris said.

The corpsman kept a straight face, handed Morris an ice pack. "Let me get Dr. Leonard. He has the duty today. He should be here in a few minutes, sir."

The ice pack was comforting. His lip must be the size of an inner tube, Morris thought. He studied his reflection in the glass door of a cabinet. The rictus of a smile clenched his teeth. What would Ellen say? And Beth? The smile faded. Why had Robby gone to see Turner? Morris could not believe that Robby had so quickly found out about his time with Ellen. The attack had to be related to something else. But what?

After ten minutes, Morris threw the ice pack in a corner, started out the door of the treatment room, and bumped into Jim Leonard. "Excuse me," Jim said.

"You mean for taking so long to get here?"

"I was with another patient," Jim said. He glanced at Morris's lip, then at his name tag and insignia of rank, then back at his lip. He did not dare to smile. "Let's take a look at that," he said.

"I've already seen it."

In ten seconds Morris Archer had lived up to his advance billings, Jim thought. He sat Morris on a low stool, studied his face as much as his lip. Morris's eyes looked everywhere but at him, Jim thought, and recognized an indiscriminate anger. "Three stitches should do it," Jim said.

"The corpsman already figured that out."

"Would you prefer to go somewhere else?" Jim calmly said.

"Where? Downtown? Why should I go there when you're getting paid to take care of me here?"

Did he ever let up? Jim wondered.

Morris said, "I have this theory. Doctors think the air force built a runway and put airplanes here because it was close to the hospital."

Jim ignored him.

"What do you think?" Morris said.

The corpsman entered the room and Jim briefed him, then said to Morris, "This might be painful. Would you like a shot of xylocaine? It works like Novocain."

"I'd rather have a shot of scotch."

The corpsman grinned.

"Xylocaine," Jim said, "yes or no."

"Suit yourself."

Jim paused for barely a moment. "Then it's no."

Training overcame desire: Jim sutured the lip as gently as possible. However, on the second stitch, beads of sweat popped forward along Morris's brow, stood out like rows of rivets. His hands squeezed into fists, their knuckles white. His eyes locked on Jim Leonard's eyes. But Morris did not flinch, remained stoically silent.

And now it was Jim who avoided Morris's eyes, green eyes of fire. Was he calculating vengeance? Jim wondered. "Sure you don't want a shot?"

"For only one more!"

Later, Morris would tell Charles, "That doctor didn't even use Novocain." Would he be complaining or bragging?

Now, Jim Leonard trimmed the final black silk stitch. "That's it. Come back in a week, we'll take them out."

"I can take them out," Morris said.

"Suit yourself."

"Just snip and pull," Morris told the corpsman. "Anybody can do it."

The corpsman grinned again.

"Thanks a lot," Morris said to nobody in particular. "I hope I didn't take too much of your time."

After Morris was gone the corpsman said, "You really took it easy on him but it still had to hurt like hell."

When he saw Morris, Chuck Charles said, "You look like you have a swarm of flies on your lip." During the walk to the car, he said, "Colonel Turner's secretary phoned. He

232

wants you in his office tomorrow morning at oh-eight-hundred sharp."

"Did she say what for?"

"No, just that you better be on time."

Archer said, "Maybe he wants to give me another spot." He was surprised when Chuck laughed and patted him on the back.

❧CHAPTER 40

Was Ellen Robertson's game an adult version of the childish pastime of poking a stick into an anthill? Didn't the resulting confusion quickly grow out of proportion to the energy expended? Was that the game's pleasure, so much for so little?

Not yet out of her teens, Ellen would have had difficulty explaining the compulsion to play the scurrying game with Morris Archer and Robby. All she knew was that the results gave a sensation of power, as if she grasped controls that steered other people through life. She'd definitely run Morris Archer off a high cliff, she thought, and she'd manipulated Robby as easily as leading a little boy around by his little dick.

Later, she wondered if she had led him or he had led her. She knew he was tired of her, had been tired of her since pilot training. Their marriage license was the chain that made it difficult for him to lose her, she thought. A new idea struck her: Had Robby enticed Morris to her so he could divorce her for being unfaithful?

It wouldn't be the first time she had been thrown away. When her parents signed for her to marry Robby, even that hadn't been a first. . . .

On her tenth birthday, her father called her outside and threw a rusted bicycle at her feet, one that looked like it had come from the city dump, told her, "Don't ask for anything from me ever again." That year her two older brothers had received new red two-wheelers for their birthdays. "Beginning today, you're on your own," her father said. It was one of the few times he spoke directly to her.

That evening Ellen's mother led her into the big bedroom, unlocked a dresser drawer, withdrew a blue revolver. (Ellen still dreamed about the copper snake eyes of the bullets in the cylinder.) She pointed the loaded gun at Ellen's face, jabbed it toward her as if shooting her. "This is your father's," Mother said, "and one of these days he's going to kill you with it. He hates your guts because you're not his child."

"Whose child am I?" Ellen wondered aloud.

Her mother answered by again jabbing the gun toward Ellen's face and then poking the gun's steel barrel into her belly.

That same evening Ellen's mother moved her into the half-finished attic above the garage. "Maybe he'll forget about you if you're out here, out of his sight," Mother said. Living outside the house gave Ellen freedom to come and go as she pleased.

Docile at home, Ellen at school was a tomboy, was the one usually sent to the principal's office for failing to do homework, or for talking back or, twice, for fighting. Once she scratched a girl's face after the girl sat in Ellen's chair and refused to move. The other time, Ellen punched a boy, bloodied his nose for calling her son of a bitch. That time the principal lectured her and the boy, explained the insult within the term: "A bitch is a female dog. When you call a person a son of a bitch you are calling his mother a dog. That is a terrible, terrible insult." Ellen was confused. She thought the name had insulted her: "I'm not a son," said

235

Ellen. "That's true," the principal said, "you're a daughter; therefore, the name doesn't apply to you." Was she a victim of ignorance?

A few months after moving to the garage attic, Ellen began breaking into churches late at night. She liked Catholic churches best, pretended they were castles; she draped herself in priestly garments and became the ruling queen. Randomly she carried on her escapades for nearly a year until a policeman caught her in the act. Ellen's mother disavowed her. Juvenile court authorities sentenced Ellen to a year in a school for wayward girls.

When she returned home, she was only twelve but she had the developed body of a young woman. Her father (but he really wasn't her father, she knew) studied her and then moved her into the house, gave her an upstairs bedroom. The first night he came to her, she expected him to kill her. She was prepared to do anything to save her life. To her, the little he asked and the enormous pleasure he derived from it seemed out of proportion. Yet her reward seemed out of proportion too: He told her, "I love you." He taught her ways to please him so that she didn't have to fear becoming pregnant. He pledged his love daily. After a month she tested him by asking for a new bicycle. Two days later he gave her a heavily chromed three-speed that he uncrated himself.

What started as begrudging respect from her mother developed into friendship. Ellen's mother helped her to look attractive, encouraged her to date boys her own age, to go to dances, to have a life outside the home. That was how Ellen eventually met Robby. Until he came along she had dated only timid little boys who were as afraid of her as she was of them.

When Ellen announced that Robby had asked to marry her, Mother gave delighted approval; Father flatly refused permission. Ellen accepted his decision. Mother didn't. Mother said, "She's marrying him and getting out of this house. Otherwise, I'm calling the police." She leered at her husband. "You're going to jail." She turned on Ellen. "And you, whore . . ." She released her pent-up fury in a flurry of punches to Ellen's breasts. "You're going back to reform school where you belong."

Ellen looked to her father (but wasn't he more than a

236

father?) for help. Without returning her look, he said, "Do whatever you want." Why was he abandoning her without a fight? Ellen wondered. What had become of his love? Was the whole world false? Then Ellen saw that only one question mattered: How could she avoid going back to reform school?

"I'll marry Robby," she said.

After they were married, Ellen had an urge to tell Robby about her relationship with her father. Leading up to it, she said, "My father liked to look at me when I was naked."

Robby's face took on a scarlet mask of rage. He hit her with questions faster than she could answer: Where was your mother then? Did he watch while you undressed? Did he make you dance in front of him? Is that all he did, just look? Did he touch? Did he ever try anything?

Confused at first, she made her father's attention appear innocent. "No, nothing like that," she said. "He'd just accidentally walk in when I was taking a bath or changing for bed. . . ." Why was she defending the man who had abandoned her? ". . . and he'd stop and stare for a minute."

"A minute's a long time," Robby said.

"I think he was surprised by how fast I grew up."

Ellen got the idea that the descriptions of her standing naked before her staring father both angered and excited Robby. For weeks he pestered her for details: When was the first time her father saw her naked? What was she doing at the time? How was she posed? What did he see? As a result, Ellen learned that Robby's jealousy was a tremendous weapon to be used against him. Playing with it was a perfect means of gaining his concentrated attention.

But now with Morris Archer, had the weapon backfired?

CHAPTER 41

AFTER THE CHILDREN had cleared the supper dishes, Jean Turner carried her coffee cup and saucer to her husband's end of the dining-room table and pulled up a chair beside him. Axel smiled, pleased by the manner in which she sensed that he needed her opinion. Most often, after the children departed, they sat at opposite ends of the table and made jokes. Now she came to him. He supposed that on the days that he needed support he was obviously contemplative during the meal. It was reassuring that she still noticed his signals after years. "There was a fight this afternoon in one of the squadrons," he said, "between Archer and Robertson."

"Aren't lieutenants supposed to fight occasionally?" she asked. Then she remembered Archer now was a captain: Who hit whom first?

"Lieutenants can get away with fighting only over point-less things," Axel said.

She knew the answer before she asked, "Was it over somebody's wife?"

Axel sipped his coffee, said, "Ellen Robertson."

"I'm surprised it took this long," Jean said. Axel gave her time to elaborate. "She's too restless, too beautiful for her own good." Was Ellen a victim of envy?

Axel said. "If I recall, Beth Archer is no slouch."

"They're silver and gold," Jean said. Did she mean that Beth shone like silver but that Ellen glittered like gold? Or did she mean that men reacted to the differences in their beauty like men reacted to the two precious metals: Silver produced desire, gold brought insatiable lust?

Axel said, "Ellen claims Archer tried to rape her."

"Oh, dear," Jean said.

"This afternoon while Robby was on Alert."

"Where? Where did it take place?"

"At Robertson's home." Axel related the scant facts that Robby had passed on to him from Ellen's telephone call.

"It stinks," Jean said. "Have you talked to Archer?"

"First thing in the morning. I wanted time to think."

"The Robertsons live in Tye. Should the accusation be a civilian matter?"

"That's one course. . . ."

"Did Ellen call the sheriff?"

Axel shook his head. He finished his coffee while he thought about Archer's confession at Bomb Comp, about how he'd told a factual story even though it had made him look bad. "Archer's no liar," Axel said.

Jean lifted her cup, offered it to Axel. He waved it aside. "How's Robby taking this?" she asked.

"He cold-cocked Archer, sent him to the hospital for stitches. He calmed down after talking to me. I offered to replace him on Alert but he insisted it was his duty."

Ellen's call sounded like a cry for attention. As much as she was devoted to the air force and as often as she had placed duty ahead of family, nevertheless Jean recognized moments when the individual came first. "You should have ordered him to go home," she said. "Ellen should have him beside her, at least tonight."

"Well, it's too late now," Axel said harshly, hating to be second-guessed.

"You brought up the subject, dear," Jean said and kissed his cheek.

Alone in his room in the Alert bunker, Robby told himself he had done the right thing: Archer had it coming. After all, Archer was supposed to be a friend. Why would a drinking buddy sneak around behind his back? Officers weren't supposed to do that to each other. . . .

He remembered Emily Charles.

What if in the middle of *this* Charles brought up *that*. But that was different, Robby told himself: Emily had been on the prowl. Whereas Archer had gone to his *home*. But hadn't he ended up at Charles's home, in Charles's bed?

Maybe he shouldn't have run to Colonel Turner so quickly. After all, Archer hadn't really *done* anything. Or had he?

Was Ellen going to cooperate now that he'd pushed it? Last time, she'd refused to help either the sheriff or the judge advocate. She didn't want to be "smeared with it," she'd said. "In a case like this," she'd argued, "everyone considers the woman to be guilty."

If only he wasn't on Alert . . .

He should have taken Turner's offer and been replaced. He'd phoned Ellen twice. The first time he'd told her what had happened with Archer and Turner. She'd said nothing. The second time she'd complained of cramps, had hung up after no more than a minute. Now he got busy signals and knew the receiver was off the hook. Was she really sick or was she playing games?

If only he wasn't on Alert . . .

Why did he put up with SAC? He could resign his commission, get an airline job tomorrow, work a third as hard and earn three times as much money. He'd once heard a senior airline pilot brag: "It ain't only the bucks. With all the horny stews walking around, this job is better than owning a cathouse." He could be living a wild life. Why did he put up with being locked in a cage?

Morris Archer recalled a bogus Chinese proverb: *When rape is inevitable, relax and enjoy it.* Tomorrow morning he would be raped . . . he didn't care . . . but he wouldn't enjoy it. After making love to Beth, he fell into a black

240

dreamless sleep, a sleep as innocently empty as the conscience of a saint. Did lethargy again conquer him?

Ellen must have told on him, he'd decided earlier. There
was no other explanation for Robby's actions. (Rancor
grated at each recall of Robby's attack. Instinctively Morris's tongue licked his wound, probed his torn lip, tasted
revenge; he pictured himself knocking out Robby with a
combination of paralyzing punches, felt the shots recoil in
his tight fists and forearms.) Tomorrow's sequence of events
was ordained: face Turner . . . be punished, perhaps lose his
spot . . . face Beth . . . perhaps lose his wife.

He'd closed his mind to the consequences and plunged
silently into the abyss of night, free-fell aimlessly, made
himself ignore the waiting impact. He dropped like a bomb
that another had aimed. His plunge had the finality of a
man diving from a skyscraper, surrendering past and future,
becoming a toy of gravity. Was his untroubled sleep the
result of indifference or innocence?

Early the following morning, Morris awoke with a desire
for sex. Beth wasn't in the mood. "Let me get you in the
mood," he offered. But then Beth said she heard Beverly
stirring and scampered out of bed, left a warm burrow for
him to enter. Spirit of woman. Hadn't he settled for less in
the past?

Did he dare to go to Ellen at this gray hour? Was it
possible that his conclusions from last night were wrong?
Perhaps the meeting with Turner had nothing to do with
Ellen. Could he afford to be late for the appointment?

Images and sensations from the previous day drifted back
to him. He saw Ellen with a halo of golden sunlight. He felt
her tongue tracing the outline of his lips. He never had
tasted a tongue as soft as hers. How could it be so different?
Then her hands stroked his arms, reached beneath his shirt,
grasped his erection. Again he rolled back blue sky and
found her true blondness. . . . The focus of today's dream
was as intense as yesterday's action. A bellow swelled and
collapsed inside Morris's chest. For a moment he feared
Beth had heard, then he wished she had, wished she would
return and see the stains of morning infidelity.

Suddenly he was remorseful, not for what he had done
but for what he had not done with Ellen. He had acted the
timid fool. Why had he not consumed her, used her com-

241

pletely, exhausted every trace of desire he felt for her? Instead, he had allowed her to toy with him, control him as if he were a virgin. Her rule of silence . . . returning his touch like a robot . . . that mask. How was she positive who was with her? Did it matter?

Beneath his emotions was a foundation he'd barely touched upon: He was ashamed of being stupid, of being caught.

At the breakfast table, Morris had an impulse to clear the air and salvage what he could of his marriage. He said, "I love you, Beverly," and when his daughter immediately answered, "I love you, Dada," he took it as a good omen. He said to Beth, "I have to see Colonel Turner first thing this morning." Beth nodded, found no interest in the statement. "It's an important meeting," Morris said. Beth nodded again and inventoried a list of chores she had neglected. Which one was he leading to? She decided she had forgotten to iron a dress shirt. Facing a silent Beth, Morris didn't know how to continue. His pause brought back a classic story from pilot training days. . . .

A wife of one of the instructors took their children on a month-long trip to visit grandparents. While she was away, the instructor locked into a morning-noon-and-night affair with a tiny nurse from the base hospital. One evening, a week after the wife returned, she greeted her husband with a crooked smile. "What's this I hear about you and your little girlfriend?" That afternoon the wife had learned that while she was away, the next door neighbor's preteen daughter twice baked cookies for the instructor.

In the instructor's guilt-cluttered mind the term "little girlfriend" instantly represented the nurse. Without another word to urge him, he blabbed a confession that the most jaded inquisitor would have relished. To atone for his breach of trust, he elevated his wife to the status of a queen: He promised her clothes and jewelry and a new car; he sentenced himself to years of carpools and scout meetings, dishes and laundry; he pledged himself to any additional slavish contracts that she desired. When he ran out of promises, was on his knees in supplication, then his stunned and tearful wife said, "But I was talking about the little girl who baked cookies for you."

Morris decided he could not chance repeating such a vulgar mistake, committing matrimonial suicide when stone sober.

Beth said, "What's the problem?"

"I don't know," Morris replied. "I guess I'll find out at the meeting."

They stared at each other like two strangers who happened into a restaurant at the same time and were unintentionally seated at the same table.

The morning was topped by a dirty low cloud deck that repelled sunlight. Morris drove with the Thunderbird's headlights turned on, a minority of one. A strictly radar day. Morris noticed that drivers were inching up behind, then whipping around him. What was the rush? Didn't these people have anything to think about while on their way to work? What sort of work did they do?

Morris couldn't name a single civilian job that would satisfy him. He'd rather die than sell cars or insurance or real estate. He pictured Julius MacDuff and the men at the cookout. His grading system didn't classify them as working people. Consequently, he despised them. Subversively, he categorized them as greedy capitalists, leeches that bled the honest workingmen within a democracy. Then he saw that he didn't know one person he'd classify as an honest workingman—carpenter or cowboy, plumber or plowman, roofer or roustabout—not one man who stood in sun and rain and earned a living with hands and back. Discounting crewchiefs, of course; even so, he couldn't name one of them who was truly a friend.

And where did he fit?

Another driver honked his horn at Morris, passed narrowly, squeezed in tightly ahead. Morris recognized that he was driving much slower than normal. Was he suffering a gallows mentality, a sort of foot-dragging last-mile syndrome? He imagined a condemned man strolling along the route to his execution, pausing to write a line of verse or to smell a flower, detouring to capture and then release a butterfly—borrowing a nickel to phone and cancel a dinner reservation. Along the horizon the members of a firing squad were waiting for him, picking their teeth, having to go

243

to the bathroom and complaining, checking and rechecking that their rifles were loaded—making everyone jump by carelessly firing a round or two.

Was the scene too absurd?

What would Turner do if Morris simply did not show? They could kill him only once. By then, however, Morris had reached wing headquarters, twelve minutes early.

Training had betrayed him.

CHAPTER 42

PHYSICALLY, COLONEL TURNER'S office intimidated Morris Archer. The faded walls, the plain chairs, the bars of the venetian blinds combined to create a prison atmosphere. The oversize desk and executive chair weren't out of place: They formed an island of authority within a sea of punishment.

A residue of psychological intimidation also was present. Morris had been drunk the last time he'd faced Turner. Their conversation ended when Turner called him "asshole" and marched into the night. Did any respect remain between the two men, other than that dictated by the difference in rank?

The foundation of Morris's emotions rumbled: He was ashamed of being stupid, of being caught.

Seated to Turner's left was a sandy-haired major, a man big enough to be a college football lineman. Positioned at a corner of the desk, the man leaned so that he appeared to be behind the desk, alongside Turner, when Morris entered the office. Two against one, Morris thought and halted two paces from the desk, clicked his heels, saluted. "Captain Archer reporting as ordered, sir."

Turner returned the salute, stared at Morris's stitched lip, softly said, "At ease." He had hoped to run into Archer before this, had hoped to excuse his outburst when last they met. Now was too late. "Captain Archer, this is Major Crowley."

Crowley stood, grasped Morris's hand, shook it with powerful sincerity: "Ed Crowley. I read about your success at Bomb Comp. My belated congratulations. Amazing results."

Morris frowned. Was this a social visit? The recognition pleased him. Crowley's ruddy face made Morris suspect that the man was a drinker, but he could not recall seeing him at the club bar.

In Turner's mind, Crowley's greeting was grossly inappropriate considering the purpose of the gathering. Turner put a threat into his voice. "Major Crowley is from the judge advocate's office."

Crowley sat, leaned to his left, shifted position so that he moved from behind the desk and seemingly joined Morris's side of the room.

"Be seated," Turner said. Morris had a choice of two chairs; he selected the one that aligned with Crowley.

Crowley smiled. "You needn't answer any question that might incriminate or tend to degrade you." He edged his chair an inch forward, toward Morris. "You understand?" Morris nodded. Under current military law, Crowley's warning was adequate. A Chinese proverb said: *An innocent man needs no lawyer.* Crowley said, "Tell us, if you will, what you did yesterday, during duty hours, starting with when you arrived at work."

Morris's mind leaped back and forth between answers that might incriminate and what he had done yesterday. He saw no way to talk about one without talking about the other. Yet he could not balk, could not remain silent: Silence was equated with guilt. Morris recited his activities of yesterday prior to noon, included the fact that he was an hour late for work.

Crowley asked, "Any reason you were late for work?" and

Morris explained that he got a late start because he slept at a friend's home after his wife drove off without him, left a party in anger. "What made her angry?" Crowley said.

"Is that important?" Turner asked.

Crowley nodded, walked his chair another inch toward Morris, leaned forward and narrowed the conversation to the two of them. "What made her angry?"

"I pointed my finger like a gun and pretended to shoot her."

"That's all?" Crowley said, honestly amazed.

"Some things had been said before that," Morris said. "I thought everybody was joking and then Beth got angry."

"What were you joking about?"

"Crazy things. You know . . . we'd been drinking."

Crowley smiled crookedly. "Such as?"

"Things—like what you'd be willing to do for a lot of money." Had Robby already told them?

Crowley's head nodded understandingly. "I've been in a similar conversation. Could you give an example?"

This was not the line of questioning Morris expected. "A bunch of different things," he said. Because Colonel Turner was present, he stopped. He felt naked, exposed before God, or before his mother.

Crowley cocked his head. "Such as?"

Hadn't Robby told them? "Sex things," Morris said and wondered if he would have been better off answering "Murder." What a slim choice he had.

Crowley acted almost as if he hadn't heard, said, "Who was the friend who let you sleep at his house?"

Morris tried to speak the name clearly, unemotionally, but it came out raspy: "Lieutenant Robertson." He wanted a drink of water. He dryly cleared his throat. Why had Robby started this? For a moment he again experienced a doubling of reality. Was he inside or outside the mirror? Morris said, "He made up suppositions about murder too." Was he now to pay the price for his conscienceless mirror apparition? "That was when Beth got upset. . . ."

"When you pretended to shoot her, of course," Crowley said softly. Did he intuitively understand or had he heard the story before? Morris wondered. "Where did you sleep, that night at Robertson's?"

"In the den."

247

"How come Robertson didn't drop you at your house?"

Morris corrected a previous statement. "Look, we weren't at a real party, I mean, a big party." He set the stage: foursome for drinks and dinner, at Robertson's. Abruptly he felt a loss of energy that brought a jolt of unconcern. Was he tired or disinterested? How much was he going to have to explain and then explain again? Hadn't Robby given the details?

"Did you sleep alone in the den?"

Morris hesitated. The questioning was all wrong. His answer was going to sound queer: "No. Robby slept there too." He spoke the words and wondered what lies Robby had told. He had to clarify the statement, regardless of how dissolute the additional facts made him appear. "I drank until I passed out. Robby did too."

Crowley grinned. "How do you know what Robertson did? You said you passed out."

"I did. But Robby passed out first."

"Where did Mrs. Robertson sleep?"

"Upstairs." *Was there something else that he should know?* "I guess. She went upstairs after Beth left."

"Did you sleep in the den the entire night?"

"Yes."

"You didn't get up, wander around the house, anything like that?"

Morris shook his head.

"Where in the den did you sleep? Chair, couch, floor?"

"On the couch." Morris again felt a need to clarify: "Robby slept in his recliner." How was it possible for a man to sleep and shower side by side, day after day, with other men while in the Alert bunker, and then to feel suspect after sleeping fully clothed near another man during one drunken night in a private home?

"Did Mrs. Robertson enter the den during the night?"

"I don't know." *Was he supposed to know?*

"You ever sleep at Robinson's—Robertson's before?"

"That was the first time."

"The Robertsons ever sleep at your house?"

"No." Morris felt weighed down by the chain of questions. What had Crowley said about answering questions that tended to degrade? Wasn't every question an innuendo? Answering such questions in front of Colonel Turner was demeaning, was like having his brain exposed to his mother. Morris felt humiliated, wasn't certain if Crowley was against him or on his side. Was there something he had missed? The questions had flowed so effortlessly, so quickly.

At the start of the questioning Turner had sat stiffly at attention, displeased by Crowley's questions, made more so by Morris's answers. As the questioning rambled he relaxed deeper and deeper into his chair. His eyes grew duller and duller. He came to resemble a novice deep-sea fisherman who had been adrift for half a day without a nibble. But then, there was little need for him to be there. Crowley was the professional angler of the expedition.

Now Crowley leaned back in his chair, crossed his legs. He smiled at Morris. "Finish telling, if you will, what you did yesterday, during duty hours."

Beth was soaking in the bathtub when the telephone rang. She decided the caller was Morris and she decided not to answer.

When he'd come home the previous evening she'd hardly recognized him, for reasons other than his patchwork mouth. "Robby punched me," he'd said humbly. "I don't have the faintest idea why." He'd had a lost little boy look and she'd felt an urge to hold him, but had kept her distance. Had he sensed her sympathy? Unexpectedly he'd staggered against her, wrapped his arms around her, hugged her to him, and spoke into her hair: "I'm sorry for last night. I was drunk. I didn't mean what I did. Don't you understand? I love you."

She hadn't believe him, not one word. She had sensed a deeper problem hidden behind his remorse.

"Can't you see how I feel?" he'd asked and there was pained puzzlement in his voice. Had he been speaking to Beth or thinking aloud? "Look how much I've accomplished and how little I've gained." Over and over, like a lost wayfarer, he'd circled the tangled jungle of his own misery. "Promotion to captain. Moving on base. That's nothing. New furniture. The car. They're burdens, not rewards."

They were rewards to Beth. She nearly had said, "It's more than most men your age have." (Later, Beth agreed that moving on base was no reward. Base housing was closer to the heart of SAC, closer to the bull's-eye of a thermonuclear attack.) Morris complained he had nothing, she'd thought, but he'd once had her love and could have kept it forever, if he had valued it. Was that what he now had been seeking, what Beth now had denied?

Rather than generate anger in response to Beth's indifference, Morris had transferred his attention to Beverly, had coaxed a dividend of "I love you" after investing a dozen or more of his I-love-you's. "Wouldn't it be easier to look in a mirror?" Beth had wanted to ask. But she'd been afraid: This strangely humble and bewildered person was still her tyrant husband. She'd preferred being spectator to his self-pity than victim of the misdirected wrath of his unhappiness.

Now the phone was ringing and she knew it was Morris and she wasn't going to answer. Did he think everything was back to normal?

He'd made love to her the night before. Had she sacrificed her body to preserve the sanctity of her mind? She'd pretended to have an orgasm. Then, when she'd thought he was asleep, he'd asked, "Aren't you due for a period?"

"I'm a few days late," she'd said.

"You don't think . . . ?"

"No," she'd said.

"You ever think about having another?"

"Once in a while." *What did he know?*

"Tonight, when I was holding Beverly, I wondered what it would be like to have a son."

"Not from me," she had silently answered, "not in a thousand lifetimes." And then she had felt a guilt so terrifying that she'd had to turn her back to him, had feared that even in the dark her face would radiate the truth. No mask could have hidden her emotions. She stood accused of a crime she had not yet committed, and her accuser was the cause of the crime.

No, she would not answer the phone, she decided. Then Beverly toddled into the hall, picked up the receiver, said, "Mama," into the mouthpiece.

Beth wrapped herself in a towel and took the phone. "Mrs. Archer? Is that you, Mrs. Archer?" The woman's voice sounded familiar. "This is Maria Cannon. Remember? The picnic?"

The Mexican woman from the exchange, Beth thought. "How are you?"

"Fine, Mrs. Archer. But I don't feel so good to have to call you. I don't want to but I thought I owe a favor." Maria Cannon drew a deep breath. "My friend works in headquarters and she overheard about Captain Archer's trouble with Mrs. Robertson and she told me about it just now this morning."

Beth said, "Yes?"

"Mrs. Archer, she done that before."

"Done what?"

"Said somebody try to rape her."

Before Beth could ask, "Did Morris try to rape Ellen?" other questions crowded her mind. When? Where? Was that why Robby punched Morris?

"But is not true," said Maria Cannon. "Mrs. Robertson makes men come to her and then, after, she says they try to rape her." Maria Cannon then related a most unconventional story: "We were stationed at the same base as Lieutenant and Mrs. Robertson, in Georgia, when he was in pilot school. One of Ralph's friends worked night shift and he met Mrs. Robertson one day at the bowling alley. She gave him her telephone number but told him to call in the daytime. He thought she was an airman's wife 'cause she's such a baby and the next morning when he finished work he phoned her and she invited him to her house. Ralph's friend was no troublemaker, Mrs. Archer. He told us, when he got to the house, Missus Robertson was in bed with no clothes on and she was wearing some kind of mask, like a Halloween mask. And she let him do her but only—I don't know how else to say it, Mrs. Archer, and I'm sorry—she let him do her only in the wrong hole."

Beth experienced a moment of disbelief, as if the telephone call was a wrong number and did not pertain to her. Then to her horror she saw exactly how it related to her and she cringed. *Had Morris done that?* She would not put it past him. *And then afterward, last night, he'd had sex with her.* Beth felt defiled in a way she never would have imagined. She wanted to crawl back to the bathtub and scrub herself, turn herself inside out if possible, scour and flush away every trace of Morris Archer.

Maria Cannon was still talking: ". . . he drove away, Mrs.

Robertson wrote down his license number and called the sheriff and claimed he try to rape her. Our friend told the truth but nobody listened, not even his lawyer, some captain. Lieutenant Robertson graduated around then and transferred away without anything settled. Our friend, he got a bad conduct discharge later for something else, but Ralph said it really was 'cause he messed with an officer's wife.

"You see, Mrs. Archer?" Maria Cannon said. When Beth didn't reply, she explained. "Captain Archer didn't try to rape Mrs. Robertson. It's something she's making up again."

Innocent of rape, Morris was guilty of a greater sin in Beth's eyes. He'd done it with Ellen in a way that was totally repugnant. Beth believed that after a relationship died a loving partner should be allowed to retain individual pride. It was an earned right. But Morris's selfish lust had made Beth a dupe, had shattered her right and stolen her pride, had left her feeling filthy and degraded.

"Mrs. Archer, I hope I helped. I hope everything works out."

Beth managed to say, "Thank you, Maria. Thank you for calling." Morris had taught her how to hate, Beth thought.

↘CHAPTER 43

Finish telling, if you will, what you did yesterday, during duty hours," Crowley said.

"I'd rather not," Morris said.

"Why?"

Morris couldn't think of a reason other than he would incriminate himself. He didn't care to admit to that fact.

Like a bored fisherman whose drifting boat was unexpectedly spun by a change of current, Axel Turner sat erect, swiveled his chair so that he could better see Morris Archer. The chair's leather creaked loudly.

Relaxed, Crowley waited without moving, his eyes focused on some neutral middle ground.

Morris stared distantly through the prison bars of the venetian blinds. What could he tell them that they didn't know? Time ticked back and forth from yesterday to tomorrow. What was the price for having gone to bed with another man's wife?

The room's silence erupted in the blare of a klaxon: *Ah-ooooo-gah.* Conditioned reflexes made Morris leap to his feet. He grinned foolishly, then looked at his watch. Before the klaxon's second bleat ended, Turner had bolted from the room. Crowley remained seated with legs crossed.

While the klaxon blared Morris paced. *He belonged out there, not trapped in here. What if it was the real thing? Then what they did in here was totally meaningless.* Morris stopped pacing the instant the klaxon fell silent. In the exaggerated stillness that followed, he heard ground power units and aircraft engines firing to life at the far end of the runway. Colonel Turner's secretary looked in the office's open door: "The command post phoned. It's a Coco. The commander should be gone for a while."

"We'll wait," Crowley said. "Please close the door."

Morris walked to the window. "We'll be able to see them when they taxi down the runway," he said.

Behind him, Crowley said, "How come you no longer want to talk about yesterday?"

With Turner gone, Morris felt less threatened, as if God was on leave. There had been earlier moments when he'd suspected Crowley sympathized with him. Now, he easily said, "Because of your warning about incrimination."

"Afraid of incriminating yourself?"

The first airplane taxied along the runway and Morris checked his watch. "Three minutes, forty-nine seconds. That's good."

"Are you really afraid of incriminating yourself?"

"Yes," Morris said.

Morris saw the second airplane moving at a fifteen-second interval behind the first. Goosebumps sprang up along his forearms. Even though the crews were merely practicing, he longed to be in one of the airplanes. Theirs was the most important role on earth.

"Of what?" Crowley asked.

Morris turned away from the window. Crowley's back was to him. Morris said, "If I tell you that I may as well tell you everything."

Crowley said, "Do you know that Ellen Robertson claims you raped her?"

"What?" Morris's voice chirped an octave above normal. He stepped in front of Crowley, his fists clenched.

"I'm wrong. I meant to say, Ellen Robertson claims you *tried* to rape her."

In an egotistically convoluted channel of Morris's mind, "tried" indicated failure. Subconsciously, the reason for failure was important.

"Now that I've told you," Crowley said, "I have to advise you that you don't have to make any statement regarding her accusation, or regarding the offense of rape."

"Offense? Bullshit," Morris shouted.

"And that any statement made by you may be used as evidence in a trial by court-martial."

This had gone too far, Morris thought. "Listen," he said.

Crowley continued his quasi-lecture: "Rape is a serious offense. So is attempted rape. It falls under UCMJ Article eighty: 'In that Captain Morris Archer did at such and such place, on or about such and such time, attempt an act of sexual intercourse with a female not his wife, by force—'"

"Wait a minute," Morris said and sat down. Why had Ellen declared war on him?

Crowley draped an arm over the back of his chair and asked, "Did you go to Ellen Robertson's home yesterday?"

"Wait," Morris said. The anxious whine of earthbound jet engines filled the background of his mind. "Wait." He thought of Ellen's counterfeit charge and Robby's sneak attack and he saw no need to wait. If it was war, he had better counterattack. "What if I told you I didn't *try* to rape her?" Later he would agonize over his words, the self-incriminating details. As of the moment, however, truth appeared to be a panacea. "Look, I didn't have to try. We did it. When I went to her house, she was waiting, in bed, naked." He described exactly what had occurred: mask, robot reactions, silence, blondness, refusal to accept him in the usual way, promise of tomorrow.

When Morris finished he felt free, as if he was thinking clearly for the first time in days. He asked, "What about Robby? What charges are you bringing against him?"

"We'll think of something," Ed Crowley said. During the confession Crowley had been fascinated by Morris's face, the most innocent adult face in his recollection, an altogether guiltless, open face. There was in it, as foundation for it, a self-denial, a visible disbelief that the owner of the face and the owner of the mind behind it were the same person.

Furthermore, the face was guileless, without expression of ulterior motives: It held no plea for mercy, no plea for belief. Crowley's experience convinced him that Morris was recounting facts. Unless Morris was schizophrenic, his details were too bizarre to be false. Most important of all, in presenting his defense, Morris Archer provided information for a list of offenses that stretched beyond Article 80. Inwardly Crowley was sated. Truth filled and satisfied him as much as a good meal.

To save himself from drowning in a sea of punishment, had Morris Archer grasped the jaws of a shark?

If she scrubbed all day she still would not feel clean, Beth thought and drained the bathtub for the third time. The core of her hate was solidified, compressed into a critical mass. She would be rid of Morris Archer.

She dried carefully, then dressed in gray sweatshirt, blue jeans, loafers. She went outside to the storeroom, found Morris's empty footlocker, carried it into the house, opened it in the middle of the living room. She went to the bedroom, snatched an armful of Morris's clothes from the closet, returned to the living room and dropped the clothes into the footlocker, hangers and all. Approximating that there might not be enough space for what followed, Beth stepped into the locker and stomped the clothes into a bale. With that technique she had no trouble packing everything. On top she threw Morris's shoes and glossy flying boots.

She dragged the locker from the house, stood it on end at the beginning of the driveway. She returned inside, locked the doors, hooked the night safety chains, then made certain the windows too were locked.

She telephoned the command post, briefly talked to a controller, then phoned the base hospital and demanded to be put through to Jim Leonard. After some confusion on the line, Jim answered: "I have a patient in the other room. Can I call you back in a few minutes?"

"Remember what I wanted you to do?"

"I can't talk about that now."

"I want it done next Tuesday. Morris goes on Alert Monday." Jim didn't respond. "I'm not going to change my mind. I'm more positive than before."

"It won't be easy—"

256

"I don't care. If you won't do it, I'll go to Mexico. I know a girl who went over there in high school."

"You don't want to do that."

"Yes, I do, if you won't help."

Women die in those places, Jim wanted to shout. He said, "That's not safe."

"I don't care. I'd rather die than have this baby."

You don't mean that, his mind's voice told her and his mind's ear heard her answer, *Yes, I do.*

"I'm serious," Beth said.

"I know." A budding love or a flowering pity? He'd have to arrange for the use of a friend's office in town, he thought. On base was too public. "Get a sitter for Tuesday or Wednesday, for in the evening." Jim decided this was to be his role in Beth's life. She was chained Andromeda and he was Perseus who gained her freedom: Rather than escape the monster, she would not allow the monster to procreate. "Make sure the sitter can stay late."

"I love you," said Beth.

At her side, Beverly said, "I love you, Mama," and hugged Beth.

Upon returning to his office, Axel Turner found Ed Crowley sitting at his desk and talking on the phone. Turner dropped into a chair on the visitor's side of the desk. Crowley quickly ended his conversation, walked around the desk, sat in the chair next to Turner's. "How was the Alert, sir?"

"The wing's best Coco. Soon we're going to practice-launch the Alert force—test if we can actually get airborne, see how long it takes."

"That should be exciting."

"I hope not. I hope it's routine as hell. What did you do with Captain Archer?"

"Sent him to his squadron. He gave me his version of what took place. I believe him. There was no attempted rape. He and Mrs. Robertson had at it, by agreement."

Turner repeated what he'd said to Jean: "Archer's no liar."

Crowley nodded. "Then, based on what he said, he's guilty of Article One-Thirty-Four, adultery; Article One-Twenty-Five, sodomy; Article Ninety-Two, dereliction; and

257

probably Article One-Thirty-Three, conduct unbecoming."
Crowley smiled.

Turner's mind juggled the idea of Morris Archer and
Ellen Robertson having an affair. Cases such as these
irritated him because they were fundamentally avoidable.
Why couldn't people control themselves? Sorting this out
required a mind like Jean's. For what reason would Ellen
Robertson cry attempted rape? he asked himself. The action
made little sense to him. Was Ellen Robertson crazy?
Should he recommend her to Dr. Gomez? Solving Ellen
Robertson's problem wasn't his job, he told himself. He
wanted to be solving military problems. It was easier to
punish than to understand indiscretions, especially avoidable indiscretions. "I can't permit this sort of behavior in my
wing," he told Crowley. "It's prejudicial to good order and
discipline."

"Obviously," Crowley said with a pampering tone that
made Turner feel like a senile Solomon. Was his declaration
of command a platitude? Had he lazily reduced certain
aspects of leadership to nothing more than applying time-
proven formulas to age-old problems? That wasn't leadership. "What do you suggest?" Turner asked before
recognizing that he'd taken a subordinate stance. He moved
to his executive chair on the other side of the desk.

"I suggest we wait," Crowley said. "Let me talk to
Lieutenant Robertson again. And to Mrs. Robertson."

Turner wanted to discuss the problem over lunch with
Jean. "I need your suggested course of action by noon," he
said emphatically and again assumed command.

258

CHAPTER 44

BEVERLY SAID, "I love you, Mama," and hugged Beth, transmitted echoes of innocent love that reverberated along blocked channels of emotion within Beth. Beth pulled Beverly onto her lap, wrapped her arms around the child, rocked her like a metronome, crooned in tuneless bewilderment. What had Jim asked: "Would you want to do this if it was Beverly?" And she'd answered, "No. With Beverly—I was innocent then."

Why was she not innocent now? She had not changed despite Morris's efforts to convert her into a robot. Deep inside she was as pure and innocent as Beverly. *As innocent as the child deep inside her?*

She lifted one of Beverly's tiny hands, nibbled its palm with her lips, made Beverly giggle. She stared into the baby's face and saw herself a quarter century ago. Could Beverly see herself a quarter century hence? Beverly grasped Beth's thumb, squeezed gently. The loving pressure traveled to Beth's quivering heart. With a gentle forefinger Beverly stroked a tear from the corner of Beth's eye, wiped it along Beth's cheek. It was as if a person reached across half a century to dry her own tear.

Fragile baby, Beth thought and ached with the realization that another baby growing inside of her could be equally delicate and fragile. "Are you so positive it's a son?" Jim had challenged. "Yes," she'd said. Hadn't she felt the monster clawing inside her womb? Or had she felt terror? Had her grisly nightmare strangled the mother within her?

Beth saw herself seated in a field of bluebonnets, a gray mother with two curly-haired girls sprawled beside her, heads nesting on her lap. She saw only the three of them, together and alone. Nothing beyond today would be the same again. She felt as if she had fallen into middle age directly from childhood's end.

Inside of her a two-month-old baby radiated brainwaves and heartbeats, the most basic of human attributes. The baby was far more a part of her than of Morris. Would she dare to kill herself or dare to kill Beverly? What if the baby was a replica of Beverly? In the future, how could she admit to Beverly, "I killed your sister"?

Had the past months unbalanced her reason, undercut the foundation of her soul, made her at times more insane than sane?

She had been prepared to commit murder. She hid her face in Beverly's hair, her hair. Even dear Jim had not dared to call it murder. Jim must love her to risk such an act. How had she found the audacity to ask him—to demand that he do it? After Beverly, he was her only comfort in the world. She would miss him.

A wave of fear swept over Beth. She shuddered so violently that Beverly's face puckered as if to cry. "Ma-ma," she said. And the shudder passed, a black cloud across the effulgent face of the moon. Would she be brave enough to confront Morris one more time?

Robby awaited Crowley inside the Alert area entry point. Enroute, Crowley had stopped at the base legal office to pick up Second Lieutenant Clayton Barnes, the junior advocate. Crowley wasn't going to be caught without a corroborating witness twice in one day.

At the entry point an armed air policeman matched Crowley's identification card to a name on a control access roster. Crowley vouched for Barnes. "I've always heard SAC security was tight," said Barnes. "That was pretty loose."

"Try getting on one of the airplanes," Crowley said, "but first tell me where you want the body sent."

Robby saluted Crowley, told him, "I meant what I said on the phone. I talked to Ellen three times already this morning."

"Let's discuss it," Crowley said and led the way up a long, straight ramp that carried to the top floor of the two-story bunker. Equally long ramps descended to the bottom floor, underground. Barnes pointed to the building's ocher-yellow walls: "Who picked that color?" Inside, Robby led the way to a windowless room with two tables and six chairs, little free space, walls painted the same sickly yellow.

Crowley sat, waited while Barnes and Robby exchanged introductions, recalled an old saying: *Rank among lieutenants is like virtue among whores.*

Then Robby said, "Ellen wants to drop it."

Barnes said, "It isn't her choice. If a crime has—"

"Clayton, sit down and listen," Crowley said. He folded his arms, leaned on the table, stared at Robby.

Robby unzipped and rezipped the breast pockets of his flying suit, two at a time. "Ellen said the woman always gets the blame. She said it'll come down to her word against his."

Crowley said, "Not if there's evidence. Not if he hurt her. Did Captain Archer hurt her so it shows?"

"I told you yesterday. She said he pushed her around."

"Any bruises, cuts?"

"How do I know? I haven't seen her." His fingers worked the zippers. Or did the zippers work his fingers? "No," he said loudly. "I asked her this morning. She said no."

"Archer mustn't've tried very hard," Crowley muttered.

Robby leaned across the table. "What's that supposed to mean?"

Crowley saw a threat in Robby's posture but no threat in his eyes. Crowley shrugged.

Robby stood tall. "Can't we drop it?" His words were a prayer.

Barnes shifted to speak and Crowley showed him a fist.

Robby smiled at the gesture. Crowley smiled with him, then asked, "What makes you think you can play touch and go with the legal system? Yesterday afternoon you wanted Archer's head. Today you say forget it. How will you feel tomorrow?"

"It's not me. It's my wife." The zippers sang.

"Then how about you? You want to pursue it?"

"I don't know." Robby asked but he knew he was helpless. "Can I?" He had been through the exercise a couple of years earlier.

"Sure. Talk your wife into pressing charges and testifying." Why was he being perverse? Didn't he already know the outcome?

"She won't do that." Everything was different and yet it was the same, Robby thought.

"And she's a civilian and we can't force her. Right?"

Robby played stupid: "I don't know. Can you?"

"Yes. We can." But was it worth it? "Let's forget the whole thing," said Crowley. "Does that make you happy?"

Robby sat. With head lowered, he said, "I don't see what you want from me."

Crowley dropped his arms loosely at his sides. In a "pass the butter" voice, he said, "Punching Captain Archer is going to cost you. I talked with him this morning." Robby's head popped up. "And he wants a piece of you. He is your superior."

"That's debatable."

"In case you don't know it, we can charge you without his approval. And we're going to. The law's clear. You hit him, you pay."

Barnes nodded emphatically.

"Even if he deserved it?" Robby said.

"That remains to be proven. You care to prove it?"

Robby gave his zippers another workout. He left both pockets open. "Screw Archer," he said resignedly.

Crowley's mind said, "Your wife already did." Where would that lead? How had he ended up holding a bucket of rattlesnakes? If he went to court now, everybody would refute everybody else. Archer's confession lacked strength because nobody could support what Crowley had heard. By the time he reached court, Archer probably would have a lawyer who argued that there had been no confession:

Archer's word against Crowley's. With the bizarre details involved, a good cross-examiner might convince a court that Crowley had an overstimulated imagination. Ellen could be subpoenaed to take the stand but she couldn't be forced to testify against herself, vis-à-vis adultery. Even if she was granted immunity from a civil charge, Crowley would bet she'd perjure herself rather than sew on the big red varsity A in front of Robby. The charge of attempted rape would, as Robby said, simmer down to one word against another.

Crowley knew the air force also was on soft ground regarding jurisdiction. Had the poking below the belt taken place on base, authority would be clear. But nobody in Tye, Texas, cared a yahoo about what two air-force people did, as long as they didn't do it in front of the local schoolchildren. Some locals still studied people in air-force uniforms as if they were creatures loose from the zoo. Nobody in Tye was going to worry about punishing the behavior of a pair of rutting mammals: It would be as unnatural as taking the stud bull and a heifer to court.

Crowley categorized Robby as a natural victim, a slick guy who usually discovered far too late that things were wrong, the type who then compounded problems by taking the law into his own hands. Crowley decided the case started as a private spat, which, for some reason, Ellen expanded to the public domain. Had she broken the rules of a long-standing game or started a new game? Nothing forced Crowley to keep her game going. And yet he didn't want it to stop. His head was crammed with plays that lacked only an opponent to run them against.

He had a perverted urge to plunge ahead wildly, to vent his frustration on Robby by asking, "Was Archer kidding about your wife liking to take it up the keister while wearing a mask?" How many points would that score? The tactic would be as unsportsmanlike as kicking on the line of scrimmage. The question was certain to enrage Robby, who, at the moment, appeared pacified. With his sense of justice recharged, however, Robby might answer the question by providing the air force with a dead body or two. Crowley sighed.

"Now what?" Robby said.

Crowley thought about meeting Ellen Robertson, judging

if the prize was worth the battle. By his standards the woman usually wasn't. Of course, he judged on appearances. He'd never sampled the romantic techniques by which the dowdiest women caused the greatest passions, the most violent crimes. "Is there any chance your wife might answer a question or two for me?"

Robby was firm. "No. She won't talk to you. She won't talk to anybody."

Robby's certainty irritated Crowley. "Then it's up to Colonel Turner. He's the boss," Crowley said. "I'd guess you'll end up with a letter of reprimand." That was what he'd recommend to Turner. Victims didn't deserve maximum punishment, Crowley thought.

"How about Archer?"

Crowley mentally ran through options: "Probably the same."

A letter of reprimand reproved the recipient for unacceptable behavior. A copy of the letter was placed in the recipient's personnel folder. If he kept free of trouble for a year, the letter was removed from the file and destroyed.

"That's light punishment," Robby complained.

"Yeah, so is yours," Barnes told him. "You both deserve a court-martial."

The kid was a killer, Crowley thought and thanked sweet Jesus that Barnes didn't know what he knew.

Beth again telephoned Jim Leonard, said, "I'm sorry about before."

"I understand."

"No, you don't. I'm only beginning to. Meet me for lunch, please."

"The drive-in, where we went that first time," he said, "at noon." He needed to take the rest of the day off, to talk with Beth, to find strength in her resolve. After having dealt with Morris Archer, he had a new view of her life.

Crowley returned to Turner's office with an hour to spare on his deadline. He explained the facts. Turner asked several hypothetical questions before telling Crowley to prepare letters of reprimand based on Article 133, conduct unbecoming an officer and a gentleman.

Happy that the wing had avoided a pointless scandal,

Crowley said as an afterthought, "I'll bet Bomb Comp made Archer a hero to a lot of people."

Turner pointed a finger at Crowley, said, "Bomb Comp results have nothing to do with this." His declaration was not a platitude.

"I ordered," Beth said when Jim Leonard entered the car. He took Beverly onto his lap. "She'll wrinkle your uniform."

"Then I'll look like the rest of the doctors."

"I'm leaving Morris," Beth said.

Jim nodded. He wondered if his wife once had talked to another man in this way. Did Beth want his approval?

"I'm really going to do it."

"What about, you know, the other?"

Beth reached out and stroked Beverly's curls. "I can't. It's . . ." She almost said "wrong." She took Jim's hand. It felt twice as warm as hers. "Would you have really done it?"

"To help you," he said. Was this to be their final meeting? "What do you want from me now?"

Beth released his hand. "Nothing," she said and lifted Beverly from his lap.

Was she using him or was he using her? "I didn't mean that the way it sounded."

Beth had hoped to share the satisfaction of her decisions, perhaps use them as entries to the future. Why did he resent her? Why had the mood soured?

"Where are you going to live?"

A car hop brought their food on a tray. Jim reached into a pocket. Beth said, "I paid. Please."

His cheeseburger and malt were tasteless. Would anything have pleased him? He was restless, irritable, had the feeling he got from a case he couldn't diagnose. "You staying in Abilene?" he asked.

She shook her head: "I'm going to Laredo." She intended to return to her parents, live with them long enough to have the baby, then find a job and a home of her own.

"The base there has a decent hospital," Jim said.

In a fantasy, Beth already had transferred Jim to that hospital, had had her baby there. And would she then divorce Morris? The dark hand of doubt touched her: Had she made the proper choice? Would she be able to provide for two children? She stifled her doubts by reminding herself that she would not be confused by facts and statistics. She knew how she felt. Logic would not overrule her emotions. She did not expect life to be easy, but whatever her future, it had to be better than her past. Beth said, "Have you been to Laredo?" Was she inviting him there?

"On the way to the bullfights in Nuevo."

Beth watched him from the corner of her eye. "How did you like the girls over there?"

"You mean in Boy's Town?" He made an observation new to her: "They're—joyless. Men who find satisfaction in them must be the saddest creatures on earth." Did his description trigger his next thought? "I forgot to tell you. I met Morris. I sewed his lip."

"I don't want to hear about Morris." She angrily pressed the car horn. A car hop appeared and unhooked the tray from the window.

"I don't want this kind of good-bye," Jim said. "Let me see you again." Would Beth always be the one who got away? "When are you leaving?"

"Monday. Maybe Tuesday. I'll call you," Beth whispered.

Jim stretched around Beverly and hugged Beth briefly, awkwardly, then stepped from the car. He held back a hundred questions. The answers were none of his business.

CHAPTER 45

CROWLEY WAS THE only person not dissatisfied with the outcome of the Robertson-Archer affair. He had seen too many cases in which a military court was misused to settle a private dispute. He did what he could to prevent such abuse.

He remembered a case in which a female civilian had reported her former lover, a staff sergeant, for stealing government property. By the time the case reached court she and the sergeant were reunited. On the witness stand her memory repeatedly failed until a boxful of supposedly stolen tools was reduced to a single screwdriver. Crowley still heard her saying, "Honestly, I honestly don't remember," while staring into her lap. The sergeant was convicted of misappropriating a one-dollar-and-twenty-two-cent item. During the sentencing phase of the trial the board learned that the sergeant had been denied a promotion he'd earned because he was awaiting court-martial. The board decided that was punishment enough (far too much, several board members later said) and ended the farce by verbally reprimanding the sergeant.

Crowley had been defense attorney in a similar case between a jilted doctor and the nurse who spurned him. The doctor charged the nurse with theft of a seven-cent syringe. At one point in the court-martial Crowley clicked down a nickel and two pennies on the table in front of the prosecutor and said, "Will that satisfy you? Can we return to the meaningful problems of the world? Or do you want interest too?"

In Crowley's mind, principle was limited by the ridiculous. He didn't picture himself to be Clarence Darrow any more than he considered every case to be the Rosenberg Trial. Perhaps that was his shortcoming, was why he would retire as a major after twenty years.

He was satisfied with his performance in the Robertson-Archer affair. He hadn't mishandled Archer's confession. He doubted that he would have learned as much with Turner present. He could have used the confession in court. His testimony would have had merit, even without corroboration. But it could have been messy, ended with everyone covered by muck. The public didn't need to gawk at the sordid side of the air force, least of all the officer corps.

Crowley recognized that Archer would get further comeuppance from Turner, either with a derogatory comment on his efficiency rating or by some less visible method. Probably Turner would have similar punishment for Robertson too.

Most lasting, however, was the psychological punishment that participants meted out to each other. Crowley predicted a bleak atmosphere within the Robertson household for months to come, possibly years. Experience taught Crowley that married people simply did not forgive and forget. He wondered how the issues would impact Morris Archer's wife, the unknown value on his mental balance sheet. It was Crowley's opinion that unpredictable variables in personalities produced harsher punishments than those decreed by most courts-martial.

Axel Turner was displeased with mere letters of reprimand for Archer and Robertson. He thought that Crowley had mishandled the evidence against Archer and thereby destroyed the most damaging charges. Now Turner had to manipulate Archer's future in less direct ways. To begin, he decided to bury Archer on his wing commander's preference list. Turner couldn't control the spot promotion cutoff point on the list (CINCSAC set the quota) but he knew that if Archer fell below the top ten percent he was likely to lose his captaincy. To protect Charles's majority, Turner would give him a different navigator and allow him to retain the crew number and crew record. Before he did that, he'd promote Dixie Smith to aircraft commander. The changes would take place over several months and appear routine. Later, when Archer's annual efficiency report came before him for endorsement, Turner intended to write, "This officer's moral standards need improvement," and leave an ineradicable stain on Archer's record.

Ellen was upset by Turner's decision. Robby tried to explain that he'd done as much as possible. She cut him short: "I'm not happy. I'm not visiting you this week. I won't go anywhere near that base. Maybe forever."

Robby believed he deserved a lesser punishment than Archer. He willingly would accept a letter of reprimand if Archer was court-martialed. As it now stood, he thought he should go stone free. He decided he would start the paperwork to resign his commission on the day Turner handed him the written reprimand.

After Ellen declared that she would not visit him for the next five days, Robby called on Colonel Turner. "Sir, this incident has upset my wife. My marriage is in danger. I request to be replaced on Alert for the remainder of the week." He expected one day off at most.

Turner remembered Jean's advice: "You should have ordered him to go home." Furthermore, he saw a chance to use the move to his advantage. He gestured for Robby to follow him and they walked down the hall to Major Clark Devon's office, entered without knocking. Devon was alone at his desk. Turner said, "Clark, I want Lieutenant Robertson replaced on Alert, as soon as possible. Put Dixie Smith in his slot. Tell Dixie it's his last Alert tour as a copilot and that next week he'll begin upgrading to aircraft commander."

Devon said, "Sir, tampering with the Alert schedule cycle sets a dangerous precedent."

"I've thought it through, Clark. Just do it, please."

"Yes, sir," Devon called to Turner's departing back. He sat down and glared at Robby. He'd heard rumors. "Personal problems? What makes you special?"

"Colonel Turner said, 'As soon as possible,'" Robby reminded him.

"In good time."

"Call Dixie or I'll do it." Devon didn't move. Robby picked up the telephone and dialed the squadron.

Devon said, "Put down my telephone."

"Go to hell," Robby said. "I'm getting out of the air force, not trying to get in."

Devon jumped to his feet, snatched the phone from Robby. The squadron adjutant was on the line. "This is Major Devon. Hold it a minute." He covered the mouthpiece with his hand, whispered a threat: "Later, Lieutenant."

"Tell Dixie I'll be waiting at the Alert bunker." Robby double-timed out of the office.

Devon weighed the consequences of hanging up the phone, then he passed on Colonel Turner's orders.

The squadron adjutant said, "Charles's crew already left for the day. I'll ring Dixie at home. Who you want to put in the back seat on Charles's crew? They fly day after tomorrow, go on Alert Monday."

Devon said, "That's your problem," and started to hang up. Then he shouted, "Wait." His irritation with Robby had almost caused him to miss a perfect opportunity. "Hold it a minute," he said and scanned a list of names greasepenciled on a wall chart. He selected the most recently qualified and least experienced copilot, Lieutenant Don Cutter. "Put Cutter in Smith's place. If anybody complains, tell him Colonel Turner's balancing out the experience."

Devon put down the receiver and laughed because he knew that Archer would have to work twice as hard to compensate for the dozens of mistakes a rookie copilot made during bomb runs and celestial legs. Archer's days were numbered, Devon thought. He wished he could be aboard when Archer got his unreliable bomb.

* * *

Morris felt unjustly punished because he had been unjustly accused. He learned he was to receive a letter of reprimand when, on his way home, he stopped at the base legal office to confer with Crowley. He'd had a feeling that Crowley was willing to help him. "What if I refuse to accept the letter?" Morris asked.

"You can't refuse. The letter's the commander's prerogative, just like the definition of conduct unbecoming an officer. All you can do is write a letter in mitigation. We'll attach it to the reprimand."

"But what did I do wrong?"

"The things you confessed to me."

"You told on me?"

"That's my job. I warned you."

Truth was Morris's haven. As a child he was taught that truth contained its own punishment. Confessing a bad deed made a person feel worthless. Truth forced a person to cope with guilt. When a person resolved his guilt the matter ended. The self-governing philosophy was perfect control for a moral man with a healthy conscience.

"Did you tell . . ." Morris felt shame, not for being stupid or for being caught, but for the base acts he'd performed with a fellow officer's wife. ". . . everything?"

"We touched lightly on the wet spots."

What does Turner think of me now? Morris asked himself. It was as if Morris's mother had been shown a pornographic movie that featured him. There was no defense. How would Beth react to such details?

❧ CHAPTER 46

LIKE MOST MEN on the crumbling rim of a failing marriage, Morris overlooked his evident predicament, which deteriorated as steadily as a rotting tooth. While driving home, he searched beyond where he stood, scanned the horizon for a diversion to fill the near future. Was he seeking a Band-aid for a toothache? His view was distorted by limited imagination and introspection. His design for a brave new world of matrimony was contained within appeasers for his mate—a new car, a larger house, different furniture, another child—solutions born of generation after generation of male infallibility. Modifying the environment that encapsulated his fixed family relationship was his solution for escaping the past while retaining the past, hopefully dampening the descending spiral of his life. When life's focus temporarily shifted, the inevitable consequences of the unavoidable were delayed.

Was this solution limited to failing marriages, however? In a capitalistic society of expanding affluence, was constant material renewal becoming the expectation that bonded husband and wife?

Now, without understanding that he'd expended the diversions of new car and new household (his on-base quarters would be available shortly after the first of the year), Morris concentrated on the idea of a son, the single forward course he saw. Otherwise, he would have been forced to retreat, to review the past, to face his shortcomings again.

Robby reached home just before dark. The instant he set the car handbrake, the first-floor houselights went off. Coincidence, he thought: Would the lights flash on if he released the brake? He remembered a summer day between his freshman and sophomore years, a day his family had set aside for a picnic. Everyone was gathered around the car when huge, pelting raindrops unexpectedly fell from a clear sky, drove the family into the house. The volume continued unabated for minutes. Angry at the prospect of a washout, Robby leaned out the back door, looked to the heavens, and shouted, "Hey, crumb bum, knock it off," and the rain stopped in a fingersnap. His father batted his eyes, threw the car keys to Robby, and said, "If I had that much influence, I'd save it for something worthwhile."

His father had tried to talk him out of marrying Ellen, Robby remembered.

Now, the instant Robby clicked the car door closed a light came on upstairs. *Two for two,* he thought, and smiled for the second time that day, recalled Crowley making a fist at his stooge lieutenant. Crowley was a prick.

Robby entered the house through the front door, unwittingly retraced Morris Archer's meandering path through living room, dining room, kitchen, to den. Was he surveying his home to make certain his possessions were undisturbed by the intruder?

He had five days off, he thought, a break longer than any normally on the schedule. Robby was fed up with being a grease-pencil name on a board. He would write to the airlines tomorrow, he decided.

He climbed the stairs two at a time, turned on the light in the extra bedroom, glanced over the makeshift sewing table and the stacks of boxes. (A year later, after he had fulfilled

273

his obligation to the air force, after Ellen had moved back to New York State rather than follow him to Dallas, where he would be based with the airline, he finally opened the boxes. Two were filled with homemade baby clothes. In one box were clothes crudely put together, the product of a beginner. The other box held gowns and jackets and bonnets of extraordinary design, covered with embroidered flowers and animals, edged with ribbons and lace. In a third box, which was really a crib in disguise, he found a blond baby doll dressed in gown and jacket sparkling with sequins and tiny pearls. The doll was wrapped in a quilted pink baby blanket with the name Louise embroidered across the front. He had forgotten too soon that he had married a child, Robby thought.)

Now he turned off the sewing-room light and walked to the master bedroom. Ellen was waiting, pale arms resting outside the sheet, forming a ghostly V. Backlit by a bedside lamp, golden hair glowed like a halo. From the shadows her eyes glittered blackly, held the icy thrust of distant space. "I'm glad you came home," she said.

They were in the middle of making love when the telephone rang. "Leave it," Ellen said. Robby thought it might have something to do with Alert. When he answered, nobody was on the line.

The next morning his questions began: What were you wearing when Morris came over?

Morris didn't see the footlocker until he swung the car into the driveway. What the . . . ? he thought and braked too late to avoid hitting the locker and tipping it over. Had he damaged the cár? What was the locker doing there? In the headlights he saw tread marks grooved into the lawn where somebody had swerved around the footlocker. Beth? The Chevy was at the far end of the driveway. The landlord would have a fit over the ruts. What was going on?

He opened the footlocker, saw his flying boots, lifted them out and cursed. The toes were scuffed. It took several seconds before he recognized that the bale contained his wadded uniforms and civilian clothes.

In a green fury he hurled his boots at the house, hit a casement window, shattered glass. He ran to the kitchen door, twisted the knob, found it locked. He ran back to the

274

car for keys. He unlocked the back door but it hung up on the safety chain. He heard Beth say, "Go away. You don't live here." The sharp words stabbed his stomach, produced a twisting spasm that churned his bowels. He leaned his weight against the door, felt the frame bend. Through a two-inch gap he saw Beth ten feet away, holding Beverly. "Let me in," he said. His voice quivered. His chest shook like a poorly tuned engine. "Go away," Beth whispered.

The humiliation of being locked out of his home was more than he could bear. He threw himself at the door, felt the frame shiver, heard it groan. Beth disappeared from view. He hit the door again and the chain stretched the frame, made it screech. Morris kicked the door and the frame splintered loose, clattered along the floor, dangling from the safety chain.

He burst into the house and saw Beth standing in the living room, holding Beverly, looking outside through the front window. Within Morris was an outcast feeling, a fear of punishment.

She turned to him, screamed, "Don't you hurt us." Beverly gave a cry of pain. Their contorted faces were two identical, accusing masks of fright.

Morris tried to say, "I didn't do it," only to discover he did not know what he was denying.

"Get out," Beth shouted, "or I'll call the police."

"You can't throw a man out of his own home."

"You go or I go."

"What about Beverly?" he asked.

Would he steal Beverly? Beth backed against a wall. He wanted to capture the child's affection only to gratify his ego, Beth thought. He had no other use for Beverly. She hugged the baby tightly, stood hunched as if expecting to be struck by a volley. Was she so easily defeated? She had planned a week's strategy. . . . Seeking maneuvering room, she said, "I know about Ellen."

"That was a lie."

"Was it?"

Morris's face became a guiltless mask. "I didn't try to rape her." Hadn't he used the same words with Crowley? How many times would he repeat his rosary of absolution? "She took back everything she said."

"But I heard what really happened." In blunt terms Beth

275

described what Maria Cannon had told her, substituting Morris for the airman. "You're nobody special," Beth said at the end, "she even does it with airmen."

All masks fell away. Beth and Morris exchanged stares of naked hatred. He stepped forward and she flinched, turned so that her body shielded Beverly. "Who told you that?" he said. It had to have been Ellen, he thought.

He stepped into the hall, picked up the telephone, dialed Robertson's number. He needed to know why Ellen was tormenting him. Robby answered the rings and Morris was speechless. Why wasn't Robby on Alert? He put down the receiver. What was wrong with the world? Had everyone turned upside down?

He faced Beth, spoke the most remarkable words to come from the mouth of a nuclear warrior, acolyte of earth's end: "We have to go on." A rictus of a smile gripped Morris's jaw. Parts of his body and mind separated themselves from each other. He went to the kitchen and began to repair the doorframe. Beth watched in puzzled silence. After a time, he said, "On the way home I thought about having a son. So logical then, so illogical now."

Later he said, "You need time alone."

Then, even later: "As far as I'm concerned you can have whatever you want. Take everything." (Months beyond, when they faced an attorney, Morris bickered over trivial objects until Beth grew frenzied, then he gracefully conceded. Following a bitter session regarding custody of Beverly, he whispered to the lawyer, "Isn't that what God does, teases and then gives in?")

Morris finished with the doorjamb, taped a cardboard patch on the window, then went to the bathroom and packed his dopp kit. He kissed the top of Beverly's head. "I'll see you a week from Monday, when I come off Alert," he said. After tying the footlocker into the open trunk of the car, he returned to the house for a shoeshine kit and an iron. His parting words were, "Believe it or not, I love you."

CHAPTER 47

IN THE MORNING when Archer rolled out of bed he was practically at work. From his room in the bachelor officer quarters he could walk to the squadron in the time it took to drive from town. He awoke in a sour mood. Did his mood reflect his environment? The bachelor quarters exhaled a fetid odor of institutionalized sleep, the same joyless male rancidness that permeated the Alert bunker's underground level. Five days of this, then seven days of that, he thought. One was the other, the other was the one.

Morris beat Charles to work. He had maps spread and the mission outlined—the crew's annual jet-assisted takeoff (JATO) followed by a day celestial navigation leg and two bomb runs on San Antonio—when Charles walked in followed by Don Cutter. Morris said, "You're late."

Charles said, "I'd like you to meet our new copilot—"

"Are you kidding?" Morris had seen Cutter around the squadron, had disliked his washed-out features, his platinum hair, his tall and skinny body. Worst of all, Cutter wore glasses with little round lenses set in pink plastic frames that made him look like a Jap. "How did *that* get through pilot training," Morris once had said to Robby. "Where's Dixie?" Morris now asked.

"Colonel Turner gave him his own crew."

Morris pointed to Cutter with a jerk of his head. "You pick him?"

"Don was assigned by wing. Colonel Turner wants to balance the experience."

That's a lie, Morris's instincts told him, revealed the unwritten plan: Turner's going to make your life miserable little by little. To Morris, slow punishment was the worst punishment.

Charles smiled at Cutter, said, "We'll train Don, make him better than Dixie. Everything'll work out."

Morris said, "I hope so. Tomorrow's mission's easy. Day celestial. If you have trouble finding the sun, Chuck can point it out."

Charles said, "That's the one star I know."

After the following day's mission during which Cutter lagged eternal seconds behind at several crucial moments, when Morris was thankful to land with a nineteen-mile celestial leg and a 2900-foot bomb (he'd canceled the second run on San Antonio: "No more bombing until we talk," he'd shouted over interphone); then, alone with Charles in the squadron locker room, Morris said, "You let wing shit all over us, give us that sorry excuse for a copilot. You didn't even argue for us," and then he blurted out a subconscious statement that Charles ignored outwardly but could not have humanly ignored inwardly: "I don't know why I expect more from you. You can't even control your wife. You should have seen the way she acted while you were in Hawaii." Was Charles's tolerance for abuse predicated upon his stability or upon Morris's instability?

By then Morris was mindlessly functioning on spillovers of adrenaline and anger. Had he been able to see, he might have recognized the same silent symptoms in Charles's narrow red eyes and tight pale lips. The flight had been a near tragedy from the moment the bomber cleared the ground. . . .

* * *

The worst moment came when, for the only time in the mission, Cutter mistakenly got ahead of the plane's progress. During takeoff roll, he misread the airspeed indicator and caused Charles to fire the thirty-three JATO bottles too early.

Each JATO bottle was a solid propellant rocket that generated 1000 pounds of thrust for approximately twenty seconds. The bottles hung clustered from a half-moon aluminum rack called a "horsecollar," located beneath the aft fuselage midway between wings and tail. The JATO boost helped lift the B47 into the air, was vital when gross weight reached 220,000 pounds, the Alert configuration. When the bottles burned out, the pilots jettisoned them along with the horsecollar. A combat crew made one JATO takeoff each year to maintain proficiency.

When Cutter called the wrong speed, Charles triggered the JATO firing switch on his control yoke and the bottles simultaneously belched fire and smoke, became thirty-three miniatures of the large-scale rockets Americans soon would cheer time and again on television. Once the JATO bottles fired there was no method for turning them off; they burned until exhausted. With the added thrust, Charles's B47 rose heavenward as quickly as a homesick angel, smoothly poised like a life-size display model on the crest of a billowing cloud.

The bottles burned out and the nose-high airframe mushed toward a stall. Charles shoved the control yoke forward and dived the bomber to build flying speed.

In the aircraft's nose where day was night, blind to the external horizon, Morris felt his stomach float into his chest. He'd been pressed into his seat by the JATO's kick, had watched the altimeter rapidly wind from runway elevation of 1800 feet to 4300 feet. Now he had a weightless sensation as the altimeter unwound. The bomber plunged through 4000 feet, headed toward 3000.

With cold hands Morris reached between his calves, raised a red metal D-ring, and loosely curled his fingers through it, prepared to fire his downward ejection seat. All it took was a nine-inch pull.

He decided that when the plane reached 2600 feet, he was leaving. That was 800 feet above the West Texas terrain. The downward system's minimum altitude was 400 feet, with no room for error; every automatic device had to function exactly as designed. He wasn't going to remain scarecrow still while the plane plowed to earth and fireballed. He wasn't going to be found sitting in the wreckage, a charred mummy. Charles and Cutter had the whole Texas sky above them. His life was trapped in the narrowing slit of space below. He cursed the sightless silence. Why didn't Chuck explain what was happening?

Charles was in an embarrassed sweat. He'd ridden the JATO's exhilarating charge, rapt in the power of the surge. Mesmerized by the steep angle of ascent, he'd allowed the airspeed to slip away. Because of Cutter's mistake, there was no excess speed. The faintest falter of control fluttered through Charles's arms, tickled him awake, caused him to overreact and drop the bomber's nose sharply. Unaware of Cutter's error, he blamed himself for the predicament. As the airspeed increased, he leveled the bomber. He was in command again but silenced by guilt. What a horrible example he'd set for Cutter.

Cutter had recognized his error the moment the plane cleared the runway. Inexperience had frozen him with indecision: confess amid confusion or hope that Charles worked it out? Now that Charles had control, he decided the discussion could wait until they were on the ground.

At 2700 feet—with 100 feet to spare—Morris's fingers twitched, then squeezed the D-ring tightly. Could he eject without a command? What if he bailed out of a perfectly safe airplane? "What's happening?" he said loudly, heard his voice as if another spoke for him. "Where we going?"

"Up," Charles said. He momentarily leveled the B47, then began a rapid climb.

Morris provided the heading to a control area in the Gulf of Mexico where they had planned to jettison the horsecollar. He stowed his D-ring and shivered from head to toe. "Turn up the heat," he said before recognizing that the frigid touch resulted from fear. . . .

Now, back on the ground, Morris wanted an accounting for his fear and for the eternal seconds of delay that nearly had cost him an unreliable bomb. After attacking Charles's leadership, he attacked Cutter's proficiency.

Charles's response stopped him. "Why don't you take tomorrow off? I'm going to review the tech order with Don. On Alert, we can work out crew coordination."

A three-day weekend without asking, Morris thought. How would he spend so much free time alone?

↘CHAPTER 48

SHORTLY AFTER CHARLES ended his flight at Dyess, a more significant launch took place half a continent away. The December 19, 1958, issue of the *Abilene Big Country Journal* reported it under the headline: U.S. PUTS 4-TON MISSILE INTO ORBIT; ATLAS SURPASSES SPUTNIK'S SIZE. The accompanying story read:

WASHINGTON, Dec. 18—In a display of missile power, the United States today fired an 8500-pound Atlas ballistic missile into orbit. The air-force Atlas is two and a half times as heavy as the payload of the Soviet Union's Sputnik III.

The Atlas was launched from a pad at Cape Canaveral, Florida, at 6:02 P.M.

President Dwight D. Eisenhower announced the spectacular success at a White House diplomatic dinner. "The entire vehicle is in orbit," he said proudly. "This launching constitutes a distinct step forward in space operations. The success opens new opportunities to the United States and all mankind for activities in outer space."

Atlas is the fifth United States artificial satellite. Its life expectancy is twenty days and it will burn up when it falls back into the atmosphere.

Air-force officials said the Atlas launch was strictly a military test of a new inertial guidance system for intercontinental ballistic missiles. The launch had no connection with the International Geophysical Year program, the officials declared.

Sputnik III's payload weighed 2919 pounds compared to Atlas's 8500. However, the Sputnik III missile went into separate orbit at the May 15 firing. Therefore, the entire Soviet package may have weighed a total of 8800 pounds.

The Soviet Union regained the space initiative on September 14, 1959, when Luna 2 reached the moon. The *Abilene Big Country Journal* headlined the event: SOVIET ROCKET HITS MOON AFTER 35-HOUR FLIGHT; IMPACT TIME IS CALCULATED WITHIN 84 SECONDS. The first object sent by man from one cosmic body to another bore pennants and the hammer-and-sickle emblem of the Soviet government. The object was a sphere weighing 858.4 pounds. It struck between the lunar depressions known as the Sea of Serenity and the Sea of Tranquility. On October 4, Luna 3 took the first photographs of the moon's far side.

Five United States Pioneer rockets failed to hit the moon prior to Luna 2: two didn't survive launch; two were destroyed enroute; the fifth missed by 37,000 miles on March 4, 1959. Luna 1 missed the moon by 4650 miles on January 2, 1959. Following the impact of Luna 2, Vice-President Richard M. Nixon announced that the Soviet Union had "failed three times in the last two weeks" to hit the moon with a rocket. He did not reveal the source of his information.

Atlas was a surprise Christmas gift. Even the intelligence to which Axel Turner was privileged had not hinted at the colossal success. Turner was proud that an air-force missile had placed America back on top.

Before Atlas, American satellites had been products of army and navy programs. The United States had followed its three "oranges" with a fourth on July 26. However, that 38.43-pound satellite had had a threateningly unique impact: Its orbital path was the first to cross Soviet territory and its instruments measured radiation. Nevertheless, analysts still had claimed the United States wouldn't duplicate the Sputnik III feat until 1960 at the earliest. In Atlas, American scientists somehow had compressed more than two years of effort into seven months.

Lenin must be spinning in his tomb, Turner thought happily. He would have paid a hundred dollars for a photograph of Khrushchev's face taken at the moment he heard the news of Atlas's orbit.

The air force would have operational ICBMs within a year, Turner estimated. When he later read that the Atlas circular error of probability was three miles, his immediate thought was that no manned bomber was that inaccurate. But when he read of the missile warhead's yield and applied it against the softness of target cities, three miles became adequate, particularly if related to missile speed and penetration of defenses. At the same time, a flitting ambivalence crossed and recrossed his mind, made him question the need for nuclear missiles as he once had questioned the need for nuclear bombs. . . .

Early in the 1954 series of thermonuclear weapon tests, Axel Turner had been on a Pacific island 900 miles from ground zero. He had been standing on a beach in the middle of night. As if someone had thrown a cosmic light switch, night became a brilliantly blue neon noon. An eerie sensation overcame him. God was supposed to make day and night, he thought. By all his values what he saw was a sacrilege. Man had made a day and that was frightening. Gradually the light diminished, much like sunset. The blue sky turned yellow yellow, then blood red. Darkness crept from behind him. Night returned. The event was soundless, motionless except for waves splashing at his feet.

Any man who witnessed such raw power and did not question the course of history had to be a monster, Turner had thought. But his mental battle was little more than a skirmish along an isolated valley of his mind. He saw no way to alter the course of strategy. He was a simple custodian of death who prayed never to be needed. He could have objected to nuclear weapons by giving up his career, but that option retreated from his thoughts. It was preposterous to imagine what would happen if every soldier resigned.

(Turner's prejudiced guess proved accurate: On October 31, 1959, the first Atlas missile was placed on Alert at Vandenberg. By the end of 1959 the air force had six ICBMs on Alert.)

In the middle of the night following Atlas's launch, Turner awoke with the desperate apprehension of a man driving ninety miles an hour down a one-lane, dead-end street.

On January 1 he would pin on his brigadier star and assume command of the new air division at Dyess. On January 5 bombers of a second wing would begin arriving from their present base in Oklahoma. When the transfer was completed he would command two super wings, a total of 120 B47s. As part of a new SAC plan, his crews and bombers would routinely disperse to airfields in Alaska, the United Kingdom, and North Africa. By using more runways, more bombers could get airborne in less time. And the forward bases were closer to Soviet targets. Turner's command would be global.

But once his super wings were assembled, would they not immediately begin to disintegrate? Wasn't the beginning also the end? The B47 was phasing out of the inventory. The last SAC B47 wing, the "Bloody Hundredth" of World War II fame, had been fully equipped in February 1957. In October 1957 the first RB47 had been flown to the aircraft graveyard at Davis-Monthan.

Was Turner's fate to oversee a long-term disbandment? Had he attained his career destination in reaching a single star?

He calmed his midnight apprehension with logic. He had served his nation as his nation had demanded. If he met a dead end, so be it. A true soldier did not plan the course of a career. Men who schemed and manipulated their assignments were politicians. A true soldier accepted assignments as they came, conscientiously performed the related duties.

Years later he was not overly disappointed when his time had come and gone and he still wore a single star. The pyramid of officers narrowed precipitously where he stood, permitted a select few to ascend higher. Congressmen

285

carefully controlled the progress of generals, permitted fewer than 500 air-force officers to reach star rank.

Although Axel was not overly disappointed, Jean was. She should have focused her efforts on superiors rather than on subordinates, she tried to tell herself, but in her heart, she knew that she too had served as life demanded. She had done the right thing. In a tirade born of rejection and righteousness, and behind Axel's back, she wrote long letters that denounced the promotion system to congressmen and newspaper editors. Her efforts caused Axel to retire before his mandatory date.

Axel was disappointed by Jean's actions. However, he understood when she explained that she'd done it for him, not for herself. She'd forgotten the maxim that a strong leader was also a dependable follower, he thought. "As long as the United States exists as a democracy," he reminded her, "soldiers of all ranks will be subordinate to the will of the people."

"Soldiers are citizens too," she answered, "and so are their wives. They have a right to speak out."

Axel soothed her by confessing, "At this stage, I suppose it doesn't hurt to admit that there were many situations when I thought you'd be better in the uniform than I was."

While calming his midnight apprehension following Atlas's launch, perhaps Axel's logical mind should have looked beyond his situation, should have asked, Why did the will of the people tolerate nuclear weapons? When man-made sun touched man, nationalism should have vaporized. Why had common men everywhere failed to unite? Didn't they see that revolution in the United States and in the Soviet Union was the only way that they would free themselves from the threat of rulers who continued to preach doctrines of Washington and Jefferson, Marx and Lenin, dead doctrines that kept them in power? Revolution was a legacy of both nations.

↘CHAPTER 49

Morris Archer lay stretched on an endless plain that blazed like Van Gogh's sun-fired fields at Arles, a place of ceaseless light. Hot caliche dust filled his throat. He coughed and his bones rattled with agony. He was unable to move. Was he paralyzed or rooted to the ground? Had he fallen from the sky or blossomed from the earth?

The face of Chuck Charles hovered overhead, a devotional countenance guarding Morris's province of pain with its calm assurance: "Try not to move. You're injured. But you're going to be all right."

Morris's tongue twisted to reply, but his crusted lips were sealed with a cement of gray dust.

"You're going to be all right," Charles said. "But first you'll spend time here. It's the price you have to pay."

How long? Morris's mind pleaded to know, made his throat constrict.

Charles moved away, dimmed rather than distanced

himself. "It won't be long," Charles said and became a transparency.

Wait, Morris silently shrieked. *Don't go.*

"You'll be here only twelve or thirteen—"

Morris expected Charles to say "minutes," and then flashed to "hours," feared Charles would say "hours," an unendurable sentence. A century of pain filled each second.

". . . twelve or thirteen . . ." Charles vanished. His voice said, ". . . *million years.*"

Morris's heart pounded, pumped pulses of pain through his shattered bones. He madly calculated: twelve . . . thirteen million years . . . megayears . . . how many lifetimes? Would he still be there when mankind was extinct?

In the next microsecond the truth was revealed to Morris Archer and he shook with convulsive waves of hopelessness, seismic tremors of despair. With the sureness of godly revelation he saw a futureless fate. Clarity crushed his soul. He unquestioningly knew that on the plain of ceaseless light there was no way or no reason to measure time. He had fallen upon a landscape that was past, present, and future. Today was eternal.

As it was in the beginning, is now, and ever shall be, world without end.

Morris came wide-awake, covered with sweat, panting. His stomach rumbled and gurgled with a two-day load of tacos and tequila.

Was hell his future? Had God dropped into the gutter to deliver that message?

Naked beneath the bristles of a wool serape that chafed his skin, he felt goosebumps pop up along his arms and legs as his pulse slowed and his sweat chilled. A Mexican woman curled next to him, pressed against him for warmth. Her coarse bleached blond hair rasped like sandpaper against his neck. Seventeen, she'd said. A year or two from middle age, he thought. Had he been searching for Ellen?

From the light of Sunday's dawn through the sheer curtains of a single window, Morris surveyed the Villa Acuna crib in which he'd slept. Votive candles sputtered in red glasses set before a low altar in a corner alongside the head of the bed. Sanctified sex, Morris thought and his mind sang, *Holy Mary, Mother of God, pray for us sinners now and at the hour of our death.* On the opposite side of the bed a tin bucket and gray porcelainized basin stood on a small table. The corner behind the table was curtained by a faded yellow sheet.

The wall beyond the foot of the bed was still in shadow and appeared to waver, reacted like a tapestry in a breeze as morning light approached it. Undulations moved from ceiling to floor. The light brightened and the tapestry became a blanket of cockroaches scrambling over and around each other, flowing in a migration that prickled Morris's flesh.

The bristles of the wool serape and the barbed feet of the roaches became one, made Morris retract his legs, run his hands across his body to brush away imaginary invaders. The sensation of the roaches forming a blanket around his body drove him from the bed, forced the first step of a long punitive journey into the black hole of his psyche. His entry point would be light-years from his exit.

He dressed rapidly from a pile of clothes on the packed earth floor at the foot of the bed. The woman hugged the serape tightly around her, curled into a fetal knot, said, "You go?"

"Yes," Morris said and pulled Mexican money from his pockets, dropped every peso and centavo he owned onto the bed.

"Too early," the woman complained.

Morris nodded. The money was token of his final time, although he did not recognize the gesture at that moment.

Like a living nightmare the clawing blanket of roaches followed Morris across the border, wrapped about his self-respect. He hated himself and what he had become.

At the Laughlin Air Force Base officers' club, he ate breakfast enough for three men and then walked into a nearby pasture and threw up until, down on his knees, he emptied himself of the last three days, purged his body of the aftertaste of whoring and of the aura of fear that clung to him from Friday's flight.

If only he could fade back farther in time . . .

He wished to return to the day before the dinner party at Robby's . . . and then to the night he stepped off the airplane at Bomb Comp . . . and then back, back, back in life—before SAC and the air force, before college, before his first whore and his first drink, before hydrogen and atomic bombs. . . .

On bended knees, once again seven years old, he waited to receive first holy communion. He was physically hollow, queasy from fasting. But he was spiritually pure. The psychological feast that awaited him eased his corporeal hunger. The body and blood of Christ would enter him, become one with him, and he would become one with God. He was as sinless as the day he was baptized.

Paradoxically, he had been innocent the night before communion when he had made his first holy confession, had stretched his imagination to manufacture sins to admit to a priest. Later he feared that his stretching of the truth was a sin in itself.

Was the morning of his first holy communion the last time in his life that he was truly innocent?

When had he given up hope for psychic resurrection predicated upon Christ's mercy? Was it at the age of twelve when he'd fallen in love with the bomb? What was real became magical. Hiroshima and Nagasaki showed him a god on earth. How could a heavenly god be more powerful? What was human became divine. The sacrament of confirmation that followed the summer afterward had been meaningless: He'd needed no reconciliation with an invisible supreme being to seal his baptism and communion. The circle of his religious belief had been closed with the bomb.

He remembered *the* December 7 when he had sobbed in bed, sobbed with the fear of an eight-year-old child who expected the Japanese to bomb him exactly as they had bombed sleeping Pearl Harbor that morning. His mind had replayed newsreel scenes of London burning in darkness beneath the blitz of Nazi bombs. That night he suffered his first exposure to a recurring nightmare in which, like the buildings of London, his home was set ablaze by bombs, made to flare like a bonfire before it collapsed inward upon him. That night he died the first of many deaths.

Four years later he was reborn when American aircrews cremated Hiroshima and Nagasaki, repaid the Japanese for the fear with which they'd infected his childhood. The bomb was his wartime savior. Short years later, in his teens, the bomb became a national guardian angel, protector of peace. When Morris attained manhood, the bomb absorbed him, transformed him into a champion prepared to destroy those who threatened Pearl Harbors of solar magnitude. In joining with the bomb, Morris Archer became more than a part of God; he became a god.

He saw these associations for the first time and marveled at how he had blankly stored the memories for years. Why was he seeing relationships now? He unexpectedly comprehended that his frightening wake-up dream represented his life today as much as it represented his life in a hereafter. He was bound to an endless task, to an institution of fire. The shadow of his life's orbital path described a black trellis of motionless, nonproductive activities. Rather than being a savior, he was a servant to a mechanical monstrosity—a black angel with wings of fire.

His thoughts compressed and against his will he saw a motivation for his adult behavior, accepted and rejected the knowledge within the time it took to ask: Was his wartime childhood terror the rationale for his aggression? He never had been in actual danger. How could a personality be sustained upon the fragile foundation of needless revenge?

Before he arose from his knees and left the field, his mind involuntarily recited words he had not spoken in more than a decade: *O my God, I am heartily sorry for having offended Thee because Thou art so very good, and I firmly propose, by the help of Thy grace, not to offend Thee again.*

On his return trip to Abilene he discovered he had been speaking a language of fire that he did not understand. Like an innocent viewing his environment for the first time, he was conscious of the vertigo of evil converting young men into pawns of space. Heroism was irrelevant. He saw masked bomber crewmen, eyes glazed by nuclear illiteracy, tumbling out of their skins and into the inferno of thermonuclear battle. With unfeeling fingertips they groped for buttons that fleetingly turned the world to fire and gold. . . .

Within the core of a thermonuclear burst—a shattered and confined cosmos that attained many times the temperature in the center of the sun and reached the pressure of a hundred million atmospheres—there was a sea of gas so dense with neutrons that it was also a metal that contained every element below the mother elements of plutonium and uranium: tin, copper, iron, silver, gold.

King Midas' gold.

The cognizance of a valueless world created a strange affinity within Morris's mind. He saw the single gravitational trajectory—whether the weapon system was bomber or missile—that linked each pawn to his target, tied executioner to victim. Now he wondered if at the end of his trajectory he would find a child, waiting in bed, dreading Morris's existence as Morris once had dreaded the Japanese. The difference was that a Moscow child's fear was valid.

❧CHAPTER 50

Aᴛʟᴀs's ʀᴜᴍʙʟᴇ ɪɴᴛᴏ space shortened the gravitational
strands that spanned indefensible continents, that linked
superpower to superpower. SAC planners reacted as nerv-
ously as their Soviet counterparts. But wasn't that to be
expected, weren't such men identical?

On Monday morning, Major Clark Devon's opening
statement of the changeover briefing startled the forty-five
incoming Alert crewmen: "The next time the klaxon
sounds, you will launch." Over the hubbub his statement
created he shouted, "The launch will be a test."

Atlas's success magnified the missile threat. CINCSAC
decided the minimum interval takeoff concept needed an
ultimate test: A wave of bombers racing off the ground at
fifteen-second intervals was dramatically different from a
line of bombers reservedly taxiing along a runway.

"Between noon, local time, today and noon, local time,
tomorrow," Devon said, "you'll receive a Delta Alert message that will authorize launch." He explained that the —th

Bomb Wing was specially chosen, was the only unit participating in the test. The wing's fifteen Alert bombers would fly a route that kept them clear of populated areas. As soon as they burned off enough fuel to reach landing weight they would return home.

Devon handed out a checklist of special instructions headed by a warning: *During this exercise the safing/locking pin will not be removed from the U2 hook.* If he had the authority, he would weld the damn thing in place, Devon thought.

Following the briefing, Chuck Charles took Devon aside. "About our new copilot—Don Cutter." Charles lowered his voice: "The other day, we had a problem with our JATO takeoff." During their tech-order study session, Cutter had told Charles about misreading the airspeed. "I was wondering—this is heavyweight and a lot more critical— could I have Dixie back for a day?"

Devon said, "No. Dixie just came off Alert this morning." His mind clicked to a lower emotional frequency: "But I see your problem. I'll get you an experienced copilot by eleven."

The two majors exchanged friendly smiles. Charles's was genuine. Devon's was a mask: He intended to replace Cutter with Robby Robertson. Lock all the crazies in the same cell and see what happens, Devon thought.

At the same time as Clark Devon briefed the incoming Alert crews, Beth finished loading the Chevy for the day-long drive to Laredo. Her mind mockingly told her that the only thing she'd brought to the marriage and still possessed in its original condition was her imaginary monument of flawless white stone representing wifely fidelity. Throughout the day to come, her mind's eye would trick her and she would see a tip of a monument across wide-open range, a distant white rock outcrop or mirage, a goal toward which she seemingly returned again and again.

Would her monument be intact if Jim Leonard had been home when she'd phoned on Sunday? Instead of Jim, a woman had answered. Beth nearly had asked, Are you the stewardess from Dallas? "He ran to the hospital, he'll be back any minute," the woman had said. "Want to leave a message?" The clear voice had rung with confidence, had made Beth want to ask, Am I doing the right thing? Instead she'd said, "I'll call again." Later, the phone had gone unanswered while Beth imagined them making love, together ignoring her pleading rings.

(During the following months Beth wrote Jim letters that she did not mail. A few years later when she was happily married to a rancher who had lost his first wife to cancer, Beth recognized that she had done the right thing by not mailing the letters. She would have been forcing what was not meant to be. Like Morris, Jim was city; she was country. City people wanted to overturn the earth and control nature; country people were satisfied to live with the land, to follow nature's dictates. The two groups came from different civilizations.)

As Beth drove south out of Abilene, she dreamed of a sister for Beverly, a new life within her new life.

Beth had found extra hope in her mother when she'd telephoned her on Saturday: "I'm coming home for Christmas. Am I welcome?"

"You're always welcome," her mother had replied. "I wish you'd called sooner, I'd've bought a bigger tree."

It would be her first Christmas tree since leaving home, Beth thought. Beverly's first ever. Morris hated Christmas decorations, called them a waste of money.

"Can I stay through the New Year?" One week at a time, Beth had thought and offered a bribe: "I'll buy groceries."

"You don't have to do that."

"Morris won't be coming. He had to work all week. I'll explain when I see you." Beth had tendered a second bribe: "I have a surprise."

Without missing a beat her mother had said, "You're pregnant."

Beth had laughed. "Wait until you meet Beverly." Beth had pictured her mother catering to the child's every desire, spoiling her, freeing Beth to find a part-time job before the new baby came. Then Beth had abruptly realized that her father wasn't home. Otherwise, mother wouldn't've been chatting. The observation had irritated Beth. Why couldn't her mother always behave this openly? With Father in the room Mother wasn't permitted to think. "We'll be there Monday, after supper."

"I'll hold something on the stove."

"I'm looking forward to coming home. I love you, Mother."

"I love you too, child," her mother had answered.

She would be satisfied with "happy," Beth thought. She didn't expect her future to be "perfect." Perfect was for fairy tales. Happy included good and bad, the roller-coaster ride of life. She hoped never again to break down in one of the ride's troughs as she had done with Morris.

(That summer, after Beth's wish came true and she had another daughter, in a rush of guilt for bringing the child into a fatherless world, Beth named her Bonnie Morrisa. Was the name intended to tie Morris to the child or to tie the child to Morris?)

Chuck Charles's crew was drawing maps of the Delta Alert route when Clark Devon opened the door of the yellow target study room and said, "Lieutenant Cutter, follow me. I have other work for you."

Minutes later Devon returned, smiled, said, "Here's your new copilot," and pushed Robby into the room.

Morris snapped the point off his pencil. Charles stood, gestured meaninglessly. Robby stepped into the hall, called to Devon who already was twenty feet away and moving fast, "Wait a minute."

Over his shoulder Devon said, "I don't have time for personal problems." He turned a corner, went out of Robby's sight. He'd euchred them, Devon thought, and rushed to tell Fred Martin.

Robby posed in the doorway, half in and half out of the room.

Morris's mind eddied with indecision. Resolving problems in the confines of his own head was not adequate, he'd decided. And yet . . .

The previous night he'd visited Beth, had stood in the duplex's doorway exactly as Robby now was posed, had refused to enter his own home, had focused all of his willpower to tell Beth, "I came to say I'm sorry," and when she did not respond, he'd added, "about Ellen, I mean."

"That's not the problem," Beth had said.

"You're not angry about Ellen?" His voice had taken on a note of hope, but he hadn't dared to look at Beth, had shifted his eyes around the living room as uneasily as Robby now studied blank cinder-block walls.

If Morris could have seen into Beth's mind, he would have learned that she viewed his defensive posture as regret more than remorse. Her unfamiliar position of advantage had given her a burst of courage and she'd attacked: "Yes. Yes. I'm angry about Ellen. That's only part of it. Every day with you is hell." She'd caught herself shouting. "This is useless," she'd said and moved beyond his reach, sat on the couch.

"I thought you were happy. I was happy."

"Dear God," she'd said.

"Beth, I'm sorry—really—for whatever I did."

"It's too late." She'd put her head in her hands. "Please. Leave me alone."

To his and her surprise, he'd nodded and walked away.

Chuck Charles stared at vacillating Robby and his mind banked around clouds of doubt: Would he rather risk it with Cutter? Didn't safety come before personalities? How would Morris react? Didn't Alert duty come before the rumors he'd heard? Charles looked at his watch: It was too late to find another copilot and still have time to discuss procedures. Experience told Charles that the klaxon would sound shortly after noon, no later than one o'clock. Planners knew launch and recovery were safest during daylight hours. The next logical time was tomorrow morning. But today was clear; who knew what weather might blow in overnight. "Come on, Robby. Let's talk about the takeoff," Charles said.

Before Robby settled into a chair, Morris clasped his hands in front of him, lowered his head as if in prayer, and said, "I want to tell you I'm sorry for the way I've behaved." He looked up, caught Charles's eye. "Forgive me for what I did—for what I said about Emily. . . ."

Charles had never expected such words to flow from Morris's mouth. His eyes misted as if they'd viewed a miracle. It was as if a savage had suddenly spouted a Shakespeare sonnet:

> Book both my wilfulness and errors down
> And on just proof surmise accumulate;

297

> Bring me within the level of your frown,
> But shoot not at me in your waken'd hate.

Morris's next remark was so blatantly in and out of character that Charles's eyes cleared in a wink and he snorted with muffled laughter at the personality that produced such absurd reasoning: Morris turned to Robby and said, "I forgive you for punching me."

Robby said, "I didn't come on Alert to make friends," and turned away.

"Let's talk about it later," Charles said, then asked Robby, "When did you make your last JATO takeoff?"

Snarled in a tangle of failed apologies, Morris didn't hear the discussion that followed. Beth had refused his overtures of reconciliation. Charles had laughed at his sincerity. Robby had ignored his generosity. How could he begin a new life without forgiveness for the old? Didn't they see he wanted to change? A punishing question struck him: Was atonement a lifelong task?

Morris was too new to the game of atonement and could not role-play, could not tolerate being unfulfilled.

He smashed a fist down on the table. Through a green scrim that fogged his vision, he shouted, "God damn both of you. I try to say I'm sorry and—you laugh."

"Up yours," said Robby.

Morris's face reddened. "Fuck you," he shouted. "I know you. You're not perfect."

Charles rose to his feet, instantly realized he'd made a mistake because Morris and Robby stood too, with fists clenched. Fortunately, Charles thought, there was a table between them.

"Listen. Morris. I accept your apology," Charles said. "I'm sorry I laughed. If you want to discuss it further, it'll have to wait until after we fly. Please?" Charles looked at Robby, begged with his eyes for peace, turned back to Morris: "Is that all right, can we talk about it when the flight's over? Please?"

"I guess so," Morris said. Now he owed Charles an apology for damning him, he thought. When did it end?

❧CHAPTER 51

THE KLAXON SOUNDED at twenty-three minutes after noon, caught most of the crewmen in the dining room. For once they knew the category of Alert in advance, Morris thought while sprinting down the ramp toward the two rows of bombers parked perpendicular to the runway. Then he thought that it would be a coincidence, but they could be headed to war, and the possibility drove him to run faster.

He reached the aircraft ladder at the same instant as Robby, stepped back, and let Robby go first. By then Charles had arrived and Morris shoved him aboard before scampering up the ladder and slipping on the spare headset at the aisle position. He heard a command-post controller broadcast: "Twenty-three Zulu. Authentication is Mike Hotel. I say again. Skyking, Skyking. This is Offutt with a Blue Dot Four. Prepare to copy. Break, break. Kilo. Alpha. Mike. Tango. November. Golf. Break, break. Authentication time is eighteen-twenty-three Zulu. Authentication is Mike Hotel. Stand by for roll call."

With a grease pencil Morris wrote the message's letters and numbers into blanks on a checklist covered by clear plastic. Then he placed a small black plastic template over a half sheet of paper printed with a tightly clustered square of random letters, a secret form valid for only twelve hours of eternity. He aligned a notch on the left edge of the template with numbers corresponding to the authentication time. Through two square holes in the template, he saw the letters M and H. Robby and Charles were doing the same. "It checks," Morris shouted, then dropped down the ladder two rungs at a time, called, "A Delta," to the waiting crewchief who already had unfastened the grounding wires.

Around them, starters fired as the first of the bomber fleet's ninety engines spun to life. The whine of turbines rose to a controlled scream. From a position alongside the engines where he manned a fire extinguisher, the crewchief held up three fingers and nodded, indicated Charles had number-three engine up to speed. From it he could start the other five. Morris unplugged a pair of electrical cables from the bomber's fuselage, dragged the heavy lines across the top of the ground power unit, and then guided the self-towing cart clear of the aircraft's path.

A nearby bomber rolled forward, and then another. "Hurry up, Chuck," Morris shouted into the backwash of fire that swept across him from the turning bombers' engines, made him face away while jet blast shook him, fluttered and stretched his flying suit like clawing hands. The heat wave passed and he saw the crewchief pulling wheel chocks; he sprinted, leaped onto the ladder, pulled up the rungs behind him as he climbed, tugged closed the outer door, slammed its lock in place, then closed and sealed the inner door.

He was gliding toward his position in the nose when the plane lurched forward, made him stagger before he dropped into the waiting webbing. Of their own accord, his arms slipped into the parachute harness, his hands clipped straps across his chest and around his thighs. He ducked into his helmet, heard Robby say, ". . . like we're sixth in line."

"Nine behind us," Charles said. "Not bad."

Robby told him, "Number six breaks right after gear-up."

Morris's mechanical fingers wove the ejection-seat shoulder straps and lap belt together, hooked in the dime-size rings that separated him from his seat, and deployed his parachute that automatically functioned faster than human reflexes, hopefully saved his life in the event of a low-altitude escape.

As he approached the runway Charles had no regrets about replacing Cutter. Robby's experience was what he wanted in the middle of a lock step stream that placed four airplanes on the runway at the same time: the leader scant seconds from liftoff; two around midfield, one soon after and the other shortly before JATO firing; and the fourth commencing roll at the hammerhead. A fifteen-second interval didn't allow time for discussion in an emergency. Of course, once the JATO fired, decision time was ended: They were committed to fly.

Charles jockeyed the throttles, maintained spacing behind the plane he followed so that when it was his turn to take off he could roll onto the runway without braking, without losing momentum. He saw the first B47 in the stream begin takeoff. "Nav, one's rolling," he reported.

"Five minutes, twenty-six seconds," Morris said.

"You sure?" Robby said. "That seems slow."

Morris was irritated by the question, said, "It's twenty-eight and a half after now. Klaxon sounded at twenty-three."

Wisps of black smoke trailed from the lead aircraft's engines as the pilot added water injection to augment the jet fuel and increase thrust. About the time the leader's JATO bottles fired, the second bomber began to roll.

"Number two's interval was twenty-five seconds," Robby said.

The JATO boost didn't affect the lead aircraft's heavy-weight configuration as dramatically as it did aircraft at training mission weight. Instead of bouncing the bomber into the air, the JATO accelerated the bomber along the ground, provided the ten extra knots of speed needed for liftoff.

As one plane fired its JATO and the next began its roll, Charles felt he was watching a motion picture replay itself.

"Three was twenty-five seconds behind two. Can't they

301

tell time?" Robby complained. But when four rolled with an eleven-second separation, he said, "That's too close. He's gonna overrun his ass."

The first three airplanes lifted off exactly as briefed: One bore straight ahead, maintaining runway heading; the second veered twenty degrees left and the third twenty right as soon as the landing gear retracted. The dispersal pattern took each plane out of the jet wash of the one in front of it.

"Five went at exactly fifteen seconds," Robby said. "That still looks tight."

By then Charles was turning left, rolling onto the runway. With his right hand he reached down and activated the JATO arming switch. Robby said, "Fifteen seconds—ready—ready—*now*," and with his right hand Charles shoved the six throttles to 100 percent power, gave them a second push to make sure they were all the way forward. In the back seat Robby leaned his weight against his throttle controls.

The bomber accelerated slowly at first, straining against the bondage of gravity. "Come on, baby," Robby said. The bomber *felt* heavy, Charles thought, and told himself he wouldn't want to do this every day.

"Coming up on seventy knots," Robby said. "Ready—ready—now."

"Everything looks good," Charles said. His left thumb waited above the JATO firing button on the control yoke. The airplane in front had already activated the JATO bottles and Charles saw dozens of sparkling eyes in their burning exhausts.

"Coming up on ninety—ready—ready—*now*," Robby said and Charles pressed the trigger.

Axel Turner observed the Delta Alert from the control tower. Motion picture photographers were stationed at both ends of the runway. CINCSAC wanted it documented, Turner thought. Maybe he intended to send a copy of the reel to Khrushchev.

Turner was annoyed by the late spacing between the first three pilots. But when four went early and then nearly dragged a wing the moment he broke ground, Turner decided early was worse than late. When five, six, and seven were on the money, he felt better.

At the same time, Turner worried about turbulence on the

runway. By now, takeoff roll probably felt like crossing the wakes of an armada of motorboats.

Then six fired his JATO and from the tower it looked like an artillery shell hit the plane. At JATO ignition, one bottle of the solid fuel propellant ruptured in a flash that kicked loose eight bottles surrounding it, sent them flying like unguided missiles.

"What was that?" Turner asked and trained binoculars on the wounded plane.

Two of the freed bottles rocketed upward and tore through the skin of the bomber's fuselage, ripped into the center main fuel cell before deflecting away. Fire from the bottles still attached to the plane ignited the fuel that poured from the bleeding cell.

The senior controller in the tower, a gray-haired master sergeant and former pilot from World War II, spoke calmly into his microphone: "Aircraft on the roll at the four-thousand-foot marker, your fuselage is on fire."

Flames blossomed into a yellow flower, expanded to a size as large as the airplane. Petals of fire fell along the runway.

Seven already had started to roll, hesitated momentarily, and then plowed ahead, steered between the petals of flames, ignored the JATO bottles squibbing alongside the runway.

"Hold the takeoffs," Turner ordered. "This is still a peacetime operation. Safety first."

"Aircraft in takeoff position, hold your position," the controller quietly said and the eight remaining bombers bunched up along the taxiway, engines running.

To Charles the exploding JATO bottle registered as an aerodynamic tic, a tremor of power, as if a cosmic giant had given the plane's tail an exploratory brush with a toe.

In the seesaw limbo of the bomber's blacked-out nose, to Morris the distant thump impacted like a gunshot. "What was that?" he blindly called.

Charles scanned the instrument panel, found everything normal. It was too late to abort on the runway, he thought and asked, "Robby, you see anything?"

Maybe they'd hit a bird, Robby thought and stretched his neck to see as much of the airframe as possible. His heart turned to ice when he saw the fireball clinging to the fuselage behind him. The instant the controller's transmission reached them, Robby shouted, "The whole plane's on fire, from the wing root aft."

It was a nightmare emergency. The bomber carried all its fuel in the fuselage. The plane was at a point where it couldn't be braked to a halt and abandoned. And a thermonuclear weapon hung in the bomb bay.

A short lifetime of training dictated Charles's response. "Prepare for bailout as soon as we get airborne." After the JATO fired, the aircraft hadn't accelerated as quickly as he'd expected. "Morris, I'll tell you when. You'll be first. Then you, Robby." Beneath his oxygen mask Charles grinned in concentration, as if he enjoyed the challenge. He watched the airspeed indicator climb, saw it touch 140 knots. He pulled back on the yoke, breathed deeply when the nose came off the ground cleanly. He wanted 500 feet of altitude before zooming skyward, putting the nose into a steep climb that allowed Morris to eject in a trajectory that paralleled the ground.

In the back seat Robby looked over his shoulder and thought that there was no need for *him* to wait. *Charles couldn't see the fire the way he saw it.* At any second the tail might burn off, or the whole plane blow up. He imagined a fuel cell erupting or the bomb's high-explosive charges detonating. He didn't want to die inside a ball of fire. As far as he was concerned Archer was on his own. *Breaks of the game.*

Like a flaming torch the bomber passed over the end of the runway. Its altimeter showed 2000 feet—200 feet above the terrain. Robby stowed his control yoke, lowered his helmet visor, took a deep breath. He squeezed the hand trigger on his left armrest and blew off the bomber's canopy.

Hurricane winds surrounded the pilots, vacuumed dust, dirt, and every loose article from inside the plane. Charles squinted, lowered his visor against the hail of debris. He knew what had happened but before he could speak Robby squeezed the right armrest trigger and launched himself in an upward arc that carried him high above the plane's tail, leased him more than ample altitude for survival.

❧CHAPTER 52

ELLEN LOOKED AT the kitchen clock when she heard bombers starting engines in the distance. Another Alert, she thought, and in the middle of lunch too. She wished she had the money SAC spent on fuel for just one scramble.

By the time she walked upstairs to the bedroom window, the bombers were moving. She wondered how it felt to control one of the big warplanes. She felt cheated: Why weren't women allowed to be pilots?

The first bomber rolled onto the runway and Ellen nearly turned away in envious spite. She didn't care to watch the men at play. Then she noticed black smoke from the engines and recognized that the bomber was taking off. More planes .followed. They seemed to launch closer and closer together, as if crowding each other off the earth, pushing each other into the sky.

"My god," Ellen whispered. The Alert force was launching. Did it mean war? Robby was with them. . . .

An airplane on the runway burst into flames and Ellen

305

gave a short, sharp cry of fright. The plane continued its roll. From her perspective, Ellen saw a yellow fireball with wings. The crew was going to die, she thought, and then thanked God that the bomber and its weapon were taking off away from her. Was it Robby's plane? He should have been on Alert last week and home now, she thought self-accusingly.

The fireball lifted off the ground like a comet of destruction, burned its way into the lacework of exhausts from the planes before it.

Ellen saw a black dot shoot into the sky above the fireball and then break into two pieces: one tumbled to earth; the other became a parachute. Could it be Rob?

The plane emerged from the fireball and Ellen realized it was trying to climb. However, it seemed to lack energy, seemed to stop almost before it started, silhouetted against the sky. For a long moment the burning cross of a warplane hung balanced above the barren hills before tipping over, falling off on a wing, collapsing into an inferno of its own creation. The plane left an archway of black smoke across Ellen's horizon, the trailing scrawl of a final signature against a blank page of blue-gray sky.

Seconds later she heard a faint explosion, the thump of a muffled drum. The house briefly trembled. Ellen thought she saw another parachute low to the ground, but wasn't certain. Smoke veiled the landscape.

Her eyes wandered to the remaining bombers hunched along the taxiway. Their motionless tension eased a portion of her mind: They would not have stopped if war had started. Was Rob in one of them? Ellen sat on the edge of the bed and filled the only role left to her: She wished for her husband's safety.

Self-destructive insanity gripped Morris when he heard the overlapping transmissions: "Aircraft on the roll at the four-thousand-foot marker, your fuselage is on fire," and "The whole plane's on fire, from the wing root aft."

Of their own volition Morris's hands clawed between his legs, found the D-ring and trembled with the urge to pull it. His mind screamed that it was better to explode into the ground than to be consumed in the flames of wreckage. *Hell was a heartbeat away.* Then an Act of Contrition possessed his soul. His mind vowed: "O my God, I am heartily sorry for having offended Thee because Thou art so very good, and I firmly propose, by the help of Thy grace, not to offend Thee again."

From the mouth of Charles came God's answer: "Prepare for bailout as soon as we get airborne. Morris, I'll tell you when. You'll be first. . . ."

You'll be first. You'll be first. You'll be first. . . . Morris's mind chanted and tears of gratitude filled his eyes. In preparation for ejection, he lowered his visor, stiffened his back, resettled his fingers on the D-ring. He felt the airplane lift off and watched the altimeter creep upward.

When Robby blew away the canopy, a tornado effect inside the nose made Morris twitch, blink his eyes, think he'd inadvertently fired his seat. Relief and resignation hit him simultaneously: He hadn't ejected accidentally but Chuck and Robby had done so deliberately. Swept by a wave of lethargy, Morris accepted that he was to die in the grasp of the monster he had embraced.

Then, from what sounded like a great distance, above the howl of wind, Chuck's voice called, "Morris, you still there?"

"Yes," Morris shouted.

"It's all right. Hang on. I'll tell you when." Charles aimed the airplane at an uninhabited stretch of farmland. He yanked back on the control yoke, buried it in his lap.

Multiple gravities dragged down Morris's arms while the bomber's nose climbed until it pointed straight to heaven.

Charles saw the altimeter reach 2300 feet. He shouted, "Go," and flipped a switch that set the alarm bell ringing continuously.

Morris pulled the D-ring with all of his strength, pulled against the concentrated forces of nature, pulled for his life. In the first two inches of travel the D-ring lanyard released a panel beneath Morris's seat. A metal square dropped away like a trapdoor leading from one life to another. A sound of falling water, the tumble of white water rushed over him in a torrent.

He pulled the D-ring to its limit.

Like a double exposure, he was inside and outside of the airplane at the same instant. Lightning-blasted, he breached into the air feet-first, on the upward trajectory of an artillery shell exploding across the womb of space. In the arms of technology, he again traveled the first page of his history, retraced his birth.

Technology's mother-touch lifted him clear of his escape seat, deployed his parachute. Beneath the canopy blossom he oscillated through half an arc and gently landed, in a seated position, amid plowed rows of winter wheat. He tipped onto his back, then grasped a parachute riser and dragged it toward him, collapsed the canopy.

He rolled over in time to see the warplane impact the ground on wingtip and tail, then fall onto its back and erupt into a yellow and black fireball. Later he remembered feeling the earth shudder but could not recall a sound.

Where was Chuck? Morris shed his parachute harness and helmet, then jogged in a wide detour around the burning wreck. He'd gone nearly a quarter mile before he spotted the red and white panels of a parachute in the distance. He took off in a sprint through the foot-high wheat.

Charles shouted, "Go," and tripped the alarm bell. He hoped Morris was gone and, knowing he had no more time to wait, pushed the control yoke forward. He was on his back, however, and couldn't reach far enough: The yoke didn't meet the locking detent, fell back into his lap. The movement was one he'd never practiced, a feat he'd never conceived of having to perform. He told himself to stay calm, mustered his strength, pushed and failed again. On the third try, panic elongated his arms, made his legs add a kick; and he drove the yoke far enough to lock it out of the way. An unstowed yoke would catch him across the thighs when he ejected, break or amputate both legs.

In the middle of Charles's unforeseen problem, the airplane shuddered at the top of its stall, then paused, hung motionless in space and waited for gravity to recapture it forever. Charles's double delay was a lifetime too long. Gravity stretched the bomber beyond the vertical, made it reel backward like a gamefish in a final death throe.

By the time Charles squeezed the ejection trigger, he saw the horizon coming up behind him. He was nearly inverted, aimed on a downward trajectory, headed earthward.

He recognized his predicament. Not only was his ejection

attitude undesirable, but his delay also caused him to be firing from a relatively stationary platform; he lacked the forward momentum of Robby and Morris, speed that created rushing air to hasten deployment of a parachute.

Mother technology performed only within design parameters, was incapable of miracles. Charles separated cleanly from the seat; his ripcord pulled automatically. The two-foot pilot chute sprung free but the twenty-eight foot main canopy unfolded limply from the backpack. Charles saw the ground rushing toward him. He doubted the parachute would have time or distance to deploy fully.

If he could have stopped in midair, he could have lectured for hours on the conditions that led to his problems, the mistakes he'd been forced into, and the probable outcome. He recognized most of the factors working against him.

The single thing he might have overlooked, however, was a premeditated valor of which he was barely conscious, a product of his subconscious mind. His regard for the lives of others was the cause of his plight as surely as anything else. His valor was born of his selflessness, his innate tolerance that made every man equally valuable within his eyes. What else could motivate a willingness to remain inside a fiery crucible? What else could compel a man to risk his life in order to save the life of another man who did not love or respect him?

In the last moments of fall, Charles tried to assume a body position that might lessen the shock of impact, tried for a parachute landing posture he'd been taught with practice leaps from a five-foot-high platform twice a year. He misjudged the distance; the ground moved faster than he estimated. He was struggling to align his body when he hit the earth. With hips twisted, he landed half on his back and half on his side, impacted with the force of a man thrown from a twenty-story building.

Charles's pelvis shattered. His lower spine snapped in two. The long bones in both legs, above and below the knees, fractured. His right elbow drove into his body and crushed five lower ribs, collapsed the lung on that side. His right wrist snapped; his right shoulder separated. His brain concussed when his helmet split. His spleen ruptured.

* * *

To Morris the figure looked as if it were a toy of space: Arms and legs and torso were at odd angles, as if bent by a cruel giant hand and then thoughtlessly discarded.

Morris knelt beside the figure and tenderly unhooked its oxygen mask, raised its visor and removed its helmet, then unbuckled its harness.

Because of its nearness, the face looked enormous. It was a hideously ugly, unnatural ceramic white. Trickles of blood from the nose formed a crackle pattern across one cheek as if the body were already disintegrating.

Morris turned his eyes away, then forced them to look back. The figure's eyes moved and Morris said, "Chuck?"

The eyes looked beyond him, as if searching for escape out of the landscape of pain, seeking a more peaceful universe.

"Chuck?" Morris again called and was answered by the judge who sat within his mind: By every construction of your nightmares, that should be you.

"Chuck? Don't die," Morris shouted and dropped his face to Charles's chest, embraced the man with whom he had traded places. Gripped by the pain Charles felt, Morris cried in agony. "Don't die. Please don't die." He prayed, "Please, God, don't let him die."

The last image to touch Charles's eyes, to focus in his brain was a lone hawk soaring against the blue-gray winter sky. His soul reached out and stroked the bird.

With his head resting on Charles's chest, Morris heard only the hammer thumps of his own guilty heart.

EPILOGUE

JULIUS MACDUFF TOOK charge of Emily Charles's life,
helped her to organize a future when she couldn't see one.
He told her, "The air force takes care of its own. And,
honey, I'm air force—all the way."

He stood shoulder to shoulder with her at Chuck's
funeral, and at the ceremony in which General Turner
presented a posthumous Distinguished Flying Cross to
David and Becky, and at David's swearing-in as a second
lieutenant upon graduation from the Air Force Academy,
and at Becky's graduation from Abilene's Hardin-Simmons
University.

Along the way, he guided her investments and made her
into what he fondly called, "The only rich and sober woman
I know."

In 1985, Emily supported Julius on her arm, in his final
public appearance, while they watched Lieutenant Colonel

311

David Charles navigate the first B1B to its welcoming landing at Dyess, one of only two bases selected to house what many experts considered the last of the manned strategic bombers. Some experts claimed the warplane was obsolete before it flew off the drawing board.